ONE MORE ROUND

AMBER PALMER

Complete Editing Services performed by Heather Nix

Cover Design: Forensics and Flowers

It's never too late to start over. To do the scary thing for the sake of your own peace.

So take risks. Kiss your brother's best friend. Do that body shot.

You never know what may change your life.

PLAYLIST

FOR THE FULL PLAYLIST, SCAN THE QR CODE!

Father Figure - Taylor Swift
Steady as Stones - Woodlock
Man I Need - Olivia Dean
Vienna - Billy Joel
Pink Skies - Zach Bryan
Wondering Why - The Red Clay Stripes
The Prophecy - Taylor Swift
Say Don't Go (Taylor's Version) - Taylor Swift

TRIGGER/CONTENT WARNINGS

- Alcohol consumption
- Explicit sexual content
- Dying relative/parental figure
- Death of a family member (on page)
- Strained parental relationship
- Brief mention of suicidal thoughts
- Depression
- Grief/Mourning
- Suicidal Ideation (Brief, on page)

OLIVIA

MY PINK MANICURED nails clicked against the sleek glass desk as I stared back at seven men old enough to be my father. They all looked the same in their expensive yet plain navy suits. Some even went as far as to coordinate their ties. How cute.

Meanwhile, I was the breath of fresh air this industry so desperately needed, dressed in my favorite red velvet Alice and Olivia powersuit. It said I came to shake hands, not kiss asses. They might not have wanted me, but they needed me.

Being a woman in a male-dominated field wasn't easy. I was frequently dismissed from the moment I walked into a room. More often than not, most men thought I was an overdressed secretary or personal assistant rather than the CEO of Hartstrings, one of the country's biggest record labels.

While it was annoying as hell to be immediately discounted before I opened my mouth, it was, admittedly, very satisfying to see their smug faces turn pale the moment I took a seat at the head of the table.

While Hartstrings was well known in the music industry, it was often underestimated simply because we didn't have offices outside the United States. It didn't have the global reach of others. However, our board of directors was looking to change that. They pushed for new acquisitions that would not only put us ahead of the biggest names out there, but would also grow our brand to a level we'd never seen before.

It was why I'd been away from my family, trapped in stuffy offices with smaller labels, independent artists, and lawyers for the past three weeks. Every few days, a board member would request a meeting where I'd have to present what very limited information I had. Most of the time, it was a quick one-liner saying I had nothing new to report.

I glanced out the window of the high-rise, staring out at the city below. Los Angeles was beautiful and vibrant, always bustling with excitement over the next big thing. But after three weeks here, with very little to show for it, I was ready to go home to my family. I wanted to hug my daughter and friends. I wanted to wear worn-in jeans and a T-shirt, rather than an expensive suit.

I wanted some goddamn peace and quiet so that maybe, just maybe, I could get rid of the excruciating headache that'd plagued me from the second my plane touched down. These work trips were starting to kick my ass. I was away from home more days than not, forced to hear about my daughter's day via FaceTime than at the dinner table.

I may have chosen and fought for this career, but it was certainly starting to lose its appeal.

"Ms. Hart, I really must insist we wait until our lawyers can fully examine this new contract. Your legal team has made so many alterations," the man on my left said. His eyes slid down my body in an obvious perusal, a slimy smile stretching his thin lips.

"The alterations you suggested, Mr. Cavender," I countered, straightening in my seat. Out of the corner of my eye, I noticed someone waving through the frosted glass wall, but I couldn't look away from the man in front of me.

"Be that as it may, I'm sure you understand our wanting to double-check we aren't losing any rights we don't want to give away."

There was only one person in this room I was grateful for, and that was the man sitting on my right. Carl Johnson had been with Hartstrings since my uncle, John Hart, took over the company after my father's sudden passing. He was passionate about two things: this company and his salary, in that order. I never had to worry about being taken for a fool when he was at my side.

Carl pinched the bridge of his nose as I spoke. He wanted to go home just as badly as I did. "Mr. Cavender, this negotiation period has gone on long enough. Your lawyers have already worked with our team to prepare this document and have reviewed the amendments together. Otherwise, we would not be sitting here today, waiting for your signature." I slid my pen toward him with a smile. "Now, if you want this deal to go through for your company, I suggest you take this pen right here and sign on that dotted line."

His partner, a portly man with a bald head and graying goatee, snorted as he addressed my lawyer. "This is why women shouldn't be in charge of a million-dollar company. They're too emotional. Your board should rethink sending their CEO to handle deals during their time of the month."

"Billion. Hartstrings is a *billion*-dollar company. That's why we're proposing to buy you out." The man sank back in his chair, clearly pissed at my correction. "And we have no problem walking out of here today. Your misogyny is nothing I haven't heard before, but I will not be insulted by the likes of you when it is *my* company that is attempting to cut *you* a deal so you can pay off your second mortgage and outstanding child support."

"How dare you—"

"Have I struck a nerve? Hurt your feelings, perhaps?" I clicked my tongue. "Aww, is it that time of the month?"

His mouth snapped shut just as Darcy, my assistant, stepped into the room. Her face was pale as she glanced around, an apology already preparing to slip free. I held up a hand to stop her. She wouldn't have interrupted if it wasn't an emergency. "What is it?"

Darcy shifted on her feet. "Mr. Hart on the phone. He said he's been trying to get ahold of you all afternoon."

Goddammit, Lukas. It wouldn't surprise me if he was pulling this shit just to be an ass. He knew my phone was on silent during meetings. "Can you take a message—"

"Unfortunately, Ms. Hart… I think you're going to want to take this call." She held up her phone.

Standing from my chair, I buttoned my blazer and gave the men a tight-lipped smile. "Excuse me," I said, rounding the table and stepping out into the hall. The door closed behind me.

"I'm so sorry," she said, offering her phone to me. Unease settled in my gut at her pained expression, eyes glinting with unshed tears.

I took her phone and brought it to my ear as I heard my brother's voice. "That you, Livvy?"

"What's wrong, Luke?" I didn't feel like bullshit pleasantries when my heart was racing out of control. What if something was wrong with Charlie or her dad? What if they'd gotten hurt, or worse?

My brother hesitated for a moment before he uttered the four words that nearly sent me to my knees. "It's John. He's sick."

"I'll call you right back," I said, ending the call before he could argue. Turning toward Darcy, I instructed her to call the pilot and have the plane ready as soon as possible.

I was going home.

Slipping back inside the boardroom to gather my things, I turned toward the table of baffled men. "Unfortunately, I have to cut this meeting short, gentlemen."

"We're not done here!" the first man exclaimed. "There are still negotiations to be had, and contracts to sign."

"Frankly, Mr. Cavender, that offer right there is our final offer, and it is overly generous. Should you choose not to sign it today, there will be no further negotiations, and Hartstrings will walk away from this deal without so much as a second glance. Believe me when I say we have many other independent labels that would love to work with us." Turning toward Carl, I said, "They have until the end of the day to review. If you don't have their signature by then, please formally withdraw our offer to purchase Ridley Records."

Carl nodded once. "Of course, Ms. Hart. It would be my pleasure." As I moved to walk past him, he gently grasped my elbow. "Is everything okay?"

My concern must have been written on my face, because all I saw was sympathy on his own. "I'm not sure yet," I said, swallowing the panic rising in my chest. If I let it in now, I would never be able to face whatever was waiting for me at home. "That's what I'm going to find out."

OLIVIA

LUKAS:

"Hey, Livvy. Call me when you get a second."

LUKAS:

"Your assistant said you're in a meeting, but this can't wait."

LUKAS:

"Uncle John's in the hospital. You need to come home."

I STARED down at the myriad of missed texts from my brother for what seemed like the hundredth time since I boarded the Hartstrings private jet just over four hours ago. My phone had been blowing up all morning, but I'd ignored everything for the sake of closing the deal. That was just part of the job.

The flight attendant advised me to fasten my seatbelt as the pilot announced our descent to Nashville, And tucking my phone away, I closed my eyes, gripping the armrest like I did every time I flew. You'd think I'd be used to it by now, but apparently not. I hated heights, and I hated flying even more. It didn't matter that the plane was private. It just meant there were fewer people to witness my anxiety at the slightest hint of turbulence.

The moment the plane came to a stop, I grabbed my things and thanked to the crew as they dropped the stairs. The central Tennessee air was muggy, even though the sun had already gone down. Not that it made much of a difference either way. It was just as humid after dark.

I scanned the tarmac and spotted a blacked-out SUV idling just ahead. The headlights illuminated a tall figure standing just outside the door.

"Little ostentatious, don't you think? Too good for commercial these days?" my brother shouted as I walked down the stairs. I smiled as he met me at the bottom, wrapping me in a warm hug. He smelled like home, like pine sap and sawdust and good memories. "Good to have you back, Livvy. Despite the circumstances."

"Yeah, they're not great," I agreed, blowing out a breath. "How's John doing? Is there any news?"

Lukas inclined his head toward the vehicle. "Come on. We'll talk on the way." He grabbed my bags while I slid into the passenger seat. As he settled behind the wheel, he looked over at me and smirked. "Sure you don't want to sit in the back? Isn't that what you're used to these days?"

"Fuck off," I muttered. "It isn't like I have much of a choice. You try taking conference calls and reviewing profit reports while driving and tell me how that works for you."

My brother's laugh was deep and throaty. "Naw. I passed on that shit, remember? You're the prodigal daughter."

"Lucky me," I sighed, melting into the leather seat. We were silent as we drove away from the airport and merged onto the highway, heading toward our small hometown rather than the city. "Wait, we aren't staying in Nashville? I thought John was at the hospital there."

My brother paused. "He was."

I turned in my seat to face him. "*Was?*"

Lukas sighed, drumming his fingers against the steering wheel. He looked so much older than I remembered. It hadn't been that long since I'd seen him, a couple of months at most, but there were deep bags beneath his eyes and an exhaustion that seemed bone-deep.

"He said he wanted to go home and spend whatever time he had left in the town he loved, so…"

"And you let him? The doctors just let him? Can they do that?" I questioned, pulling my brows together.

My brother shrugged. "We can't force him to stay against his will, Livvy. They advised against it, but he signed an AMA and wheeled himself out this morning."

I rubbed my temple. "So, what? He's just going home to die?"

Lukas's thrumming stopped, and the silence that took its place told me everything I needed to know.

"What the hell, Lukas? Isn't there anything we can do?"

"It's end-stage liver failure. We don't have a lot of options—"

"I mean, can someone get a medical power of attorney over him? Declare him unfit to make his own decisions?" I pulled out my phone and began scrolling. "Or what about a liver transplant? That has to be an option, right?"

He shook his head, snatching my phone out of my hand. "John refused all treatment, and he's been declared of sound mind."

"What did the doctors say? Did they give him some bullshit about poor odds or something? Could we get a second opinion?"

"*Jesus* Livvy. I almost forgot how pushy you can be," Lukas mumbled. "I was there when the doctors told him a transplant was risky given his age, just like any other procedure would be, but that there was a decent enough statistical rate of survival. They offered to set him up with other doctors for a secondary opinion, but John waived it all."

"He still said no?" My voice was barely above a whisper as I settled back into the leather.

Lukas reached over and gave my hand a slight squeeze. "I'm sorry, Livvy."

"What happens now?" I whispered, voice breaking. I didn't want to think about what this meant or how many difficult conversations were looming overhead. "I mean, how long?"

"We hired an in-home nurse to make sure he's taken care of for however long he has left—"

I slammed my hand down on the dashboard. "Which is how long, Luke? Answer the question."

He ran a hand through his short brown hair, mussing it slightly. "Three to six months if he's lucky."

Three to six months wouldn't even see John through to his next birthday. There'd be no more holiday celebrations, something that he always made a big fuss out of. No more fatherly advice followed by warm hugs and total understanding.

It would be gone. *Poof.* Just like Dad.

"This is bullshit," I said as the first tear fell. I couldn't bring myself to wipe it away. The grief weighed too heavily on my heart.

"It is," he agreed. "But it's what he wanted. At the end of the day, all we can do is respect his wishes and hope he doesn't leave the world with unfinished business."

Lukas didn't let go of my hand as I cried. Not even when his emotions got the best of him, and tears rolled down his cheeks as well. It was all too much to handle. We'd lost our dad at an early age, but Uncle John had done his best to step up to the plate. He'd never had kids of his own, but Lukas and I might as well have been. Neither of us were ever left wanting for anything. He made sure to stand in for every monumental moment a dad should be present for. He even walked me down the aisle on my wedding day.

Luke and I drove in relative silence back to our little hometown. The radio wasn't even loud enough to drown out the crunch of our tires against the asphalt. I focused on the noise, trying to push away the intrusive thoughts clamoring to be let in. It wasn't until I saw the "Welcome to Pinecrest" sign that I finally asked, "Does Mom know?"

Lukas blew out a long breath. "She does."

"How is she taking it?"

"About as well as could be expected," he said dryly. "She'll probably be two bottles of Chardonnay in by the time we reach the house."

I shifted in my seat. "Does she know I'm coming?"

"There wasn't really a way around that, Livvy. You've got to see her sometime."

"I know that. I just didn't think it'd be like *this*," I muttered. "But I guess nothing brings people together like an impending death in the family."

"Morbid but true," he chuckled. "If it makes you feel any better, I've put her in the main house with me while you get to escape to the cottage by yourself."

"Oh, thank god. I can lock the doors and never come out," I said.

Lukas laughed. "Yeah, I don't think sequestering yourself is gonna work. You know how persistent she can be. She'll probably camp outside your front door until you say something to her."

"The problem isn't speaking to her. It's saying what she wants to hear." I scoffed. "I can't give her what she wants, Luke. It's a nonstarter."

"Not even now?" he asked.

I shook my head. "Especially not now. It complicates things, sure, but the wheels are already in motion. I can't stop them. I don't *want* to stop them."

Lukas nodded but didn't say anything more. I could always count on him not to push me. He knew me better than that, knew I would shut down entirely if he did.

That courtesy was something Mom hadn't extended to anyone, though. She was often lost in her own world, indifferent to others' emotions until they somehow came back to affect her. Dad's death hadn't helped, either. If anything, she'd become more withdrawn over the years and quicker to adopt a victim mentality whenever she was met with opposition.

My brother called her selfish, and my therapist called it narcissism. Po-tay-to / po-tah-to, as far as I was concerned. Whatever it was had caused a rift between us that I didn't know how to mend.

Or if I even wanted to.

"Home sweet home," Lukas said, pulling up to the large wood-framed gate at the front of our property. He rolled down the window and punched in the code as we waited for it to swing open slowly.

I looked at the empty hooks hanging from the worn cedar beam across the top with a pang of regret. When I was a kid, Dad and I had come up with a name for the property. He said it hadn't mattered that it wasn't a working ranch; everything needed a name—something that set it apart from every other plot of land that people built on. So, we'd come up with Blue Moon Ranch, and he'd had a sign made the very next day.

After he died, it was the first thing our mother had taken down. I screamed at her for hours when I realized what she'd done. Then the silence settled in. There was no sympathy or remorse in her features. Just a stony coldness that she still wore.

Lukas crept along the winding road that led past his home. It was a massive ranch-style house that looked like it had been plucked from the pages of a magazine. The exterior was made of dark rock and cedar, featuring huge windows that allowed for an unobstructed view of the sprawling acreage on each side. White pipe fencing gave the illusion of a fenced-in yard, but it was little more than a picturesque decoration.

As we drove by, I noticed the darkened windows and drawn curtains. If it weren't for the single light illuminating the porch, it would've looked deserted.

"She's fucking subtle, isn't she?" Lukas asked. I followed his gaze to where a figure sat in a rocking chair adjacent to the front door. She was hidden behind a cloud of smoke, but I didn't need to see her face to know what lie behind it.

I turned away, feeling uneasy. Despite the dark tint, it felt as though our mother's contemptuous stare was burning a hole through the window. Every ounce of her disdain and disappointment was evident. She might as well have put out her cigarette directly on my skin. "So much for quitting, huh?"

"Did you really think she was going to? She's like a fucking freight train these days. One goes out, and she's reaching for the next," Lukas said, pulling up to my temporary home.

I didn't bother with a response. Neither of us had ever believed our mother when she said she was going to do anything. Smoking had been a hot-button topic growing up. Lukas and I had begged her to stop, but she never did.

"So, you'll need to get groceries because I haven't had a chance to go to the store, but there should be plenty of drinks to choose from," Lukas said, hopping out of the SUV and grabbing my bags.

"Are we talking water, tea, and coffee? Or something stronger?" I asked, trailing slowly behind him up the softly lit cobblestone path that led to the front door.

The guest cabin I was staying in matched the exterior design of Lukas's house on the hill, but it had a cozy feel that the big house didn't have. It was small in comparison but still had two bedrooms and bathrooms for guests. The living area was an open-concept space with tall ceilings that made the room feel larger than it was, and a small office was located just off the entrance.

Lukas keyed in the alarm code and flipped on the switch as we stepped inside. He set my bags down in the entryway. "You know I always have a premium selection on hand," he said, smirking. "Especially when it comes to family reunions."

I came up behind him, wrapping my arms around his waist. "I love you," I mumbled into his back. "I knew I was your favorite sister."

He patted my hand, chuckling. "You're my only sister."

"Semantics," I said, stepping back and brushing past him.

Lukas walked over and pulled two glasses from the bar cart in the living room. "Thirsty?"

I nodded vigorously before plopping down on the couch, letting out a lungful of air as my body sank into the plush fabric. It'd been one hell of a day, and the prospect of the days to come was already exhausting me.

The clink of ice cubes against crystal pulled me back as Lukas shook the glass above my face. "Bless you," I said, grabbing it with both hands and sitting up. The amber liquid burned as it hit my tongue but finished smooth as hell. "Oh, this is the good shit."

"Nothing but the best for the bigshot CEO. I know you're accustomed to a certain level of luxury," Lukas said, raising his glass.

"And you're not?" I snorted, gesturing around the room. "I received the same inheritance as you did, Big Brother. Not to mention the very successful business you run."

Lukas had always loved working with his hands, and Uncle John nurtured that. With a little investment from our family trust and a lot of dedication on Lukas' part, he started Hartfelt Homes—a premier construction group that specialized in custom houses. When he inherited the ranch, he gave the main house a major facelift, and built this little cabin from the ground up. Most of the homes in Pinecrest had Lukas's touch to them in one way or another. If something needed fixing, he's who everyone called.

"Semantics," Lukas said, smiling. He settled into the armchair across from me. "So, how long do you plan to stay?"

That was a great question. An excellent one, really. And the answer was complicated. While I knew I could easily take the time off given the situation, I wasn't sure if I should.

I looked down at the glass, tapping the outside three times. "I don't know."

He shifted, furrowing his brows. "What's that mean?"

"It means I don't know," I said, shrugging. "It means my life has felt like a shitshow over the past few years. That this is the first time I've been able to disconnect and just exist in the silence."

Lukas hummed, swirling the liquor in his glass. "Pinecrest has been good to me, you know. Good place to raise a family—"

I snorted. Lukas talking about raising a family was laughable. I'd never met someone so hellbent on living the single life. "What do you know about that?"

"Hey! I have friends who aren't eternal bachelors."

"Sure, you do," I said, downing the rest of my drink, shaking it in my brother's direction for a refill.

"You know where it is," he said, gesturing toward the bar cart.

I rolled my eyes, pushing off the couch. "You're the worst."

"Thought I was the best?"

"I've changed my mind," I murmured, snatching the decanter from the cart.

Lukas watched as I refilled both glasses. "Speaking of family men... Does your ex-husband know you're in town?"

"Why do you say it like that? You make it sound so gross and horrible and miserable."

"Sorry... Baby daddy?"

I scrunched up my nose. "Ew, that's worse."

"Divorcée it is then," he said, leaning back.

"You know damn well we would still talk every day, even if Charlie wasn't in the picture," I said, pointing in his direction. "He's my best friend. It was never like that between us."

Lukas tented his fingers in front of his face. "And yet you have a kid."

I gave him a saccharine smile. "You, of all people, know you don't have to be in love to have a kid. We were lonely until we weren't. Honestly, I'm surprised you don't have any little ones of your own running around, given your proclivity for practice."

My brother was many things, but a bachelor would forever be top of the list. I could count on one hand the number of relationships he'd been in over his forty-two years, and that included his girlfriend from the first grade. He had quite the reputation around town as the kind to love'em and leave'em. Sometimes, I swore he tried to live up to the rumors instead of squashing them.

I leaned back, taking a sip. "And, of course, he knows. I called him before I even boarded the plane. He offered to let me stay with them."

Lukas snorted. "Isn't that awkward? I mean, he's remarried."

"It's only weird to you because you're a forty-two-year-old manchild who can't comprehend being in the same room with someone you slept with. I was the one who drew up the divorce papers. I was the one who told him to follow his dream." I shrugged. "She was it."

Grady's and my relationship was long, but not entirely complicated. We got married as a stipulation from Hartstrings' board of directors. Apparently, they believed the CEO should be married. They said it painted a picture of stability, which was rich seeing as at least a quarter of the members were on their second wives already.

Grady was my best friend. Other than one drunken, lonely night that resulted in our daughter's conception, it'd never been anything but platonic for us. Our relationship was like one of those romantic comedies where two friends get married for some kind of mutual benefit. Except, instead of falling in love at the end, we got a divorce and shared custody. Our daughter may not have been planned, but I didn't realize how much I needed her until I held her in my arms. I'd always love him for that gift alone.

Grady helped me take over my company, and I helped him get the record deal he deserved. He'd given up so much of his life so that I could live out my dream. Even if he had benefited from it too, it wasn't the same. The least I could do was finally set him free once I had it. When he'd found his forever, I didn't give him a choice. I'd had the divorce papers drawn up and signed before he could stop me.

Not long after our divorce was final, Grady married his high school sweetheart. Cleo was wonderful. I absolutely adored her. It'd been a bumpy ride to get to where they were now, but I was so damn glad to see it worked out. If anyone deserved their fairytale ending, it was them.

"You were in the wedding," he deadpanned.

"Did you know it only takes five minutes to get ordained online?" His unamused stare remained absolute. "Anyway, I told him I was grateful for the offer but that I would much prefer to drive my big brother crazy."

Lukas snorted. "Charlie excited?"

"We haven't told her yet, but I'm gonna swing by tomorrow morning—apparently on my way to get groceries—and pick her up."

"And you're bringing her here? With Mom so close?"

I let out a breath, deflating into the cushions. That was a great question. One I didn't want to answer but knew there was no use in avoiding. "I don't have a choice. I'm surprised she hasn't stormed over to Grady's house already and demanded to see her."

"This is so disappointing. I bet your daddy's rolling over in his grave right now."

"You're so selfish, you know that? How could you do this to me? How could you keep me from my only grandbaby?"

"All you do is think about yourself, Olivia. You never once consider how I might feel about your decisions."

It'd been two years since Mom had uttered those words before storming out of my door. They still stung like they did the day she said them. My divorce was just one of the many things my mother had never been able to move on from. The day I told her had been the last and final straw. Apparently, it had broken something in her brain that caused her to malfunction as a human being.

Neither Charlie nor I had seen her since. I had wanted to keep it that way as long as I could, but now the situation had changed. There would be no avoiding this one.

It was almost ironic that Uncle John's health was the thing that brought us back here. He'd tried to smooth it over countless times, but neither my mom nor I were willing to listen to reason. I guess he'd get his wish in the end.

"Well," Lukas drawled, downing the rest of his drink with a grimace. "Here's to family reunions."

OLIVIA

THE WHEELS on the rickety shopping cart rattled against the checkered linoleum as I pushed it down the cereal aisle. The Save 'N Shop hadn't changed much over the years. Even some of the staff were the same. I recognized at least three weathered faces from when I was a kid. The faint scent of old grease clung to the cream-colored walls, a casualty of butting up next to the Dairy Queen for decades.

It was like stepping into a museum honoring retro grocery stores, which honestly just added to its charm. I was at least ninety percent sure that nothing had been updated since the eighties, except for the addition of computers at the checkout counters.

"*Moooooom,*" Charlie sang, tugging on my sleeve. "Can we get Fruity Pebbles? I want some for dessert!"

I raised my brows and stared down at my daughter. At nine going on eighteen, she'd grown way too much for my liking. It felt like she was changing right before my eyes, and I selfishly hated it. I wanted her to stay this sweet little girl forever and not have to worry about all the bullshit that came with growing up.

Her blue eyes, the ones I'd always struggled to say no to, stared back. It was like she was trying to break me down. Dammit, the kid was too good. She always had been.

Since picking her up from her dad's house this morning, Charlie had been stuck to my side. She'd droned on about school and her friends and how she wanted to be captain of her soccer team next year. I didn't think I got a word in the entire time. It damn near broke my heart. Guilt was my constant friend lately. It may have only been a few weeks since I'd seen her, but that had been a few weeks too long.

Work had been more hectic than usual. I'd spent the past six months flying back and forth between Los Angeles and Pinecrest, while Grady and Cleo had moved to Pinecrest permanently. It'd been a weird change at first, going from a big house in Nashville to crashing in my brother's cabin, but we made it work. I was waiting to buy something until I knew I could settle in it properly, to make it the perfect forever home for Charlie and me.

Lately, it seemed like that dream was slipping further away.

Finding a work-life balance had always been a struggle. I spoke with my uncle at length before accepting my position as CEO, and he didn't sugarcoat how difficult it would be at first, but that wasn't anything I didn't already know. The sad reality was that I would need to bust my ass even more than my male counterparts because not only was I a woman, but also a mother. It was bullshit, but that was business.

Everyone needed something from me, yet I was constantly fighting to be taken seriously. The word "nepotism" had been thrown in my face more times than I could count. Meanwhile, our profits had been on a slow but steady incline since I took over. Not that anyone took that into account when they gossiped about my leadership, though.

Apparently, I needed a certain appendage between my legs for anything I did to matter in their eyes.

At first, it was fine. Grady and I had the co-parenting thing down. It was always easy for us. But as my job became more demanding, he had to take on more responsibilities. He didn't mind, but I struggled with our new reality. I hated not being present, but I thought it was temporary. I thought proving myself would be over by now. If anything, it had only gotten worse.

I wanted to be the one taking Charlie to her soccer practices and concert recitals. I wanted to be there for every parent-teacher conference or talent show. I wanted to already know what her favorite freaking food was, not find out while standing in the damn grocery store.

Looking back, I wasn't sure how my dad managed to do it. He loved the company, but the company never came before his kids. When my uncle took over Hartstrings in the interim, he did the same. Neither my brother nor I ever felt like we came in second. Maybe that was just a benefit of the times, or maybe it was because men didn't have to worry about doing more than was asked of them.

Every day, it was getting harder to justify the cost of my career.

"Fruity pebbles for dessert?" I asked.

She nodded vigorously. "Yeah! It's not so different from eating cake, right? I mean, it's kind of the same thing."

"Can we compromise?" I asked, coming to a stop in front of their cereal selection.

I'd planned out a whole day for us. After dropping off our groceries, we were going to go get our nails done, do a little shopping, and have lunch at a cute little sub shop on Main Street before coming home and binging movies on the couch. I still hadn't mentioned John's condition, nor did I plan on it. Not today, anyway. I wanted one good day with Charlie before I burst her carefree bubble.

I already knew how much it would hurt. She loved John. With Grady's dad living in Texas, he was like a second grandpa to her. Always taking her places when Grady or I couldn't, and he completely spoiled her rotten.

Hearing that he was sick wouldn't be easy for her.

Charlie lifted her chin and straightened her shoulders. Good lord, this kid was only nine. How was she capable of giving so much sass? "Like what?"

I scanned the shelves. Was there anything considered a healthy cereal? "What about some Honey Nut Cheerios? They're sweet, but an argument could be made that there's some nutritional value." *At least, I think?*

Charlie had never liked cereal growing up, so this phase was new.

Something I would've known if I had been around more.

My daughter studied the options, biting down on her bottom lip as she prepared to launch a counterargument. "What about Fruit Loops?"

I laughed. "Girl, I don't think that's any better than Fruity Pebbles."

"But they both have fruit in the name," she said, pouting. "Doesn't that mean they're healthy? You and Daddy always tell me I need to eat my fruits and vegetables."

I shook my head. "I wish it were that simple. That'd be pretty cool, huh?"

"If it's not healthy, then how come Harper's dad lets her eat it?" Charlie asked, crossing her arms. She was staring longingly at the overly sugary breakfast items. "Why can't I?"

Oh boy. Charlie had always been an expert negotiator. She knew how to work every angle to win us over, but she'd always respected our decisions. We didn't have to fight with her or try to force her to understand. "I can't speak for someone else's parent, baby. You know that. What they choose to do in their house is up to them," I said.

Charlie let out a big sigh, and I thought the case was closed.

"Dad lets me have it," she mumbled. "I wish I was going back to his house."

Well, that fucking hurt.

"*Ouch*," I said, looking down at her in confusion. "Thanks a lot, kid. Where is that coming from?"

"I don't understand how everyone's rules are different," she said, raising her voice an octave. "Daddy has rules. You have rules. Harper's dad has rules. Why aren't any of them the same? It's not fair!"

I couldn't help but stare open-mouthed at my daughter as she stomped her little foot against the ground in indignation. "I understand your frustration, but being rude isn't going to help your case. That doesn't make me want to meet you halfway."

"Okay, but why can't we get it just this once?"

"Because I said no, Charlie. That's why." I hated myself for saying it, for not being able to give her an actual answer she would understand. It reminded me of my mother; how quick and easy she was to say no if it meant she'd have to be sober enough to drive me to a friend's house. "You're more than welcome to get the Cheerios or nothing at all."

"Guess I'll get nothing," she said, stalking to the front of the basket.

I shrugged, fighting back tears as I grabbed a box of Raisin Bran for myself. I couldn't help but feel like the morning had gotten away from me somehow. I was supposed to have one last good day before I had to return to a reality in which the man who helped raise me was dying. Before I had to break my daughter's heart, again.

Being a mom was the hardest thing I'd ever done. I wanted

to crumble. To scream. To fall to my knees and wail about how life wasn't fair, but I couldn't do any of that. Instead, I had to put on a happy face and pretend that my daughter's cutting words weren't the icing on a fucked-up cake.

We walked down each aisle in silence. Every time I tried talking to her, I was met with a one-word answer, a clipped yes or no, or complete and total silence.

Would the guilt of my being away ever subside? Sometimes I felt like a stranger spending time with my daughter. Grady and I had both taken great care with how we explained our separation to Charlie. We'd seen a therapist beforehand to figure out what to say and how to say it. She had a lot of questions when we told her the news, but in the end, she seemed happy because we were happy.

Cleo absolutely adored her and vice versa. There were moments I expected to feel jealous of another woman being there for my child when I should be, but I didn't feel any of that. She was terrific with Charlie, and could nurture her in ways Grady and I had always struggled to.

But it didn't lessen the sting when she said she preferred being with them to me sometimes.

The sound of Charlie's squeal caught my attention, but before I could stop her, she took off running down the aisle and disappeared around the corner.

"Charlie!" I called, chasing after her, but she didn't listen. "Goddammit."

I picked up speed, nearly colliding with another cart as I tried to slip past. "Watch it!" someone muttered, but I didn't pay them any mind. I grabbed my purse from the child seat and left everything else behind.

"Charlie? Charlie!" My voice rose when she didn't answer me. Rationally, I knew she was safe. The Shop 'N Save was small. A bell rang every time someone entered or left. It was likely that she saw a friend from school and had just gone to say hello or something. It didn't matter what I told myself. None of it worked to calm my fears, especially when she wouldn't stop and answer me.

I could just make out the color of her scrunchie as she disappeared behind the last aisle, her little hand waving at someone down the way. "Char—"

My words came to an abrupt halt as I turned the corner and ran smack-dab into something hard. I threw my hands out to stop myself from falling, but whatever I grabbed slipped free. It felt like it happened in slow motion, like a train wreck you can't help but watch, as a gallon of milk clattered to the floor and exploded all over me.

OLIVIA

"OH MY GOD!" I screeched, looking down at the mess I'd made. Milk soaked my clothes and seeped into my shoes. I bet when I tried to walk, it'd make a disgusting squelching noise like it did in the freaking movies.

My eyes drifted up to someone standing in a pair of sneakers just ahead of me. Sneakers that were also covered in a stupid white liquid I now despised.

"I'm so sorry," I said in a rush, bending forward to pick up the loaf of bread I'd knocked to the ground. "I wasn't paying atten—" My words cut off as I noticed who the large, broody figure in the sneakers was. A figure that definitely wasn't supposed to be there and *definitely* wasn't supposed to look as handsome as he did. "Duke?"

He studied me closely, bright green eyes carefully combing every inch of my face. Something about it was unnerving. Unnatural. His hair was longer than I remembered, touching the collar of his T-shirt and tucked beneath a dark ball cap. Dark stubble along his chin blended in with the thick mustache framing his lips.

"Well, I can see you haven't gotten any more graceful as you've gotten older," Duke mused.

"Nope," I said, chuckling dryly. "Just as clumsy as ever."

"Try watching where you're going next time," he said, bending back down to pick up my purse. He held it out, shaking it when I didn't immediately take it.

"Uh, okay. I'll try to do that." *Freaking asshole.* I wasn't sure why the interaction struck me the wrong way, but it did. Something in the way he spoke put me on high alert. Sure, it wasn't ideal to be covered in fucking milk, but I'd apologized. It was an accident. I was too worried about Charlie and the way she'd run from me to notice where I was going.

"Mom, you ran right into Harper's dad," Charlie said, crossing her arms. The hint of worry in her voice from earlier was gone. I was clearly back on her shit list. And honestly? She was on mine now, too.

"Maybe I wouldn't have if you hadn't run off. Seriously, Charlie. I know this is a small town, but I called your name, and you didn't stop. I was scared."

She rolled her eyes. "Nothing ever happens here, Mom. Dad says it all the time. So does Mr. Bennett."

"Okay, well, if you could hold off on giving me any more heart attacks today, that'd be great," I said, turning my attention back to the man in question.

"Olivia," he gritted out, tipping his head in greeting. It was forced. Like it was taking everything in him not to run and hide from me. "It's been a long time."

"It really is you, huh?" I said, letting my gaze rake down his body.

Duke and my brother had been best friends growing up. Where one went, the other followed. They spent the summers running amok and causing absolute havoc in Pinecrest. One time, they'd gotten banned from the summer fair. Apparently,

Duke stood guard outside one of the abandoned booths while Lukas got frisky with the old mayor's daughter. Needless to say, Uncle John smoothed things over with a nice donation, and Lukas and Duke spent the rest of the summer working to pay him back.

"In the flesh," he said.

I poked him in the center of his chest, staring at the spot where the tip of my finger met his body. He was the perfect mixture of hard lines and soft edges.

"You done?" he asked, knocking my hand away.

"I don't know. I feel like I'm in the Twilight Zone or something," I answered honestly.

Someone tugged on my sleeve, and I looked down at Charlie. "Mom, can Harper and I have a sleepover?"

I glanced at the small girl at my daughter's side. Her fair complexion made her long auburn hair, pulled back in an unruly ponytail, stand out. There was a dusting of freckles across her nose, and she had gorgeous green eyes.

That sweet girl was Duke's daughter? I recalled Lukas saying something about him getting married, but that was ages ago. She looked nothing like the grumpy bastard in front of me. Lukas never mentioned anything about it, and to be fair, why would he?

She lifted one hand in a shy wave. "Hi. I'm Harper," she said quietly.

I smiled. "Hi, Harper, it's so nice to meet you—"

"*Moooooooom,*" Charlie interrupted. "Please?"

Duke just stood there, covered in milk, awkwardly staring at the three of us. His arms were crossed over a wrinkled t-shirt, muscular legs on display in a pair of athletic shorts that looked like they'd seen better days.

"Sunshine, they might have plans today—"

"They don't. Harper's soccer game is over. Dad usually takes me to it. I wanted to go today, but he said we couldn't because you were coming to get me."

I tried not to let her words affect me, but they did. Goddammit, they did. I wasn't sure how a day that started so great had led to her looking at me like I was the worst person in the world for telling her no to some fucking cereal.

"Not today, Charlie. I just got in, and I want to spend time with you," I said, forcing a sense of cheer to my voice that I didn't feel. "What about our day together? We were going to have so much fun!" Charlie's face turned bright red, and I could tell she was preparing to have a total meltdown, so I added, "How about I get Mr. Bennett's number, and we can arrange something for later?"

Calling Duke "Mr. Bennett" was so weird. I hated the way it rolled off my tongue, but it also felt way too intimate to be using first names with a guy I hadn't seen since my wedding. Especially when he was staring at me like I'd done something wrong.

"She can come with us," Duke grunted. "I don't care."

Charlie and Harper began whooping and hollering like they'd just been told they could eat cake morning, noon, and night, but I held up my hand. He couldn't just come in and undermine me. I'd already said no. And this was my day, dammit. I missed my daughter and wanted to spend time with her.

"I'm sorry, girls. It really will have to be another time."

"What's it matter if she stays with us?" Duke asked, shifting on his feet. "I said it wasn't a problem, and I meant it. Just let the girl have some fun, Olivia."

I turned toward him. "Because I haven't seen my daughter in nearly three weeks, and I'd like to spend some time with her. What part of that is unclear?"

He scoffed, shaking his head. "Maybe that's your problem."

"Excuse me?" I asked, blinking in confusion. What the hell was happening right now? How did this day go to shit so damn fast?

"Maybe you shouldn't go so long without seeing your daughter. Maybe," he growled, taking a step, "you should realign your priorities. Make time for the things that matter."

As much as I wanted to shrink away, I held my head up high. Sure, this may not have been my finest moment, but I'd gone toe-to-toe with bigger assholes than him before. I wasn't about to back down now. Not for him. Not for anyone. "Kind of rude to throw around accusations when you don't know what you're talking about, isn't it? I mean, I could do the same to you, but I'm not."

"I know enough about your type. Always chasing another high. Always putting other shit and other people in front of the things that matter," he spat. "And please, enlighten me on what judgments you could throw my way. I'd love to hear them."

I pointed at his chest. "Your shirt is wrinkled, there's a mustard stain along your collar, and you look like you haven't showered or shaved in days." The last line was a low blow, and I instantly felt bad as his shoulders slumped ever so slightly. Guilt set in immediately, making me feel sick. God, what was I even saying? As if I had any right at all to talk about the state of someone else's life when my own was a mess. "Look, I'm sorry. That was way beyond rude, and I—"

"No, I get it. Wouldn't want your daughter hanging out with someone so unkempt," he muttered before turning toward Charlie and Harper. "Come on, Harper. I don't feel like cooking. How about we grab some lunch in town?"

His daughter nodded, turning to Charlie and wrapping her in a big hug. "See you next weekend at the game, Charlie."

I stood in silent, embarrassed shock as Duke tucked his daughter under one arm and walked away from his cart filled with groceries. What the hell just happened? The whole scenario was like a strange fever dream.

"That was *so* mean. I can't believe you'd say that. You don't even know him," Charlie said.

I *did* know him, but that wasn't the point. It wasn't worth arguing. Her little fist was clenched at her side, and she was looking at me like she'd never seen me before, like I was the worst person in the world.

Honestly, I felt like that, too.

I didn't know why I said the things I did. I could blame it on exhaustion or frustration, but that didn't make this sickening feeling go away.

There was something unnerving about the way Duke stared at me. Like he could see down into the depths of my soul and had already determined that I was a horrible, judgmental, selfish person. As much as it pained me to admit it, there may be some truth to it. Maybe my job had turned me into someone else—someone I didn't recognize.

"Charlie..." I began but stopped as her posture deflated, and her head hung low.

"Let's just go home," she muttered, stomping ahead of me. "I just wanna go home."

I stared at Duke's cart full of groceries, guilt tugging at something deep within. Grabbing hold of the handle before thinking better of it, I followed after my daughter, feeling my hope for the day wither away until it was nothing but ashes, crumbling in the wind.

DUKE

"HEARD YOUR DAY WAS SHIT," Lukas said, amusement coloring his voice as I picked up my phone.

"Understatement of the fucking century," I muttered beneath my breath, drying my hands on a dish towel on the counter.

It was so much more than just a day. Two years ago, I had everything figured out. My life was better than it'd ever been. My wife and I were happy. Harper was thriving in school. I gave back to my community, and my community gave back to me, supporting the dream I was chasing. Because of them, I quit my job at the mechanic shop to ensure Frank's Bar—a Pinecrest legend—was restored to its former glory and gave the lost and weary a place to call home.

Little did I realize I would soon become one of them.

In the blink of an eye, my life crashed and burned like an old country song. Everything good was tainted. I was weak. A coward. So goddamn beat down by life and circumstance that I could barely stand to look at myself in the mirror most days.

Today, it just happened to hit harder than most. My world lost focus the moment I ran face-first into Olivia fucking Hart.

The Harts were Pinecrest royalty. Everyone knew their name, knew how much money and power came with it, and fawned over them accordingly. Even though my family lived paycheck to paycheck, I was lucky enough to consider Lukas my best friend. We were inseparable growing up, still were, but his sister? That was a different story.

God-fucking-dammit. Out of all the people I could've run into, it had to be her? Olivia Hart had always been a pain in my ass. From being forced to spend time together as kids, to saving her ass when she got her jeep stuck in the mud after I told her it was shit weather to cruise in. The girl was one headache after another.

"Were you able to get the milk out of your favorite New Balance sneakers, Grandpa?"

I pinched the bridge of my nose. "I don't know what the fuck you have against them. They're comfortable. Sorry I don't wanna kill my feet when I'm on them all day."

"That's why they make inserts for your other shoes. You can be stylish and comfortable at the same time," he mused. "A concept I know has been long since lost on you."

His words hadn't stung exactly, but they were another reminder of how my life had changed. My outfit was simple and to the point. I didn't see the need to dress up when I was just going from the cabin to the bar or to Harper's school. It wasn't like I was going on dates or anything. Even when I had that one damn time, I knew five minutes in there wouldn't be a number two.

"Maybe when you have a kid of your own to chase around, I'll convert you."

Lukas laughed. "Yeah, that'll be the day."

"You talking about wearing New Balances or having kids? Kinda hard to tell," I said, grabbing a bottle of cleaner and spraying it over the counter. Harper had gotten jelly everywhere while making herself a sandwich And while she'd tried to clean up, she ended up leaving a sticky mess along the surface that wouldn't be conquered by anything less than industrial strength solvents.

"Both," Lukas chuckled. "But I'm an awesome-as-fuck uncle. How is my niece doing, by the way? Haven't seen her around much lately."

My hand faltered as I let out a sigh. Lukas always offered to watch Harper when I needed him to, and she loved going out there to visit his hoard of animals. "Yeah, it's rough this time of year, ya know? This is about the time Sarah—"

"Walked out," Lukas finished quietly. He knew every sordid detail of my ex and I splitting. He'd been there to take care of Harper when I physically couldn't get out of bed, and he'd made sure I ate when I'd rather have wasted away. "No, I get it. Losing a parent is rough. When my dad died… Well, it wasn't his choice to leave us. I knew that. Could rationalize it, even."

"Can't really rationalize this, though. Makes no goddamn sense, walking away from your own kid," I groused.

Ever since the divorce, my daughter had struggled to find balance. Her life had been uprooted, torn from her childhood home because I couldn't afford the mortgage payment by myself anymore, and her mom wanted nothing to do with us. Sarah moved to the city, choosing to follow dreams of her own, which apparently didn't include her husband or her child. These days, Harper was lucky to get a text on her birthday. Her mom never called. Never sent gifts. It was like we didn't exist. While I wasn't wasting my days pining for a woman who, looking back, I knew was never going to stay with me, our daughter felt the absence of her mother something fierce.

"You know I'm always here for you," Lukas said after a beat. "Y'all can stay in the guest house—"

Before he could finish, I was already shaking my head. We'd

had this argument more times than I could count. "We're good here, Luke. Told you that."

"You're sleeping on your goddamn couch, Duke. A couch I know damn well isn't comfortable."

He was right, but I wasn't about to admit it and acknowledge another failure. Another thing I couldn't fix.

Six months ago, Harper and I moved into the small cabin behind Frank's bar. It came with the property, so I figured I ought to make use of the damn thing. There was only one bedroom, which meant I was, in fact, sleeping on the too-small couch every night so my daughter could have her privacy. I thought it might help get her back to her old self, but it only seemed to make her sadder. The only time I saw her smile these days was when she was around her best friend.

"How goes things with you?" I asked, changing the subject. If there was one thing Lukas wouldn't do, it was push things after I'd drawn a line in the sand.

Lukas blew out a long breath. "John's sick."

"Aw man, I'm sorry. What's he got? The flu or something? Heard that's going around."

"No," Lukas said after a long moment. "End stage liver failure. He's declined all treatment. Doc said three to six months."

My eyes closed as I processed the news. John Hart was a stand-up guy. Literally one of the best I'd ever known. After Lukas' dad died, he took on the parental role Lukas and Olivia needed while their mother lost herself to grief. Not only that, but John had helped my uncle since he was elected mayor of Pinecrest over fifteen years ago. Together, they'd helped transform our little town into the tight-knit community it was today.

Why did the worst things happen to the best people?

"Christ, man. I'm so sorry. What can I do?"

Lukas laughed, but there was no warmth to it. "Want to see if you can convince the old bastard to do a liver transplant?"

"He refused?" I asked in shock. "Why the fuck would he do that?"

"He said he's lived a good life. That there's no point in postponing the inevitable. We all die in the end, after all. Fuck if I know. It's idiocy if you ask me. He's got all the money in the world and yet won't use it to save himself."

Suddenly, it made fucking sense. "That's why Olivia's back, isn't it?"

"Picked her up last night. I don't think she's handling it well, to be honest. She's putting on one hell of a front, but you know how she is. Stubborn as a goddamn mule and never willing to ask for help."

She was sure as shit stubborn alright.

"She'll be fine," I bit out. It came out more harshly than I intended, but Lukas didn't seem to care. He was too lost to his own battles to hear about the one I was currently waging with his sister in my head.

Once upon a time, I'd been glad Olivia left this tiny town to chase her dreams. I listened as Lukas talked about all her accomplishments. Even followed her career on my own a bit, too, but times had changed. Now, I resented her for leaving. For the fame, the fortune, the too-good-for-Pinecrest attitude. It reminded me too much of Sarah. The way she disappeared without a second thought, leaving Harper and I to pick up the pieces. A divorce was one thing, but how could a mother walk away from their kid? Their stories were too similar for me not to compare.

If I'd passed her on the street, I would've known it was Olivia immediately from the fancy way she carried herself. She might've been wearing a Hartfelt Homes T-shirt, but the skintight jeans painted on powerful legs gave her away. They hugged every goddamn curve of her body like a masterpiece. Silvery blonde hair was piled into an artful bun on top of her head, giving a perfect, unobstructed view to her slender neck. I could still smell the faint scent of her expensive perfume. Sweet berries and warm vanilla. Thank god for the cold milk that had shocked me out of my stupor, otherwise I might've stood there gawking like an idiot.

"Liv's a fighter, but I still worry about her. I invited her and Charlie over for dinner tonight, but she declined. Told me that as long as our mother is staying under my roof, she wouldn't be stepping foot inside," Lukas muttered.

"She can't get over herself for five minutes? Not everything is about her." I was being an ass, but it was true. Their mother was a barely functioning alcoholic in designer clothes. The only reason she wasn't living out on the street is because of John's generosity. But sometimes you needed to set that shit aside for family. They were blood after all. Whatever she'd done couldn't have been that bad.

"It's complicated, but I'm not getting between them. Tomorrow will sure as fuck be interesting, though."

"Why's that?"

Luke was silent for a second. "Liv and I are going to visit John. I wouldn't put it past our mother to make an appearance. Especially if I told her to stay her ass home."

"Better take two cars," I mused. "Have an exit strategy just in case. Liv just might leave your ass behind."

"No shit," he chuckled. "Might need a deputy on standby. Think your cousin could give us a hand?"

"Not if you want to keep that shit quiet." My cousin, Beau Campbell, was one of the biggest gossips in town. When he wasn't on duty at the Sheriff's Office, he was usually at some book club in town with our grandma, chatting up all the old ladies and making them blush.

"On second thought, I think I'll pass. Don't need to watch him drool over Liv, and then hear about it all over town."

"Dad, who're you talking to?" Harper rounded the corner, a crumb-filled paper plate in one hand, and an empty soda can in the other.

"Uncle Lukas. Wanna say hi?" I asked, holding the phone out for her to take. She nodded and I took the trash from her, throwing it away quickly before heading out of the kitchen. I needed to get ready for work and my buddy could talk anyone's ear off, even my introverted daughter.

I walked into the bathroom and took a good look at myself before brushing my teeth. It had really chapped my ass when Olivia had called my appearance out. Her voice was cold, words slicing deep. It would've felt better if I just laid down and let her kick the shit out of me. What did it matter at that point? I was already hanging on by a thread.

What hurt most of all was that she was right. I looked like a goddamn mess.

It'd been over a week since I last shaved. My stubble had grown into the makings of a beard. I couldn't even remember the last time I'd cut my hair, which was normally hidden under a ratty old baseball cap anyway. My clothes were stained because I'd forgotten to start the laundry the night before, and had to dig through the pile until I found something halfway decent. I hadn't noticed the stain until we were already on our way to the game. By that time, it was already too late to change.

"Dad? Someone's outside." Harper's soft voice sounded from the other side of the thin, wooden door.

"Alright, sugar. I'm coming." Giving myself a final onceover in the mirror, I sighed and opened the door. My daughter's hair was still tangled from riding home with the windows down in my truck. It was early spring, which meant the weather was still nice enough to enjoy the cool mountain air without feeling like you were suffocating.

There weren't many similarities between my daughter and

me. Her fair complexion and auburn hair were all her mother. The two things she had were my eye color—a green so light and cutting that it often resembled gray—and my quiet demeanor. Our introverted tendencies were often a hindrance now that it was just the two of us. It was one of the reasons I liked her spending so much time with Charlie. That girl could get Harper giggling and laughing like no one else.

"Did you see who it is?" I asked, stepping around her toward the front of the cabin. There was one large window in the living area, but the curtains and blinds were drawn tight.

Harper shook her head, handing me back the phone. "It was dark and the light wasn't on. I just heard a knock when I was going to my room."

Pulling back the plaid curtains, I could see that the bar was already packed for a Saturday night. It was going to be an all-hands-on deck situation. Sawyer, my bartender, usually covered the rowdy crowd until it got dark. Then I'd lock up and walk over to finish the shift while she graciously watched Harper. It wasn't an ideal arrangement, but it was what we had. It was why I preferred when Harper spent Saturday nights with Charlie and her family, but that went to hell the minute Olivia crashed in and changed our plans.

"Who's out there?" Harper asked.

"No one that I can see. You sure you heard a knock?"

She rolled her eyes. "Yes, Dad. I know what I heard."

"Okay, okay." I held my hands up. The attitude was something new, but I didn't mind. Not if she was talking to me. "Guess it could've been one of the tree limbs knocking against the roof. Might need to go out tomorrow and take a look."

Harper shrugged and silently trudged back to her room. I turned just in time to see her close the door. She'd been quiet since we left the grocery store. More reserved. During lunch, she'd hardly said two words to me. Just sat and ate her sandwich quietly like I wasn't even there.

She's ashamed of you.

You're never here.

She wishes she was with her mom.

She doesn't love you.

Vicious words and cruel taunts filled my head as they always did when we had a day like this. I struggled with fatherhood more than I ever wanted to admit. Struggled to connect with any role other than protector and provider in the most basic sense. When Sarah was here, she could do all the fun shit with Harper that I swore I didn't have time for. Now, I was kicking myself in the fucking balls thinking about all the opportunities I'd missed to figure out what else she needed to live the life she deserved.

At the end of the day, I just wanted to be a good dad. I wanted my daughter to be happy and healthy and full of love. If she ended up in therapy fifteen years from now, I didn't want it to be because I was a piece of shit who never showed affection. I loved that girl with everything I had. Every broken, shattered piece of me.

She was the only reason I was still breathing. My sole purpose.

Heading back to the bathroom, I quickly changed my clothes and combed back my hair before tucking it beneath a hat. I was just gonna sweat my ass off anyway. Plus, it wasn't like Frank's was a fancy establishment. Hell, a man came in once wearing nothing but a hospital gown.

Walking over to Harper's door, I knocked gently. "I'm headed out, sugar. Sawyer will be over in a bit."

"'Kay, Dad."

I rested my forehead against the wood and closed my eyes. A

two-word response was better than none. I should be grateful I got that much. "Love you. I'll see you in the morning."

I waited for a response, but nothing came. Silence greeted me like a slap in the face. With a sigh, I turned and made my way to the door. The last thing I wanted to do was go look over a bunch of rowdy drunks, but I didn't have another option. I put my entire savings on the line to buy Frank's. Letting it go wasn't an option.

I'd just have to add this day to the pile of other shit days and move the fuck on.

Opening the door, I nearly faceplanted as my feet got tangled up in something on the first step. I turned and stared at the obstacle, cursing under my breath when I realized what it was.

Paper bags overflowing with groceries sat upright at the doorstep. There was a folded card on top, but I didn't need to read it to know who they were from. Still, curiosity got the fucking best of me. I snatched it up, scanning the neat cursive lines.

Duke,
Dinner's on me. Hope this is everything you guys needed.
— Liv
P.S. The Fruity Pebbles are for Harper

OLIVIA

BEING home came with a whole list of challenges I'd never anticipated. I was used to strict schedules and deadlines in my professional life, but everything changed the moment I boarded a plane and stepped foot in Pinecrest. There was an unpredictability here I wasn't used to. Change was everywhere I looked.

Buttercup Bakery, home of my family's favorite lemon cupcakes, had closed last year, and in its place was a fucking Starbucks. And the floral shop, Forget-Me-Not, had a 'For Sale' sign on the front door. Main Street was once filled with local favorites, some that had been around since my grandpa was a boy, but nearly half of them had either been turned into something else or closed entirely.

It nearly broke my heart strolling through town with Charlie yesterday—seeing all the hard work people had put in for years, decades even, gone in the blink of an eye. Those small businesses were what made a town like Pinecrest the gem it was. Everyone knew one another, helped their neighbors as though they were family. Property developers from big cities always hovered like vultures, but businesses had fought them back with pride. Now, the empty buildings might as well have been dead carcasses on the side of the road, ripe for the picking.

While I'd been able to somewhat salvage the rest of our day together, my daughter was still distant. We talked and laughed and goofed around, but her smile didn't reach her eyes. She didn't open up about school or friends. Anytime I got a morsel of information, it was because I literally pried it out of her.

It was all made worse by telling her exactly why I was back in town. Somehow, I managed to keep my tears at bay as I told her that John was sick. She voiced all the things I couldn't. How it wasn't fair and that she didn't understand why he wouldn't fight harder. I held her in my arms as her tears soaked through my sweater, doing my best to soothe every painful, horrible sob ripping from her chest. At least, in that moment, I felt like I could do one thing right. I could comfort my daughter and let her fall apart knowing she was in a safe space.

But as her tears subsided, she told me she wanted to go to bed early instead of watching her favorite movie, and that hollow feeling in my chest felt deeper. Disappointed as I was, I didn't have any fight left in me. So, I just tucked her in, giving her forehead a quick kiss, before trudging outside, pouring a tall glass of wine and allowing myself to cry.

I couldn't remember the last time I'd let my tears fall like this. It might have been the night I found out I was pregnant with Charlie, scared shitless that Grady wouldn't be happy about our little surprise. Maybe it went further back. Maybe it was the night a police cruiser pulled up in front of my school instead of my dad. The way I instantly knew something was wrong.

Was it bad that I couldn't remember?

I had hoped letting everything out like that would make me feel better come morning, but it didn't. Instead, I woke up with dark circles beneath my eyes and that same nail-biting dread in the pit of my stomach.

I'd blame it on the wine if anyone asked.

"Delivery incoming," Lukas boomed, walking into the kitchen with a tray of insulated coffee cups. His eyes landed on the homemade plate of cookies on the counter and like a heat seeking missile, he homed in on them before I could stop him. "Oh my god, yes."

"Hey, I didn't say I would share," I said, ripping one of the cookies from his grip. "Cleo and Charlie made those for me, not you."

Lukas plopped down on the stool across from me. "You can't spare one for your poor, lonely brother?" he pouted, softening his eyes. "I don't have anyone to make me cookies."

"And whose fault is that? Certainly not mine." If he wanted someone to bake him cookies, he could find his own Cleo because mine was off limits. I snagged one of the cups, brought it to my nose, and inhaled. "Alright, you can have *one* for bringing me this."

"I'm surprised you didn't grab some coffee yesterday. Didn't you go to the store?" he asked, groaning as he took a bite. "Fuck. These are so good."

I followed suit, closing my eyes as the perfectly balanced sweetness landed on my tongue. I wasn't sure what she did to make these taste so goddamn good, but they were perfect. "Must have slipped my mind given the fiasco."

Lukas, being the shit-stirrer that he was, already knew about my run-in with Duke yesterday. I'd called him the moment I walked out of the store with my groceries in one cart and Duke's in the other. There'd been no plan in the heat of the moment, just guilt from knowing he'd left them all because of what I'd said. I wanted to make it right. But once I paid for them, I realized I didn't know where he lived. Charlie told me about Frank's Bar, and I'd thought she was joking around, and called Lukas instead hoping for some clarity. Instead, I'd driven toward Frank's feeling like more of a dick than I already had.

Duke and I were never close by any stretch of the word. I had no right to know about his life or his business, but I couldn't imagine what would push him from living in the gorgeous house Lukas built for him in town to the tiny shed behind Frank's. None of it made any sense.

While he and Lukas got into their fair share of trouble growing up, Duke seemed to have his head on a little straighter. He was the captain of the football team, an A and B student. He pulled my brother from fights and steered him away from the darker aspects of his personality after our dad died. Other than a warning they got for getting caught underage with a case of beer, there wasn't a mark on his record as far as I was aware.

So how the hell had he ended up where he had?

"Earth to Liv." Lukas snapped his fingers in front of my face, bringing me back to the present. "Hello?"

"Sorry," I muttered. Not even the warmth of the coffee was enough to ward off the chill of unease I felt. "Thousand miles away."

"I see that," he said slowly. Though I wasn't looking at him, I could feel his eyes on me all the same. "You sure you're okay to do this today? We can hold off—"

"No. I want to see him. I need to. Putting it off won't change things. It'll just leave me with regrets."

As much as I didn't want to see John in such a frail state, Lukas was driving Charlie and me over to visit him this afternoon. Though he still owned the ranch Lukas lived on, he'd bought a couple of hundred acres across town when we were kids. It had become his sanctuary, of sorts. Ours too. Especially in the early years after Dad's passing.

Tucked away at the edge of the forest was his large

craftsman style house. Beautiful tapered cedar columns sat atop thick stone plinths, carefully crafted to blend in with the surroundings rather than stand out. On one side of the house was the woodshop he'd built for Lukas, and beneath that had been a soundproof music studio for me. He enjoyed fostering that kind of passion in both of us. Encouraged us to follow our dreams, no matter what it entailed.

"I just want to warn you… He's not in the best shape." Lukas' face was grim. "It may be hard—"

"I said I want to do this, Lukas." I met my brother's steely gaze as my voice broke. "He was there for us when we had no one, and I'm going to be there for him. I don't give a shit what he looks like."

Lukas' eyes softened a fraction. Reaching out, he rested his hand on mine. "I know you don't, Livvy. I'm just worried about you."

"Well, don't be. Focus that concern on our uncle. Maybe it'll be enough to make him reconsider." I tried to smile, but it didn't feel right. We both knew nothing would change his mind. John was a stubborn man, even on his best day. If he had made a decision, it rarely ever moved.

My brother echoed the hollow gesture. "Yeah. Maybe."

THANKS TO CHARLIE, the ride to John's house was anything but silent. She and Lukas chatted about anything and everything, cracking jokes and making plans. It hurt more than I cared to admit that neither of them extended an invitation to me, assuming I wouldn't be around.

It wasn't an unfair assumption. I was always on the road, but I was here right now, after all. And I had no plans of leaving anytime soon. My job had taken a lot from me, but it wouldn't take these last few months with John. I wouldn't let it.

"And I was just cast as the lead in the big musical in school!" Charlie exclaimed proudly. "Mrs. Anson said I have the voice of an angel. I don't know what that means, but I think it's good."

Hearing them talk so freely stung more than I cared to admit, but I kept smiling anyway.

"Hell yes," Lukas chimed in, smiling. "You're gonna blow all those other kids out of the water. I might even have to make a sign!"

Charlie giggled. "Uncle Luke, you know you can't hold signs up in the auditorium. You got yelled at last time."

"Last time?" I asked, turning toward my brother. "What happened last time?"

My brother grinned. "Well, Grady and I might have gotten a little carried away and made a six-foot-wide sign that said, 'Charlie Hart's Number One Fans.' But they told us we couldn't bring it inside, wouldn't even let us stand in the back with it."

"I'm guessing that didn't stop you."

"Nope. We got a little creative and snuck it inside under our jackets. It was a little worse for wear, but it got the message across."

"Uncle Luke and Daddy almost got banned from the auditorium," Charlie said, giggling. "Mrs. Anson said if they ever did that again, they wouldn't be able to step foot inside the building. She was *so* mad."

"Worth it," Lukas said, sharing a wink with Charlie in the rearview mirror.

My smile slipped as I took in the easy way they bantered over core memories. Memories I wasn't a part of, nor could ever get back. I shouldn't have been jealous of the bond they shared. If anything, I should be thanking all the stars in the sky that my daughter was so loved in my absence, but since when did emotion ever make sense?

As if sensing the direction of my thoughts, Lukas reached over and gave my hand a squeeze. "Can't wait for you to see our shenanigans this year. We go all out for our Charlie girl. You just gotta promise not to rat on us."

Charlie's head jerked up. Her blue eyes cautious. "You'll be there?"

I hated the skepticism in her voice. The waver that said she wouldn't quite believe me if I said yes. And even if I had no clue when it took place or what my life would look like at that time, I knew one thing with absolute certainty. "I wouldn't miss it for the world, baby. I'd love to come."

Charlie's cheeks pinked, a huge smile spreading across her face. "Really? That would be so cool. And maybe afterward, we could have a party! Like a really big party to celebrate school being over. We could invite everyone like Harper. Oh, and Mr. Bennett! That's okay, isn't it, Mom?"

"Anything you want, superstar. It's yours." Hope bloomed in my chest as my daughter launched into a whole new conversation about over-the-top party themes and elaborate invitations. Right now, no matter what she asked for, I would've given it.

But that hope died as we pulled up to John's house, and a familiar pearlescent white Mercedes caught my eye. The driver stepped out and stared in our direction as we came to a stop. Though her face was concealed by giant sunglasses and a satin scarf draped over perfectly polished hair, I knew precisely who it was.

"What the hell, Lukas?" I muttered beneath my breath as he killed the engine.

Lukas, to his credit, looked just as irritated as I felt. "I told her not to come—"

"Did you tell her we would be here?" I snapped, thankful

Charlie was too lost in her grandiose plans to notice the shift in atmosphere.

"I—"

"Momma, who is that?" Charlie asked, peering between Lukas and me at the person standing in front of the car. Then her little face scrunched up. "Why is she wearing that funny thing on her head?"

"Deal with that," I muttered to my brother before stepping out of his truck. He followed suit, rounding the vehicle. Without so much as a glance at her, I stepped to the back and helped Charlie out of her booster seat. She gripped my hand tightly but didn't question anything else as I offered a tentative smile.

Though I couldn't make out exactly what my brother was saying, I heard words like *leave* and *not welcome* as we came face-to-face with a woman I hadn't seen since she'd broken my heart for the last time. I couldn't see her eyes, but I felt her piercing, judgmental gaze all the same. It was one I was all too familiar with.

"Hello, Mother."

DUKE

"GIMME ANOTHER," Too Drunk Johnny said, holding out his empty beer mug.

It would seem my workday was starting off with a bang if the town drunkard was already three sheets to the wind. I snagged the mug from his grasp, moving to fill a fresh cup with water. "How 'bout one of these instead?" Ice rattled against the chipped glass as I shook it in his face.

"Bah! You're not getting soft on me now, are ya, boy? I 'member when you were just this tall," he said, holding space between his thumb and pointer finger, which made no goddamn sense.

Setting down the rag I was using to wipe the bar, I forced my eyes wide. "Dad? Is that you? Mom said you went out for milk—"

Johnny rolled his eyes, jerking the water from my grasp. "Dick," he mumbled between desperate gulps. "You know what I meant."

"Just like *you* know we're not gonna overserve your ass. Get sober and get a ride, Johnny. Don't make me call Beau," I groused, snatching his keys. With a loud clatter, I dropped them into the steel canister behind the bar we'd lovingly nicknamed "the drunk tank."

Every night was the same. Johnny came in, drank as much of the cheapest beer I was willing to serve him, and then tried to push his luck for more. The man had been battling demons for as long as I could remember. As much as I hated enabling his bad habits, at least I could keep an eye on him here and get him home safe if he got too drunk.

"I swear I've only served him a couple of beers, Duke," Sawyer said, looking warily around me at the grumbling man who was more than likely flipping me the bird behind my back. "He wasn't this bad earlier. Need me to call Beau?"

I shook my head. "Not worth it right now. Make the call if he tries to snatch his keys back." I thumbed over my shoulder to the canister. "I've seen him make a mad dash over the bar before."

Sawyer smiled and nodded her head, turning back to the steaming dishwasher. "I'm just gonna finish putting these away and then I'll head over to the cabin, okay?"

"Sure thing. I made lasagna for dinner. Help yourself to as much as you want."

"You didn't have to do that, Duke. I brought a sandwich."

I leveled her with a glare. "You insulting my cooking?"

"Of course not," she hurried to say, wringing her hands in front of her. "It's great! I just mean—"

"Be sure to take a plate for your grandma, too. You know where the Tupperware is. I happen to know Maeve loves my cooking," I added.

Sawyer looked away, chewing on the inside of her cheek. The poor girl didn't have the best home life growing up. Her mom got mixed up with the wrong crowd when she was just a baby. The best thing that woman ever did was drop Sawyer off with her grandmother before disappearing from her daughter's life. While Maeve might not have had much, she gave Sawyer the best life she could.

The least I could do was treat the eccentric old woman to an occasional free meal.

"Duke—"

I shook my head. We went through this almost every week. "You help take care of my bar and my kid, Sawyer. I can cook you some damn dinner." Her lips twitched at the exasperation in my tone. "Consider it a perk of the job if you have to. Just don't argue."

"You know how much I adore Harper. It's an honor to watch her." Sawyer's eyes always softened when talking about my daughter. Sometimes I wondered if it hit a little too close to home, but I didn't dare pry. Not when Harper enjoyed Sawyer's company so much. "I appreciate it."

"I appreciate you," I said, placing my hand on her shoulder. "Now get out of here, will ya?"

Sawyer gave a two-finger salute as she closed the dishwasher and headed for the door. I moved behind her, watching through the dirty back window as she trudged up the walkway to our cabin. Once she was safe inside, I walked back to the bar and studied the room.

Sundays were usually quiet. So much so that I rarely worked them. Regulars lined the bar top, gossiping like old hens. I swore some of them were worse than the ladies at bingo. Behind them, the tables were empty save for one or two lone patrons. I almost glossed over the person in the back booth, but the flash of color stole my focus.

I wasn't sure what caused Olivia Hart to be drinking alone at three in the afternoon on a Sunday, but it couldn't have been good. Her back was to the bar, shoulders hunched forward. Silvery blonde hair was pulled back in a low bun at the nape of her neck, allowing me to see her side profile. She stared straight ahead, eyes seemingly unfocused. The only movement she made was to occasionally lift a glass to her lips.

As much as I didn't want to, I decided it was best to say something to her. We may not have reunited on the best terms, but I could swallow my pride and thank her for the groceries. I'd intended to pay her back anyway. Might as well suck it up and get it over with now.

After checking on the regulars, I rounded the bar and touched the other tables one by one. There weren't many, which meant it was a shitty way to procrastinate. Two empty glasses sat on the worn wood. Her water was untouched. As she finished what was left of the third, she closed her eyes and sighed.

"Are you stalking me?" I asked, crossing my arms. It was my piss-poor attempt at a joke, but judging by the glare Olivia sent my way, it didn't land.

"Lukas said you didn't work on Sundays," she muttered, circling one perfectly manicured finger around the rim of her glass. There was something about her that was different than before. For how tense she was, you'd think I just asked her to defuse a bomb.

"Usually don't, but here I am." I wasn't going to tell her that the only reason I was here today was because of her. How I couldn't stop wondering what she had thought of Harper and I living in that tiny ass cabin, or the fact she'd driven clear out of the way to make the delivery in the first place. I needed to do something other than sit around and let my mind run rampant. There was only so much laundry a man could do while keeping his sanity intact.

"Here you are," she echoed with a sigh. Those same deft fingers rubbed at her temple as though trying to dissolve a headache. "Just give me a minute and I'll be out of your hair."

"You've been drinking."

Olivia snorted. "Very observant. I have been."

I crossed my arms. "Well, you can't drive."

"No shit, Sherlock. I was going to call Lukas." Then she groaned, hanging her head. "Nope. Scratch that. If I call Lukas, then he'll give me a lecture, and I really don't want one of those. Maybe I could call Cleo… Or Grady, even. Lord knows I've picked him up from this bar more times than I could fucking count."

Her voice trailed off as she reached into her expensive purse and pulled out her phone. I wasn't sure if I should give her privacy or not, so I decided to be useful instead. "Give me your keys."

Olivia turned to me, eyes narrowing. "Why?"

"So I can put them up knowing you're not a danger to yourself or others," I bit out. "Bar rules."

Honestly, those were only the rules for Too Drunk Johnny and the occasional rowdy out-of-towner that crossed our path, but I wasn't taking any chances with Olivia. Knowing her, she'd slip out without so much as a word and walk home just to spite me. Then I'd be stuck calling everyone we knew to make sure she got home safe. This seemed like the safer option.

"Since when?" She leaned over, giving me a perfect view down her shirt. The perfect breasts hidden beneath the tight cotton blouse.

What the hell was I doing?

I tried looking away, but it was too late. The way Olivia's lips curled told me she'd caught me staring. I was seconds away from apologizing when she cut me off. "Well, Duke? Since when has that been a rule?"

The way she said my name, accentuating the K in that flirty fucking tone of hers, had my dick twitching behind my jeans, which took me by surprise. Since Sarah left, I hadn't so much as looked at another woman. I was too jaded and too goddamn tired to even entertain the thought of hooking up with someone. Besides, it wasn't like I couldn't scratch that particular itch myself. My hand worked perfectly fine and it didn't come with expectations.

"Since I took over and got sick of drunks trying to dip out on tabs and get behind the wheel," I gritted out. It wasn't a total lie. Johnny had nearly taken out the big ass neon sign out front on more than one occasion. But I'd never needed to use the jar for anyone else.

"Are you worried I'll leave you with the bill?" she asked, quirking a brow.

"No, but—"

"What about drunk driving? Does that seem like something I'd do?"

I pinched the bridge of my nose, letting my eyes slide closed for one blissful moment of silence. "Always a pain in my fucking ass." When I glanced back at Olivia, she was waiting patiently for a response as though she didn't have a care in the world. This morning, I would've believed the lie. Would've let her keep the façade going. Seeing her drunk in my bar at three in the afternoon told another story, though.

"Well?" she asked.

"I'll let you keep your keys if you tell me why you're here," I countered, widening my stance. There was no point answering her previous question because no, I didn't think she'd drive drunk. Especially not after what happened with her dad. It may have been over twenty years ago, but I knew how his death affected both of his kids.

There was a brief flash of surprise before Olivia masked it with sarcasm. She picked up her empty cup, ice rattling against the glass as she shook it slightly. "It's a bar. Why do you *think* I'm here?"

I wasn't sure if she was looking for honesty, but I was going to give it to her anyway. "Seems to me like you've had a shit day and are trying to drown out the noise in your head." I looked around the room. An old country ballad came from the jukebox, breaking up the silence save for the soft hum of conversations at the bar. "You knew we'd be slow. That people would be too preoccupied to notice you slipping into the back booth. Your back's turned to the bar, signaling you don't want to be bothered except for the occasional refill. And you seemed specifically bothered by seeing me standing in my own damned establishment, which makes me believe Lukas either doesn't know you're here or doesn't like that you are."

If my best friend knew his little sister was getting drunk in the afternoon, he would've tagged along so that she wasn't alone. Unless something had happened between them. Was he the reason she was here? Had they gotten into a fight?

Olivia's face screwed up so tightly, I almost thought she swallowed something sour—not that I really wanted to think about her swallowing anything. If I did, I might just embarrass myself in my own bar. I couldn't seem to keep my head on straight around her.

"I didn't realize you were a fucking therapist," she said.

"I tend a bar. Of course, I'm a therapist."

That was something I'd had to get used to when I started here. I wasn't the type of guy people normally spilled their secrets to. Sarah always said I had "RBF," whatever the fuck that meant. But once I stepped behind that bar and poured their drinks, people couldn't help but tell me all their problems. Sometimes I'd try and help them work it out. Sometimes I just listened.

Olivia snorted. "Well, I pay top dollar for a professional to tell me how fucked I am. I don't need you piling it on for free."

"Is this your way of saying I'm not getting a tip?"

The tiniest twitch of her lips was enough to not make me feel like a complete asshole. What the hell did she mean she paid someone to tell her she was fucked up? Was that truly what she thought? Granted I didn't know her like I used to, but Olivia gave off the impression of having her shit together. I never would've assumed anything less.

"The other bartender was better company and quicker with the refills."

"Well, she's gone for the day. If you're planning on sticking around, you're stuck with me."

Olivia turned around as though to verify that Sawyer was, in fact, not behind the bar. With a huff, she faced me once again. "Well, where is she? I promised her a tip when I sat down. I don't want her to think I was lying just to keep the liquor flowing."

I could've easily told her some bullshit about Sawyer going home or her shift being over. Instead, I found myself saying, "She watches Harper in the evenings while I work."

"Really?"

I shrugged. "It isn't an ideal arrangement, but it's what I've got for now. Sometimes Lukas watches her when Sawyer can't."

"My Lukas?" Olivia asked, shock coloring her features. "As in the bachelor extraordinaire?"

"Being single doesn't make someone incapable of watching kids. You trust him with Charlie, don't you?"

"In a pinch, sure, but she's normally with Grady or Cleo." The way she was staring was unnerving. Like she was trying to unearth all my secrets and figure me out. It made my skin crawl.

As she opened her mouth to speak, I cut her off. "Give me your keys and I'll get you another drink." I held out my hand, waiting for her to hand them over.

Olivia's gaze dipped to my waiting palm before flitting away.

"No, that's okay. I think I'll call someone to get me." She offered a tight-lipped smile. "Thanks, though."

For some reason, disappointment hit me hard and square in the chest. I wasn't sure why I wanted her to stay. It wasn't like we were friends. Hell, we were barely acquaintances. I should be celebrating her getting out of my hair.

"Just doing my job," I muttered, dipping my head and heading back to the bar.

As I checked on the other patrons, I found my gaze wandering to her slouched form in the corner. She was on the phone with someone, smiling softly as she spoke. I couldn't help but wonder who was on the other line. If she were calling Lukas or Cleo or Grady like she said she would, or if this were someone else. Someone who was probably much better company than I was.

Why the fuck does it matter, Duke? Why do you care?

Before I could dig too deeply into that downward spiral, Too Drunk Johnny stood up. His barstool clattered to the ground, sending every head in the room his way. "Damn legs fell out from under me," he cursed, swaying as he bent forward to set it upright. "Need some better chairs here."

"Maybe if you weren't drunk off your ass, it wouldn't be a problem," I said, rubbing my temples. "You're a fucking liability."

"That's not a very nice thing to say."

"Yeah, well, it's not very nice to fall off my furniture. I'm calling you a ride, and they're taking you home." Pulling out my phone, I put in his address and ordered a cab. "They'll be here in ten minutes. That water better be gone by the time they get here," I said, pointing toward the still full glass I'd given him earlier.

"Yeah, yeah, yeah." He waved me off. "Quit your whining or I'll go to the bar across town."

Gerald, one of my regulars, shook his head. "Johnny, you've

been banned from that shithole since 1997 after you started that bar fight. 'Member? There was a goddamn town meeting 'bout it."

Johnny's lips tipped up. "Oh yeah. Forgot about that." He faced me again. "Guess you're stuck with me then."

"Lucky me," I muttered. "G, make sure he finishes that drink for me, yeah? I gotta run to the back."

Gerald reached down and grabbed his cane, raising it above the bar and shaking it in Johnny's direction. "I'll beat him if he doesn't."

I turned my back to the men, praying like hell there wouldn't be a goddamn dead body on the floor by the time I grabbed more napkins. That was the last thing I needed on my plate. Thankfully, the two were still bickering like an old married couple and Johnny's glass was half-empty when I returned. I listened to them trade barbs as I refilled the dispensers along the bar.

"Oh, Duke," Gerald said, cutting into my focus. "Blondie wanted us to tell you she was gonna hitchhike home with a random stranger."

"The fuck?" Instantly, my gaze shifted to the booth Olivia had occupied not even five minutes ago. Had she really snuck out while I wasn't looking? Surely she got a ride home and wasn't really going to be that reckless?

Gerald and the guys busted out in laughter at my reaction. "Oh shit, man. I'm sorry. I had to. She said she'd cover my tab if we said it." He pulled a bill from his wallet and flashed it my way. "Keep the change, loverboy."

I narrowed my eyes on them. "You just like stirring the fucking pot, don't you?"

He flashed me a shit eating grin. "An old man's gotta get his kicks where he can. Not much excitement left in these bones."

Blowing out a breath, I grabbed the cleaning supplies and

headed over to the booth. To hell with them, and to hell with Olivia. It wasn't like I was disappointed she skipped out without saying goodbye. In fact, it was better that way. No more awkward small talk necessary. Just the transactional relationship between a bartender and his patron.

It wasn't until I was laying my head down for sleep that night that I realized I was a fucking liar.

OLIVIA

NEARLY A WEEK HAD PASSED since I left Duke's bar, and each day I wondered if he was as bothered by my sneaking out as I seemed to be. In my slightly drunken stupor, I thought having the old men tell him I was hitchhiking with a stranger would be funny, but now it just felt rude. Given, though, that he hadn't tried to contact me to verify I was, in fact, still alive, I guessed he was fine with it.

He doesn't even have your number to contact you, you fucking idiot.

Try as I might, everything about that day still unnerved me. Though Lukas swore he hadn't invited my mother, he'd clearly let something slip. And while I knew avoiding her entirely wouldn't be possible forever, I'd hoped I could get away with it for a little while longer.

She had barely nodded a polite hello in my direction before her attention snagged on Charlie. I hated the way they stared at one another. They might as well have been strangers, and for all intents and purposes, they were. The last time I'd seen my mother—the night we'd both traded insults we couldn't take back—I'd vowed she would never know my daughter. That she'd have no chance to dig her talons into Charlie's mind, warping and twisting it until she was as lost as I had been growing up under her care.

Lukas, true to his word, had intercepted before she could say a word to my daughter. I ushered her into John's house, closing the door on my brother so that he could get rid of her, even if only for that day. I was struggling enough as it was and I wasn't allowed to break down the way I wanted to. I had to hold it together for Charlie, who'd run right up to the man she loved so much.

The silence in the house had been unnerving, immediately setting my senses on alert. John was the type of man who you could hear from a mile away. He was loud—obnoxiously so. He'd never learned the concept of an inside voice, not even when it came to business. Typically, when I came over, it felt like home, but that day it felt like a tomb. The house was mourning right along with us.

Seeing John in such a frail state, the way his chapped lips cracked as he spoke, the yellow pallor of his skin, had rattled me to my very core. He always seemed infallible growing up. But then again, I'd once thought that about my own father, too. Turned out he was just as mortal as the rest of us.

Though he'd tried to put on a show for our sakes', I could tell how much pain he was in. Seeing Charlie helped, I think. There was a glimmer of something in his eyes as we left. Unshed tears that would likely fall when he was alone. I hated the thought. Hated leaving him, but his eyes were growing heavy, and Charlie was pulling into herself, watching the man who'd been like a grandfather to her disappear before her eyes.

Before we left, I texted Grady and Cleo to ask if Charlie could come over for a few hours. I knew it was my weekend with her, knew I'd just gotten back in town, but I needed a moment to wrap my head around everything. My life felt like it was spinning out of control, and I desperately needed some space to spiral so I could eventually pick up the pieces of my new reality and piece them back together. Even though, eventually, there would be another piece of me missing.

The decision to show up at Frank's wasn't taken lightly, but Lukas had assured me that Duke didn't work on Sundays. It was the one day a week that he dedicated solely to Harper. I hadn't heard from him after we'd dropped off groceries, so I wasn't sure if I'd overstepped. The last thing I wanted to do was suit up for another fight. My armor was broken and needed repair. I didn't trust myself not to make a complete and total ass out of myself.

But apparently, the universe had it out for me, because he'd shown up after all. I'd wanted to die when he walked up to my table and asked if I was stalking him. Of course, that was what it seemed like. Accidentally assaulting someone in the grocery store and then buying and delivering their groceries probably wasn't something a sane person would do.

He'd looked better than the last time I saw him. Still tired, but show me a parent who wasn't, and I'd call them a liar. And with his wife apparently no longer in the picture, Duke was left to do it all on his own. Even though Grady and I were divorced, I'd never considered myself a single parent. I wasn't doing it on my own. I couldn't, in fact. Because of my job, I was forced to rely on others for support. If I didn't have Grady and Cleo, I wasn't sure what I would have done. Charlie would certainly suffer for it.

Who did Duke have save for the sweet bartender who also apparently filled the role of a nanny? His mom had a stroke a few years ago and was unable to care for herself. I remember Lukas telling me about how hard it'd been to find a good care facility with the space to take her. John fronted the money for her care to ensure Duke didn't have to make concessions. His uncle, the former mayor, had recently moved to an oceanfront state to enjoy his retirement. And even though I wasn't quite sure what the situation with his ex-wife was, she seemed to have completely removed herself from the picture.

By the time I'd left the bar, I had more questions than answers. I wanted to help him in whatever way I could. Not that he would accept it, especially not from me. He was too proud. It didn't take a fucking rocket scientist to figure that out. If I couldn't outright ask him, then I'd have to find other ways around it. Ways he couldn't say no to.

I remembered what he said about Harper's soccer games. How Charlie showed up to every one to support her best friend. Grady offered to take her this morning, but I told him I would do it. Honestly, I was thrilled to experience this dose of normalcy with my daughter. If I were home more, it could be a regular occurrence. Though I didn't want to impede on Grady's time with her, the prospect of stepping into a real routine with them had me jumping out of bed this morning.

Now, we were on our way to the game, rocking bright pink t-shirts with coffees and donuts in hand. Charlie was strapped in behind me, singing loudly to whatever song was playing on the radio. I sometimes saw so much of myself in her. She had a true talent for music. Always had, even as a toddler, dancing to the beat. The music producer and CEO in me was salivating at the potential she could have if she pursued a career in music, but the parent in me was nervous. I didn't want her to feel the pressure of the media and fans like her father and I had.

When we pulled up to the park, I paused, watching all the kids run to the field as their parents strolled leisurely behind them, lawn chairs in hand. "What happened to the stands?" I asked, brow furrowing. I hadn't thought about seating.

"They took them down last month. They're supposed to be

putting new ones in, they haven't." Charlie looked behind us at the empty trunk of my SUV. "I thought Dad told you about that."

I sighed. If he had, I must've missed it. Honestly, I was too excited when I asked if I could take her, I might've blacked out entirely. *Shit.* "I'm sorry, sunshine." How could I have already fucked up something so simple? Why wouldn't I think to bring chairs as a precaution? I was severely out of practice.

"It's okay, Mom. I like sitting in the grass by the team anyway." She looked down at my cream joggers. "But you might want to stand so you don't get stains on your butt."

I laughed, unable to help myself. If grass stains were the price I had to pay, so be it. I'd gladly do it to see her smile.

"I'll be fine. These are old anyway." They most certainly were not. And they were expensive to boot, but they were just clothes. Clothes could be cleaned or replaced.

Time with my daughter could not.

Charlie smiled and opened the door. She took off at a dead run toward the team before I could utter a word. Like so many others, I let her go without too much worry. It wasn't until I got closer to the parents that my nerves kicked in.

While I was used to being social for my job, I'd never really mastered small talk with other parents. Maybe that was why most of the information I gleaned was second-hand from Grady or Cleo. The majority of conversations I overheard in passing were about PTA meetings and school pick-up complaints, none of which I had experience in. I didn't even know what the PTA did, so I couldn't even begin to contribute.

Sticking to the outskirts of the crowd seemed like the safer bet. I didn't want to feel judged for being so unprepared. I could still see Charlie sitting on the sidelines, chatting to girls I assumed were her friends. On instinct, I found myself scanning the kids for a pop of copper hair. Because Harper was who we were here to support. It definitely had nothing to do with my sudden interest in her father.

That would be ridiculous.

I was just about to sit down when a hand, calloused and warm, caught my elbow. "You should probably pay more attention."

I whipped around, finding Duke staring down at me. Gone was his unkempt beard, in its place was a goddamn mustache that'd make Burt Reynolds proud. The stubble around his jaw only added to the hotness somehow. Like he was unbothered or just rolled out of bed.

When I didn't say anything, he glanced down at my feet. "You were about to sit in dog shit."

"Oh," I said, following his trail to where a relatively fresh pile was steaming on the ground. "I swear that wasn't there 30 seconds ago." I lied. I hadn't looked at all. But admitting that felt wholly irresponsible, and I didn't want him to think worse of me than he already did.

"Right," he muttered, hand still lingering on my skin. It wasn't until a whistle blew behind us that he quickly dropped it to his side. "I'm guessing you didn't bring a chair."

It wasn't a question. It was a statement. Fact. Though he might have disarmed me at first, his accusation had my skin prickling.

"For your information, I happen to like sitting on the ground. I like the feel of grass beneath my fingers. It's soothing."

His expression almost seemed bored. "I don't really give a shit. It's okay to admit you forgot—"

"I didn't forget," I interrupted.

"Yeah, okay. Sure." Duke rolled his eyes. "Here. Take mine." Before I could object, he roughly unfolded the chair between us. Both of us stared at it, unmoving.

"I don't want—"

"Christ, woman. Are you always so damn stubborn? Just sit your ass in the chair." His voice was loud enough that everyone around us turned to stare. While he certainly didn't seem to give a shit, I felt the burn of my cheeks as they turned bright red. To save myself further embarrassment, I plopped down in the seat with an audible huff.

"Well, what're you going to do? Just stand there?" I mumbled, crossing my arms. I wouldn't admit it to him, but I was actually relieved not to ruin these joggers after the first wear. The lining was incredibly soft.

"Yup." That was it. That one single word had me clamping my mouth shut so hard, my jaw hurt. I could feel him behind me, feel the heat coming from his body. It wasn't even that chilly this morning, but it was welcome all the same.

Every move I made, every single shift in the stupid chair, was a reminder of his presence. He seemed to adjust with me. Minute arrangements that always kept him at my left shoulder. It wasn't that I was uncomfortable. It was the fact that I could smell his cologne each time the breeze picked up. There was a hint of spice to it, like burning sage and freshly cut cedar. Without thinking, I found myself leaning closer. When I realized what was happening, I'd pull back.

"Do you and Harper have plans after this?" I asked after a particularly long stretch of silence.

"What?"

"I asked if you had plans after this. I'm sure the girls are probably hungry. We could go to lunch. Harper can come over, too. I know you said Grady takes them sometimes." I added the last part so it didn't seem like a half-assed invite, but I wasn't sure it landed as I intended.

When he didn't say anything, I peeked up at him. His jaw was set, the muscle beneath fluttering as he gnashed his teeth together. "I know what you're doing."

I raised my brows in question. "Being nice?"

Silence stretched for a beat before he muttered, "I don't need your pity, Olivia."

Is that what he thought this was? "Good, because I'm not giving you any. I'm trying to show you that last week was a one-off. I'm not trying to step in and change the girls' routine with my presence. If they normally get together after soccer, I'll gladly take them." When he still didn't respond, I continued. "Lunch can even be on you."

He made a noise that was somewhere between a chuckle and a scoff. Like he wanted to laugh, but his pride wouldn't allow it. "It won't be fancy, then. Sure you can handle that, honey?"

Honey. The nickname rolled off his tongue like butter and made me feel all sorts of warm inside. It was meant to be patronizing, but there was a certain lack of conviction to it. Like he changed his mind at the last minute, yet couldn't stop himself.

"Please, Duke. I grew up in this town. I went to Dairy Queen every Friday night after high school football games just like everyone else. Contrary to whatever belief you have, I'm still that same girl." I pulled my YSL purse from beside me, shaking it his way. "Just with slightly better accessories."

His green eyes bore into me, searching for any hint of a lie. When he found none, his gaze flicked back to the field. "I can see that."

Taking that as my cue, I turned around in my chair. I didn't want to fight. And despite the people-pleasing tendencies screaming in my mind, I didn't need Duke to like me. We were going to be around each other whether we wanted to or not. His best friend was my brother, and our daughters were just as close.

His sigh was so heavy, I couldn't help but smile. I knew what he was going to say before he even uttered the word. "Fine."

DUKE

"THAT LAST GOAL was so sick, Harp!" Charlie said, hooking her elbow with Harpers as they skipped ahead of us toward the diner. "You were totally unstoppable!"

Harper blushed, but her smile was as a mile fucking wide. "I *felt* unstoppable. I just hope Ashley isn't too mad about it at school on Monday."

"Who cares?" Charlie replied, shrugging. "You were awesome. That's all that matters."

Olivia and I strolled behind our girls, both keeping an amicable distance between one another. After the game ended, the girls were thrilled when Olivia told them about lunch. Even more so when she asked if Harper wanted to spend the night. Both girls elected to ride with her so they could make plans for the evening.

Just as well for me, because I needed a goddamn minute to get my head back on straight.

I'd spent the entire drive to the soccer field this morning worrying so much about what to say when I saw Olivia that I'd decided it was better if I didn't say a damn thing at all. When I spotted her standing at the outskirts, looking so fucking lost and out of place, I knew my plans to stay away from her were headed directly out of the window.

Given my general lack of manners toward her, I was surprised she even mentioned lunch. If I were her, I'd want to spend as little time in my company as possible.

Yet here we were, walking into Lucy's Diner side-by-side. Lucy herself called out a greeting as our daughters blew through the door and headed for the only open booth. The diner was always busy on Saturday mornings, so seating was a gamble.

I would've preferred a table. Somehow it seemed a little less intimate, but I could manage for an hour. How hard could it be to sit directly across from the brown-eyed woman who—to my utter chagrin—kept showing up in the most unexpected places?

That single thread of optimism came crashing down the moment Harper and Charlie slid into the same side of the table, leaving Olivia and me no other option but to sit next to one another.

"Oh. Um..." she stammered. We stared at the glittery red bench seat as though it'd personally offended us. "Girls, why don't we—"

"Slide in," I muttered, stepping to the side so she could move past me. She hesitated a moment longer, clearly looking as apprehensive as I felt, but we didn't need to make a big deal out of a seating arrangement. "This is the only open table."

Olivia's eyes scanned the diner in confirmation before flicking back to mine. She straightened her shoulders and offered me a polite smile as she glided past me. I held my breath as I followed suit, keeping as much space between us as possible. It wasn't enough, though. Her sweet perfume somehow mixed perfectly with the scent of pancakes and syrup, making my mouth water for something other than food.

"Good morning, you four!" Lucy said, dropping four menus on the turquoise table top. "Did you girls enjoy the game? Heard there was quite an upset."

We followed Harper and Charlie's gaze to the table where that Ashley girl was sitting with her parents. She had her arms crossed tightly over her chest and was glowering at her stack of pancakes as though they'd kicked her puppy.

Harper's shoulders fell, and Lucy clapped her on the shoulder. "Don't let her get you down, sweetie. It's a competitive sport. And you were clearly the better player today."

My daughter tucked a loose strand of hair behind her ear and smiled. "Thank you, ma'am."

Lucy tutted. "None of that *ma'am* nonsense. How many times do I have to tell you that? Now, what're we having to drink?"

"Two chocolate milkshakes and two waters for us," Olivia said, winking at Charlie.

"Ooh, Dad! Can I have a chocolate milkshake, too?" Harper asked, widening her green eyes. When my kid was as cute as that, how could I say no?

"Make that four," I said. Fuck it. Why shouldn't we indulge a little bit?

"Four shakes and four waters coming right up!" Lucy dashed off to put our drinks in, and the girls immediately jumped back into their planning, leaving Olivia and me to sit in silence.

I should say something—anything, really—but nothing came to mind. I'd never been much of a talker to begin with, and that hadn't changed as I'd gotten older. I saved my words and my breath for shit that mattered and didn't feel the need to yap just for the sake of it.

Olivia, though, did not share my opinion apparently. I could feel her knee bouncing anxiously beneath the table. She was making the whole damn seat vibrate with her fidgeting.

Without thinking, I reached out my hand and braced it on her knee before giving it a squeeze.

Fuck. Fuck. Fuck. Why did I do that? And why was I still doing it?

Olivia turned to me, wincing as she took in my stern expression. "Sorry. Nervous habit."

"Don't see what there is to be nervous about," I said.

Still, I kept my hand in place.

She laughed. "Well, this is a bit awkward, isn't it? I mean, we're just sitting here in silence."

"It's not silent. The girls are talking right there, and we're surrounded by about forty people having their own conversations."

"But we're not."

"What do you want to talk about? The weather? Oh yeah, it looks really nice out today. Heard there's gonna be a storm next weekend, though," I said sarcastically. "How is that any better?"

She blew out a breath. "Guess it isn't. Especially not if you're gonna be an ass about it."

"Honey, being an ass is my default." There it went again. The same slip of the tongue as earlier. I hadn't meant to say it, and I definitely hadn't meant to be a repeat offender. At least this had a bit more bite to it than before.

Olivia scanned my face. I wasn't sure what she was looking for, but I didn't like it. That woman had an uncanny ability to slide beneath my skin. I was defenseless against her. It pissed me off.

Yet my hand was still on her goddamn knee.

"Well, it doesn't have to be," she said, shifting in her seat. The movement caused her legs to close, trapping my hand right between her thighs. Her skin was hot, even through the fabric. It was enough to snap me out of whatever stupor I was in.

I pulled back, quickly placing my hand in my lap to cover the situation taking place in my jeans. For the second time in a week, Olivia Hart had me thinking about everything I shouldn't be.

I liked sex just as much as the next person, but it'd never been a necessity for me. It wasn't something I thought about every minute of every day. During college, I dated a few women before meeting the one who'd eventually become my wife. It wasn't like I was inexperienced or anything, but I wasn't what she wanted.

Sarah always said I wasn't affectionate enough. That I didn't show her the right amount of physical attention. So, I tried. I tried to be conscious of every move, every touch, just to try and make her happy. It was never enough.

So, color me fucking shocked when I had to stroke myself multiple times in the shower two nights ago because I couldn't get the infuriating woman in front of me out of my head. When I realized what I'd done, I panicked.

I'd known her damn near my whole life and had never seen her as anything other than my best friend's little sister. Why now? Why, when I truly couldn't afford any distractions, did she decide to waltz back into my life and fuck with my head?

The worst part was that it wasn't even on purpose. Olivia hadn't done a single thing to make me spiral out of control like this. She hadn't insinuated anything. Hadn't offered anything, either. Save for a few lingering glances on both our parts, she'd been completely appropriate.

It was maddening. She was maddening. This whole situation was maddening.

"Uh, Dad?" Harper's voice pulled me back to the present.

I jerked my gaze away from Olivia, realizing Lucy was standing at the head of the table with a notepad and pen, a knowing smile on her face. "What can I get you, Duke?"

"You sure you're okay with taking her?" I asked, walking through the front door of our cabin.

After lunch, Olivia and the girls followed me back home since Harper needed to pack a bag. I wasn't thrilled about the prospect of anyone else seeing where we lived, but it wasn't exactly a secret anymore. She knew I didn't live in some fancy house anymore. Knew Harper and I were doing what we could to make ends meet.

"Positive. We're gonna do mani-pedis. Watch junk television. Eat *so* many sweets," Olivia paused, smiling as I turned toward her with a raised brow. "Oh, relax. It'll be fine!"

"I just don't want to impose."

Olivia held up her hands. "Duke, I swear. It's not an imposition. I'm happy to do it, and the girls are ecstatic. Take the night off and relax."

Truth be told, I could use a night to myself. The house was a mess, which didn't take much. It was a grand total of 600 square feet. Most of my chores had been pushed aside since Sawyer had come down with the flu last week. She was back now, but I had to rely on our part-time help more than normal and fill in the rest of her schedule with my own time.

Or what little of it still existed.

Running a hand through my hair, I nodded. "I can pick her up first thing in the morning—"

"Or I could bring her home in the afternoon when Charlie and I head over to Grady's. It's on the way," she said, looking around.

That was bullshit. Grady's place was on the other side of town, and we both knew it. But rather than argue, I just nodded again. "Alright. I'd appreciate that."

Olivia's head swiveled in my direction, her jaw slack in surprise. "Did you just… agree with me?"

"Alright. Let's calm down now," I said, turning toward the kitchen. I needed to put some space between us.

Much to my dismay, she followed.

"Maybe I should jot this date down. You know, for the history books." She cleared her throat and held her hands out in front of her face. "The day Duke shut up and didn't argue."

I couldn't help it. My lips twitched. "Feels like a mouthful."

"Thank god I can fit a lot in mine," she shot back with a playful smirk.

Goddammit. Now I was thinking about what all she could do with that mouth. How she'd look up at me from her knees, brown eyes glistening with desire. The way her lips would look wrapped around my—

"Ready!" Harper announced, running into the living room with Charlie hot on her heels.

Oh, thank god. There was no way I could've continued that train of thought without embarrassing myself any more than I already had today.

I hadn't realized how close Olivia and I were standing to one another until Harper's voice had us jumping apart.

"Got everything you need, kiddo?" I asked, turning toward my daughter. She was staring at Olivia and me, no doubt wondering why I was acting so strange.

Get in line, kid. I was asking myself the same thing.

She hiked the strap of her bag higher on her shoulder. "Yup. I'll only be gone a night, Dad. It'll be fine."

"Alright," I conceded. "Give me a hug before you go."

She rolled her eyes, but came over anyway. I was sure that to someone like Olivia, whose family was borderline overly affectionate, our little side-hug looked awkward.

To me, though, it was everything.

Like her old man, Harper wasn't particularly keen on physical affection. So, whether I asked for it or not, every time she didn't argue or grumble was monumental to me. At least for a moment, I could pretend I was doing something right. That I wasn't completely fucking up this whole parenting thing.

I took the bag from her shoulder, holding out my other hand to gesture the girls forward. While I want to believe I did it because I was a gentleman, the truth of it was that I could easily slide my eyes to Olivia's ass as she walked.

I'd hate myself for it later, but not now. Not when I knew this would likely be the only time I could openly stare and not worry about being caught.

Maybe I could satisfy my curiosity with just one look, though I doubted it.

I followed Olivia to the trunk of her fancy SUV, putting Harper's duffel inside and closing the hatch. The girls had already climbed into the back, leaving the two of us alone once again.

"So, you'll bring her home tomorrow?" I asked, already knowing the answer but needing to fill the silence anyway. I wasn't quite ready for her to leave yet.

"Yeah, probably around two or so, if that's okay. We're going to Grady's for dinner. I'd invite you and Harper, but—call me psychic—I can imagine you'll say no."

I dipped my head. "Maybe if the whole CEO thing doesn't work out for you, you could join a traveling circus as a fortune teller." It wasn't that I didn't like Grady or his cooking. I'd been invited to their house several times over the past few years. With Olivia there, though, it felt weird. Like I'd be intruding somehow. They were a family, and I was the outsider.

Also, a small part of me didn't want to spend time with her in the presence of her ex-husband.

Not that I should want to spend time with her at all.

Olivia's expression faltered for a second before clearing. Had I said something wrong? I thought it was funny. "Right. Do you want my number so that you can text me if things change?" she said, wincing. "Or, I guess you could get it from Lukas if you need it. I'm sure you don't really want me having that kind of easy access to you."

I didn't, at all, but it would be the responsible thing to do. You know, in case of an emergency or something. At least, that's what I told myself as I fished my phone out of my back pocket and handed it to her.

Olivia took it hesitantly, her fingers flying over the keys, before handing it back to me. "There. I programmed my number and sent myself a text so I've got yours."

"Great. That's great."

We stood there for a second, neither of us knowing what to say. Finally, she snapped her fingers and pointed behind her to the driver's side door. "Better get going. These girls have a lengthy list of things they want to do, and we're definitely going to need to stop by the store."

"Right," I said, following as she stepped inside the car. With my hand on the door, I leaned in to talk to Harper in the back, but I realized my mistake too late. Olivia's breath fanned out against my neck, causing goosebumps to crop up along my skin. "Uh, be good for Olivia, okay, Harp?"

What was I saying? I'd never done this when I sent her off with Grady. Never drew out our goodbye or lingered in his car.

"I will, Dad. I promise."

"Alright. Well, yup. I'll just let you girls go." My eyes dropped to Olivia's as I pulled back. "Let me know if you need anything."

She smiled, albeit shakily. "Everything will be fine. Now, stop being so overbearing and enjoy your night."

Olivia closed the door the moment I stepped back, turning the ignition over and reversing out of the spot next to my truck.

I watched them leave, waving to the rearview mirror as they pulled onto the highway and headed into town.

Fishing out my phone, I was curious about what she had texted herself. Knowing her, it wasn't a simple "hi" or "it's Duke." No, Olivia would've tried to add humor to the situation, whether to cover up some kind of embarrassment she felt or to make someone—me, in this case—smile.

DUKE

Knew you'd look.

I couldn't help but laugh. It was ridiculous and stupid, but god, it made me smile. What was worse, it felt good. I wasn't sure what that meant. Feeling like this, feeling the walls I'd built so high lose a brick or two, made me nervous. But there was also something freeing about it.

That terrified me most of all.

Without thinking too much more about it, I went inside, turned the water of my shower as cold as it would go, and stepped beneath the icy rivulets.

OLIVIA

"OH MY GOSH, you've been to *the* Met Gala?" Harper asked, eyes wide with excitement.

I bit my lip to stop from laughing. The last thing I needed was to spill bright red nail polish all over Lukas' cream colored couch. "A few times, actually. And yes, it's just as insane as it looks on the internet. The outfits are out of this world."

Charlie, who was examining the rhinestones I'd dotted along her toes, said, "Some are really weird, though. When I go, I'm going to make sure mine is the best."

I shrugged. My girl didn't hesitate to call it as she saw it. And if she had big dreams, who was I to deny her? "They can be a little... strange, yes."

"Wow." Harper slumped back into the cushions and stared at her feet. "That's so cool."

Putting the cap back on the polish, I sat back on my heels to examine my handiwork. Both girls had wanted nail designs. While I was no artist, I was surprised at how well the flowers came out on Harper's toes, and the polka-dotted placement of Charlie's rhinestones.

"What do you think, girls? Should we make some ice cream sundaes and settle in for a new movie?" The one they'd put on at the start of our spa day was already over. We hardly paid attention to it, considering our time had been spent laughing and giggling as I worked.

Charlie jumped from her seat, bounding into the kitchen to rifle through the ingredients we'd picked up at the store. She never needed to be told twice about sweet treats. "Uh, duh! I want to make mine the biggest ever."

I stood, holding my hand out to help Harper up from the couch. She stared at it for a second before accepting. I wasn't sure whether she'd take it. And when she never dropped it, dragging me into the kitchen, there was a weird twisting sensation in my stomach.

I never wanted to pry, but I was curious about Harper's relationship with her mom. She rarely mentioned the woman. Anytime she spoke about her past, it was always her dad. How he taught her to braid her hair, or would get up in the morning on her birthday to cook chocolate-chip pancakes and bring them to her in bed.

While her mother's absence was apparent, her dad's presence was noted.

In every story, every memory in which Harper mentioned her dad, she smiled. And it wasn't some grand "I just won the lottery" smile. It was the simple twist of her lips. The kind that portrayed comfort and stability.

I wondered if Duke saw the same thing I did. I wondered if he realized that through everything—the divorce, the cramped living spaces, the long work hours, the inevitable parental breakdown after his daughter went to bed—Harper loved him fiercely.

I hoped, for both their sakes, that he did.

By the time Harper and I made it into the kitchen, Charlie

was in the middle of building her dessert monstrosity. "Oh my god, child. What are you doing?" I laughed, shielding my eyes from the mess along the counter.

She stared at a jar of maraschino cherries, brows furrowed and lip bitten in total concentration. "I'm trying to get a cherry," she said, not taking her eyes off her prize.

"I can see that," I said, putting my hands on my hips. "You do realize, though, that there are, like, six other cherries above the one you're trying to get, right?"

"Yes, but this is the biggest one in the jar. And it's the one I want."

Harper and I both bent forward. "How do you know?"

"Because I have eyes, Mom. And this is clearly the biggest one."

Harper just shrugged. I nudged her shoulder with my own. "That's your friend," I muttered.

She giggled. "Yeah, but she's *your* daughter."

I straightened up and sighed. "Have I raised a monster?"

Charlie, clearly not finding our jokes funny, met my gaze. "Sorry that I want the best for myself," she deadpanned before going right back to what she was doing.

Thankfully, my daughter's attitude was interrupted by a knock at the front door. "I apologize for questioning your desires, daughter. I shan't do it again." I pointed toward Harper. "Think you can handle that diva while I see who's here?"

Harper giggled and gave me a thumbs up before I turned and headed toward the entryway. I could hear them mumbling to themselves and digging through the kitchen drawers as I opened the door.

Cleo stood at the threshold with what looked like a dozen freshly baked cookies, two large pizzas, and a smile. "Sorry, I'm—"

I grabbed her hand and pulled her inside, setting the food on the accent table before hugging her. "My savior. Thank you, thank you, thank you!"

She laughed and returned the gesture. "Well, I couldn't let my favorite girls go without those," she said, gesturing toward the sweets.

While I hadn't met Cleo until I showed up unannounced in my ex's hometown, I'd heard about her the entirety of our marriage. Understandably, it took her a little bit to warm up to me. I couldn't imagine how weird it must've been for her to find out the man she'd been in love with since she was sixteen, who had married and had a child with another woman, had been pining for her just as much as she had for him.

But now? Now, Cleo Wilde was one of my best friends. I couldn't imagine my life without her. There wasn't a single thing she didn't know about me, and I her. We had spent many girls' nights on the couch drinking way too much wine and sharing every high and every low.

She was the best bonus mom and loved my daughter as fiercely as if she were her own. Grady and I never wanted her to feel left out or that she didn't have a say in how we raised Charlie.

I pulled back, taking her in. She wore a Black Springs Ranch sweatshirt and black leggings. Her long blonde hair was tucked behind one ear, framing her face in loose waves.

"I want one of those," I said, dropping my gaze to the cute little horseshoe embroidered on the sleeve. Cleo's family owned the massive ranch in Texas, and ever since her sisters had taken over the day-to-day operations, they'd come up with the best merchandising ideas.

"Oh, this?" Cleo asked. "I'll have Lennox send one over. They just got the sample stock in. Mom is thrilled at the prospect of organizing and selling merchandise. I don't think my dad's retirement suits them very well."

I snorted. That sounded about right. Her dad, Doug, was one of the busiest bodies I'd ever met, and I could imagine he was likely driving his wife and kids crazy. "Don't blame her, honestly."

"Me either. How's it going?" Cleo kicked off her slides near the door. "I don't hear screaming."

"That's because you saved Charlie from herself with your impeccable timing. I made the mistake of asking why she was digging toward the bottom of the cherry jar instead of using the ones on top."

Cleo smirked. "Trying to get the biggest one?"

"Don't tell me she learned that from you," I groaned.

"Blame your ex," she said, shooting me a wink as she moved past me.

Fucking Grady. I should've known. I grabbed the food before following her into the kitchen. "Honestly, that explains so much."

Both girls looked up from their cherry endeavor, grinning when they took in our new guest. "Cleo! You're here!" Charlie exclaimed, abandoning her mess. She took off running toward Cleo, nearly knocking her over as she slid to a stop. "Wait... Are those for us?"

Cleo wrapped Charlie in a hug. "Well, when your mom mentioned y'all were having a girls' night, I couldn't resist crashing. I hope that's okay?"

"Well, you brought cookies and pizza, so duh." She shrugged, digging into the box and grabbing a slice of cheese.

While Cleo and the girls got settled in the living room, I stayed behind to clean up the mess. I couldn't help but smile as I watched them all together. Charlie was flipping through the movie selection, trying to find the perfect film to end the night, as she spouted off movie facts about nearly every one. Cleo, of course, was fussing over everyone's comfort as she always did, but instead of stress or worry in her face, I only saw genuine peace. Harper sat between the two of them with the widest smile I'd ever seen, watching them banter back and forth playfully about which 2000's romcom was better.

And me? I stood there, happier than I had in a long time, surrounded by mess and chaos, wishing Duke could see the way his daughter shone.

Despite the time, when we pulled up to Duke's cabin the next day, he was waiting outside with a cup of coffee. Cleo left before we did, running to town for the hamburger buns Grady had forgotten to pick up earlier.

I glanced in the rearview mirror, watching Harper smile as she unbuckled her seatbelt. Duke met her at the door, pulling it open and helping her out. "Hey, sugar. Did you have fun?"

"Dad, we had the best time! Miss Olivia and Miss Cleo gave us mani-pedis," she flashed him her fingers, "and they bought pizza and ice cream—"

"Don't forget the fresh cookies!" Charlie interrupted.

"Right! The cookies. They were so good. Oh my gosh. And we watched movies until, like, midnight."

Duke's face was alight as his daughter chattered on and on about everything that happened last night. It was literal word vomit. I found myself laughing as I got out of my seat and walked to the truck, hefting her bag over my shoulder.

The two of them seemed so relaxed, so at ease. It was a jarring contrast to the way I'd seen them interact before. Maybe they both just needed a break. I imagine living in such a small cabin probably felt like it was impossible to get out from under the others' space.

"Damn, that does sound pretty fun." Duke's eyes softened as they locked with mine over Harper's head. "I'm a little jealous."

"Next time, you can come too, Mr. Bennett. I'm sure my mom wouldn't mind, right?" Charlie and Harper both turned to me, eyes pleading.

"Can my dad come to the next sleepover?" Harper asked, lip jutting out.

"Oh, I don't think so," Duke said at the same time I stammered, "S-sure." The man in front of me widened his eyes at that, clearly not impressed by my response, but what was I supposed to do? "I mean, we can figure something out," I added quickly. "Not like we have to decide anything today."

"Definitely not a sleepover," he muttered.

Harper turned toward him, face scrunched up in confusion. "Why not, Dad? It's on Uncle Lukas' ranch. We go there all the time."

"Maybe the boys could cook us dinner before we shoo them out, huh?" I glanced over at Duke's hands—a massive mistake, honestly—and added, "Although, your nail beds could definitely use some help." I was desperately trying to bridge the gap so as not to disappoint the girls, but also keep some semblance of distance from Duke. The last thing I needed to think of was having a sleepover.

I doubt there would be much sleeping...

That's what scared me the most about Duke. It wasn't his gruff, pain-in-the-ass attitude. Or even the constant scowl that marred his face.

It was the fact that I hadn't been able to stop thinking about him since we ran into one another at the store. If the girls hadn't been with me last night, I would've had a long date with my favorite vibrator, going round for round with his name on my lips.

If I knew he was only a room over, sleeping or not... Well, neither I nor my vagina could be trusted.

Duke glanced between the three of us. Both our girls held pleading looks in their eyes, as though this was the most important and exciting decision that could ever exist.

"If I say yes, will you stop staring at me like that?" he asked his daughter.

She nodded enthusiastically. "I promise."

He pinched his nose and sighed. "Fine, but—"

Charlie and Harper both let out hoots of victory, effectively cutting him off. When he turned to me, I just shrugged. "Kids want the damndest things."

Duke didn't say anything as Harper and Charlie said their goodbyes to one another. Before I could hand over her bag, Duke stopped me. "This isn't a good idea."

"What isn't?" I hoped that playing the fool would help me get out of this situation. I knew as well as he did that this little flirtation held no future. It was a recipe for disaster. My time in Pinecrest was limited, no matter how much I didn't want it to be. And Duke didn't strike me as the kind of guy who wanted to do long distance to make things work.

Not that there was anything to make work, anyway.

I was getting way too caught up in my head over the whole affair. So what if we'd flirted a little bit? Two people could be attracted to each other and choose not to act on it. In fact, it happened all the time.

"You know damn well what," he growled.

God help me, that shouldn't have been so hot. What was wrong with me?

"Listen... It's not like anything has to happen. We'll tell the girls our schedules are conflicting, and that'll be that. No adult sleepovers to worry about."

"I don't like to lie to my kid, Olivia."

"Neither do I, but have you got another solution? Because I sure as hell don't see one."

The muscle in his jaw ticked. I absentmindedly wondered how he had any teeth left, given how hard he ground them together. "Then I guess that's what we'll do," he grumbled.

He dropped my hand and stepped back, leaving me utterly confused as to what transpired. "I'm sorry. We'll do what now?" I asked.

Duke paused, and the pained look that crossed his face was almost enough to make me regret poking fun at him. "Look, it's been a long time since I've seen Harper smile like that. Clearly, it was good for her. And I know it may come as a shock to you, but I try to do what I can to make sure she doesn't feel like she's missing anything by only having one parent present."

"It doesn't." Though he said it as a rhetorical statement, I couldn't help the words from spilling out. Because it didn't come as a shock at all. Despite only being around him a handful of hours at best, I already knew that Duke would do whatever it took to make Harper happy.

Duke shifted on his feet, looking uncomfortable at what I'd said, but he continued. "If doing this sleepover thing will make her happy, then I'll do it. Maybe you could teach me a thing or two about nail beds or whatever." He waved his hand in the air awkwardly and I laughed.

"Alright. I'll see what I can do. Hopefully, you're not a lost cause."

Duke grabbed the bag strap, tugging it free from my grasp. He hesitated beside me, dropping his head so his lips grazed the shell of my ear. "I may be an old dog, but I can still learn new tricks, honey."

Then, as calm as ever, he turned and walked into his house—

leaving me standing in his driveway with soaked panties and a sudden desire to see exactly what new tricks he was referring to.

DUKE

"DUKE, would it be okay if I leave a little early tonight?"

I turned to see Sawyer standing behind the bar, twisting her hands in front of her. We'd been doing inventory all morning, but she seemed quieter than usual.

"You good? What's wrong?" I asked, wiping my hands along my jeans.

"Everything's fine!" she said, rushing to assure me. "It's just that my grandma's car is ready to be picked up from Jim's shop, and he closes at six on the dot. I can come back afterward!"

Yesterday morning, Sawyer told me her grandma's car had broken down on the way to the grocery store. Thankfully, I was still in town after dropping Harper off at school, so I swung by and picked both of them up before calling Jim, the local mechanic, to haul the car in and take a look. It cost me a month's worth of free drinks to convince him to move it to the front of the line, but it was worth every penny.

"Take the night off," I said, turning back to survey the contents of our fridge. "You deserve it."

"What about Harper? Ryan called in, so I was supposed to watch her so you could cover his shift."

Shit. I'd forgotten about that. But I couldn't very well go back on my word now. Sawyer deserved a night off more than anyone else I knew. I just needed to rearrange some things. It wouldn't be the first time I'd been forced to bring my daughter to work with me. I could stick her in one of the back booths so she could do her homework.

The bar would just have to close early when I put her to bed.

"I'll take care of it, Sawyer. You have more than enough on your plate right now." She opened her mouth to argue, but I stopped her. "Do you wanna argue, or do you wanna get out of here and enjoy an early evening?"

Sawyer smiled tentatively. "You know, you're a pretty great boss."

"God, that makes me feel old," I muttered.

"Well, you are in your forties…"

I pointed toward the back exit. "Get out."

She raised her hands in defense, holding back laughter. "Sorry, I had to."

"Can't believe this is the thanks I get for letting you leave early," I said, turning back to the bottles of liquor on the shelves.

When I first took over this place, I had to start from scratch. The previous bartender and owner had run off to Texas, leaving behind a whole lot of nothing for me to go by. In a strange turn of events, that same owner ended up marrying Olivia's ex-husband's sister—which gave me a headache if I thought about it too long.

When Sawyer came looking for a job, I'd been hesitant to hire her. She was young and had no previous bartending experience. Her resume was sparse, but I knew her grandmother and wanted to give the girl a shot. It was one of the best business decisions I ever made.

Now, being around Sawyer was like being around family. As an only sibling, I sometimes envied the relationship Lukas and Olivia shared. They bickered and bantered but had each other to lean on when shit got tough. Sawyer was as close as I had to a little sister, and I was grateful for her.

I couldn't view Olivia that way anymore.

I wasn't sure what the hell was happening between us, and I didn't know if I'd ever figure it out. Going there with her would be a colossal mistake for so many reasons.

Then again… I knew without a shadow of a fucking doubt that not at least *considering* taking a chance would haunt me for the rest of our lives.

Over the past couple of weeks, we had settled into a routine. Since I was usually stuck at the bar during the day, Olivia had been picking up Charlie and Harper from school most afternoons. She'd take the girls to Harper's practice every Tuesday and Thursday, occasionally taking them to the diner for supper before bringing Harper home.

When I could, I'd do the same for her. Sometimes she'd get stuck in a work meeting, or need to stay late with John. I figured the least I could do was return the favor so she could take care of whatever shit she needed to.

Thankfully, tonight was her night. I didn't have to worry about juggling the bar and dad duties until after seven, which would be fine. I could spend the night catching up on paperwork instead.

WHAT I THOUGHT WAS GOING to be a chill Tuesday night turned into a goddamn fiasco. After Sawyer left and I flipped the neon open sign on, nearly the entire town descended onto my little bar. I didn't know what kind of fucking memo I missed about the goings-on of this town, but clearly, everyone was finding a reason to raise a glass tonight.

Thankfully, everyone knew I ran a bare-minimum crew as it was. It didn't come as a surprise to find me behind the bar alone, and most customers were patient. If they weren't, they usually caught the side eye of old Gerald, or even Too Drunk Johnny on occasion.

It was enough to make whoever was about to kick up a fuss shut their damn mouth and wait for me to pass back by.

However, because I'd been so busy, I hadn't been able to check my phone all afternoon. I didn't realize what time it was until I saw Olivia, Charlie, and Harper walking through my door.

Olivia looked around, brows furrowed at the busy tables. She ushered the girls up to the bar, waiving hello to the old men sitting across from me. "Busy night?"

I checked my watch, dropping my head back and groaning when I saw it was half past seven. "Shit. I'm so sorry. Sawyer needed the night off, and Ryan wasn't scheduled. It's been a little busy tonight."

"You're working all of this alone?" she asked. Across the room, someone started singing a very off-key version of a George Strait song, causing all of us to cringe.

"Don't have a choice," I said, filling three cocktail glasses with ice and pouring a double shot in each one. "It was either this or shut down for the night." And that wasn't an option. Especially not now.

Olivia's hand landed on Harper's shoulder. "What about Harper?"

I scanned the room, hoping there was still an empty table nearby, but every single one was full. There wasn't even a seat at the bar. Fuck. I should've marked one as reserved when I had the chance, but it had happened so fast that the thought never crossed my mind.

"Give me your keys," Olivia said, holding out her hand.

I stared down at her waiting palm. "What?"

"The keys for your cabin. Give them to me," she said, not moving a muscle.

"Olivia, it'll be fine. I'll clear out a table in just a minute, and Harper can hang out there until I close down early."

It wasn't ideal. Honestly, I hated the idea of Harper hanging out here while it was so rowdy, but with no one else to watch her, I didn't have another choice.

"You have ten seconds to fish those keys out of your pocket and put them in the palm of my hand before I break a window and climb in." Olivia leveled me with a stare that was a warning not to fuck with her. I imagined it was the same one she used in meetings to get her way. "Ten. Nine. Eight—"

"Fine, okay. Here," I said, sticking my hand in my jeans and producing the simple ring. "What are you—"

"Don't worry about it. I'll take care of the girls while you handle this. What time do you normally close?"

"One, but—"

"Dammit, Duke. Just shut up and let someone help you for once. I'm not asking for a kidney," she snapped.

Gerald chuckled next to her. "Stubborn ass might be more inclined to give one of those suckers up than accept an ounce of help."

Olivia turned to the old man and smiled. "He *is* a stubborn ass, isn't he?"

"You're not helping," I muttered beneath my breath, unsure of who I was really talking to.

Grabbing the drinks and placing them on a tray, I turned to

say something else to Olivia and the girls, but they were already gone.

BY THE TIME I turned off the lights and trudged back over to the cabin, it was nearly two in the morning. I had to stay later than usual to tidy up, or Sawyer would've walked into a nightmare come morning.

Olivia's car was parked next to my truck. Through the curtains, I could tell that the lamp was on inside the living room, but Harper's room was mercifully dark. Guilt gnawed at me, knowing Olivia had Charlie in tow.

The thought of them driving home so late was out of the question. It was dangerous on these roads at night. They wound up and down through the pitch-black mountains, and she'd have to take the backroads to get over to Lukas' ranch.

It was all-too-common for folks to hit an animal or swerve off the road and crash trying not to. Sometimes they ended up with nothing more than a few stitches or bruises, but others weren't so lucky. Casualties happened every year. I'd never forgive myself if Charlie or Olivia ended up as one of them.

The first thing I noticed when I entered the house was the lingering smell of fresh pine cleaner. Even in the dim lighting, I could tell the difference. My kitchen was a mess when I went to work this morning. I never had the chance to clean. And there had been paperwork spread over the coffee table, too.

Olivia was curled up on the couch, an open book splayed out in her lap. Her neck was bent at an odd angle, lips softly parted. She'd done all of this without me asking. Done it all out of the goodness of her heart just because she wanted to.

I walked over, crouching to place my hand on her shoulder and shake her awake gently. "Olivia," I whispered.

She grunted in response, burrowing herself further into the cushions and tugging the blanket up around her shoulders. She was always like this when Luke or I had to wake her up after football games. Sometimes, she woke up ready to fight. Others, she'd sulk until we unloaded all our gear from the truck, and she was able to climb into her own bed.

Mumbling a curse, I decided to leave her be and check on my daughter instead. The sound of soft snores met my ears, and I smiled as I looked in to see Charlie and Harper fast asleep together.

The soft glow from the pink flower lights hanging above their heads showed me all I needed to see. Charlie slept just like her mother, sprawled out with her mouth wide open. If Harper seemed to mind, I'd have never known. She was just as chaotic, her sheets wrapped around her legs, clinging to the stuffed bunny she'd had since she was a baby.

There was no way in hell I could wake them up and tell them to leave. Not after everything Olivia had already done for Harper and me. When she stopped by, I should've just asked if Harper could stay the night with her instead. At least that way the girls would've been more comfortable, and she wouldn't wake up with a headache from sleeping like a goddamn pretzel.

I was also embarrassed for her to see the way I'd been living. To see how much I'd let things slip lately. I hadn't gotten groceries this week because I'd been too busy, so Harper and I had been living off of PB&J for the past two days.

Olivia wouldn't ever judge, but she was like her brother in the way she always wanted to help. Neither of them could leave well enough alone. Most of the time, I didn't mind, but going through this divorce was different. I felt like a failure on so many levels, telling myself that accepting help was a sign of weakness.

But when I stopped and asked myself what the worst that could happen was, I drew a blank. This town had rallied in support of Harper and me on many occasions, even if it was just stopping by the bar for a drink or smiling when they passed us in the grocery store. Leaning on someone to get by was normal. I didn't want Harper to grow up thinking otherwise.

Closing the door to my daughter's room, I decided to take a shower. I could worry about everything else in the morning. There were some spare blankets and pillows in the hall closet that I could grab. Sleeping on the floor for one night wouldn't kill me. Maybe it'd finally convince me to invest in an air mattress for emergencies.

Not that I ever planned to have Olivia over like this again.

Turning on the shower and shedding my clothes, I let the small space fill with steam before stepping inside. I really needed to shave the stubble lining my jaw, but I'd do that later. All I wanted to do now was sleep.

I washed my hair and body quickly, trying my best not to focus on Olivia sleeping just in the next room. I'd spent too many nights thinking about her in this shower, and my dick did not need the reminder. Last thing I needed was to be in here all night, fucking my fist and wondering what she'd sound like coming on my tongue.

After rinsing with cold water as an extra measure, I stepped out, patted myself dry, and secured the towel around my waist. These were the times I wished for luxuries like the fucking warmer we used to have at the old house.

Tennessee nights could be chilly as fuck.

I'd just begun brushing my teeth when the bathroom door opened. Olivia stood in the doorway, sleepy chocolate eyes widening as they trailed slowly down my body. She didn't try to hide her perusal. It was far too blatant to pretend it was anything but what it was.

And even though I knew it was a bad idea, I let her.

There was something exciting about the way she was staring at me. It made me feel a prickle of pride. For the first time in years, someone was seeing me as a man—not just Harper's dad or the owner of Frank's Bar. And it wasn't just anyone. It was Olivia fucking Hart. My best friend's sister and the object of all my recent desires.

"I-I'm so sorry," she stammered, voice raspy from sleep. "I should have knocked, but I must be dreaming."

I waited for her to slam the door, but she didn't. She stood there, chest heaving, staring at me with these big doe eyes that made me want to sink to my knees in front of her.

"Do you need the bathroom?" I asked, trying to focus on the situation at hand.

Olivia watched with rapt attention as I spat out my toothpaste before turning to face her. There was a subtle flush creeping across her cheeks and down her neck. I wondered how far it went beneath her wrinkled blouse. If it covered the pale expanse of her chest like I imagined it did.

I really needed to move, to stop standing here like some fucking creep. The longer we stayed like this, our restraint crumbling by the second, the harder it would be to walk away from her.

Thirty minutes ago, I could've given any number of reasons we shouldn't be alone together. Yet now I couldn't think of a single one.

"Y-yes." Olivia cleared her throat. For the first time since she walked into the bathroom, she met my gaze. "Yes, I did, but I'll... go."

As she turned to head back into the living room, my hand reached out on instinct to stop her and landed on the bare skin of her arm. "It's all yours," I said, gesturing behind me. "I was just finishing up."

I hurried past, trying not to think about how soft she felt until I finally heard the bathroom door snick shut. Making quick work of my time alone, I grabbed a clean pair of boxers and a shirt from my makeshift dresser and changed.

By the time Olivia emerged from the bathroom, I'd already made my bed on the floor. There wasn't much space in the cramped room, leaving me lying just beneath her.

Her steps faltered as she noticed me on the ground. "What the hell do you think you're doing?"

I turned over my shoulder. "Going to sleep. Looks like we're having that sleepover a little earlier than intended. I pulled a blanket out for you, too. It gets a little cold at night."

"No. I'm not talking about that. I meant what're you doing on the floor?" she asked, crossing her arms over her chest.

"Dunno if you've noticed, honey, but there isn't another place to sleep unless I plan on spending the night in my truck. So sit your ass down on this couch and settle in for the night."

"You're not sleeping on the floor."

"I'm good here." She didn't move. She just stared at me in that impossibly bossy way of hers until I asked, "Do you have a better idea?"

Olivia's gaze flicked between the couch and my makeshift cot for a moment before ripping the blankets from my body. I scrambled to grab them back, but it was too late. "What are you doing?" I hissed, grabbing a pillow to cover my crotch.

"Come on. We'll share." She sat down, curling her feet beneath her body and situating the blanket I had laid out for her. Then she patted the cushion beside her. "Your turn."

"Olivia…"

She rolled her eyes. "My god, Duke. It's either this or I'll be the one sleeping out in my car. You're being an idiot."

"You wouldn't dare," I growled.

She flicked her gaze toward the couch in challenge, practically begging me to call her bluff. "I think we both know I would."

With a sigh, I pushed off the ground and took my seat, ensuring my body was as far as it could be from hers. She handed over the blankets with a saccharine smile before grabbing the pillow I'd dropped and handing it to me. "Happy now?"

She settled into her spot, eyes slipping closed. "Very."

OLIVIA

"DO YOU THINK THEY'RE OKAY?"

"Dunno. They look a little… tangled."

"Should we wake them up?"

"We're already late for school…"

"Dad's gonna be so mad."

I groaned, burrowing further into the warm cocoon I found myself nestled in. Voices whispered around me, trying their best to rouse me from sleep, but it was no use. Pine and pepper filled my nose, and I relaxed, comforted by the scent. I wasn't even sure what it was, because it definitely didn't smell like my lavender laundry soap.

The blankets snugly wrapped around my waist tightened, pulling me closer to the source of heat. Duke was right. It did get a little cold at night.

Duke.

Last night.

His scent.

Oh my god.

My eyes shot open, finding Harper and Charlie both staring

at the couch as though it'd grown two heads. It was only then that I realized the blankets around my waist weren't really blankets at all.

They were arms. Strong, muscular arms that held me as though whoever they belonged to was frightened I might run away. Arms that, I realized with startling clarity, belonged to the man snoring beside me.

I sat up in a hurry only to be pulled back against Duke's chest. His body was like a freaking furnace. I was beginning to sweat with our daughters staring at us like we were crazy.

"Duke," I hissed, trying to pry his grip loose. He didn't budge. I smiled awkwardly at the girls before trying again. "Duke." This time, I accentuated my words with a sharp jab to his side.

He let go with a groan, rubbing his eyes to clear away the sleep before leveling me with a glare. "Ow. What the—"

"Morning, Daddy," Harper said, breaking out into a fit of giggles next to Charlie.

Duke coughed, grabbing the nearest pillow to cover his lap. Morning wood was nothing to be ashamed of under normal circumstances, but honestly... I didn't want to try to explain that to two nine-year-old girls. That would've been too much for me to handle.

"We weren't sure if we should wake y'all up, but," Charlie glanced at her phone, "we're both late for school."

"Yeah, like super late," Harper added.

"Shit," I cursed, hopping up to the sound of Duke's muttered, "Fuck."

"I should've set my alarm," I muttered, hopping up from the couch. It was nearly ten.

Duke grabbed his phone and sighed. "I thought my battery would last until morning, but apparently not."

"I kind of thought y'all were dead," Harper said. "Dad never sleeps this late."

"Neither does my mom," Charlie added. She still had a shit-eating grin on her face.

Since I was a kid, I'd always run on minimal sleep. I was too much of a night owl to go to sleep early, but try as I might to sleep past sunrise, it never worked. No matter what time I went to bed, I was up by seven with no exceptions.

"Come on, girls. Let's get you to school," Duke said, pushing to his feet. I covered my laugh with the back of my hand as he dragged the pillows and blankets with him, earning a pointed glare.

"So… About that," Charlie said. "Today was our field trip to the park. If you take us to school, there will be no one there because everyone left at nine."

"Oh my god, that was today?" I groaned.

The girls nodded. "Yup."

Duke cursed, still standing there holding the blankets and pillows at waist height. Honestly, it was sort-of adorable seeing him so disheveled.

Charlie turned to Harper and loudly whispered, "We should really start a swear jar."

Harper nodded. "Then we'll definitely be able to afford the ponies we want."

"Ponies?" Duke and I turned toward our daughters.

"As in plural?" I asked.

"One for each of us. Duh," Charlie deadpanned.

Right. Yes. Silly me.

"You know I've wanted one for years now, Mom. Dad keeps saying he'll get me one, and then he doesn't."

I wasn't opposed to Charlie having a horse, especially since she'd learned how to ride thanks to Cleo a few years ago. But that was a big responsibility I wasn't entirely sure she was ready for. It was a miracle Grady hadn't caved yet. Normally, Charlie just needed to bat her long eyelashes at her dad to get whatever it was she wanted.

Duke shook his head. "Where would we even keep a horse, sugar? In your bedroom?"

"No, we'd need to build a barn out back," Harper said. To her credit, she looked deadly serious.

His long fingers came up to scratch at the stubble along his jaw. Stubble that'd grown out significantly over the past few days. I noticed he never seemed to fully get rid of it. Not that I minded. I liked the sexy pornstache with a five o'clock shadow look.

Duke had always been attractive, but the way I was seeing him lately put his younger self to shame. He was muscular and yet soft. Handsome and yet rugged. There were no overpriced flashy accessories. The man didn't even own a smartwatch, and his phone was at least four years old, given the cracked screen and shitty battery life.

He preferred stained T-shirts and a worn flannel to five-thousand-dollar suits. The boots by the door looked as though they were in desperate need of a resoling. There was no pomp or circumstance. Just a simple man with simple needs living a simple life.

When was the last time life had been simple for me? I'd operated at an all-or-nothing, breakneck speed since the day I graduated high school. John sent me away to college, where I majored in business operations and minored in music theory. He had me out on scouting trips before I'd even graduated because I had an ear for talent.

That was how I met Grady, after all.

But even after I left school and started shadowing him at Hartstrings corporate office, I never took a break. The only vacations I went on were weekend trips I could get away to visit Grady on tour, but that was years ago.

This was the first time since I'd started my career that I'd been able to slow things down and relax, but it wasn't the same. I still had to check my email. Still had frequent meetings with lawyers and others, not only for business matters but also for John's estate planning.

I didn't realize how desperate I was for a change of speed until I woke up late in Duke's arms on a Wednesday morning.

"Looks like we have no choice but to play hooky," I said, stretching my arms above my head. Duke turned toward me, eyes homing in on the sliver of exposed skin where my shirt had ridden up.

Both the girls cheered as the grump in front of me cocked a brow. "Hooky?"

"Are you unfamiliar with the concept? See, it's when you take off work or school just because you can."

"I know what it means," he muttered. "But I can't just decide not to work today. There's a bunch of shit I didn't get to finish last night. Sawyer's probably over there already." He walked toward the windows and pulled back the curtain. "Yup. Her car is out front. I have to go."

With a sigh, he began walking toward the laundry room to drop the blankets, which I'm pretty sure was just an excuse to grab some pants. Charlie and Harper turned toward me, frowning.

"What if the girls and I came with you today?" I asked.

Duke stuck his head out of the kitchen. "What?"

"Yeah. I'm sure there's something we could all do to pitch in, right?"

His brows furrowed. "Well, no. Not really."

I shrugged. "At least you'll have the best help around," I teased. His lips twitched, and I considered that a win. "Come on. They can't go to school now, and I've always wanted to know what it was like to work in a bar."

"Why?"

I shrugged. "Blame it on Coyote Ugly."

Duke barked out a laugh. "You know it's not that kind of bar, right?"

"Any bar is that kind of bar if you just believe in yourself and the sturdiness of the structure you're dancing on," I said, tossing in a wink for good measure.

"What's Coyote Ugly?" Charlie whispered, looking to Harper. Thankfully, she just shrugged.

"You're too young to know, and you'll never find out!" Duke called out.

The girls and I waited on bated breath as the silence stretched on. I wasn't sure why my stomach was in knots. It was better if he said no, anyway. My email was likely overflowing, and I had several missed calls I needed to return as soon as possible. Yet, here I was, not-so-patiently waiting for him to say yes.

Duke's loud sigh was all the confirmation we needed to start cheering. "Christ. I'm going to regret this," he said, walking back into the living room. He'd changed his shirt from last night. It was slightly wrinkled, but I loved that he didn't care.

"Nope. We'll be the best helpers ever. Isn't that right, girls?"

"Totally," Harper and Charlie agreed.

As the girls ran to drop their backpacks in Harper's room, Duke turned to me. "About this morning..." He ran a hand through his thick hair. "I don't know what happened. I'm sorry if that made you feel uncomfortable."

I couldn't hold back my laugh. "You're apologizing for cuddles?"

The blush that crept across his cheeks was adorable. "I mean, yeah. I didn't mean to cross any lines, or—"

I put my finger to his lips to stop him from talking. I may

have lingered *slightly* longer than felt appropriate. "If I didn't like it, I would've said something."

"You liked it?" he asked, dubiously.

I nodded. "Do you know how long it's been since I've been held like that?"

Alarm bells sounded in my head, warning me to slow the fuck down. We were stepping into unfamiliar territory. I wasn't sure if I should give him this piece of honesty or let it die with me.

"How long?" His voice was no more than a low rumble.

"Nearly ten years."

A line formed between Duke's brows as he did the math. "But Charlie is—"

"She just turned nine," I confirmed.

In the entirety of my life, I'd only been with two men. The first was a random guy I met at a frat party my first year of college. I put no stock in the idea of virginity. I had no desire to wait until marriage or for Mr. Right to come along. For me, it was just one more thing to check off a list, honestly.

The second and last was Grady.

Charlie was the result of one of our lowest moments. I'd picked Grady up from the very bar Duke now owned. We came home, both feeling sorry for ourselves for different reasons, and let our bodies work out our frustrations. Then, in the aftermath, we realized we'd foregone a condom.

Nine months later, I gave birth to our daughter, who turned out to be the best thing to ever happen to either of us. It wasn't planned. Kids weren't even something we thought would be in the cards for us, honestly. But Charlie had changed both our lives.

It'd only happened once, though.

I thought about dating after the divorce, but it was different now. Social media was full of weirdos looking for a handout, and now that I had a kid, I wasn't about to trust some random guy I met off the internet. The whole concept seemed like too much work. I didn't want to spend what little time I had on anyone other than my daughter.

Until now. Until I was staring up into bright green eyes that made my heart race every time they met mine.

Feeling that way was dangerous. Duke and I had no future. Eventually, I'd have to return to my job and leave Pinecrest behind once again. Each day I stayed, each moment I let myself indulge in the freedom I'd been gifted, was one step closer to the end.

I wasn't sure if he felt the same curiosity I did, but for my sake, I should've made up some excuse to leave his house before I spent another day wishing I could stay.

But I didn't.

Charlie and Harper came bounding into the room, both laughing about god only knew what, as Duke and I stepped apart. He cleared his throat, forcing a smile, before he said, "Y'all ready to work?"

They nodded enthusiastically as we walked out of the house. The girls each grabbed one of my hands. Harper reached out for her dad's, waiting patiently for him to take it. The smile he gave her, soft and full of tenderness, made me weak at the knees.

We walked like that, hand-in-hand, the short distance to the bar. Charlie hummed some song that was stuck in her head while Harper bobbed along to it. I looked over to Duke, who was fully grinning. The sun shone down on the four of us, bathing us in warm light.

As we stepped into Frank's, Charlie and Harper immediately went over to the jukebox to pick a song.

"So much for helping," Duke muttered.

I patted his chest, trying hard not to focus on the heat seeping through his clothes. "You knew that wouldn't last long."

"Hey, guys!" Sawyer said from behind the bar. She paused when she saw me, a knowing smile playing on her lips. "Olivia, right?"

I walked over and held out my hand. "Right! And you're Sawyer?" The young girl nodded. "I hope your boss gave you the tip I left last time I was here," I said, giving her a wink.

"You know damn well I did!" Duke called from somewhere in the back.

"I don't know..." Sawyer drawled. "How much was it again? He only gave me a twenty."

I gasped. "Duke Bennett, how dare you pocket the other eighty!"

Sawyer and I broke out in a fit of giggles as Duke rounded the corner, a scowl already forming. "That's a damn lie, and you —" he paused, pointing between the two of us. "I can already tell this is a bad idea."

"Why, sir, whatever can you mean?" I asked, thickening my accent. "Whatever you're accusing me of is slander, and I won't stand for it!"

Duke pinched the bridge of his nose, which only had us laughing harder. "Yup. Terrible idea."

"I don't know," Sawyer said. "I think it's the start of a beautiful friendship."

"Or a definite pain in my ass," he sighed. "Listen, the mop and bucket are in the closet over there. Why don't you make yourself useful and leave my staff alone? She's got work to do."

I gave him a salute as he disappeared into the cramped storeroom. "Sir, yes, sir." Leaving Sawyer to finish what she was doing, I walked back toward our daughters. "Alright, girls. Let me teach you a thing or two about Coyote Ugly."

While I couldn't be sure, I swore I heard Duke cursing beneath his breath.

DUKE

WHEN JOHN HART called me this afternoon, I wasn't sure what to expect. Sometimes, I'd run errands for him if he wasn't feeling well. Other times, I would help him with things that needed fixing around the house or yard. If there was a big project, Lukas would haul my ass out to help with whatever needed to be done.

But today, John hadn't given me a single clue as to what he needed. The bar was slow enough that Sawyer could handle it on her own until Ryan showed up later this afternoon. So, I'd jumped in my old truck and driven across town to his property.

When Lukas told me his uncle was sick, I never expected it to be terminal. The man felt infallible. He was bigger than life itself, and every single person in town would feel his absence.

If it hadn't been for John, I never would've been able to help my mom get set up in a care facility after her stroke. I damn sure couldn't have afforded it after my divorce, when it was taking everything I had to keep Harper and me afloat in the aftermath.

Looking back, the signs of his illness were there. The low

energy, the bruises across his skin. It shouldn't have come as a surprise, but it did. I hated that he was refusing to fight. It wasn't fair to him, and it wasn't fair to us.

As I pulled onto the property, I noticed Olivia's black SUV parked outside. I stopped beside it, hesitating with my hand on the ignition, wondering if it was too late to drive away or if I'd already been noticed. My truck wasn't that loud. Surely I could just sneak off.

As if on cue, I saw movement through the large arched window in front of me. The curtains pulled back, and a very familiar face peeked through the fabric. A face that had started haunting my dreams at night.

Guess that answers that.

Since our little sleepover, my mind had run rampant with thoughts of Olivia. Showers were my favorite time of day. A moment to reflect on the way it'd felt to have her in my arms and wonder what noises she'd make if things had been different.

I shook my head. Olivia Hart was a goddamn distraction. The worst part was not knowing if this pull was mutual. I mean, I wasn't ignorant. I noticed the way she looked at me from time to time. The chemistry was there, but was it enough to tempt her?

That was the million-dollar question.

It was best if I never found out the answer. If the attraction wasn't reciprocated, I'd rather take my secret to the grave. And if it was? Well, that would just be the cruelest form of torture because I could never act on what I wanted anyway.

Lukas would kill me if he knew I was lusting over his little sister. He'd always been protective of her with good reason. Anytime she'd brought a boy around as a teenager, he found something wrong with them. When she introduced Grady as her fiancé for the first time, I thought he was going to have a fucking aneurysm.

Not to mention the fact that Harper and Charlie were best friends. What if whatever this attraction was between Olivia and me affected that? It'd sure as fuck make pickups and drop-offs awkward if we couldn't even be in the same room as one another.

So, no. I wasn't convinced it'd be worth it to try and blur the lines of friendship between myself and my best friend's little sister.

No matter how tempting she was.

Stepping out of my truck, I headed for the door. I didn't even get the chance to knock before it swung open, revealing a smiling Olivia.

"Duke, I didn't know you were coming over." She stepped aside, ushering me in. "Is everything okay?"

What had I just said about not wanting to rock the boat with Lukas? Because I was ready to call myself a fucking liar after being in her space for only a second.

Olivia really was beautiful. Her hair, normally pulled back, was down, making her bare face seem more relaxed. It matched the slightly baggy Hartfelt Homes t-shirt and loose-fitting jeans she was wearing.

It made me wonder what she'd look like waking up next to me one morning, freshly fucked and satiated, wearing nothing but my shirt from the night before. How it'd hang nearly to her knees, and I'd only need to slide the fabric up a few inches to satiate my appetite.

And her scent. God. The sweet perfume hung in the air, wrapping around my senses and holding my thoughts hostage with images of her head thrown back in ecstasy as I—

"Duke?"

I blinked away the thoughts, focusing back on the woman in front of me. "Sorry, what?"

Olivia gave me a coy smile. "I asked what you were doing here."

"John asked me to stop by, so"—I reached up and scratched the back of my neck—"here I am."

"Oh. He didn't tell me." Her full, glossed lips drew together in a pout. The way they glistened in the light captured my attention. "But, then again, I've been so busy this morning that he might've said something in passing, and I forgot."

She gave me her back, motioning for me to follow as we went down the hall and through the living room. I'd been in this house a thousand times since I was a kid, and it never failed to leave me in awe. High ceilings and viridian walls were accented by cedar beams and leather furniture. It was a mountain getaway dream. Large, arched windows were situated all throughout the house, leaving each room steeped in natural light.

As we stopped short of his room, Olivia paused. "It's not been a good day, just so you know. He's been a little out of it."

I nodded, not needing any details. It wasn't my intention to sit around and gossip with the old man. I was just here to do my job—whatever that may be. "Noted."

She knocked once before entering, and I followed her inside. It was quite a bit darker than the rest of the house. The only light came from a single lamp on his bedside table.

It'd been about a month since I'd seen John Hart, and the decline was shocking.

He was sitting up in bed, trembling hands folded neatly in his lap. His olive skin was jaundiced, and his normally warm brown eyes were clouded and sunken. It reminded me of the bad FX makeup at our local haunted house that popped up every Halloween.

Except this wasn't fake. It was real. John was dying.

I already knew that. Lukas had told me as much when we

spoke, but it was different seeing it in person. Suddenly, whatever sadness I'd felt before returned tenfold.

"Took you long enough," John said, breaking into a coughing fit. Olivia went to his side, eyes filled with caution, and brought a glass of water to his cracked lips.

When she pulled it away, she tutted. "I told you to keep the sass to a minimum, and what do you do? You make some smart ass remark and start coughing."

John looked to his niece and smiled weakly. "I'm not sorry."

"I know you're not." She patted his hand. "I'll leave you two boys to yap now. If you need anything, just tell Duke to yell for me."

"If he needs anything, I can get it for him." I strode across the room and sat in the chair next to his bed. "I know my way around the house just as well as you do."

Olivia stood there, mouth parted slightly, an argument already forming on her lips. "But—"

"Take a break, Olivia. I've got him." There was no malice in my words. No insistence that she couldn't take care of him when I knew damn well she could. But I also noticed the way her shoulders fell in relief when I told her to rest.

If I could give her a few minutes of peace, I'd consider my day well spent.

She slipped out the door and closed it behind her. When I turned back toward John, his eyes were trained on the spot she just left. "That girl has always been so damn smart, but stubborn, too. Sometimes stupidly so."

"That doesn't seem very nice."

"The truth almost never is," John grumbled.

I leaned back in my chair. "Dying really changes a man."

He chuckled lightly before gesturing for his water, which I helped hand over. We sat in silence for a long moment until he finished. "That's true. Makes you see everything in a different light. What's important, what's not, and all the shit in between." He paused, pointing to the door as he struggled to catch his breath. "I fear that girl won't learn that lesson until it's too late."

What shit could John possibly be talking about? He lived a good life. Devoted time and energy to his family and his company, catapulting it into a success no one could have ever imagined.

From what little I knew, Olivia had taken her role as CEO seriously. While I had judged her for it previously, before I saw the way Charlie hung onto every word she spoke and how she loved that girl more than words could ever say, I now knew there was no way she would've taken the job if she felt her daughter would suffer.

"She's got a good head on her shoulders," I said. "She'll figure it out. Give her some credit."

John snorted. "Weren't you in my office crying over that no-good ex-wife of yours not six months ago?"

I remembered that day with startling clarity. Despite Sarah packing her bags two years ago, it'd been moving into that goddamn cabin that'd nearly undid me—the look on Harper's face as she watched so many of our things be sold or put into storage because we couldn't fit them in our place.

Grady offered to take her for the night to help ease the transition, and I hadn't argued. While I wanted to reach for the bottle, I'd found myself sitting in my truck out front of John's house instead. He'd always been like a dad to me, so it was natural to turn to him.

I stormed into his office, dropped to my knees, and sobbed for the first time in my life. I told him every deepest fear I had. That I was ruining my daughter's life, that she would grow up to resent me when she was older. How I wished it would all stop, and I wanted to be better than the miserable, pathetic bastard I was turning into.

And then I told him how I wasn't sure I could go on anymore. That I struggled to get out of bed most mornings, and how Harper would be better off if she were in someone else's care. Someone who could give her all the things I couldn't. Who could make sure she lived a happy and fulfilled life.

I desperately wanted to make the pain go away, because goddammit… It hurt so fucking bad. Ripping my heart out of my chest would've been less painful than the disappointment on Harper's face when she looked around at her bedroom.

John hadn't said anything. Not right away, at least. He let me cry and bitch and moan until the room descended into an eerie silence and I'd caught my breath. Then he stood from his desk and walked over to me. I watched him, wondering if he was going to slap me and tell me to get my shit together, or tell me I was nothing but a disappointment to him.

Instead, he put his hand on my shoulder and pulled me into him. How long had it been since I experienced a touch of comfort and not disdain? Too fucking long. I lost it again, in his arms, as he stoically told me I would be okay. There were no flowery words or platitudes, just the truth.

I would be okay. Harper would be okay. Everything would be okay.

Of course, he offered to loan us money. When I refused, he offered to put us up in a better place. I couldn't accept because I knew John, and I knew it wouldn't be a small two-bedroom rental somewhere in town. It'd be an over-the-top property that I'd never be able to pay him back for.

I couldn't take anything else from him other than his reassurance. That was the day I knew things had to change. I needed to get my head straight. Not only for my sake, but Harper's as well.

"That was different," I said, shifting in my seat. "And you were cheerier yourself back then, too."

"Because I knew I'd lived my life in a manner I could look back on and smile. A fact I'm grateful for today. Could you imagine being on your deathbed and having regrets?" He shook his head. "I couldn't. Regrets are for fools."

Regrets are for fools.

I had so many regrets in my life. Too many, probably. Regret that I'd tried so long to make someone happy who wasn't happy with herself. Regret that I'd held on in hopes things would change, that they'd get better.

Regret that I'd never be able to find out what Olivia's kiss tasted like.

"Philosophical, too." I smiled, but it wasn't genuine. "Is that why you won't agree to treatment or a transplant?"

John looked down at his hands. His fingers, which had once been calloused from hours working in the woodshop with Lukas, had grown soft. There were bruises on top where he'd had bloodwork done at the hospital. An undeniable reminder of the sickness that was killing him.

"That's part of it," he said quietly. "I'm an old man, Duke. An old man who has lived an extraordinary life. I've traveled the world. I've loved and lost and loved again. I've helped build one of the greatest music empires in the country." I saw the tears in his eyes before the first one fell. "None of that compares to the joy Lukas and Olivia have brought me. Though I was not blessed with children of my own, I helped shape them into the brilliant people they are today. I've seen them do extraordinary things in this life, and they will continue doing so when I'm gone. They are my legacy. I couldn't give a shit about the rest, if you want the truth."

"So, why not stay for them? Why not fight?"

He shook his head. "I'm tired, Duke. I've been fighting this disease for longer than either of my kids knows, and I don't have it in me to fight much more. I just worry they'll let my death hold them back."

He took a breath before continuing. "Olivia, well… She'll work herself to the bone if no one tells her not to. And life will pass her by in the blink of an eye. I know how much she loves the *idea* of her job—Hartstrings wouldn't be what it is today without her—but it's killing her. She hasn't been happy there in years. Every time I try to talk to her about it, she shuts me down. There was a time, not long after Charlie was born, when I thought the tides were turning for her."

"A woman can have a career and be a perfectly good mother, John," I said, defensiveness sharpening my tone. Who was I? I barely recognized myself. "It doesn't have to be one or the other."

"Don't lecture me on sexism. I'm well aware. Olivia's problem is that she lets the job consume her. The career she thought she wanted when she was a kid? She's finding out that it doesn't fuel her fire, but she doesn't understand why. So she pushes herself harder and harder, but one day, she will break. When that happens, I won't be there to help her pick up the pieces or realize why it didn't work in the first place."

I sat with his words for a moment, thinking back to the day I found Olivia sitting alone, drunk, in my bar. She'd looked so exhausted, and I'd been a dick to her for no other reason than I could be. In fact, I'd been a dick most of the time I'd spent in her company as of late.

Could it be possible that she was just as goddamn exhausted as I was? That she was just trying her best to give her daughter the best life she could, even if it was at the detriment of her own well-being?

"Come to think of it, I do have one regret," John said softly.

"What's that?" I asked, leaning forward in my seat. Whatever wisdom he was about to impart, I wanted to memorize it.

The pause stretched on until I worried something was wrong. His clouded eyes were haunted by something I couldn't see or hear. A moment in his past that obviously caused him great pain. "I regret not telling Olivia that following in her father's footsteps won't bring him back. She should know. I should tell her."

Reaching out, I covered his hand with my own. He felt so frail. "You will. You have time."

This time, his laugh was brittle. "What a cruel thing to say to a dying man."

"I'm choosing to believe it's true. What can I do for you? I'm sure you didn't just invite me over to talk about your feelings."

"Is it so hard to believe I wanted company?"

"The company you had before I walked in is much better than my cranky ass."

John tilted his head to the side, observing me closely. "Ah, that's true. Nicer to look at, too." My cheeks flushed, earning a smile from the man watching me so closely. "No, I didn't need anything. I just wanted to see you. It's been too long since you've come by."

Guilt pricked at my conscience. It'd been over a month since I'd seen him. I kept telling myself I needed to stop by, but something else always popped up. Harper's school and soccer kept me busy. Not to mention everything at work.

And I'd purposely avoided any place Olivia might have been just so that I wasn't tempted to do something I'd regret.

"How about I bring Harper by this weekend after her soccer game? I'll cook lunch. Maybe roll your ass out to the garden to eat?" I offered.

John nodded. "I think I'd like that. I do have one favor to ask of you, while you're still here."

"Whatever you need. I brought my tools, just in case."

"That won't be necessary. I'd actually like you to get Olivia out of this house for a few hours. She's driving me crazy. Ever since she got here, she's been in and out of my office. Going through shit I haven't seen or touched in nearly a decade, and wanting me to tell her if it's important or not. I'm exhausted. I just want to rest."

I blinked, clearly not expecting that ask. I mean, what? Was he asking me to take her out on a date or just tell her to leave?

"Why don't you just tell her you've had enough for the day?"

John sighed. "Because then she'll want to move on to some other menial task instead of just sitting down and enjoying the silence of the country. She's forgotten what it's like, I think. To enjoy life. Help her remember."

"And you think *I* can help with that?"

"Maybe not, but you can take her out for lunch or something, can't you? Give an old man a break."

I pushed to my feet, smiling at the man in question. "That I can do. Want us to bring something back for you?"

He shook his head. "Nothing for me. Meds have me feeling a little tired. Think I'll just rest my eyes for a bit."

I wasn't sure why, but I stepped forward and held my hand out for him. "I'm grateful for you, John. You're an amazing man."

He smirked. "You're just saying that because I talked the sheriff out of hauling your ass to jail when you and Lukas got caught drinking at the football fields."

"That's certainly high on my list, sure."

"Go on. Get out of here." He jerked his chin toward the door. "And make sure to take care of my girl."

"It's just lunch. I'm sure I can handle it," I said, turning for the door. I paused at the threshold, looking back at the man who'd guided me through so much of my life. His eyes had slipped closed in the few steps I'd taken, and his breathing evened out. For the first time all day, he looked peaceful.

The house was eerily silent as I stepped into the hallway,

save for some quiet muttering coming from John's office. I took my time, looking at the memories hanging on the wall. There were pictures of all of us from over the years. Lukas and me after our football team won the state championship. Olivia and Grady when they brought Charlie home from the hospital. The last Christmas we had together right before Lukas and I ran off to college. It was all here, from damn near birth until now. And I was in all of them as a real member of the family.

It wasn't until I was standing there, looking at Olivia's ass bent over the table, that I realized I'd made it to the threshold of John's office.

Even though I knew I shouldn't have, I couldn't help but stare. She was rifling through papers, talking to herself in a way that had the filthy curses leaving her mouth seem cute. Though the jeans she was wearing weren't tight, they hugged her curves every time she moved.

What the fuck is wrong with you, Bennett?

I cleared my throat, chuckling as Olivia whipped around with wide eyes. Her hand flew up, pressing gently to her chest in shock. "Fuck, Duke. I'm sorry. I didn't hear you come in."

"Oh, I just got here," I lied. "No apology needed."

She leaned back against the desk, arms folded in a way that pushed her breasts up. The little gold necklace she was wearing glinted in the light.

"How'd your visit go? I'm sure he was happy to see you. It's been a constant parade of unfamiliar faces around here lately. Lawyers, nurses, board members." She rolled her eyes. "Though I just wish they'd stay away. He shouldn't be focusing on anything other than his health."

There was so much I wanted to tell her. The things he told me in confidence were all things she should know, but I couldn't be the one to say them. John would need to cross that bridge sooner rather than later. I supposed the good thing about knowing you're dying was that you could plan those kinds of conversations.

"It was good. I thought he had some work for me, but I think he just wanted someone to talk to."

Olivia straightened at that. "I'm excellent company. And Lukas should be home soon."

I raised my hands, sensing her defensive nature kicking in. "I'm not implying you're not. But I think maybe he wanted to talk about something other than his impending death and all the goddamn paperwork surrounding it." I looked around the office at the countless boxes and stacks of paper. "I mean, I understand why you're doing it, but..." I trailed off, shaking my head. "Look, he asked me for a favor. One I know you're gonna fight me on."

She narrowed her eyes. "What is it?"

Taking a deep breath, I said, "He wants me to get you outta the house for a bit. Take you to lunch or something."

Shit. Suddenly, this felt so stupid. I mean, I had no idea what to do. And what were we going to talk about? Other than the bar, this was the most time we'd spent together without the kids. Maybe this was a bad idea.

"He wants me... out of the house?" she asked slowly. A little line formed between her brows, one I wanted to wipe away. "Why?"

"You want the truth?" Olivia nodded. "He says you're driving him crazy."

I waited for a rebuttal, a tantrum. For her to tell me to get the fuck out of his house, but she didn't do any of that. Instead, her luscious lips parted, and she threw her head back in laughter. I was swept up in the beauty of it, unable to do anything but join in myself.

She looked around the room, nodding. "Honestly? I could use a break. And," she checked her watch, "the girls will be out of school in a few hours, so I'd need to leave soon anyway to run a few errands. Maybe we could pick them up together and get ice cream?"

The way she effortlessly included Harper and me in her plans was monumental. Like my coming in didn't completely ruin or derail her day. Sarah would've thrown a fit if I'd done that to her. She would've called me selfish or asked why I hadn't asked her sooner. For a woman desperately seeking something new and fresh, change was something she hated.

"Yeah, that'd be great," I said, shoving my hands in my pockets. "I'm sure they'd love that."

"Honestly, so would I. Ever since we went to Lucy's diner the other day, I've been craving another milkshake. I just want to stop by John's room and tell him bye."

"Then that's what we'll do. Whatever you want."

The smile she gave me as she stepped forward was blinding. Her finger lingered on my chest as she moved past me. "Better be careful with that offer, Mr. Bennett. I just might take you up on that."

As I followed her back down the hallway, I couldn't help but thank the fucking universe for John Hart and high-waisted jeans.

OLIVIA

THE FAMILIAR CHIME of the bell sounded out as Duke, Harper, Charlie, and I stepped through the door of Lucy's. Thankfully, it wasn't nearly as busy as it was after Harper's game.

"Sit where you like, sweeties! I'll be right over," Lucy called from the register.

The girls looked at one another with knowing smiles before running to the same booth as before. And just like last time, they sat on the same side, leaving Duke and me to squeeze in together.

Only this time, it didn't feel awkward.

When I told Duke I needed to run errands, I was expecting him to bail. I wouldn't have blamed him if he had. Instead, he jogged over to his truck, moved Harper's booster seat over to my car, and told me to get in the passenger seat.

I had half a mind to argue, but then he draped his hand effortlessly over the steering wheel to back out of the drive, and I lost every coherent thought I had.

Duke wasn't classically handsome. He was rugged. Ridiculously so. He reminded me of the videos I saw on social media of a lumberjack competition in Alaska, where every guy wore flannel, had a beard, and was muscled up to perfection. Sometimes, I caught a faint whiff of pine when he walked by, so it fit the bill.

Except this lumberjack wore a tight-fitting black t-shirt, had a mustache, and a permanent scowl stretched across his face. One I noticed slipping more and more lately.

Today alone, I caught him smiling at least four times. Not that I was counting, of course. That would be ridiculous. But it did make me curious to see if I could make it happen again.

For science, of course.

When we pulled up to the school and told the girls we were going to grab an early dinner, they giddily piled in the back of my SUV. I wasn't sure they'd stopped talking since we picked them up, which warmed my heart.

Though Charlie and I had a rough start when I first showed up, we had settled into a groove. I was grateful for the co-parenting relationship Grady and I shared. He didn't mind that she stayed with me most days. It let me see a side to her I never got to see in the stolen moments I was home before. Like how grumpy she was when I woke her up for school every morning, or the small burst of energy she got after dinner. Every now and then, I'd find her curled up in bed beside me without any recollection of when she'd crawled between the covers.

If I wasn't careful, I could get used to this kind of easy life.

"Not that I'm complaining about such fine company, but it's not a Saturday afternoon," Lucy said, sidling up to our table with a smile. She sat two coloring mats and crayons on the table for the girls. "Are we celebrating something?"

"My uncle told Duke to get me out of the house," I said, rolling my eyes. "Apparently, I've been driving him crazy, so we thought we'd take the girls out for a treat."

Lucy's eyes lit up at the use of the word 'we.' She glanced between Duke and me with a barely concealed smile. "Well, what a wonderful way to spend an afternoon. Are we gonna do the usual?"

"Burgers, fries, and shakes for the table, if you don't mind," Duke cut in before I could say anything. He turned to me. "Chocolate, right?"

I blinked, surprised he remembered. "Right. Is that okay with you girls?"

Both of them nodded before excitedly trading crayons.

"Perfect! I'll put this in for y'all. Be back shortly." Lucy winked and strolled off, leaving Duke and me to stare at the girls.

"Here. Y'all can do this one." Charlie shoved the second coloring mat and crayon pack toward Duke and me. "We'll see whose is best before we leave."

I stared down at the page. I'd never been much for coloring books, not even as a kid, but I downright loathed them as an adult. Cleo tried to get me into it one night after one too many glasses of wine. By the end of the night, I'd nearly thrown her coloring book and fancy markers in the trash because I'd gotten so mad.

"Oh, I don't need to do this to know yours will be better, sunshine," I said.

Duke bumped my shoulder with his. His green eyes damn near sparkled with mirth. "What? You're not up for some friendly competition?"

"Not when I know I'll lose," I muttered.

"Mom's a sore loser," Charlie added. *The little shit.*

I turned toward her. "So are you, dear daughter. The apple doesn't fall far from the tree."

She just shrugged. "At least I'm not afraid to try."

Jeez. Getting kicked out of my uncle's house and put in my

place by my nine-year-old wasn't on my bingo card for the day, but it looked like I didn't have a choice.

I reached forward and yanked a blue crayon from the cheap cardboard box, pointing it at my daughter. "Alright, smarty pants… Let's make a deal. Whoever loses has to do dishes for a week."

Charlie narrowed her eyes. "What about Duke and Harper? That's not fair if they don't have the same rules."

I turned to Duke. Charlie was right. If it was going to be a team event, he had to be on board. "Well?"

Duke looked at Harper, who had a smirk on her face. A dare. A challenge. With a simple nod, he said, "Alright. I'm in."

LUCY STARED between our two art pieces, tilting her head back and forth as though she was a famed art critic instead of a restaurant owner we'd paid twenty bucks to judge us impartially.

Twenty bucks was a good investment if it meant I won.

Of course, there was no way to tell whose was whose. Our mats had been face down when we asked her if she'd be willing to do it. Then we mixed them up a couple of times for good measure.

"Well?" Charlie asked. Her big blue eyes were so wide; it was the perfect puppy-dog pout. Lucy looked her way, visibly softening under my daughter's gaze.

"Oh, no, you don't." I snapped my fingers in front of Charlie's face. "That's the oldest trick in the book, and it's not allowed."

"She doesn't even know which one is mine, Mom. How could I possibly cheat?"

Okay, so she had a point. But I knew my daughter would do some shady things to get out of doing dishes for a whole week. I couldn't trust her when so much was on the line.

"No tricks. Keep those big, blue eyes to yourself," I said, leaning back in the booth.

Out of the corner of my eye, I noticed Duke shaking his head in silent laughter at our banter. There was something different about him today. He seemed lighter. Less guarded. And I'd counted two smiles since we sat down.

Our newfound camaraderie felt an awful lot like friendship. Being able to spend time with someone who not only understood the pressures of being a parent but also the impending demise of my uncle was freeing somehow. It had been a long time since I had a friend who understood.

My only problem is that I wasn't sure friendship was what I wanted. At least, not entirely.

I didn't have much experience with relationships. Before I married Grady, I had a handful of boyfriends who never made it past the six-month mark. Then I married my best friend in a ruse to take over my family's company and help his music career. We were only supposed to stay married a few years. Enough to satisfy the press and the Hartstrings board of directors so they'd allow me to assume my position as the company's CEO.

But as the years passed, neither Grady nor I had any interest in going through the divorce process. He would forever be pining over the one who got away, while I was convinced I'd be the really cool single aunt someday.

And then came Cleo.

I personally had zero interest in dating. Which was fine, seeing as I also barely had time to fly home and see my daughter a couple of times a month. For whatever reason, being around

Duke was changing things for me. And it wasn't just the realization of how lonely I'd been since the divorce.

It was *him*.

His looks. His smell. His moody demeanor. His stupid slutty little mustache. His deep voice. His calloused hands.

Oh god, his hands. They were massive and looked like they were carved from marble. On more than one occasion, I'd found myself wondering how they'd feel as he ran the rough pads along my body gently. Reverently. How he'd grip my hips, bruising them with each mindless thrust.

I'd had to charge my little pink bullet twice since I got here.

While I could blame the sudden horniness on the fact that it'd been a very long time since I had sex, it wasn't that simple. Nothing and no one else made me feel the way I did when I was with him. Not even my trusty book boyfriends, which I found extremely frustrating as I tried to relax one evening with my favorite one-handed read. A mustache showing up on my favorite fae prince really put a damper on things.

"You good there?" Duke asked, pulling me from my thoughts. The entire table was staring at me with concern.

"Sorry. Must have zoned out there for a minute," I said, smiling weakly. I looked toward the girls and Lucy. "Did you pick a winner?"

Lucy shook her head. "You know, this is a lot of pressure to put a single person under," she muttered. "But I suppose if I had to choose, I'd go with..." Her eyes darted between the two sheets. "This one."

I closed my eyes to the sound of Harper and Charlie whooping loudly. Everyone turned towards our table as Duke and I launched into our complaints, demanding to know why theirs won over ours.

"They colored in the lines, and you didn't," Lucy said, slapping down our bill on the table. "Come see me at the register when you're done so I can take care of this bill for you."

"You're cruel," I said as she walked about. "This was rigged."

Across the table, Charlie and Harper wore smug expressions. "Looks like we're off dish duty for the week." Then they turned to one another and did some kind of handshake that looked like a strange secret code.

"Braggarts," Duke mumbled, looking down at his empty milkshake glass.

Harper leaned forward and placed one hand behind her ear. "What's that?" she asked. "I can't hear you over the sound of sweet, sweet victory."

I turned toward Duke in horror. "Who raised these monsters?"

"Yours is the ringleader," he said.

Charlie beamed at his distinction. Typical. Only my daughter would take something like that as a highly distinguished honor.

As I reached across the table for the check, Duke grabbed it first.

"You ran errands with me all afternoon," I said. "The least I could do is pay. Especially since I got you stuck on dish duty."

While I knew he wouldn't give it back, I thought he'd put up more fight than he did. Instead, his lips quirked, and he said, "Running errands with you isn't something I need to be paid to do. I enjoyed it."

"You enjoyed running errands?" I asked, brows furrowed.

"With you," he corrected, sliding out of the booth. "I said, I liked running errands with you." Before I could utter another word, he strode to the counter to pay our bill.

I was vaguely aware of Charlie asking me something, but I wasn't sure what I said. I wasn't even sure I replied at all. While she was talking, my attention was elsewhere. I knew I shouldn't gawk at Duke in front of our kids, but I couldn't help it. I loved watching him, seeing the occasional tilt of his lips, or hearing a smart-assed quip.

Surprisingly, I loved doing normal, everyday things with him. And he apparently loved them, too.

"Earth to Mooooom," Charlie sang.

"Huh? What?" I turned toward my daughter. "Sorry. Zoned out again."

She rolled her eyes playfully. "Yeah, you seem to be doing that a lot today."

"Alright, you have my full attention. Hit me with it."

"I asked what we were going to be doing after this, and if Harper could come over? I want to show her the treehouse Uncle Luke is building for me."

"Uh," I said, chancing a glance back at Duke. He was tucking his wallet in the back pocket of his jeans. "We'll head back to John's after this so Mr. Bennett can get his truck, but it's fine with me if they come over."

The girls whooped again as Duke turned toward the table. They flew past him to the quarter machines at the front. He stopped in front of the table with his hands stuffed in his pockets. "I swear to god if you bet them anything else…"

"Not this time. The girls were asking if you wanted to come over once we got your truck from John's. Charlie wants to show Harper the treehouse Luke is building for her," I said, sliding toward the end of the seat.

"And what'd you say?"

I wasn't sure why, but I was suddenly worried he thought that I'd committed him to something he didn't want to do, so I hurried to offer assurances. "I told them it was up to you, I swear. You're not obligated to—"

"The answer's yes."

For what felt like the millionth time today, I wondered who

this man was and what happened to the Duke Bennett I thought I knew. Because the one I met a few weeks ago wouldn't be caught dead spending more time with me than was required. "You don't have to—"

"I know I don't. I *want* to." As if remembering himself, he added, "Plus, I think it'd make Harper happy."

"Yeah, it'd totally make Harper happy." We were trapped in a moment, neither of us willing to break eye contact.

It'd make me happy, too, I thought. However, I kept that comment to myself.

As I tried to exit the booth, I thought Duke would move. He didn't, of course. When I straightened, our chests were nearly touching, and his breath mingled with my own. The scent of spearmint gum filled the small space. I leaned closer, trapped by his piercing green gaze against my will.

Something clattered to the ground behind him, causing me to jump back on instinct. His arms shot out to steady me as I almost fell backward into the booth. It was only when he was sure that I wasn't going to fall over that he relaxed his grip. "Careful. Don't go falling for me now," he murmured.

Oh my god. Was Duke *flirting* with me?

What did it say about me that I was in my late thirties and had no idea if a man was flirting or not? I couldn't remember the last time it'd happened, which may have been even more pathetic.

"Well, you make it hard not to," I laughed, gesturing toward his body. He smirked, and I rushed to cover my tracks. "I mean, you know, when you don't move out of the way," I corrected.

Smooth, Liv. Real fucking smooth.

Duke let his hands travel down my biceps and to my hands, lingering there for a moment before stepping back and clearing his throat. "We should probably get going. I'm sure the girls are wondering what's taking us so long."

"Yup. Good call." I moved in front of him, and his hand found the small of my back. The hem of my t-shirt had ridden up just enough while sitting that his fingertips brushed against my bare back. The simple touch had my skin prickling and my senses on alert. I was so keenly tuned into his body placement, relishing the stupidly giddy feeling in my stomach at his nearness, that I didn't even notice we made it to my car.

Duke guided me to the passenger side door of my SUV, gesturing for me to step inside. For once, I did as he asked without question. "Such a gentleman."

"Sometimes," he said, giving me a fucking wink before checking the girls' seatbelts.

He got in the car, placed his hand on the back of my seat, and turned over his shoulder to back out. Why was that so hot? I caught a whiff of his cologne as he leaned close, the masculine scent drawing me in. Being near him was clearly making my brain go fuzzy. I needed to get it together.

But how could I when he looked so effortlessly hot and was a gentleman to boot? The more I got to know him, the more I wanted to be around him. Sure, he could be a grumpy ass sometimes, but I'd seen a different side of him today. One I wasn't sure existed.

One I found way too intriguing.

By the time we made it past Main Street, Charlie and Harper had both taken over the role of DJ, blasting pop music that made Duke cringe. "Who listens to this shit?" he asked, glancing my way.

I rolled my head along the headrest. "You do realize I'm the CEO of a music label, right?"

He shrugged sheepishly. "I'm guessing that's one of your artists?"

"Sure is," I laughed. "We found her singing at karaoke bars

around Nashville. The moment I heard her voice, I knew she was going to be a chart topper."

Duke was quiet for a second. "Do you love it? Your job, I mean."

I wanted to tell him how badly I *wanted* to love it. That I'd worked my ass off and even married a man I knew I'd never love as more than a friend to ensure the position would be mine.

But I didn't. I hated it.

I hated the fact that it took me away from my daughter, my family, and my friends. That I couldn't promise anything other than a handful of stolen moments with them a month. I hated that it didn't allow me any room for error. That the fate of the entire company, and the livelihood of every employee and artist under the umbrella, was sitting on my shoulders.

Most of all, I hated the way it made me resent my father the longer I stayed on, a man whom I'd idolized and built my life around since I was a young girl. A life I no longer wanted. Not the way it looked currently, at least.

Instead, I wanted soccer games on Saturday mornings and lazy pancake breakfasts on Sunday. I wanted to get pissed off at the dumb shit parents did in the pick-up line at Charlie's school. To have the luxury of getting kicked out of my daughter's end-of-year play because her family loved her too loudly.

And I wanted a man I could rely on. Who would add to my life instead of taking from it. The kind of man who was kind-hearted and loved deeply.

I wanted a man like Duke Bennett.

"Olivia?"

"No, I don't love it," I responded honestly, unable to stop the laugh from bubbling out of me.

Duke likely thought I was losing my mind, but admitting something like that felt like lifting the weight of the world from my shoulders. I hadn't admitted it to anyone. Not even Grady. The last person I tried talking to about it shamed me and called me a disgrace to my father's memory, so I learned quickly to keep it to myself.

"Then why are you doing it?" he asked.

I searched for any hint of judgment, but found none. Just careful curiosity. "It's all I know. It's what I've worked for my entire life. Seems kind of pointless if I don't follow through." My gaze fell to my lap, to the chipped manicure the girls gave me during our sleepover. "Besides, there's no one else in the family to take over. If I don't stay on, it'd be the first time a Hart wasn't CEO."

"You can't live your life for someone else." Duke's voice was soft. Reassuring. It nearly had me on the verge of tears.

Before one could fall, I pushed forward. "Tell that to my family. My dad was adamant about me following in his footsteps. And John's dedicated just as much of his life to ensuring the transfer of power from him to me was as smooth as possible. I can't let all of that go to waste just because I don't love it anymore."

Duke's fingers tapped against the wheel, but he didn't say anything right away. It wasn't until we were pulling onto the last stretch of country road that he spoke again. "You should talk to John about how you're feeling. I bet the thing that he wants more than anything in this world is for you to be happy."

There were so many things I wanted to say but didn't know how to voice. Of course, I knew John wanted me to be happy. He had spent his life helping me chase a dream I thought I had, stopping at nothing until it came to fruition. But how could I tell the man on his deathbed that all his hard work had been for nothing? Instead of wasting his time on training me to fill his shoes, he could've given his energy to someone else. Someone worthy of the role who wouldn't want to throw in the towel after only a few years in the job.

"Eh, it's fine," I said, forcing a smile. "No one loves their job all the time. It's just a part of life." I turned to him in my seat. "I mean, can you honestly tell me that you've never hated a single moment of owning the bar?"

"I hate the time I spend there that takes me away from Harper, but I've never hated my decision to own the bar or regretted it in any way. It was what I wanted, and I made it happen. Why should I hate that? And if I did, why would I stay in a situation that makes me unhappy?"

"Okay. I guess you're the anomaly then," I muttered, sitting back in my seat.

Was he right? Was it as easy as telling John I didn't want this life anymore?

"I've learned a lot in therapy, you know." His gaze flicked to the backseat where Harper and Charlie were thankfully still distracted. "After Sarah left, I was in a bad spot. Like, a really bad one, Olivia. I struggled to get out of bed. Struggled to shower. There were some days that I had to beg someone to take Harper for a night or two because I'd drunk myself into a stupor and couldn't even pick her up from school. But I got help. I talked to John about what was going on and the horrible thoughts swirling around in my head. He was the one who helped me find a therapist and get my shit straight."

I chewed on my lip, trying to keep my surprise hidden. Did Lukas know that Duke had struggled like that? "John helped you?"

"Honey, he's helped me more times than I could count. It was just my mom and me growing up. She did what she could to give me the best shot at life, but it wasn't easy being a single mom and having to raise a restless kid on her own. John stepped in, paid for anything he could. Sports. My first truck.

You name it." He glanced at me, smiling slightly. "How'd you think I paid for school? A scholarship?"

I shrugged. "I guess I never really thought about it."

Duke was always just... *there*. He and my brother were inseparable. I didn't consider us growing up any differently because he often stayed with us more than he did at home. But thinking back, it made sense. John and my parents always made sure that Duke had a pile of presents waiting for him on Christmas, and he accompanied us on every single family vacation we ever took.

"I know what it's like not to want to disappoint someone. After all John had done to help me succeed, going through the divorce and losing the house felt like I was slapping all his generosity in the face."

"I guess I'll have to take that into consideration. Got a good recommendation for a new therapist? Preferably not anyone in a fifty-mile radius?"

Duke pulled onto the property and headed up the short drive to John's house. He parked beside Lukas's truck and cut the ignition. The girls didn't waste any time unbuckling themselves and rounding the corner to where I was sure they'd find my brother hard at work.

I went to follow them, but Duke's hand on my elbow stopped me. "I know you're gonna play this off as a joke, but I still think you should talk to him about how you're feeling. I promise you, he wouldn't want you to look back in twenty or thirty years and regret living a life you didn't love. I know you don't want that either."

No, I didn't want that. While I respected Duke's attempt to— I don't know—give me a pep talk, our circumstances were different. I'd told John more times than I could count that all I wanted was to be like my father. Like him. It felt weak walking away so soon. Like I hadn't actually tried to make the job my own.

And if I didn't take it, who would?

"I'm going to go check on the girls and say hi to Luke," I said, pulling my arm free from his grip.

Duke nodded, but didn't push the change of subject. He stepped out into the sweet afternoon air with me. "I'll go check on the old man," he said, gesturing toward the house. "Let him know we're home."

I watched him disappear into the house and debated following him. It was my daughter's lighthearted giggles that changed my mind.

Rounding the corner of the house, I saw Charlie, Harper, and Lukas beneath the old oak tree. Once upon a time, Lukas and I had our own treehouse here, but it had been torn down years ago.

Charlie had been begging my brother for years to rebuild it, and he finally started a few months ago. It was a slow project since Lukas only came by on his occasional day off to work on it. Lately, though, it seemed like he used it as an excuse to come by and see John.

"What is going on here?" I asked, planting my hands on my waist. Charlie and Harper were both soaking wet while Lukas looked guilty as he dropped the water hose and raised his hands above his head.

"They started it," he said, sending a pointed look in the girl's direction.

"No, we didn't," they said in unison.

"Yes, you did."

"I tripped," Charlie said, examining her nails.

Lukas leveled her with a glare. "And managed to soak me in the process?"

She shrugged. "I don't know how it happened, but it did."

I covered my smile with the back of my hand. "So, you—the forty-two-year-old adult—decided to get revenge on two nine-year-olds? Am I understanding this correctly?" Lukas opened his mouth to argue, but snapped it shut. "That's what I thought." I looked toward the girls. "We'll talk about this later. For now, please go play. I need to talk to your uncle."

Harper headed off to the treehouse first, but Charlie turned around and shot daggers at my brother before shouting, "Snitches get stitches. You better sleep with one eye open, Uncle Luke."

When she turned around, Lukas looked at me with wide eyes. "What the hell are you teaching that kid?"

"Hopefully not to take any shit. I dealt with enough from you growing up."

"Yeah, yeah," he said, shaking his head. Water droplets flew everywhere.

"Oh my god, stop it," I hissed, stepping away from him. "You're worse than your niece."

He winked. "Must be where she gets it from."

God. I didn't even want to think about the hell she'd raise as she got older. She was a handful as it was.

"Did you say hi to John?" I asked, looking toward the house. I could see movement from inside, but couldn't tell if it was Duke or one of the nurses we had on staff.

"He was sleeping when I got here, so I decided to work out here in the meantime. Would you mind going inside and getting some towels while I make peace with your daughter? I don't want to wake up to her standing above my bed with a knife sometime in the future."

I looked back toward the treehouse where Charlie was still shooting daggers at Lukas. "Yeah, that might be best. She seems like she'd play the long game. Really make you lose your mind before she attacks." I patted him on the shoulder. "Don't worry. She takes bribes."

Lukas blew out a breath. "Why do I feel like this is going to cost me an arm and a leg?"

"Might cost you more than that," I laughed, heading toward the house.

Duke was standing on the porch, pacing back and forth and speaking quietly on the phone to someone. When he saw me, he quickly ended his call.

"Olivia, wait," he said, sticking his hand out so I couldn't get inside.

Unease prickled at the back of my neck as I tried to move past him, but he wouldn't budge. "I need to get in the house."

Duke shook his head. "I can't let you do that."

I glanced past him through the open door. John's nurse sat on the stairs, her eyes red-rimmed and glassy. I recognized the girl from school. She was a few years younger than me but had grown up in the area. We'd been grateful to hire someone from town to watch over him. Figured that might make him more comfortable on the days he woke up confused.

But I didn't understand why she was crying. Why Duke wouldn't let me past. There would be no reason I couldn't go inside the house, unless…

But no. That couldn't be. Duke and I had seen John this morning. Had talked to him only hours ago.

Duke's gaze softened as the realization hit me. His eyes were so full of sorrow.

Of apology.

"No," I said, shaking my head. "No."

"Olivia, I—"

"Get out of my way, Duke." I pushed at his arm, but it was no use. He was immovable. "Goddammit. Get out of my fucking way." I tried again, raising my voice as I attempted to force my way through.

The nurse on the stairs began crying louder. The keening wail grated on my nerves. Why was she crying? She had no business crying. I was John's family. His next of kin. I was the one who should have broken down in tears.

I could feel them coming, but pushed them down, down, down, until all I felt was anger.

Anger at the caretaker who'd been here when I wasn't.

Anger at Duke for keeping me from going inside the house.

Anger at John for dying.

Because that was what happened. We'd enjoyed the day to ourselves. Gotten lost in each other's company while John had died alone in his bed.

John was dead.

I ducked beneath Duke's arm, but was quickly caught around the waist. He pulled me into him, murmuring apologies I didn't want into my ear. I fought him, kicking the air and punching his arm to no avail. I screamed, but had no idea what was coming out of my mouth.

Nothing made sense, and yet I knew what was waiting for me in that house. Nothing.

Duke said something to the nurse, who hurried past us and out of the house. I kept fighting against his hold, but he kept me held tight to his chest as I let out a scream. The tears had already begun, and everything was spinning rapidly around me. I couldn't catch my breath, couldn't do anything other than thrash and scream in Duke's arms as a police siren sounded behind us.

"I'm sorry, honey. I'm so sorry," Duke whispered in my ear. Suddenly, the one place in the world I felt safe was crumbling around me. I was scrambling to regain any semblance of control and failing. He rocked me back and forth, rubbing circles along my back. I'm sure he meant for it to be comforting, but it wasn't his comfort I longed for. It wasn't his voice and words I desperately wanted—no, needed—to hear.

But I'd never get the chance. Not in this lifetime.

DUKE

IT'D BEEN three days since John's passing.

His death still didn't feel real. I woke up every morning, praying that our new reality was a bad dream, but I was left disappointed instead.

When I'd walked into his house that day, it had been quiet. Too quiet. The kind that immediately puts your senses on full alert. My body could sense something was wrong before I ever laid eyes on him.

His nurse was kneeling at his bedside, a prayer of mercy and comfort on her lips as she looked up to see me standing in the doorway. I braced myself on the wall, hoping he was just sleeping. How could he be gone when we were talking only hours before? This couldn't be right.

The heart monitor wasn't making a sound, but I saw the static line. He was gone.

My mind immediately drifted to Olivia and Lukas outside. They believed they were living in a world in which John Hart was still alive, and I had to be the one to tell them otherwise.

It wasn't fair for them or me. It wasn't fair that he was taken before he said goodbye. Everything he said to me—the things he wanted to tell Olivia earlier—he'd never get the chance.

I'd never forget the look on Olivia's face or the way she screamed and clawed at my arm to let her go. I held her tightly until she calmed enough for me to safely hand her over to Lukas. When the transport van arrived, the nurse handled the arrangements, ensuring John's body was safely transferred to the stretcher and taken out of the house discreetly. I wasn't sure where Lukas had taken Olivia, but I knew they were still in the house.

I stayed with the girls while we waited for Grady and Cleo to take them home. I noticed the tear tracks on both of their faces when they stepped out of Cleo's SUV. My heart ached for everyone, but I was hit hardest by Olivia's haunted silence as Lukas escorted her out of the house. She didn't speak to me. She wouldn't even look at me.

It was like I wasn't even there.

In the days that followed, Harper and I brought meals to Lukas's house every night, staying late into the evening, shooting the shit with my friend and reminiscing about old memories. The only person absent was Olivia.

She refused any and all invites to dinner, forcing me to drop a separate plate off at her doorstep before I left. Thankfully, Charlie was staying with Grady and Cleo so Olivia could focus on the funeral preparations.

I didn't pretend to know what she was going through. Not only had she lost her second father figure and idol, but also her boss and mentor. Luke had contacted the family lawyer and the Hartstrings board on the night John passed away, so everything that needed to be arranged could be taken care of. Despite the time he had prior to passing, John hadn't planned any aspect of his funeral.

A task that Olivia had taken solely upon herself. Lukas and I had both asked if we could do anything to help. We begged for her to give us a task, no matter how menial, but she refused.

Rolling over in bed, I grabbed my phone and checked my messages. Nothing. Just like I expected. Despite knowing better, I had sent Olivia at least two texts a day to check in. She hadn't responded yet, but that didn't stop me from typing out another one.

DUKE:

How are you?

As soon as I hit send, I cursed. *How are you?* What kind of stupid question was that? Her world had just been turned upside down. While I was trying to turn it around, I was clearly doing a piss poor job of doing so.

Quickly, I tried again.

DUKE:

Sorry. That was stupid. I just meant that I was thinking about you.

Jesus Christ. Just when I thought it couldn't get any worse. I'd gone from oblivious to overbearing in a matter of seconds.

I tossed my phone on the couch cushion and let out a low groan, rubbing my hands over my face. Respecting her silence and her space was becoming increasingly difficult because I knew it wasn't what she really wanted. I told everyone the same thing after my divorce—that I was fine. That I didn't need help. That I could handle the crushing pressure of being a newly single dad with ease.

And then, when everyone left me to my own devices, I spiralled out of control to the point I almost lost myself entirely.

I didn't want that for her. Especially if I could do something to help.

Without overthinking too much, I pushed to my feet and

hollered to Harper that we were leaving in ten minutes for school.

I FOUND myself sitting outside the local flower shop, staring at the front door as though it were a taunt. Forget-Me-Not might have been closing up, but I knew the owner, Margaret, didn't let that stop her from keeping a few fresh blooms on hand.

Like most others in this town, I'd known Margaret since I was a kid. My uncle used to hire her shop to decorate the city's floats for every holiday parade. It was one of my favorite memories. You'd think she was designing for some big city instead of a population of four thousand with the way she was executing these massive, over-the-top designs. And after she was done, she and her daughter would carefully deconstruct them and send them to nursing homes in the surrounding area.

Knowing her as well as I did was precisely my problem. For as loving as the woman was, she was also one of the biggest gossips in town. If I walked my ass inside and bought flowers, it'd be everywhere by noon. It wouldn't matter the occasion. It wouldn't matter that John just died. Rumors would fly, and the accusations would follow.

I didn't give too much of a shit for my sake, but I did for Harper's. Charlie and Olivia's, too. I remembered the days Harper would come home from school with dried tear tracks on her cheeks because some kid in her class had been running their mouth about her mom just up and leaving her. They said awful things. Some true, and some not. I'd heard the same things from patrons in my bar, but I'd been able to shrug them off.

If I bought Olivia flowers, there was a risk of stirring the pot again, but it was one I was going to have to take.

With a final exhale, I climbed out of my truck and bounded up the steps. The bell above the door chimed as it opened.

"Be there in just a minute!" Margaret called from the back.

Seeing the displays empty and moving boxes packed up behind the register left me feeling hollow. I'd meant to stop by for weeks but hadn't had a chance. Being here now made it feel too real.

"Sorry 'bout that, sweetie," Margaret said, wiping her hands on her polka-dotted apron as she appeared around the corner. Her hair, which had always been bright red, was beginning to show signs of gray. "Final delivery just got in. I wasn't really expecting anyone." She paused, realizing who I was. "Especially not you. How are you, young man?"

"Young man?" I grunted, cracking a smile. "Don't think I've been called that for a minute."

Margaret scoffed. "Well, if you're not young anymore, I don't even wanna talk about what that makes me! Now, what brings you to my doorstep?"

I glanced around, not knowing where to start. I was hoping for a small pre-made bouquet I could grab quickly. I didn't know the first fucking thing about flowers.

"Would you call me a smart ass if I said flowers?"

She gestured toward the sign on the door before crossing her arms. "I could tell that much. I'm old, not blind."

"Thought we weren't talking about ages?"

"Do you want to waste my time some more, or do you want some damn flowers?" she asked.

I chuckled, shoving my hands in my pockets. "I want some damn flowers, but I don't know what kind or anything. I was thinking you might have some put together already that I could grab."

Margaret's narrowed eyes widened as I spoke. "This is for a woman, isn't it?"

"Yes, but—"

I didn't get a chance to explain before she started clapping excitedly. "Oh, I just knew you'd get back out there someday! You know, Donna Harrison told me I was crazy for even thinking about it—she thought you'd take your sulking to the grave—but look at you! Absolutely glowing." Then she cackled. "And now I'm twenty bucks richer!"

This was exactly what I was afraid of.

"Margaret, it's not like that," I began, but she shook her head.

"Sure it isn't," she said with a wink. "Now, what are you thinking? Roses for a proposal, perhaps?"

"Christ, woman. No. Nothing like that," I said. "It's for Olivia Hart. John just died, and I just wanted to do something nice for her."

Margaret's face sobered. Something like regret flashed in her eyes. "Oh, it's just awful. I didn't believe it when I heard. Though I'm not really supposed to be taking on any extra work right now, I called Lukas that very day to offer my services. Imagine my surprise when it was sweet Olivia who called me back. Offered me far more money than I'm worth, I'll tell you that much." She paused, lips pursed in concentration. "I don't have much, sweetie, but I'll make you the best bouquet out of what I've got. Don't you worry. Give me just a few moments."

Without hesitating, she hurried to the back. The store was quiet, so I could make out the sound of Margaret chattering to herself under her breath as she worked. Every now and then, she'd let out a loud curse before apologizing and continuing on. Hearing her made me curious as to what she looked like while she was in the zone, but I knew if I stepped foot in her space, I'd likely have a pair of scissors thrown at my head for disrupting her.

So, instead, I stood in the awkward silence, waiting until the moment I heard her give a triumphant little yell and the patter of footsteps. "I've got it!" she said, rounding the corner with her creation.

While I'd been expecting some giant monstrosity, I was surprised to see she'd come up with something both modest and elegant.

"Margaret, it's beautiful," I said, taking in the myriad of pink, yellow, and orange hues amidst the long, fragrant green leaves. "What is it?"

She smiled. "Daisies and eucalyptus. These big ones are gerrondo daisies—I get them imported from California—and mini gerbers." She lowered her voice. "Those I actually grow in my greenhouse."

"It's perfect," I whispered, tearing my gaze from the bouquet. "She'll love it."

Margaret nodded and handed it over before I could pull out my wallet. "Don't even think about it, young man. This one's on the house."

"I can't accept that," I protested. "Let me pay you."

She swatted my arm. "Boy, didn't you hear me when I said that family has already paid me more money than I'm worth for John's service? The least I could do is this. She needs a pop of color more than I do." Before I could say anything else, she grabbed my shoulders and turned me toward the door. "Now go get the girl."

I smiled, but didn't argue. There was no point to it. And I happened to like how it sounded. Olivia might not have been my girl right now, but I was beginning to wonder if I could make her mine one day.

I THOUGHT BUCKLING the bouquet in would've been enough to stop it from sliding, but I was wrong. I'd barely made it out of town before I had to rethink my strategy.

Unfortunately, that meant holding the steering wheel with a white-knuckled grip while the other hand was on the precious cargo in the front seat. I let out a sigh of relief when I pulled up outside Lukas's guest cabin.

At least I did that right.

After calling Lukas this morning, I knew he had to visit a job site near Knoxville this afternoon, which meant he'd be gone most of the day. At least I wouldn't have to worry about him seeing my truck and getting nosy.

Grabbing the bouquet, I hopped out of the truck and walked to the front door. Though I knew she likely wouldn't answer, I rapped my knuckles against the wood and waited.

Though muffled, I heard the unmistakable sound of her voice from the other side. The curtains next to the window snapped back, giving me a sign of life. I smiled, holding the flowers up for her to see. It was probably enough of a shock to warrant an investigation, and thankfully, I was right.

The door opened, giving me my first glimpse of the woman in hiding. I wasn't sure what I was expecting, but it wasn't this.

Olivia was dressed in a relaxed pair of tan slacks and a simple black short-sleeve shirt. Her hair was pulled back out of her face—a look I'd quickly associated with her public, busi-ness-like persona rather than the smiling woman who drank chocolate milkshakes and laughed out loud. Though she tried to cover them with makeup, the pale purple half-circles beneath her eyes gave away how much sleep she was losing.

"H-Hey, honey," I said, keeping my voice low. "Wanted to bring these by for you."

Olivia's eyes dipped to the bouquet, but she made no move to take it from my hand. Instead, her fingers tapped against the doorframe. "What're you doing here, Duke?" There was an edge of annoyance in her tone, but I didn't let that deter me.

"Like I said, I wanted to bring these to you."

"You drove all the way out here to bring me flowers?" I nodded, tamping down the anxiety coursing through my body. "Why?"

"Consider it a welfare check. You weren't answering any of my texts or my calls. When I come by at night to drop dinner off, I never see a flicker of movement inside."

"While I appreciate the concern, my brother knows I'm alive. You can get your little welfare updates from him." Without so much as a goodbye, she began to shut the door in my face.

I reached out, stopping it with my free hand. Olivia glanced up, our eyes meeting for only a second before I pushed past her and stepped inside the house. "Duke, what are you—"

I didn't stop until I was standing in the middle of the kitchen, looking around for something, anything to be out of place. A sign she was struggling. Instead of finding a mess, however, the entire space was immaculately clean. The marble countertops damn near sparkled beneath the early afternoon sun streaming in from the arched window above the sink. There were no streaks on the stainless steel appliances. All the pillows on the couch were perfectly placed, the blanket neatly folded and draped over the arm.

Hell, there was even a fucking simmer pot on the stove, filling the space with notes of apple cider and citrus.

"What the hell do you think you're doing?" Olivia asked, hot on my heels. "You can't just barge into someone's house like you own the fucking thing."

I set the flowers down in the middle of the island before turning toward her, matching the tense energy. "It's not your house. It's Lukas's. And I helped him build the damn thing."

She gave a slow clap. "Oh, well, ignore me then. Come on in and make yourself at home, why don't you?"

This woman was infuriating. She was clearly deflecting. I'd gotten to know her well enough over the past few weeks that I could tell.

"Olivia," I said, pinching the bridge of my nose. "We're worried about you. You haven't been talking to anyone. Lukas said you haven't even left the house since—" *Since John died.* "You can't blame people for being worried."

She looked away, rolling her lips together. "Well, maybe people should quit worrying about me."

"Honey, you know it's not that simple."

"God! And stop calling me that. I'm not your honey. I'm not your anything." Her dark eyes were nearly black, cool and indifferent, and so at odds with the version of her I knew. "When a woman doesn't respond to your text messages, it's because she doesn't want to talk to you. You should take the fucking hint."

Her words were primed to wound, and they struck me at my core just as she intended. It would be easy to storm out, to let my frustration get the best of me and turn me into someone I didn't recognize, but I didn't waver. I didn't let her see how much her words killed me inside.

Olivia's anger was valid. It was warranted. While she knew his death was inevitable, she thought she had more time. We all fucking did. It killed me knowing we were all robbed of that, but none more than her.

But what I wanted—what she needed—was to direct that anger toward something. Someone. Toward me. I wanted her to get it all out because holding it in was going to make the wound left behind by John's death fester until she rotted from the inside out.

I leaned forward, bracing my hands on the countertop. "I'm not a stupid man, Olivia. I know you don't mean that shit.

You're angry right now, and I get that, but you don't have to be angry alone. You have family. You have friends. You have *me*." I stressed that last word, pushing every ounce of pleading I had into my voice.

"You need to leave, Duke," she said, pulling her bottom lip between her teeth. "I have a meeting in fifteen minutes."

"Olivia," I began, but she cut me off.

"Can you not push me right now?"

"No, because that's exactly what you need. You need someone to push you. And you need to throw all your anger at them to see that they won't leave because of it." I placed my hand on my chest. "I'm not leaving, Olivia."

"You will eventually, so let's just cut the bullshit, alright? This isn't a therapy session. I don't want to talk about my goddamn feelings. I want to be left alone."

"Tough shit." I walked around the corner until I was standing right in front of her. She refused to look at me. "Talk to me, Liv. Tell me how to help."

All of a sudden, she exploded. Her eyes burned with fire. With anger and rage and fury. "And how, exactly, do you think you can help me, Duke? Huh? Please tell me."

"Just talk to me—"

"I. Wasn't. There." Each word was punctuated with a jab to my chest. "He died, and I wasn't there because we decided to go out to play one big happy family. I wasn't there when he took his last breath. I wasn't there to say goodbye," her voice broke on a ragged sob. "I wasn't fucking there, and I will never forgive myself for it."

I surged forward, taking her into my arms as her cries got louder and louder. She tried to break free, but I held her as tight as I had three days ago. As though it could somehow piece her back together.

"I hate myself for that day. And not just because he was

alone, but because, up until that moment, I was happy. God, I was so fucking happy. And when I think about what happened before, I want to smile at the stupid fucking coloring pages and all the things we shared, but then I remember what came after and I get so fucking nauseous that I spend my time between meetings with my head in a toilet."

I ran my hand up and down her back as she spoke about grief and fury and all the unfair bullshit that life sent our way sometimes. She was right; it wasn't fair that she didn't get to say goodbye.

And the worst part was that I was the last one to spend time with him. His last words were meant for Olivia, but I got them instead. They might have set her free from the prison she was keeping herself in.

"When I got divorced," I began, clearing my throat. "I alienated myself. I hated everyone and everything that seemed happy when I was so clearly in hell. I've spent the past two years of my life utterly miserable, but lately... Lately, things have been better. I appreciate the little things I'd been taking for granted. Like sunshine and chocolate milkshakes and an absolutely maddening woman who doesn't realize how much control she has over me."

Without overthinking, I pressed a kiss to the top of her forehead. Olivia's eyes closed as though savoring the contact.

There was something monumental about the moment. A tender touch between friends on the brink of something more. I wanted it to last forever. Wanted to pull her into my arms and kiss her until we lost track of time and the bullshit that plagued our day-to-day lives.

But I didn't.

"I know you're an independent woman, and I'd never want to take away from that. I'd rather take a thousand verbal blows than exist in your silence. But if you don't want to take it out on me, take it out on Lukas. Take it out on Grady. You have so many people who care about you."

Olivia buried her head in my chest, crying harder. Her hands clutched at the fabric of my shirt, stretching it tightly across my shoulders and neck. I could feel her body weakening, going limp in my arms.

Without asking, I scooped her up the best I could and brought her over to the couch. She sat in my lap as I rocked her back and forth slowly. Deliberately.

The phone rang somewhere in the distance, but she didn't move. She simply sat there and let me hold her until her eyes drifted shut and her breathing evened out.

We stayed like that for nearly an hour, me holding her as she slept. I would've stayed longer if I hadn't needed to pick Harper up from school. Though I tried to be as gentle as I could as I rolled her onto her back, she blinked up at me in confusion.

"I've got to go pick up Harper, but I'll bring dinner by at seven," I said.

Olivia dipped her chin in acknowledgement as I draped a stray blanket over her body.

As I stood up, her eyes had drifted closed. I headed to the door, but paused when I heard her softly whisper, "Thank you for the flowers."

OLIVIA

THE EARLY SPRING air was crisp as I watched the pallbearers set my uncle's casket on the lowering mechanism. Flowers of every color decorated the white tent covering the burial site. It was only a fraction of what was brought over from the actual ceremony.

Honestly, I had no idea what we'd do with all of them. It seemed like a waste, especially when I couldn't fathom taking a single bloom home.

Today wasn't one I wanted to look back and remember.

My brother turned his back to the casket, and I saw tears shining in his eyes. Duke, who graciously agreed to be one of my uncle's pallbearers at Luke's request, clapped him on the shoulder. They mumbled something to one another, but I averted my gaze, not trusting myself to keep my composure.

Instead, I stared down at my feet. They'd grown numb hours ago during the drawn-out funeral service as countless members of the community and the board of directors eulogized my uncle. He would've hated the whole affair if he were still alive, but how was I supposed to tell people they couldn't pay their respects to a man who was so universally loved?

Lukas took the seat next to mine, but neither of us spoke. There wasn't much left to say. We had been barraged with condolences all day, which, despite the lovely sentiments, left me feeling drained. Regardless of how well I'd been trained to hide my true feelings in public, there were only so many times I could force a polite smile and thank people for coming by to pay their respects.

Charlie's presence was the only thing keeping me centered. I tightened my hold on her hand, squeezing gently when I heard her quietly sobbing. Tears streamed down my daughter's face. I pulled her into me, draping an arm around her shoulders. Grady and Cleo were on her other side, both wearing matching red-rimmed expressions, staring straight ahead as the pastor spoke.

Though I could feel her gaze on me, I ignored my mother's presence at the end of the aisle. Just like I'd been ignoring her for the past week and a half since John's death.

The calls began the day after and were easy enough to ignore. I added it to the list of things I'd been avoiding since Lukas carried my limp body into his guest house and let me rest in the stillness of the dying daylight. The voicemails that followed were drunken tirades. Harsh accusations and questions about what was going to happen to the company and if I was going to burn everything my family built to the ground for my own selfish desires.

After the first three, I blocked her number.

I thought that put an end to it but then the knocking started. I ignored it still, trying to focus on planning John's funeral between meetings with the Hartstrings board. Then the knocking turned into pounding. Lukas had to come down and drag her away from the cottage at one in the morning, only two days ago.

Every day was something new. It was why I refused to leave the cottage to eat dinner with them at Lukas's house, why I ignored Duke every night when he dropped off a plate just for me. Why I'd almost ignored him the day he came by with flowers.

I almost threw them out in an angry rage just because it was the only thing I had control over. They'd been in my hand, hovering over the trash can, before I set them back on the counter and crumpled to the floor in shame. I didn't deserve them. Didn't deserve his kindness either.

What killed me most was the relief I felt at seeing him standing on my doorstep, looking so goddamn nervous. And then I hated myself for adding to his pain, knowing he was grieving my uncle just as much as the rest of us were.

I was no stranger to death or grief, but losing John was different than my father. Though both tragic in their own ways, my uncle had become the father I chose. He spent the past twenty-two years of his life ensuring neither Lukas nor I ever felt as though we weren't loved and supported.

It was much more than my mother did, choosing to check out when we needed her most.

I glanced down at Charlie and pressed a kiss to the top of her head. This was her first dance with death. While I'd hoped to shield her from it as long as I could, it snuck up on us anyway. We all thought we had more time with John. The doctors said months, but those months turned into weeks at best, and now we were sitting at a funeral surrounded by a sea of black coats and dresses.

The massive crowds at both the funeral home and the burial site were testaments to how loved he was. How many lives he touched. More people spoke at the gravesite service, but I didn't remember what they said.

As the pastor asked everyone to stand, the first tear I'd shed all day slipped free. I quickly wiped it away before anyone could notice, finding myself wishing it were the brush of Duke's fingertips instead.

Everyone lined up to give their final condolences. One by one, I saw faces I recognized. Faces that had rallied together to make sure today went as smoothly as possible. Lucy, who closed the diner to cater the celebration-of-life gathering at Lukas's house after the burial. Margaret hadn't hesitated to order thousands of dollars' worth of flowers when I called. Even Too Drunk Johnny was standing at the back of the crowd, sober for the first time in my life—though something told me he wouldn't stay like that for long.

By the time Duke and Harper made it to us, the burial site was nearly empty. People loitered by their cars, their sorrowful glances back at us a reminder we were still being watched. Lukas' tears fell freely when they walked up. Duke clapped his shoulder before pulling my brother into a hug. Though I couldn't make out what they were saying, Lukas squeezed his eyes shut and nodded his head before they separated.

And then Duke was standing in front of me, green gaze swimming with unshed tears. Somehow, I knew he was holding them at bay for me. I wasn't sure I would've been able to contain myself if I saw them fall. I wasn't that strong. Not anymore.

I gave him a watery smile, voice wavering as I spoke. "Thank you for coming, and for"—I gestured toward the scene behind him—"agreeing to be a pallbearer. He would've loved that."

The longer Duke stood there, the harder it was to keep my composure. I needed him to move. To stop staring at me with such sorrow and grief, or else I was going to lose it right here and now. There was only so much I could take, and I was already at my limit.

"Honey…" His voice was low, cautious, as he reached out and pulled me to his chest. Everything in me crumbled at that one single word. It was like the breaking of a dam. I let myself go, unable to keep him at arm's length any longer. My hands found their way around his waist as I clung to him like a life raft on turbulent waters. When the first sob broke free, I couldn't stop myself from sinking completely into his embrace.

This wasn't the time or place for such a display, but that didn't stop us. I was so tired of being strong for everyone else. Tired of pushing everything to the side as I carefully treaded around their grief as though it mattered more than mine. All I'd wanted since that day was to call Duke and ask him to come over. To hold me. To press another kiss to my forehead like he had when he pushed his way into my house only days ago.

"He's gone," I whispered into Duke's chest. "He's gone, and I don't know what to do."

"I know, honey…" he said, cupping the back of my head with a large, warm hand."I know. I'm here."

My eyes were closed, but my family's curious gazes burned a hole in my back as they stared. There would be questions later. Questions I wasn't sure even had answers, but that was a problem for future Olivia, because I didn't plan on letting go of Duke anytime soon.

"Where's your car?" Duke asked, letting his hand trail down my back in soothing circles.

"I can drive," I began to protest, but stopped the moment he placed his finger beneath my chin and tilted my head up until I was staring up at him.

"Let me take care of you. Where's your car?"

My throat worked, full of grief and other emotions I wasn't sure I'd ever felt before. How could this man I'd grown up with have suddenly become one of the most important people in my life in less than a month? What did that say about me, that I turned to him in my grief rather than my friends? "I'm parked by Lukas."

Duke looked toward Lukas, who pointed toward the cemetery's entry gates. Then he glanced at Grady. "I assume you're going to the house?"

Grady nodded. "I'll take her SUV, and Cleo will drive my truck."

I was vaguely aware of them making plans, talking about moving over Charlie's booster seat to Duke's truck, but instead of pushing them away and telling them I'd handle it, I let them take care of me.

"Come on, honey." Duke wrapped his arm around my shoulders, never letting me go as we walked toward his truck.

Charlie's hand found mine, squeezing gently as I had done to her earlier in the day. Glancing down, I worried if I wasn't being strong enough for her. If I should've stood my ground and driven us home instead of being cared for. The last thing I wanted was to become my mother, so dependent on everyone else around her that she'd forgotten how to live.

But then I realized I never wanted my daughter to grow up believing she had to do everything herself as I did. I didn't want her to lose her gentle heart, the one I found myself constantly in awe of. We had a solid support system—one that others could only dream of having. Why shouldn't she learn that a vital part of taking care of herself meant leaning on those who love you to get through hard times?

Duke helped me into the passenger seat, reaching over to grab my seatbelt and buckle me in. I mumbled a quiet thank you as he quietly closed the door and moved to the back to help the girls get settled. By the time he made it to the driver's side, Lukas' truck was idling at the exit, waiting for us.

As he started the engine, soft music began filtering out of the speakers. Fresh tears filled my eyes as I recognized it as one of my uncle's favorites. Duke reached over without hesitation and took my hand over the console, briefly bringing it to his lips before interlacing our fingers and letting them rest out in the open.

For the first time in a week and a half, I believed things might be okay.

DUKE

FROM ACROSS THE ROOM, I watched Olivia as she spoke to a round man in an expensive-looking suit. Gone were the tears from earlier. They dried up the moment we drove onto Lukas' ranch. In their place was a look of perfectly practiced poise.

I wasn't sure who the man was, but he looked important. Lukas told me that most people here were members of the board. While I understood their desire to pay their respects, now didn't seem like the time or place for them to be hovering over the family like vultures.

When we pulled up to Lukas's house earlier, the girls had quickly jumped out of the truck, leaving Olivia and me alone. Neither of us spoke. We sat there in the silence, holding onto one another. It'd taken every bit of self-control I possessed not to drive us away. If Lukas hadn't knocked on the window, maybe I would've acted on it.

I wasn't sure how long he'd been standing there, but his gaze snagged on our interlocked hands before Olivia pulled hers away like we'd been caught doing something we shouldn't have.

Once we got inside, Olivia had put as much distance between us as she could. Anytime I drew near, she found an excuse to leave the vicinity. Eventually, I grabbed a beer and parked my ass on Lukas's couch, sinking into the leather.

At least this way, I could keep an eye on her without feeling like I was being overbearing.

If there was one thing I'd realized, it was that I didn't want to continue living the miserable existence I'd trapped myself in. Olivia brought light back into my life and made me feel hopeful about the prospect of an infinite number of tomorrows. It wasn't just my life, but Harper's as well. I couldn't remember the last time my daughter had been so happy.

I couldn't—no, *wouldn't*—go back to the way things were. I refused.

It didn't matter if I had to spend the rest of my days trying to convince Olivia of the effect she had on our lives. I'd fucking do it.

Holy shit. The realization was sudden and fast and hit me like a goddamn truck. I wanted Olivia Hart, and not just as a casual fling or one-night stand.

I wanted her light, her laugh, her warmth in my life every single day.

I wanted to shake my head at every ridiculous thing that came out of her mouth knowing this was her world and I was just living in it.

I wanted *her.*

The woman was a mess, but in the best and most beautiful way imaginable. I'd been so wrong about her when she first came home, so ready to jump the gun with some bullshit opinion, I hadn't even stopped to consider if my judgment may have been clouded because of my past.

Seeing her with Charlie and Harper one time was enough for me to realize she was nothing like my ex-wife. Sarah would never have sat on the ground during a soccer game to support her daughter's best friend, but Olivia hadn't balked. That was the moment I realized I could see her sitting there every week—cheering Harper on alongside me. I could see her being part of our lives long-term.

When she crashed into our lives at the grocery store, I'd stupidly believed she'd somehow ruined everything I built when in reality, she seemed to right all my wrongs. She chased away the darkness and pulled me into the light.

The couch dipped beside me, and I turned to find Lukas sitting next to me with a beer in hand. He'd discarded the black suit jacket and tie at some point, wearing a crisp white shirt with the top buttons undone. Even though I'd seen him nearly every day for the past week and a half, there was something about him that looked even more tired than normal.

Maybe the reality of the situation was finally hitting home.

"He would've hated this shit," Lukas said, bringing the bottle to his lips. "Everyone dressed to the fucking nines, talking about how great he was." He shook his head. "Biggest bunch of kiss asses I've ever seen."

I followed his gaze back to the man talking to Olivia. "Who is he?"

"Edward Montgomery. He owns a property development company in New York. Liv told me he's been sniffing around John's property for years, trying to convince him to sell." Lukas's face curled in disgust. "I'm sure he's here out of the kindness of his heart and nothing else."

If I hadn't been paying such close attention to Olivia these past few weeks, I would've thought the conversation she was having was entirely normal. She was smiling, nodding her head at all the right times. Hell, there was even a bit of polite laughter now and then.

But the problem was that I knew her better than that now. I

studied her movements, her ticks, every time we were in each other's presence, trying to figure out if this attraction was all in my head or if it was something else entirely.

The smile she wore didn't reach her eyes. It was the polite, forced one she often gave when she felt uncomfortable. And there was no warmth to her laughter. She stood rigid as a goddamn board while this prick attempted to work his charm for his own benefit. Occasionally, her gaze would drift around the room as though searching for someone. When it landed on me, I expected her to look away quickly, but she didn't. Instead, it lingered, warming me up from the inside.

"I'll be right back," I murmured to Lukas.

I didn't wait for his reply before pushing to my feet and striding toward Olivia. Neither of us broke eye contact as I slid around the dick in a suit and placed my hand on her lower back. On instinct, she sidled up next to me, soaking up my warmth.

"Need anything, honey?" I asked, turning my head so my lips brushed her temple.

Her eyes closed momentarily. "No, I'm okay. Thank you, though." I was prepared to make an excuse to get her out of there when she said, "Duke, this is Edward Montgomery. Edward, meet Duke Bennett."

Edward's smile faltered as he took us in, but his polite, business-like demeanor won out. He thrust his hand forward. "Pleased to meet you, Duke."

I glanced down at it for a second before taking it. His shake was weak and a little clammy. "Can't say the same, Eddie."

Olivia's head spun my direction, and the man blanched, snatching his hand back. I couldn't tell if she was going to have my ass for that comment or not, so I added, "You know, because we're at a funeral."

"Yes. Very unfortunate," Edward said, glancing toward Olivia. "I was just telling Ms. Hart here that her uncle and I go way back. Further than I care to mention." He chuckled, slipping one hand into his pocket. "There were some business negotiations still taking place, in fact. I know it's not the best time, but—"

"Maybe we should wait until the dirt fills his grave before we go talking business, Edmond?" I interrupted, pulling Olivia tighter to my side. "Seems pretty fucking insensitive to try and bring it up before then, if you ask me."

"My name is Edward," he hissed through clenched teeth. "And how dare you speak to me like that!" His unbelieving gaze traveled to Olivia, waiting for her to jump to his rescue. "Ms. Hart, I really must insist we take our conversation elsewhere. I will not tolerate such ill-mannered behavior from someone who couldn't even begin to understand such matters."

Oh, this motherfucker was just begging to get his ass handed to him. A task I was more than willing to take care of, but it turned out that I didn't need to. Olivia's body went rigid at his tone, turning her full attention to the small man in front of her.

"You talk about ill-mannered behavior as though you weren't plucking up the courage to ask me about my uncle's estate and the land that comes with it on the day we buried him," she snapped. "And while he may have entertained your business propositions for fun, allow me to make one thing very clear, Mr. Montgomery. I am *not* him, and I don't give a shit about what you were trying to swindle him into before his death because I am here now to protect his legacy, and that doesn't include business dealings with Montgomery Holdings."

Edward stammered, but nothing came out. I stepped closer, placing my hand on his shoulder. "I'd make sure the next words that come out of your mouth are carefully chosen. My girl deserves respect."

He glanced between Olivia and me, giving us both an awkward nod before turning on his heel and exiting the house without so much as a backward glance. Lukas, who was still watching us closely from his seat on the couch, raised his beer bottle in a silent salute.

"What a fucking dick," Olivia muttered. I shifted, looking down at her.

Though clearly haunted by the events of the day, the corner of her lips lifted a fraction as we watched Edward's car disappear, turn onto the main road, and head back into town.

"At least he's gone," I said.

My hand still rested on her back—something others around us were beginning to take notice of, judging by the number of curious glances our way. While I knew I should move it, I couldn't. Not when it was giving her comfort.

Not when I wanted it there.

She blew out a breath. "I don't know about you, but I could use a drink after that."

I gestured toward the empty kitchen, following closely behind as she walked down the short hallway toward the counter bar.

"What'll you have?" I asked, turning on my best charming smile.

Her lips twitched. "Oh? Are you a bartender or something?"

"I've been known to make a stiff drink from time to time."

She leaned back against the counter. "Tequila soda, please. Extra lime."

I nodded. "Coming right up."

We were quiet as I worked. I could feel the tension still weighing heavily on her shoulders. The least I could do is be a safe place to exist in silence. She looked out the window, giving off an air of indifference, but I didn't miss the way her fingers dug into her forearms.

"Here you go." I walked over, holding the drink out to her.

She quickly took it, holding it up in thanks. "Nice touch

there at the end." Olivia chewed on her bottom lip, staring up at me through thick lashes. "You know, the whole put some respect on my name thing."

"You liked that, huh?" I asked, smiling.

"I did." She hesitated, clearing her throat before adding. "And the territorial, 'my girl' thing was nice, too. I mean, completely unnecessary and untrue, but still."

"Doesn't have to be." My beer was lukewarm at best now, but I took a swing anyway. I needed something to do with my hands other than fucking touch her. It was hard enough trying to focus on the fact that the only thing separating her skin from mine was a thin scrap of fabric.

Olivia's silence only increased my anxiety, yet I didn't push her. If the roles had been reversed and she claimed me as her own, I wouldn't know how the hell to react either.

"It'd be reckless to be anything more than friends," she whispered. "We're both divorced with kids."

"So? Is that supposed to mean we can't enjoy ourselves?"

I wasn't sure what happened to the man I'd become after my marriage ended, but I hadn't seen him in weeks. Being here, with Olivia, was the closest I'd felt to my old self in years. Even before Sarah and I separated, I'd noticed my walls climbing higher and higher. Maybe that was one of the reasons we hadn't worked out in the first place.

I always felt like I was doing something wrong. Like I wasn't enough for her. Unfortunately, those thoughts had become reality when she left me for a life I never even knew she wanted. I vowed never to put myself in a position that could hurt Harper and me again, yet here I was, opening myself to potential danger.

Olivia averted her gaze. "Enjoying ourselves is one thing. Anything more is out of the question, and you know that."

I did know that. God, did I fucking know that. But I also

knew that the past week and a half without her had been the longest days of my life. Her silence, her absence, was fucking killing me. If I were going to die, I'd rather do it knowing the taste of her.

I placed my hand on her stomach, crowding Olivia until she was gently pinned against the counter. Conversations were a soft hum in the background. Loud enough for us to know we weren't alone, but quiet enough to give us a sense of security we didn't have out in the open.

Olivia's chest heaved as she took quick, shallow breaths. Those wide, luscious lips I'd been dreaming of parted as I invaded her space.

"What I know, honey, is that being around you is turning me into a very impatient and greedy man. One of these days…" I let my fingers play with the buttons of her dress, tugging ever so slightly. "I just may snap."

Her gaze dipped to my mouth for a moment before I stepped back out into the open. If people were looking, wondering what we were doing around the corner, I didn't give a shit. Let them see what we did to one another. Let them see just how much of a sucker I'd become in a short amount of time, because I was damn sure enjoying the view of Olivia looking fully flushed.

"That's not fair," she breathed. Her voice was barely above a whisper. Heat bloomed across her cheeks, turning them a bright pink as she finished her drink.

"What's not?" I asked, cocking my head to the side.

She waved in my general direction. "This. You. Whatever just happened."

"I don't know what you're talking about," I said, winking as I finished off the warm beer. "I'm going to grab another drink. You want one?"

She nodded. "Please."

OLIVIA

I BROUGHT my glass to my lips, sipping tequila on the rocks and sitting on the porch swing, as the last of the mourners left. Lukas and Duke were in the house, cleaning up while Charlie and Harper ran around the yard. They'd been playing tag for the last thirty minutes without showing the faintest hint of slowing down.

God, what I'd do to have even an ounce of their energy right now. Maybe then my life wouldn't feel like I was getting crushed beneath the weight of everyone else's fucking expectations.

I'd spent every day since my uncle's passing doing everything but dealing with my grief surrounding his death. If I wasn't in meetings, I was planning his funeral. And if I wasn't planning his funeral, I was answering emails. And when I wasn't answering emails, I was funneling what little energy I had remaining into raising my daughter. Then I went to sleep and started everything over again.

When I woke up today, I mistakenly assumed those expectations would end. There would be no meetings. No bullshit schmoozing. No false pretenses. Just people coming together to mourn the life of a great man. One fucking day of silence.

How wrong I was.

Though I made it through the funeral and burial unscathed, I couldn't say the same about his celebration. From the moment Duke and I showed up, I was not only swarmed by members of the board but also slimy pricks like Edward Montgomery, whose only interest was growing their portfolio in our time of despair.

From the moment he cornered me this afternoon, I'd been searching for someone—*anyone*—to save me from his over-the-top compliments and praise for not only John's work, but mine as well. Unfortunately for Mr. Montgomery, my uncle ensured I knew about the particularly nasty vultures who would use his death as an opportunity to sink their claws into a piece of the Hart legacy. He was at the top of the list of people not to work with, so he'd wasted all his time and energy coming out here and kissing my ass for nothing.

Small mercies, and all.

The screen door swung open, drawing my attention as my mother stumbled out into the fresh, pine-laced air. She didn't say anything, just removed her pack of cigarettes from her pocket and pulled one from the carton. The stench of smoke filled the space with her first puff and she sank onto the swing next to me.

Despite us being in close proximity all day, it hadn't been difficult to ignore her. She kept to herself for most of the day, sneaking off to sip from the flask she always kept on hand. The rest of the time, I'd been too busy in conversation to pay her any mind.

But now that the mourners were gone and there were no bullshit business transactions to take care of, I was forced to succumb to her presence.

"She looks just like you, you know," my mother said, breaking the silence.

I hummed, not sure how to respond. If you looked at pictures of me when I was Charlie's age, we were almost indistinguishable. Same long blonde hair. Same wide smile. The only difference was our eye color.

Thank god she took after her daddy on that one.

"Your father would've loved her."

I let my head fall back against the swing. "He would've."

She took another drag from her cigarette. "I would've loved her too, if you had let me."

There it was. The comment I'd been waiting for since she sat down. She had an uncanny ability to find the tiniest crack in my armor and blow it wide open. "How long have you been waiting to use that line?" I asked, tapping my fingers along the glass.

"It's not a line, Olivia. It's the truth. Your little tantrum has gone on long enough, don't you think? How long can you reasonably expect me to keep my distance from my own granddaughter?" She turned to face me, but I refused to look at her. "My own daughter?"

I took another sip. The burn of the liquor was nothing compared to the pain of the conversation. I knew where it was headed. It was the same one we had every time she managed to corner me. Only this time, John wasn't here to step in and comfort me like he always had.

"Maybe you should've thought about the consequences of your actions before you called me a selfish bitch who only thought about myself," I said, managing to keep my voice level. "Maybe then you'd still have access to the people you claim to love."

My mother gasped loudly, and I rolled my eyes. Her dramatics knew no bounds. At least she'd waited for everyone to leave before she began kicking off. I could only imagine the reaction people would have if they saw the way we interacted with one another. She would undoubtedly play the victim, blaming my cruel ways for our distance.

Finally, I turned to face her. It was the first time I'd truly taken her in. The face I used to know and love, the one full of youthful radiance and beauty, had grown weathered. Whether it was the alcohol or the cigarettes or her general disdain for her own wellbeing, I couldn't be sure. She was almost unrecognizable. If I passed her on the street, I wouldn't have known her face. The only feature my soul knew was the precise shade of her eyes because they matched mine.

"You think I don't love you?" she asked before breaking out into a coughing fit. "I said what I said because I don't want to see you squandering this family's legacy, not because I don't love you. Honestly, Olivia. You're painting me to be the bad guy here."

"Because you are," I said earnestly. "My god, Mother. Are you so narcissistic that you can't see that? I see the years of silence have taught you nothing."

"If that were true, your brother would have nothing to do with me, and yet here I am, staying in the same house I raised you both in, while you have refused to step foot inside until you were forced to today. I have tried multiple times to talk to you, but you've ignored me every time. You've gone as far as to block my number. How am I supposed to fix a relationship when the other person is so disinterested in doing so?"

"Our relationship isn't something that can be fixed with a conversation. Especially when you refuse to take responsibility for the hurt you caused."

"Is that what you want?" she asked with a huff. "An apology? That's rich, Olivia. I'm sorry I tried to help you. I'm sorry, I wanted what was best for not only you, but also your daughter. I'm sorry—"

That was it. My threshold for bullshit had been hit, especially when she brought Charlie into the mix. I stood up from the swing, turning on her in a red haze. "You don't give a shit about my daughter or me. You're worried about yourself, about the monthly allowance Dad set up for you in the event that anything happened to him. An allowance, might I add, that was meant to be used to raise the two children you had and not to drown yourself in expensive liquor and cigarettes." I flicked my gaze down her body, stopping where I knew the flask was hidden inside her jacket. "If it weren't for Uncle John, who knows what would've happened to me. You certainly didn't give a shit if I made it out of the hell I was living in."

Lukas had been away at school when our father died, so he had somewhere to go back to after the funeral. I, on the other hand, was in my sophomore year of high school. I had nowhere to escape to. Trapped in my childhood home.

She rolled her eyes. "You are so dramatic."

"Am I? Or did you forget the time you left me alone for a week after Dad died because you were on a bender? Or how about the time I came home from prom with my friends to find you passed out on the front lawn with cigarette burns all over your chest and reeking of cheap vodka?"

"So I'm not allowed to grieve?"

I pinched the bridge of my nose. "Of course you're allowed to grieve, but that doesn't mean you're allowed to stop caring for your children. It doesn't mean that you are allowed to stop being a mother. A fucking responsible adult. It would've been better if you'd given me up entirely, rather than leave me to call John when you didn't show up at dinnertime."

My chest was heaving as I tried to hold back the tears threatening to spill. I was vaguely aware of the silence surrounding us. There was no laughter, no joy, no merriment from Charlie and

Harper in the yard. The music that'd been playing in the house had stopped.

I should've stopped there. I should've walked away, but I was too angry. Too tired. Too everything. No matter how many times I told myself that I wasn't the problem, that was how I felt. Why couldn't she love me? Why couldn't she get help to be better for me?

But with sudden clarity, I realized that I was never the problem. It was always her. She would rather play the victim than own up to all the years of neglect she put me through. I had to make her see that her choices had consequences, and I was done living my life wondering what she would say next to drag me down to her level.

"For years, Mother, for fucking *years* I have tried to convince myself that our relationship was mendable. That we could come back from the way things were if you cleaned up your act and apologized, but that was my mistake because now I know you were always a lost cause." This time, I couldn't stop the tears from falling.

"The last time we talked, you said you wished you weren't my mother. Since that day, I have been piecing back the parts of me you broke. I spent years believing no one would choose me. That no one would stay. So you know what? That's fine. If you have no interest in being a mother, then I have no interest in being a daughter." She opened her mouth to argue, but I cut her off. "I hope you've gotten a good look, because this is the last time you'll ever see me. The last time you'll ever talk to me. Don't write. Don't call. Don't even send a fucking text message."

"Livvy?"

I looked up and saw my brother and Duke standing in the open door with Charlie and Harper between them. My daughter's eyes were red-rimmed from crying. She clung to Duke as though she was scared. Of me, of my mother, I had no idea.

Guilt gnawed at my insides, making my stomach churn from fear I'd gone too far.

"Excuse me," I whispered. My voice broke as a sob wrenched itself free. I stumbled down the porch and ran into the gray evening light, unsure of where I was headed. One thing was sure. I couldn't stay here. Not anymore.

Behind me, someone called my name. There were raised voices followed by the slamming of the screen door. And then footsteps fell in sync with my own. I knew it was Duke without looking. Lukas would have tried to talk to me. He would've wanted me to recount every detail and play devil's advocate.

I loved my brother dearly, but I couldn't be around him right now.

For all his greatness, he never fully understood my crumbling relationship with our mother. Part of me was grateful for that. No kid should ever have to feel like a burden to their parent.

But that often left me feeling as though I really was the problem. That I was being too hard on her or overreacting about how she made me feel. I couldn't handle feeling like that right now. Not after whatever that fucking disaster was.

I wasn't sure where we were headed, but Duke walked beside me. For the first time in my life, the silence didn't feel suffocating. I didn't feel the need to talk just to pass the time or to apologize for any discomfort the other person might have felt. He didn't try to touch me or offer me comfort.

He just let me be.

Eventually, my vision blurred too much to go on, and our pace slowed. My chest screamed at me to stop, to let my body rest. Strong arms wrapped around my middle as my knees gave out, helping me to the ground. It was so similar to the day we found out John had passed that it brought a whole new wave of grief I couldn't stop. And again, it was Duke who caught me when I fell.

"I've got you, honey," Duke whispered, pressing a kiss to my temple. "Let it out. You're safe with me."

I knew that more than I knew anything, especially in this moment. My heart, my body, my soul—everything I was would be safe with this wonderful man. He held me through every sob, through every scream. He held me until the sun dipped behind the pines and coyotes howled at the moon. He held me until my mind quieted and I took my first breath in what felt like days, all the while whispering that I was safe.

"You didn't have to follow me," I whispered. My voice was hoarse from exertion.

"I know, but you would've made too tempting a meal to whatever's lurking in the darkness," he said, lips curling into a smile against my temple.

"I think the screaming would've scared them off."

Duke let out a huff. "You're probably right." We sat there in silence for a moment before he whispered, "Do you want to talk about it?"

What could I say that hadn't been said before? Duke knew the struggles I encountered with my mother. Sometimes I called Lukas in tears in the months following Dad's death, freaking out because our mom hadn't been home in days. I kept waiting for the sheriff's department to show up at our door and tell me she'd wrapped her car around a telephone pole after a night of binge drinking.

Honestly, it was a miracle it never happened.

But I'd never voiced my issues with my mother to anyone other than Lukas or John before. While I knew I could trust Duke, I wasn't sure where to begin.

"It's crazy how fast things can change. One moment, your

family is whole, and you're left feeling invincible, and the next..." I mimed an explosion with my hands. "Everything changes. Dad's death shook every single one of us, but I think it hit my mother and me the hardest. We were so close before it happened. Always laughing, always making plans. She supported my endeavors the way all parents should, but when he died... I don't know. I think a part of her died, too."

I leaned back into Duke's chest as his arms tightened around my middle.

"Instead of clearing that part out, she let it rot until it completely destroyed the person she was before. That's the trouble with grief. It's a tragedy for someone to lose their life, but it can be so much worse for those left behind because there is no way to heal from that. You feel that missing piece of your soul every single day."

Duke nodded, his voice solemn. "I would rather be the one leaving than the one being left."

"If it wasn't for John, I don't know how my life would've ended up. We had plenty of money. There wasn't any concern about what I would need to do to make ends meet, but having my own mother disregard me at such a young age really fucked with my head. I acted out a lot, doing whatever I could to get attention. I was always a loud personality, but as I got older, I felt the need to change myself to become someone people wanted to be around. I wanted to amplify who I was so I couldn't be ignored. When I did, everything changed. Suddenly, women wanted to be like me. Men wanted to date me. I ran with it, creating the Olivia Hart you see today. Confident. Brash. Loud. Outgoing." I paused, wiping away a tear. "Scared and lonely."

"When I became CEO of Hartstrings, I thought I'd be able to let the mask slip. After all, I'd done it. I'd finally made my dreams come true. Even my mother seemed proud. She showed up to that shiny high-rise in Nashville stone cold sober. I couldn't believe it. I thought maybe now that I'd done it, now that I'd made her proud, I could just be Olivia. But I was wrong."

Nausea churned in my gut as the words tumbled out. My mouth was moving quicker than my mind could keep up. "Everyone preferred the new and improved version of me to the person I actually was. Nobody knew me, Duke. Nobody. And that meant"—a ragged sob tore from my chest—"nobody loved me. Or, they loved me, but they didn't love *me*. Does that even make any fucking sense?"

Duke nodded, squeezing my hand, and I could see everything he wanted to say reflected in his eyes. But before he could, I kept going. "I worked my ass off. I succeeded despite those who told me I couldn't do it, even if succeeding was fucking killing me. I'd worked so hard for the life I'd dreamed of, but my dream was killing me."

It still was, and there was nothing I could do about it. What difference would it make? Nothing was going to change now that John had passed. No one understood. Not even my brother. He'd been the one to turn down the family legacy to build one of his own. I wasn't afforded that luxury.

I wasn't sure I ever would be.

"I've been living a lie for so long that I don't know who I am without it." I rested my head on Duke's shoulder, tipping my chin to the sky above, and stared at the stars. "I became CEO because my parents wanted me to. It's the last connection I have with my father, and now I have to protect John's legacy. I refuse to let someone ruin what he built."

Duke's fingertips gently trailed up and down my arm, leaving goosebumps in their wake.

"When I told my mother I was getting a divorce, she lost her shit. She told me I was throwing my life away. That I was too old to find a husband at the tender age of—what? Thirty-five?" I laughed, but it was as hollow as I felt. "I told her it was my life and I wanted to live it as I saw fit. That I refused to live a life that didn't suit me. I was done pretending to be someone I wasn't, and I wanted to resign as CEO of Hartstrings immediately. I *tried.* But she said if I stepped down, it would ruin our family. That *I* would ruin our family. How can anyone say that to someone? Let alone a mother to their daughter?"

Duke tugged me closer. If he could take away the pain, I knew he would. "I'm so sorry."

"The worst part is that it didn't even come as a surprise to me. Today was the first time I've seen or spoken to her in over two years. I thought maybe things would have changed in the time that'd passed, but clearly they haven't. I'm still the same disappointment I've always been."

Even though I knew it wasn't true, I couldn't shake the cloud of shame hanging over my head. No matter what I did, none of it was good enough for her.

I wasn't good enough for her.

"Do you want to go egg her car?"

The question caught me so off guard, I couldn't help but laugh. It was absurd. Absolutely ridiculous.

"Egg her car?"

Duke shrugged. "Lukas and I did it to the high school principal when we were seniors—"

"That was you?" I asked, turning my head to look up at him.

"And your brother. It's important to remember that."

"Are you sure you should be telling me this?"

"The statute of limitations is only seven years," he said. "I think we're safe."

"But now I know one of your secrets."

He sighed, tucking my head beneath his chin. I could hear

the rhythmic beating of his heart in his chest, the steady thump lulling me into a sense of calm. "I'd give you as many as you needed, as long as they made you feel better."

His admission felt so heavy. Somewhere, there were promises behind his words. Promises neither of us dared to speak, promises we knew we couldn't keep.

There was one thing I wanted, but was too afraid to ask for. It felt wrong on so many levels, but baring my heart and soul to a man who sat and listened without judgment gave me a quiet sort of confidence. One unlike any I'd ever had before. "Would you," I paused, clearing my throat. I could do this. I could ask for what I wanted without guilt. "I—I don't really want to be alone tonight."

"Then you won't be." Duke's answer came swiftly. Instantaneous. As if he already knew what I was going to ask before I ever got the words out.

"You don't have to," I quickly added. "I—"

Duke pulled me around to face him. I straddled his waist, letting my hands fall between us as his palms cupped my cheeks. "I told you I've got you, honey, and I fucking mean it. Whatever you want, whatever you need, it's yours." His thumb brushed my cheek, gently wiping away the remaining tears. "You can trust me, Olivia."

I nodded, leaning into his touch. "I know. I do."

That was the most terrifying thing of all.

Out of all the words I spoke tonight, those scared me the most. I hadn't fully trusted a man since Grady, but even that was different. We knew exactly what we were to one another, but I had no idea what I was to Duke.

No matter how hard I tried to remember he was Lukas's best friend or Harper's dad, deep down I wanted him to be something else.

Something to me.

Without another word, he pushed to his feet, lifting me in his arms. "I can walk," I protested, pushing at his chest. "It's too far—"

"Shut up, and let me do this," Duke said, pulling me closer. "Let me carry you. And all the rest too."

DUKE

OLIVIA REMAINED silent as we headed back to the house. With her head on my shoulder and the soft sound of her breathing, I would've thought she was fast asleep were it not for the occasional tightening of her grip on my shirt collar.

I wasn't sure what made me follow after her as she stumbled off the porch steps of Lukas's house and headed out into the middle of a field. It was like a gravitational pull I couldn't ignore.

I would never forget the way her brown eyes widened when she saw all of us standing in the doorway. The moment her gaze snagged on Charlie, she was done for. Hell, I was, too.

When the girls had come running in through the back door to find us, I knew in my gut something was wrong. They had been playing out there for the past hour, but the mood had shifted. Something had happened.

That was when we turned the music down and heard Olivia's raised voice and her mother's pathetic attempts to bait her into an apology she wasn't owed.

Growing up, I knew all I needed to know about Susan Hart.

When her husband was alive, she put on a good front at being the perfect, doting mother and wife. As we got older, I couldn't help but notice the way she'd excuse herself during dinner and come back a few minutes later, glassy-eyed with vodka on her breath.

When her husband died, her addiction had spiraled out of control. I remember when Lukas got the call about his sister being left alone. John had been out of town on business for the week, and he stopped by on his way home to find Olivia all by herself. Her mother was gone. No note. No phone call. She was barely fifteen. I'd never seen Lukas so angry in my life. The guilt ate him alive for weeks to the point he nearly dropped out of school to come home and care for his sister, but John wouldn't hear of it.

It'd taken time, but he had eventually mended the bridge with his mother. I couldn't help but wonder if it had less to do with wanting a relationship and more to do with making sure he wasn't burdened with guilt if she drank herself to death.

Though after the shit she pulled tonight, I wasn't sure how much longer that would last.

Porch lights cut through the darkness as we neared the house. Olivia lifted her head, staring warily toward the house. Lukas, Harper, and Olivia sat outside on the swing. The girls laughed as he sang incredibly off-key to some old country music song on the radio.

"I can walk now," she mumbled quietly, releasing her grip on my shirt. I nodded, letting her slip carefully down my body until her feet touched the ground. Even then, I kept my hands on her waist to keep her steady. I felt her absence, the lack of heat, and instantly wanted it back.

Unable to help myself, I intertwined our fingers and gently tugged her forward. "Come on. I'm sure there's someone who's been worried about you."

"Honestly, we should be worried about them. Luke might have ruptured an eardrum."

We walked hand in hand until we reached the bottom of the steps. Charlie leapt off the swing and ran towards her mom, nearly knocking her over in the process. Olivia placed a hand on top of her daughter's head to steady them both. "Are you okay, Mommy?"

Olivia blinked, her smile faltering as she stared down at her daughter. "Yeah, baby. I'm feeling a little better now." She glanced up at her brother. "I'm sorry you had to listen to your uncle's horrible singing."

"Hey now," Lukas said, coming to stand by the porch railing. "It wouldn't have been fair if I had a good voice. I already won the genetic lottery as it is."

Olivia rolled her eyes, the tiniest smile playing at her lips. "Whatever you say, big brother."

Lukas's gaze snagged on our hands, which were still joined. At some point we'd have to talk about my sudden infatuation with his sister, but now wasn't the time. I just hoped he could see that while I may have been just as confused as he was, my intentions were in the right place.

"Y'all want to come in?" Lukas asked, pointing behind him. "I was just about to make dinner."

Olivia tensed beside me.

"She's not here," he added, softening his tone. "I wouldn't do that to you, Livvy."

"I know," she said, glancing toward me. "But I think we'll head home. I'm sure the girls are tired."

We. *We'll* head home. All of us.

Lukas nodded, rocking back on his heels. "Let me know if you need anything."

Yeah, he would definitely have questions—sooner rather than later if his tight-lipped smile was any indication. Hell, I didn't even know what I was going to tell him. But it didn't matter because that was tomorrow's problem, and I sure as fuck wasn't going to borrow trouble by asking about it today.

"We will," I said, placing one hand on Olivia's back and waving goodbye with the other. I wondered if she knew how much that *we* meant to me and Harper. How long it had been since either of us had anyone but each other.

I led her to the truck, opened the door, and helped her into the passenger seat before doing the same with Charlie and Harper in the back. They were already deep in discussion about their sleepover plans by the time I climbed inside and headed down the short distance to the guest cottage.

The girls were out of the vehicle the moment I cut the engine, bursting through the door like a goddamn tornado. Olivia and I sat in silence for a moment, watching them go before slowly following suit.

I wasn't sure who reached for who first, but our fingers found each other's as I led her into the house. I flipped on the lights as I went, heading straight through the living room to the kitchen I was all too familiar with. The girls clambered onto the tall seats at the island.

Olivia paused, leaning forward onto the counter and resting her chin in her hand as she watched me rifle through the refrigerator and pantry until I found what I was looking for.

"What're you doing?" she asked. "If you're looking for food, you probably should have taken Lukas up on his offer. I don't have much in there."

I peered at her from around the freezer door, pulling out a pound of frozen Italian sausage. "But you have the essentials to make regular old spaghetti. That sound good?"

I could see the rebuttal forming as her stomach let out a loud rumble that had our girls breaking into a fit of giggles. She tried to hide her face in her hands, but I saw the smile there.

"Figured as much. So, here's what we're going to do. You girls," I turned to Charlie and Harper, "are going to go take showers, put on your pajamas, and pick out a movie for us to watch." They took off before I had the last words out. "Good talk!" I called after them.

Olivia watched me carefully. "You really don't have to do this. It's fine. I don't think I'll be able to eat much anyway."

I knew what she was doing. Downplaying how much pain she was in so as not to seem weak. Hell, I'd been living the same way since Sarah left Harper and me to fend for ourselves.

I rounded the corner in four large strides. She turned around, giving me the perfect opportunity to cage her in against the marble countertop. Being this close to her was intoxicating. She pulled me in without even trying.

"What did I say earlier?" I asked, bringing one finger up beneath her chin so that she was staring directly at me. "I told you to let me take care of you. Cooking dinner isn't some big thing. If I weren't doing this here with you and Charlie, I'd be doing the same damn thing for Harper and me at home. It's easy, Olivia."

"Then let me help," she said, attempting to break out of the cage I trapped her in.

"Listen to me… You're going to go into your bathroom, run yourself a nice, hot bath in that oversized monstrosity Lukas calls a bathtub, and you're going to relax. No kids. No worries. No obligations."

"But—"

"I'll let you know when dinner's ready. Then, we're all going to pile onto the couch and put on whatever agonizing movie the girls picked out while we enjoy the gourmet meal I've prepared. Got it?"

Olivia's lip twitched. "Gourmet meal, huh? Aren't you going to use sauce from a jar?"

I pushed off the counter, gently swatting her ass in the process. "Get out of here before I'm forced to do something drastic."

"Oh yeah?" she asked, quirking a brow. "Like what?"

Smiling to myself, I took my time popping the microwave open and tossing the meat inside to thaw. Then I turned over my shoulder, letting her see all the heat and sexual frustration that'd been pent up for fucking weeks. "Like strip you down and throw you in the water myself."

My gaze dipped to her delicate throat as she swallowed her rebuttal. Nothing could happen between us right now. Not with our daughters in the other room. But it was tempting. God, it was so fucking tempting to do it anyway.

"I'm not used to people telling me what to do," she admitted.

"Well? What's the verdict?" I asked.

She was silent for a minute, blowing out a long breath before saying, "I think I like it." Her gaze met mine. "When you do it."

THE ENTIRE TIME I was making dinner, I was trying—and failing miserably, might I add—not to think about Olivia's words and the fact that she was just down the hall in the bath. Naked. Wet. So goddamn perfect.

How the fuck she could drop a line like that and just walk away as though she hadn't just completely fried my brain was beyond me.

I was used to being in control in all aspects of my life. I wasn't sure what that said about me, but it'd been true since I was a kid. As I got older, I quickly realized my control didn't just extend to my day-to-day, but to every part of my life. It was the one aspect of Sarah's and my relationship that we actually seemed compatible.

Occasionally, she'd want to change it up and take charge. I tried to indulge her, but I couldn't get out of my head. It always felt wrong. Now, I wondered if it really was just a case of two people who weren't properly suited for one another, because if Olivia had ordered me to follow her into that bathtub, then I would've gone like a dog on a leash.

The girls showered and changed quickly, barrelling into the living room before I'd had a chance to boil water for the pasta, so I decided to enlist their help. Harper was used to being my helper during dinner, but Charlie seemed lost. She admitted she could bake a mean cookie, but she didn't know the first thing about cooking a meal.

As we put the finishing touches on dinner, I reminded them to pick a movie while I checked in on Olivia. They gladly agreed, running for the remote without another word.

My bare feet padded against the hardwood floor as I made my way to the master suite. The door was cracked open. I rapped my knuckles against the frame, hearing a soft, "Come in," from the other side.

I blew out a breath before pushing it open and looking around. The room was tidy, but looked inherently lived in. When he built the place, Lukas was adamant about adding minimalistic touches everywhere so it felt cozy enough to stay for a few days without making anyone feel too at home.

Olivia didn't seem to get the message.

Her clothes were all over the place, strewn haphazardly along the floor and the reading chair in the corner. The bedding had been replaced, going from a soft cream to a sage green. Small picture frames were placed on her nightstand and the dresser against the far wall. Most of them were of Charlie growing up, but the two that weren't immediately caught my eye.

The first was of Grady's wedding. Olivia was standing at his side with Cleo on the other. Charlie stood between them. All of them were wearing the biggest smiles I'd ever seen. That was what true happiness looked like.

It was the second that gave me pause. Three people posed in front of a lake. It was nearly dusk, the sky in the background a faded pink hue. I remembered when it was taken, but I'd never actually seen the picture itself.

Lukas and I were holding a newly graduated Olivia between us, preparing to toss her off the dock and into the frigid water below. All three of us had just graduated from school, so we'd decided to camp at the lake to celebrate. John rented some ridiculous house he called a cabin, even though there were something like six bedrooms to choose from.

On our final night, John begged to get one single photograph to commemorate our time together before we all went our separate ways. Olivia, the darling she was, had immediately stepped between us and smiled. Her brother and I had other ideas.

We each bent down and grabbed one of her legs, dangling her dangerously close to the water. John snapped the picture right before we tossed her in, all of us with our heads thrown back in laughter.

God, everything seemed so much simpler back then. There were no rules, minimal expectations. We had our whole lives to look forward to. While Lukas and Olivia dreamed of creating big, exciting futures for themselves, I'd wanted to take a simpler approach.

I wanted to find a good job—maybe open my own business one day. I wanted to get married, have kids, and do all the boring, mundane shit together as a family. And for a while, I'd made those dreams a reality until they all came crashing down.

My life now looked so different from what I'd imagined. It was hard not to mourn what could have been. Regret had followed me around for years, even after I married Sarah. I should have done more, dreamed bigger, loved harder.

But I didn't.

Regrets are for fools.

I could hear John's words clearly. Only a fool would waste what little time he was given lamenting on the past. But it was hard not to sometimes. Especially when I looked at my daughter and wished I could give her so much more than I was able to.

"Duke?" My head snapped toward the cracked bathroom door at the sound of Olivia's voice. "Is that you?"

"Y-Yeah," I stammered, clearing my head. "It's me. I wanted to let you know dinner's ready."

"Perfect timing." I heard the sound of the stopper popping free and water draining. "I'll be out in five."

"Sounds good," I called, taking a step back from our photo.

I turned to head back into the living room, but stopped short as I realized there was a perfect line of sight into the bathroom from where I was standing. The lighting was dim. I could see the flicker of candlelight along the wall, interrupted only by a shadow. The silhouette of a woman rising from the bath.

I should stop.

I should look away.

I should leave.

But I couldn't. Not when Olivia stepped into view, giving me a perfect view of her exposed back. Rivulets of water ran down her curves, settling into the dimples just above her ass.

She moved the towel gently along her body, starting at her neck and working her way down. Her hand came up, kneading the tense muscles along her shoulders. My gaze traveled down the length of her. I was entranced, wishing I could step through the door and take care of her myself, but knowing it would cross too many lines if I did. Lines I wasn't sure either of us should be thinking about crossing in the first place.

As my gaze traveled back up her body, I realized she was looking at me over her shoulder with those warm brown eyes I'd spent my nights fantasizing about. My mind screamed at me to move, but I couldn't. I was trapped here, too lost in the moment to feel an ounce of shame.

Our gazes remained locked as she turned to face me and dropped the towel to the floor. God help me, I couldn't help myself. My eyes dipped to the blush of her cheeks, to her neck, to her exposed collarbones and the freckles dusted against the skin at the hollow of her throat. Then lower to her perfect breasts that would fit in the palm of my hand, and her rosy nipples ripe for plucking. Bluish-purple stretch marks lined her stomach, a reminder that her body had once carried life.

I wanted to drop to my knees, to kiss each one and remind her of how strong she was. I wanted to give her the chance to let go of control for once. To create a space where I could carry all her fears and worries, even if only for a night.

Behind me came soft footsteps on the hardwood floor, followed by Harper's voice. "Dad, Miss Olivia, we're hungry!"

The moment was broken, and I quickly stepped out of the room, giving Olivia her privacy. My daughter greeted me on the other side, staring up at me in question. "Why is your face so red Dad? Are you coming? We're starving"

Clearing my throat, I forced a smile and prayed to whatever fucking god may exist that she didn't notice the current problem I was having. "Yeah, sugar. I'm coming. Did you pick out a movie?"

Harper nodded. "Yup. And we got the blankets and pillows out to make a nest."

"A nest?" I asked. "You mean a fort?"

"No, Dad. A nest! Come see." Harper grabbed my hand and dragged me into the living room. Charlie popped up from the other side of the couch, arms splayed above her head in proud display. "See?"

I was, indeed, looking at a sort of nest. The entire couch was layered with blankets in different colors and pillows in different shapes. I was pretty sure they raided the whole damn house, save for Olivia's room, for materials to make this.

I had to admit, it looked comfortable.

"We wanted to make a fort, but the TV was too high, so we settled on this instead. I thought my mom would like it best. She always curls up with a soft blanket, even if it's warm outside," Charlie said. She peered behind me. "Where is she? I'm so hungry." She dragged the word out dramatically and I couldn't help but smile.

"Right here, sunshine." I turned to see Olivia striding into the room, fully clothed, much to my disappointment. She was wearing a pale green matching pajama set, and her hair was clipped up, leaving her neck on display.

I wasn't sure why that particular part of her drew my attention so much, but there was something so soft and delicate and feminine that captivated me.

Harper walked into the kitchen, holding something up. "We already got our plates—"

"Paper, for less clean-up," Charlie interrupted.

"—and there are two more right there," Harper said, nodding to the edge of the counter.

Olivia stopped beside me. I could feel the heat coming off her skin, fresh from the bath. It made my hand itch to touch her. "This looks amazing, guys. Sorry to keep you waiting."

Charlie shrugged. "Mr. Bennett kept us waiting, too. He went to get you, and then Harper had to go get him."

I glanced at Olivia, who was suppressing a smile. "Is that right?"

Harper nodded. "Yeah, I'm not sure he was feeling good after he left your room cause his face was like, really red and sweaty."

Fuck me. Kids were too observant for their own good.

Olivia hid a snort behind her hand. "We'd better feed him then." She met my gaze. "I'm sure he's starving."

We stayed like that, locked in a silent battle of wills while our daughters grabbed their food and ran to the couch. Olivia was the first to break, walking around me to get a plate of her own, and I stopped her, wrapping my hand around her wrist to pull her back.

"Go sit down," I said, nodding toward the couch. "I'll bring you a plate."

"You don't know how much I want."

"Well, you can eat what I bring you. If you need more, I'll get you more. But right now, you need to go sit your ass down. I'm not done taking care of you yet."

Her lips parted, but she didn't argue. Instead, she did exactly as she was told and found a spot on the other side of her daughter while I made quick work of the plates, piling a decent amount of spaghetti on both. If she didn't eat it all, that was fine with me. At least I'd know she'd eaten something today.

Coming back to the couch, I went to sit on the other side of Harper, but she quickly put one of Charlie's stuffed animals there. "Sugar, can you move this so I can sit down?"

"Sorry, Dad. That's," she looked over at Charlie and whispered, "what's her name again?"

"Miss Sprinkles," Charlie said with a mouthful of spaghetti.

"Right. That's Miss Sprinkles' spot. You'll have to sit over there." She pointed to the other side of Olivia, who narrowed her eyes at her daughter but didn't say anything, opting to clear the spot for me to sit next to her instead.

Careful not to trip and fall on the fifteen blankets piled everywhere, I carefully navigated my way around the coffee table to my designated seat and handed Olivia her plate. She took it with a polite nod.

For some reason, I suddenly felt nervous about her trying my food. It wasn't like this was anything complicated. It was literally the easiest form of pasta I could make. But I still wanted her to like it.

I watched as she brought the fork up to her mouth. She closed her mouth around the tines, humming softly.

"Well, what do you think?" I asked.

"Honestly?"

"That's why I asked. Don't worry, you can't hurt my feelings any more than this one can." I nodded toward Harper. "When she doesn't like something, she isn't afraid to say it."

Harper shrugged. "It's true."

"I'd have to say this is the best basic ass spaghetti I've ever eaten," she said, chuckling.

"Really?"

"Oh, I don't lie about food. Harper and I have that in common." She reached over and gave my daughter a high-five.

I glanced between the two of them. "This feels dangerous."

"Come on, Dad. We make a great team."

"Yeah! Girl power," Charlie chimed in. "You're outnumbered three to one."

I liked the sound of that. For the first time in years, it felt like having a family again. Which was alarming considering we weren't anything close to that. We were playing house at best, being reckless at worst.

With each passing day, it was getting more and more difficult to remember that Olivia's time here would come to a close. I'd have to settle for the occasional check-in when she stopped by to see Charlie, and that was even if she wanted to. She'd probably rather spend time alone with her daughter than with me.

"What movie did you girls pick out?" Olivia asked, helping herself to another bite of food.

"Um, I think it's called The Parent Trap? I don't know. It's, like, really old."

Olivia placed her hand over her heart. "Jeez, kid. Way to hit me where it hurts. I remember when this movie came out."

"That tracks," Charlie muttered. A pillow flew over, smacking her gently on the head.

Thank god she'd put her plate down already. Lukas would have had a fucking fit if he'd found red stains on his cream colored couch.

"Hey! What was that for?"

"For calling me old, you brat. Your poor mom can't take any more heartbreak right now," Olivia said.

It was meant as a joke, but the sobering look on Charlie's face tugged right at my heart. She leaned over, resting her head on Olivia's shoulder, and draped her arm around her stomach. "Sorry, Mom."

"Oh, Charlie..." Olivia wrapped her up in a hug. "I'm sorry, sunshine. I didn't mean to make you sad. This right here? With you guys? This is the best I've felt in days."

Charlie nodded, but didn't let go of her mother. I grabbed the remote and pressed play, settling in beside them. The longer it went on, the closer everyone drifted to one another.

Charlie and Harper passed out first, their snores nearly drowning out the TV's low volume. Olivia followed quickly after. Her body melted against my own. I tried to keep her upright, but it never lasted long. Eventually, I gave in, wrapping my arm around her shoulder and tucking her into my side.

We stayed like that until the credits rolled, and my own eyes drifted shut.

OLIVIA

THE SOUND of a shrill ringing pulled me from the deepest sleep I'd had in weeks. I looked around, blinking to clear my vision. The living room was still bathed in darkness, telling me it was early morning.

I felt so warm, so safe, lying here, sandwiched between three bodies. Duke wrapped me under his arm, pulling me as close to his body as was appropriate, while Charlie and Harper occupied my other side. We were a tangled mess in all the blankets the girls had piled around us. Even though I was sweating through my pajamas, I was content.

When the noise started up again, I carefully extricated myself from between them. I followed the sound to my bedroom, angrily swiping the device from the dresser and glaring at the screen.

It was barely six in the morning, and my assistant was already calling. My stomach dropped as I swiped to answer. "Hello?"

"I'm so sorry to call this early," she rushed out. "And I know the timing is horrible given what happened yesterday, but—"

I rubbed at my temples, already feeling a headache begin to bloom. "It's fine. What's wrong?"

Darcy hesitated. "The board is going to call a meeting. Today, if the buzz around the office is to be believed."

"Today?" I echoed. "Are you fucking kidding me?"

"I tried to put them off. I told them the funeral was only yesterday and you needed more time—"

"They already knew that," I muttered. "Most of them were in attendance." Christ. Couldn't they give me one fucking day before dragging me back into work? "Do you know what it's about?"

"Mr. Montgomery called a few of the members yesterday after the funeral. Apparently, he wasn't happy with the conversation the two of you had."

"Fuck me," I muttered. "What is he asking for? My removal?" I laughed because it was such an incredibly vile and petty thing to ask, but I knew if anyone was capable of it, it was him.

Despite how enjoyable it had been to watch Duke hand him his ass on a platter, I knew it would come with consequences. I didn't, however, think they would come so soon. Leave it to this prick to waste no time in stirring the pot.

"I don't know exactly," Darcy said. "Anything is possible with him. He's used to getting what he wants, and what he wants—"

"He's not going to have," I finished. "He's been trying to take a bite out of my family's hard work for years now. John warned me about this. He knew he'd come sniffing around."

"You're the executor of his will, aren't you? So you have control of his assets?"

I teetered my head side-to-side. "Yes and no. I'm in charge of ensuring his final wishes are carried out, and his estate is taken care of, but that doesn't mean I've taken control of everything." While I'd taken on the role of CEO, John had remained the majority shareholder when we took the company public. Despite my position, he remained in control of Hart-strings.

I didn't know how his shares would be split or who was getting what. Lukas and I had a meeting with the lawyers in three weeks to discuss his wishes. For whatever reason, John had been explicit in his instructions that nothing was to happen until that time had passed.

"What do you want to do?"

I had absolutely no idea. "My hands are tied. Even if the board calls a meeting, no decisions can be made until John's will is finalized and we know how his shares will be split. As the majority holder, his vote is needed to make any decisions," I said, chewing on my thumbnail. "Try to hold them off. Tell them the family is in no position to meet at this time."

Darcy hesitated. "And if they push it?"

"Then conference me in, and I'll set them straight. I'm not entertaining this bullshit today."

I could hear the smile in Darcy's voice as she said, "Yes, ma'am. I'll take care of it."

When the line went dead, I threw the phone on my bed and ran my hands over my face. I knew those vultures were bound to come calling sooner rather than later, but to try to call a meeting the day after John's funeral was diabolical. What was their goal? To hope I was so exhausted and overcome with grief that I did whatever they asked? Or maybe they were simply searching for any sign that John's stocks would be going up for sale.

There was a point when Hartstrings wasn't simply about profit. It was about family, connections, and helping artists build something they were proud of. My uncle knew growth could take away from that, but he tried to be intentional about who and what would lead the company into the future.

When he decided to step down as CEO and take the

company public, he'd already laid the path for me to follow. But those around him weren't happy with the change. Whether it was my age or my sex, nearly every person on the board had argued against my appointment.

It hadn't mattered that Hartstrings bore my name, nor the fact that I had been training for this position since I was eighteen years old. They saw a woman who was strong-willed enough to block whatever bullshit they tried to push if I believed it didn't align with our company's core values.

"You okay?"

I looked up, noticing Duke leaning in the doorway. He looked like he'd just woken up, his hair mussed, shirt askew, and pants hanging low on his hips. I very intentionally refused to look at the impressive bulge making itself known.

"Yeah, just—" I waved my hand toward my phone "—work shit."

A line formed between his brows. "It hasn't even been a day."

I laughed, but it was dry. "Considerate of them, huh? No matter how long I've been in the business, the callousness of others will never cease to amaze me."

"Tell them to fuck off. You're grieving."

"It doesn't work like that. Even if it did, well, I doubt that would go over well. It's fine, though. My assistant is fantastic. She'll take care of it the best she can and buy me a few weeks to take care of things here before I have to go back."

Even if I didn't want to go back.

Duke pushed off the ledge and walked toward my bed. He paused, taking the seat next to me. We didn't talk at first, letting my words settle over us like a weighted blanket. Only, instead of comfort, it felt suffocating.

"What if you didn't?" he asked quietly.

I turned my head towards him, noticing the way he kept his gaze trained on his hands in his lap. "What if I didn't what?"

"Leave. What if you didn't leave?"

I wanted that. God, I wanted that more than anything else in the world. And not just because I'd found myself drawn to the man sitting next to me, but because being home was the happiest I'd felt in years. Seeing Charlie every day and going to Harper's soccer games felt so normal, and so right. Having my brother on hand for any emergency that might come up was comforting.

And Duke? Duke made me feel alive. He made me feel like a woman—one with needs and desires and dreams. He made me feel seen—not just the face I showed the world, but *me.* A woman who could do anything, be anything, she wanted.

Even if what I wanted was to live an inherently average life without paparazzi following me around and men in suits looking down on me every time I walked into a room.

I shook my head. "I can't stay. The company needs me."

"And what about the people here?" he asked, staring straight at the wall. His jaw set in a hard line. "Don't they need you too?"

"And who would that be?"

"I can think of two perfectly good reasons in that room in there, and one right here." He turned his head, letting me see the way his bright green eyes burned with fire. "Including Lukas, Grady, and Cleo."

Duke's words made me want to cry. Why couldn't he see that my hands were tied here? I couldn't throw away my life—my family's legacy—for someone I wasn't even sure I had a future with.

This conversation was too much, too deep. I wasn't prepared to be poked and prodded before I'd even had a cup of coffee in my system.

"Duke—"

He put his hands up in surrender. "It's just something to think about, honey. I just want you to know you have options."

I could walk away from the company with little effort, settle down here, and live out the rest of my days in comfort. But why couldn't anyone ever try to understand the way my guilt gnawed at my conscience, telling me that the option didn't exist? Or that if I did walk away, it would be met with smug judgments and "I told you so" whispers.

I didn't want to be a failure. I didn't want to let anyone down, other than myself. At least then, I had no one to blame but the woman staring back at me in the mirror every day.

"I don't suppose you're going to get some more sleep, are you?" he asked, and I shook my head. "Figured as much. Why don't I make us some coffee? We can sit on the back porch and watch the sunrise."

Duke pushed to his feet, turning to hold his hand out for me to take. My gaze dipped to his open, waiting palm. "You don't have to do any of this, you know. Last night was amazing, and I'm so appreciative of it, but—"

"I'm not just doing this for you, Olivia. I'm doing it for me. I like taking care of people I care about, and it's been a long time since I've had anyone save for Harper." He moved, cupping my jaw and letting his thumb trace my bottom lip. "Let me take care of you a little while longer. Let me pretend there isn't an expiration date on whatever the fuck this is." His gaze dipped to my mouth. "I don't make a habit of begging, but I will if that's what it takes."

The thought of him begging—regardless of what it was for— had me squeezing my thighs together to stop the ache blooming between them. And then I remembered last night. How he'd been so enraptured by me, by my body, that he couldn't move. Having that kind of power over someone was a heady notion. One I didn't take lightly.

But it left me wanting more. Craving more.

"It would be reckless to pretend," I whispered. "We'd both end up hurt."

His tongue darted out, wetting his lips. They gleamed in the low light of dawn peeking through the windows. "I can't possibly be any worse off than I was when you showed up."

I leaned into his touch without thinking. "But I don't want to hurt you, Duke."

Duke paused, searching my face before he said, "I think it's too late for that." And then, slowly, he bent his head toward mine. Our lips brushed, sending electric currents through my body. Never had a kiss felt like this before. It was devastating.

Before I could think better of it, I closed the distance, sealing our mouths together in a tender kiss. I felt the urgency, the need to claim and be claimed, but neither of us rushed things.

Was this a goodbye? A way to put our curiosity to bed once and for all? If so, it was a shit way to go. Thirty seconds ago, I hadn't known what I was missing. Now, I was acutely aware of what it was like to kiss Duke Bennett.

Even though I knew it would hurt, knew that I would spend the rest of my life replaying this moment in time, I couldn't bring myself to regret it.

Duke pulled back with a sad smile. I waited for the apology I didn't want to hear to leave his lips, but it never did. "I had to know," he murmured. "At least once."

I stared up at him, trying to calm my rapidly beating heart. "Know what?"

"What you tasted like."

I exhaled, letting out a low curse in the process. How could he stand there so calmly and say something like that to me? How could he not realize this connection was turning me upside down until I couldn't think straight?

I finally understood all those stories I read as a kid where the princess woke up from a kiss from the prince, because the simple graze of Duke's lips would have me clawing my way back from the grave.

"That's not fair," I said, crossing my arms. "You can't just kiss a girl like that and walk away."

Duke shrugged, moving backward toward the hall. "I'm not the one walking away, honey."

"You're doing it right now," I deadpanned. "Literally. As we speak."

He smirked. "No. I'm just giving you a reason to follow. What's it gonna be? Are you gonna sit there and mope, or are you going to come have coffee with me?"

"I'm mourning, not moping," I shot back.

"Christ, woman. Always with the smart ass comebacks. Are you coming or not?"

I should say no. I should tell him to leave. I should go ahead and prepare my heart for the inevitable fucking pain leaving Pinecrest would bring.

But I wasn't ready for that. Especially not on the heels of John's death. I didn't trust myself to be alone with my thoughts because I would inevitably spiral into a pit of despair from the weight of the responsibilities on my shoulders.

With a sigh, I pushed to my feet. What was a little more pain, anyway? "Is your coffee any good?"

"Come find out."

"Goddammit, this is good," I hissed, blowing along the top of the mug that read, "World's Best Uncle" with Lukas's face in the middle.

Duke raised his own in salute. "I told you it was worth it."

When he'd gone outside to pull coffee beans from his truck, I thought he'd lost his mind. I mean, who keeps something like that on hand, anyway?

"This is so good that I don't even mind being wrong." I glanced over at Duke, who was looking out into the pasture at a pair of grazing horses. "I didn't take you for much of a coffee snob. You seem more like a Folgers guy."

He chuckled. "I used to be. I blame this on your brother. He started carrying the good shit with him to every job site because he was tired of drinking watered-down nonsense his guys drank."

"Sounds like Luke," I snorted. "I swear to god, he's more high maintenance than I am."

"He really is," Duke laughed. "Always has been."

"Y'all talking shit?" my brother asked, strolling through the French doors to the patio. He came over to me, kissing the top of my head, before tossing a large white box onto the table in front of us.

"Complimenting your fancy coffee, actually." I held up my mug. "Duke let me in on your secret addiction."

Lukas plopped down in the chair across from us, shrugging. "I like what I like. I don't see what's wrong with that."

"If what you like is this good, then there's no problem at all." I took a long sip, closing my eyes to savor the hint of pecans from the freshly ground beans. "You may need to share your supplier, though."

"What? There's no fancy pants coffee in Nashville or LA?"

"None that I can drink black like this."

Lukas leaned forward in his chair, glancing between Duke and me. "Wait... You're drinking it *black*?" We looked at one another and nodded. "What kind of monsters are you? You can't drink it like that. What about the milk? The cream? Half-and-half? Sugar, at the very least?"

Duke got closer and loudly whispered, "There's that high-maintenance thing we were talking about."

"Total diva," I agreed. "I'm not sure how he survives out here in the wilderness."

"If you don't quit your shit, I'm going to wake the girls so they can eat all the donuts I just brought before you can even apologize."

Narrowing my gaze, I asked, "What kind of donuts?"

Lukas reached forward and opened the lid, showing a variety of two dozen donuts. "Yes, dear sister. I got those horrible cake ones you love so much. Don't worry."

Before he could snap the lid closed, I reached forward and snagged the glazed blueberry and took a large bite. "You're still high-maintenance."

"Honestly, I get no respect."

"Not with as much fru-fru shit as you put in your coffee," Duke said, following my lead and grabbing a chocolate with sprinkles.

My brother threw up his hands in surrender. "I don't have to take this abuse. My nieces would praise me as the hero I am."

The fact that he referred to Charlie *and* Harper as his nieces warmed my heart. Duke belonged here with or without me. Blood didn't define family. It was the ones who showed up when you needed them that did.

While that should have comforted me, it didn't. Knowing that I was going to walk away from everyone here while their lives went on without me was depressing. What if Duke met someone? Dated? Got married? I'd have to watch as he moved on with someone new, knowing all I would've had to do was stay.

If I stayed, he could be mine. Harper, too.

Oh my god. What was I thinking? It wasn't like Duke and I were a *thing*. We flirted. Occasionally. Sometimes he held me tightly to his chest while I cried, sometimes he carried me when my legs gave out from grief, sometimes he listened to my deepest secrets, but that was it. Totally normal. *Totally.* Except for the kiss—and the accidental voyeurism—things were totally innocent between the two of us.

Could things be innocent if you saw someone naked? I wasn't an expert on these things.

"So, what are y'all up to today?" Lukas asked, glancing between the two of us. "Any big plans?"

"I've got nothing on the books," I said, taking a sip. "I might curl up and read a book or something. Just hang out here at the house."

"Sawyer and Ryan are covering the bar today, so I'm free. Is there a reason you're asking?"

Lukas shrugged. "I don't know about y'all, but I don't really want to sit in a house all by my lonesome, and I don't want to busy myself with work." He sighed dramatically. "What's a man to do?"

I rolled my eyes. "And people say I'm the dramatic sibling."

"You are," my brother and Duke said at the same time.

"My point, dear sister, is that it's a beautiful day outside. What if we opened the doors, pulled out some board games, and just chilled together? Later, Duke and I can fire up the grill or something."

I glanced over my shoulder to where the girls were still passed out on the couch, sleeping soundly. Lukas had a point. It'd be nice to spend the day surrounded by the people we loved the most.

Even if I was going to ignore why I was putting Duke in that category.

"Fuck it. I'm in," Duke said, slapping his thighs.

Lukas turned to me. "What about you, sis? Up for some friendly competition?"

"It's never friendly with you because you're a sore loser, but sure. Why not? It'll be fun to kick your ass."

"One," Lukas said, holding up his pointer finger. "I'm so glad you said yes. Two," this time he flipped me off, "You're not going to kick my ass."

Before I could ask him why he was glad we said yes, he stood and walked around to the backyard fence. "She said yes! Come in!"

"What in the—"

Lukas went inside, winking as he walked by when the front door opened. I turned in time to see Cleo and Grady stroll through the door, carrying bags of groceries and a tote filled with different board games. They both waved at Duke and me before heading straight to Charlie, who was still asleep.

I watched as Grady placed his hand on our daughter's back and gently shook her awake. She blinked, clearly disoriented, before surging up and wrapping her arms around his neck. Watching the two of them never got old because they loved each other so damn much.

She definitely had him wrapped around her finger, though.

I hadn't realized I was tearing up until Duke reached over and thumbed away the fallen tear. "Oh god," I laughed. "Sorry. I can be a big softie sometimes."

"Naw, I get it," he said. "I'd probably do the same if I were in your shoes."

"I'm sorry Harper doesn't have that," I whispered, looking back at Charlie and Grady. "I'm sorry you don't either."

Duke was silent for a moment, studying the scene just like I was. "I don't mind it so much for my sake. I've made peace with what happened. But Harper doesn't quite understand why Sarah walked away and never looked back." He shook his head. "I don't believe in things like fate, but I do believe it'd have been worse in the long run if she'd stayed just for the sake of staying."

"You're probably right. Doesn't make things easier, though."

"No, it doesn't," he agreed.

Lukas came walking out, hands spread wide. "Y'all just gonna sit there like two old biddies, or are you gonna come hang out?"

"Oh, you mean kick your ass?" I asked.

"You couldn't if you tried. Duke, back me up here."

"Naw, man. You don't have a horse in the race." He stood to his feet, holding out a hand to help me up, which I graciously took while Lukas's face turned beet red.

"You traitor! You're supposed to be on my side."

Duke started walking inside, turning over his shoulder to say, "My money's on Olivia every time."

DUKE

LUKAS HAD BEEN in a stare-off with his niece for the past five minutes. He narrowed his eyes, glancing between his cards and the stack of chips she had piled in front of her.

He slammed his cards down on the table, displaying a flush. "I fold."

Charlie's lips curved upward in a knowing smirk, laying down her hand for all to see. She had nothing. Absolutely nothing, and yet she'd played her uncle for a fool.

Again.

"Who the hell taught you to play Texas Hold 'em?" Lukas asked, sitting back in his chair. The man had always been a sore loser, no matter what he was doing—cards, sports, you name it.

Charlie reached forward, adding the winnings to her already impressive pile. "Uncle Bishop. He told me it was a valuable skill for me to have, and to make sure I can take all the boys for their money when I get older," she said very matter of factly, dipping her chin.

Cleo and Olivia reached across the table to give her high

fives. "Lennox would be so proud," Cleo said, and Olivia nodded.

At the mention of her aunt, Charlie perked up. "Can we call her and tell her I took all of Uncle Lukas's money?"

"I'm sure she'd love to hear from you, sunshine," Cleo said. "Let's go in the kitchen to give the boys room to pout." Charlie and Harper followed them into the kitchen, where Olivia topped off her wine glass while Cleo called her sister.

"We're not pouting!" Lukas called after them. He crossed his arms, grumbling, "She didn't take *all* my money. And it's not like it's real money anyway."

Grady and I stared at one another. "Yeah, okay."

"Walk away while your pride is still intact, man. Cause she'll take you for all you're worth." Grady grimaced. "Ask me how I know."

"Oh, you're shit at cards," Lukas mumbled. "Always have been."

"That's because you're the one who taught me," Grady shot back. "Not my fault, my teacher was shit."

"Fuck you," Lukas said, pounding his fist on the dining room table.

I brought my beer up to my lips. "If the boot fits... You gotta wear it."

"Whatever this is," he said, pointing between Grady and me, "needs to fucking stop."

Grady leaned back in his seat, bracing his hands behind his head. "Don't be mad because you suck. Be thankful for the precious memories we made tonight."

I nudged Grady's arm. "I, for one, will always think back on the time you got your ass handed to you by a nine-year-old with a smile."

"Fuck you both," Lukas muttered. "I'm glad Olivia divorced

you." Then he slid his gaze to me. "I pray to god she doesn't end up with you next."

Unease settled in the pit of my stomach as I took a sip of beer. I knew Lukas would want to talk about how affectionate I'd been with Olivia over the past few days, but I sure as fuck didn't want him doing it in front of her ex-husband.

To call me out, not only while Olivia was in the same room but also while Grady was now staring at me, was uncomfortable as fuck.

"I'm gonna grab another beer. You want one?" I tried to stand, but Lukas grabbed my elbow and tugged me back down.

"Oh, no you don't," he said, narrowing his gaze. "Don't think I haven't noticed the way you and her have been canoodling lately."

"Jesus Christ. What are you? Eighty? Who the fuck says *canoodling?*"

"And now you're deflecting," Lukas said. "Wonder why that is?"

I levelled him with a stare. "I'm not deflecting. It's a weird fucking word choice."

Grady placed his elbows on the table. "What exactly are your intentions with my ex-wife?"

"Yeah," Lukas said, matching Grady's posture. "What are your intentions with my sister?"

"I don't have any. We live entirely different lives," I mumbled, picking at the label along the bottle.

Our conversation this morning had been running through my mind all day. How she'd looked so pained at the thought of kissing me, of saying goodbye. There was no way we weren't going to end up hurting one another. Especially when she was still dead set on leaving.

But my restraint was hanging on by a goddamn thread, and I'd needed to kiss her at least once for my own sake. There was no way I could let her walk away without confirming what I already knew: I was well and truly fucked when it came to Olivia Hart.

The kiss was selfish on my part, but part of me hoped it would have been enough for her to at least consider staying. To figure out if this connection was worth exploring. But when I pulled away, I knew the decision had already been made. No amount of kisses or sweet words would be enough.

So, I decided that was it. I had to stop pining for Olivia and be the friend she needed.

Or so I hoped.

I glanced up, noticing Olivia's eyes locked on me. The smile she'd been wearing earlier had slipped ever so slightly. Now, she looked deep in thought.

I couldn't help but wonder if she was as torn up as I was about her decision. Likely not, since it remained absolute, but would she end up regretting that? Would she think of me every night before she went to bed, like I already did? Or would this flirtation simply be a fleeting memory? An anecdote we kept to ourselves?

Lukas tapped my arm, bringing me back to the unfortunate conversation at hand. "Stop ogling my sister right in front of me. It's fucking weird."

I turned toward my friend. "No, what's weird is your vocabulary. Maybe I'll get you a thesaurus for Christmas."

"Look, I'm just trying to prepare myself for the inevitable conversation we'll have where you tell me you're sleeping with her."

"Well, you can prepare yourself all you like, but that conversation's never going to happen."

"Don't think I didn't see the carrying or the hand holding yesterday," Lukas said.

I rolled my eyes. "Forgive me for offering comfort to a friend."

"And you slept here," Grady pitched in, trying not to smile.

"Olivia said she didn't want to be alone," I muttered. "And the girls wanted to have a sleepover."

"And where, pray tell, did you rest your head?" Lukas asked, finishing his beer. "Was it on the couch, or next to Olivia?"

"Both, smartass. We all fell asleep watching a movie. I trust you noticed the fucking nest the girls built in your living room?" Lukas didn't say anything, just continued staring daggers at me. "Look, I don't know how else to tell you that nothing happened between your sister and me last night." *Because we kissed this morning. And I would have kept kissing her if I had the chance.* "There's nothing between us."

Lie, lie, lie. It was all I seemed to be doing. And not just to my best friend, but me. Trying to convince myself I wasn't falling for Olivia was futile. It was happening whether I wanted it to or not.

And I did want it. I wanted her so badly I could hardly breathe. She'd completely taken over my life until I was just as concerned about her and Charlie's wellbeing as I was mine and my daughter's.

Both men were silent for a moment before Grady spoke up. "Do you want there to be?" He raised his hands as I turned to him, ready to attempt to convince him—and myself—that I only viewed Olivia as a friend. "For what it's worth, I kinda hope you do. Liv deserves someone great. You kinda seem to fit the bill. And Charlie already knows and adores you, so it's not like I have to worry about what you're like with our daughter." He shrugged. "That's all I'm saying."

Having his approval felt monumental. Like some major breakthrough I didn't even know I was trying for.

I just wish it mattered.

Every person at this table knew there was nothing capable of rooting Olivia to one spot. Her sense of duty was too great for her to ignore. It was one of the things I admired most about her. At least, it had been until I realized it was what was keeping us apart.

"As much as I appreciate the pat on the back, there's nothing to report." I stood up, collecting the empty beer bottles from the table. There was no way I could keep having this same conversation. Eventually, I'd fold like a damn lawn chair and spill all my secrets. I'd tell them exactly how much Olivia meant to me and how desperate I was for her to stay. "No intentions. No secret plans. Nothing."

"Doesn't mean you don't want there to be," Lukas said, softening his tone. "And I'm just gonna go on record and say that I agree with my former brother-in-law. My sister only deserves the best, and you're the best man I know." He gestured between himself and Grady. "Present company excluded, obviously."

"What about the present company?" Olivia asked, walking over and bracing her hands on the back of her chair.

Lukas smirked, jerking his head my direction. "Oh, you know… Just telling Duke what a great guy he is, and how any woman would be lucky to have him in their corner."

Olivia looked toward me suspiciously. "That's a weird topic of conversation."

Fuck. Now she was going to think I had something to do with it, when I'd been trying to shut it down all along. The last thing I wanted was for her to think I was trying to manipulate her into staying.

"Why's it weird?" Lukas asked. "Can't a man compliment his friend? Women do that shit all the time."

"I mean, yeah, but—"

"Thank you. Point made."

Olivia turned toward Grady. "What's your excuse?"

"Duke and I are friends," he added. "I'm with your brother on this one."

I stepped away from the table. "This conversation took a weird turn. I'm grabbing more beers."

Without waiting for an answer, I headed through the French doors to the beer fridge on the patio. I reached inside, grabbing three beers before turning to head inside. Only, I was surprised to see an angry blonde waiting for me.

"Fuck," I cursed, nearly dropping the drinks. "Warn a guy next time, won't you?"

She reached out, grabbing my arm and pulling me around the corner and out of sight. "What did you say to them?" she hissed.

Oh, she was pissed alright. I could see the fire raging in her eyes, begging to be let out, and I was the fucker crazy enough to take the brunt of her wrath so long as it made her feel better.

"I didn't say anything. Your fucking brother and ex-husband kept asking what my intentions were and, despite me denying everything until I was blue in the face, they wouldn't let it go."

She blinked up at me in surprise before forcing back on a cold mask. "Well, why were they talking about how great you were? Did you ask them to change my mind or something?"

I tilted my head to the side. "If you really think I'd do that, then you don't know me as well as I hoped." As much as I wanted her to stay, I didn't want it to be because I pulled some fucking trick. I wanted it to be because *she* wanted to stay. Because *she* wanted *me*.

I tried to push past her, but she grabbed my arm. "Wait, no! I'm sorry," she said in a rush. "I don't know why I said that. Of course, I know you wouldn't do that."

I clenched my jaw tight, giving a terse nod. "Thank you."

Her hand fell away from my elbow, exposing me to the cool evening air. I hated it. Hated being reminded of her leaving.

Even if she hadn't brought it up in the first place, it still hung in the air between us like a rotting, rancid smell.

Olivia groaned, leaning up against the side of the house. "I wish you hadn't kissed me."

"Just what every man wants to hear," I scoffed, hanging my head. The kiss had been stupid, but hearing her say she wished it hadn't happened was too much. "Don't worry. It won't happen again."

I only made it two steps before her voice stopped me dead in my tracks. "It isn't because I didn't enjoy it." Slowly, I looked over my shoulder to find her staring at me with pleading, pain-filled eyes. "You should know that."

"Then why did you say it, Olivia? Why twist the knife even more?"

On trembling legs, she stepped forward. "Because that kiss made me want things I shouldn't. Things I have no business wanting." Another step. "I hate that I haven't been able to stop thinking about the way your lips felt on mine since you walked away. Not even when my entire family is just inside. And you're everywhere. I haven't been able to get a moment alone because you're here, in my house, and invading my space."

"Then I'll leave," I said. Not like it was that easy, given I'd been drinking. "I'll stay with Lukas tonight so I'm not bothering you any more than I already have."

"God, you're stupid," she grumbled, closing the distance between us. "The problem isn't me not wanting you here. The problem is that I want you too much." Her gaze flicked to my mouth. "I want you so much I can barely stand it."

Our lips were so close. All I'd need to do was lower my head a fraction to capture her mouth in a searing, brutal kiss. A kiss, I hoped, that would show her just how much I wanted her back.

I brought my hand up, cupping the base of her throat. My thumb hovered over her pulse. "Honey, I—"

"I'm getting thirsty in here!" Lukas began to yell, though he was quickly cut off by his mumbled curses. "Ow. Jesus! What was that for?"

I groaned, dropping my hand and stepping back, leaving Olivia panting in front of me. "I can't do this," I whispered. "I can't kiss you again knowing you're just gonna walk away from me." Once was my limit. It was a deal I cut with myself, which was a cataclysmic mistake because it had been too good. Felt too right.

"Duke—" she began, but I quickly shook my head.

"I'm going to leave with Lukas tonight. If Harper wants to stay with Charlie, I'm okay with it, as long as you are. I'll pick her up in the morning."

Her bottom lip trembled, the sight nearly sending me to my fucking knees. "What if I don't want you to go?"

"And what about what I want?" I asked, turning her question back on her. "What if I asked you to stay?"

"It's not the same."

"Isn't it? You want me to stay the night here, and for what? We aren't going to cross that line, and it's not going to change the fact that whenever your work calls, you'll get on that fancy private jet and answer." Forcing a smile, I said, "And that's okay. I don't understand it, but I can't change your mind. Just like you can't change mine."

The image of her horror-stricken face was burned into my mind as I slowly backed away and headed into the house.

OLIVIA

"ARE you sure you have to leave?" I whined, watching my brother pack his suitcase. "Surely your crew can handle the fiasco by themselves."

Lukas sighed. "Livvy, I already told you they can't. The flooding is extensive, and I've got to figure out what the fuck went wrong and how to get it back on track." He closed the hardshell, turning to look at me. "It's only two days. Three tops. You'll be fine here by yourself."

That was where my brother was wrong.

Since the funeral, I hadn't spent a moment alone. Most of my days were spent with Lukas, helping him with whatever menial tasks he had going on at work, while Charlie slept in my bed every night. Unfortunately for me, Duke had been true to his word and kept his distance, so there'd been no time alone together.

But now, Charlie and Harper were having a sleepover with Grady and Cleo while my brother was leaving to address some emergency at one of his job sites, leaving me to occupy my time on my own.

Pre-funeral Olivia was used to being on her own. In fact, she quite enjoyed the time to do whatever she pleased. But that felt like a lifetime ago.

Now, it was the last thing I wanted.

I didn't want to think about John's death or the repercussions awaiting me when I returned.

I didn't want to think about leaving my family behind for a career I didn't want.

Most of all, I didn't want to think about missing out on the first thing that'd made me feel alive in years.

"What if I came with you?" I asked. "I'm sure there's something I can do to help, right?"

Lukas set his suitcase down and turned to look at me. "Spill. What's going on?"

I laughed, but he didn't. "What do you mean? I'm just trying to help."

"No, you're trying to distract yourself. You do this every time you're experiencing anything resembling big feelings."

"Um, no, I don't."

"You're such a liar," Lukas said, shaking his head. "Livvy, you set yourself up in a marriage of convenience because you were so goddamn impatient to prove yourself to the board. You didn't want to have to worry about falling in love, or getting your heartbroken."

"That was a business decision," I said, crossing my arms. "And it worked out for not only me, but Grady as well."

"Do you remember what happened when you found out you were pregnant with Charlie? Because I sure as fuck do."

Honestly, I was hoping he'd forgotten about that whole fiasco because it definitely wasn't my finest moment. In a moment of absolute and blind panic, I asked Lukas to do a complete renovation on mine and Grady's house just outside of

Nashville. I paid him double his fee just so he'd drop everything to get it done, but I didn't tell him I was pregnant.

When it came time to decide how to decorate what was to become Charlie's room, I panicked, blurted out that I was four months along, and left the room. When he tried to talk to me about it, I insisted the pregnancy wasn't a big deal.

And then I cried in his arms for over an hour.

It got so bad that he had to call Grady and beg him to come home just to console me. When my crying had subsided, I moved on as if nothing had happened.

"Vaguely," I said, shifting my weight from one foot to the other.

My brother sighed, rounding the corner of his bed to stand in front of me. "Livvy, I know you're scared of being forced to confront John's death alone."

"I am not. I've already made peace with it." No, I hadn't, but I couldn't very well admit that to him while I had a point to prove. "We knew it was going to happen; it was just a matter of time."

"Knowing it was going to happen doesn't lessen the hurt," he said, bracing his hands on my shoulders. "A fact which I know drives you nuts."

I batted his hands away. "No, I just wanted to spend more time with you because I know my time here is coming to an end. That's all."

That part wasn't a lie, but it wasn't the whole truth either.

"Why don't you call Duke, then? I'm sure he could keep you company."

"Why would you think that?" The words left my mouth in a rush. "That's a bit weird, don't you think?"

"I know you think I'm an idiot, but give me some credit," Lukas deadpanned. "I have two eyes and a working brain."

"I'm not so sure on that last part," I mumbled, breaking away from his gaze.

My brother stepped back and walked toward his suitcase. "I'm not here to tell you what to do. You're a grown ass adult and can make your own decisions." He paused, waiting for me to meet his eyes. "I just hope you don't regret them one day."

AFTER SPENDING hours attempting to distract myself, I wasn't sure how I ended up here. One moment, I was pacing the length of the guest cottage, chewing my lip anxiously until it bled, and the next I found myself sitting in my car, staring at the bright red neon sign that read Frank's Bar.

Realistically, I knew exactly why I was there, and it was a bad idea.

A horrible, incredibly stupid bad idea that didn't stop me in the slightest.

Reaching up, I flipped my visor open and stared at myself in the tiny lighted mirror. I left my hair down, only curling back my bangs so they framed my face better. I told myself it was only because it was easier than perfecting my signature updo, not because a certain bartender seemed to prefer it that way. My makeup was minimal, but flawless. A little bit of concealer and mascara went a long way to hide the fact that the last few nights had been restless. If I wasn't lying awake, overanalyzing every single detail that led me to my current predicament, I was getting kicked in the shins by Charlie as she tossed and turned all night.

Good luck to her future partner.

I glanced at my purse, grabbing the iconic red lip stain I kept on hand for emergencies before I could think better of it. "It's fine," I murmured, running the applicator over my bottom lip. "You're only doing this to add a bit of color to your face."

Even the lie felt pathetic.

A group of rowdy patrons walked by my SUV, laughing as they made their way into the small bar. The parking lot of Frank's was packed, even for a Friday night. That was the beauty—and sometimes curse—of living in such a small town. There wasn't much else to do other than head to your local bar for a few drinks after work.

As the door opened, I got my first glimpse of him.

Duke was wiping down the bartop, laughing at something some brunette was saying. Her legs were on full display in a pair of shorts that barely covered her ass. Hair perfectly curled and styled.

I bet she was gorgeous.

Looking down, I only ended up criticizing my outfit choice. Despite trying and failing to convince myself I was going out for me and me alone, my clothes didn't necessarily reflect that. I opted for a short, red dress that cut off mid-thigh and a pair of tall black cowboy boots I hadn't worn in years. They made me feel sexy. Noticeable, even. But now I wanted to bang my head against the steering wheel because there was no way to make my outfit look casual.

You should turn around and head home, Olivia. Make your way back to the house before anyone sees you.

My hand hovered over the ignition, ready to turn it over when the door opened again, giving me a view of little Miss *Legs For Days* twirling her hair as she downed the shot Duke set in front of her.

Suddenly, I found myself stepping out of my car, slipping my purse over my shoulder, and marching into the bar like I had something to prove.

Here goes nothing.

Duke looked up the moment I walked through the door. His bright green gaze turned molten as he slowly let his eyes travel down the length of my body and back up. The girl was still talking, laughing shrilly and twirling her hair just to earn a scrap of his attention.

I didn't blame her. I'd been strategic in my approach for his attention just like she was. But the key difference was knowing I had a horse in this race, while she wasn't even competing.

Straightening my shoulders, I marched over to the opposite side of the bar where a young man was pouring a round of shots. It was impossible to ignore the weight of Duke's gaze, but I tried not to think about it too much as I slid onto an empty stool.

The young barback looked up, offering me a kind smile. "What can I get ya?" he asked.

"A shot of tequila, and," I took a quick survey of the beers on tap, "a Banquet, please."

The man nodded. "Want some salt and lime with that shot?"

I said, "Yes," the moment Duke walked up and said, "No."

Our eyes met, warming me better than the liquor ever could. "Hi, Duke."

"Move," Duke grunted, forcing the kid out of the way. He gave me an apologetic smile and did as requested, switching to the side where the disgruntled brunette stood, glaring in our direction.

Duke leaned forward, bracing his hands on the bartop. While the weight of his attention made me feel uncomfortable, I didn't balk, didn't shift as he finally asked, "What're you doing here, Olivia?"

I let my hands rest in front of me, hoping he didn't catch the slight tremble in them at the sound of his voice. "Can't a girl go out for a drink without a reason?"

His laugh was hollow. "Sure, but not you."

"What's that supposed to mean?"

"Don't play dumb. It's not a cute look."

"What about desperate?" I asked, tilting my head toward the other side of the bar. I felt horrible speaking about another woman like that, but his comment had me aching to dig at him the way he'd just done to me. "You seemed to like that look very much. Tell me, what color were her eyes?"

"Couldn't tell you."

I clicked my tongue. "Ah, because you were too busy looking elsewhere, perhaps?"

"Because I couldn't give a shit about her eyes or her tits or her smile," he said, leaning forward. "And I think you know that."

I wished I could forget, honestly. Maybe then I wouldn't be sitting in a bar, in a short dress, no less, in fucking March.

"Charlie is with Grady, and Lukas left on a work trip, so…" I shrugged, shifting under the weight of his gaze. "I figured I deserved a night out."

"You didn't want to be alone."

I broke away, grinding my teeth together because there was nothing to say. No rebuttal I could offer. He was right. I didn't want to be alone, so I'd come here hoping for what? To talk? To drink myself into a stupor and sleep in my car?

"You're right," I muttered, slipping off the stool. "I'm just going to—"

"You know, Grady called me this afternoon. Asked if Harper could spend the night with Charlie at his house." I turned toward him, furrowing my brow. "I said yes. Thought it would be fun for the girls. He even offered to keep them for the whole weekend. Said I needed a break."

"He said the same to me." Grady had been adamant about keeping Charlie over the weekend. Gave me some story about

Cleo wanting to try a new cookie recipe she thought our daughter would love.

"So, we're both child-free," he said slowly. "And you're here. In my bar." His gaze dipped down my body. "In that dress."

I leaned toward the bar, unable to help myself. The pull I felt toward him was unmistakable. "Looks like it."

"When you need a drink, you come to me." Duke kept his eyes on me as he reached beneath the bar and pulled out two small glasses. He grabbed the tequila, pouring a double shot in each before sliding one my way. Then, as if in synchrony, we reached for the glasses and brought them to our lips.

"To tonight," he said.

I dipped my head. "To tonight."

DUKE

THE NIGHT WAS WINDING down as patrons paid their tabs and wandered out into the chilly spring evening. The only folks left were my regulars, Ryan, and me. I watched from behind the bar, unabashedly staring as a carefree Olivia danced by the jukebox, shaking her ass to All She Wants To Do Is Dance by Don Henley. Her hair was frizzy, curling slightly from the sweat beading down her forehead and neck.

It was the hottest fucking thing I'd ever seen.

Olivia had only had a few shots to calm her nerves before moving about the room, talking to people she hadn't seen in years. She played a game or two of pool, losing each time and yet still smiling as though she was the happiest she'd ever been.

And then she decided to dance like no one else was watching, even though every single person's eyes were on her.

Ryan was clearing out the tables, shaking his head as she strutted over to him and started singing along to the words. It was slightly off-key, but she didn't care. Especially not as he joined in, his voice terrible in comparison.

My regulars watched in awe. Johnny had been so enraptured, he'd barely finished his second beer. I was no better, struggling to keep my eyes off her and take care of my customers like it was my goddamn job—which it was.

"That girl is something else," Gerald said, turning around in his seat and pulling out his wallet. "Been a long time since I've seen anything that pretty up close."

His brother, Tommy, nodded. "Sure wish the women we dated back in our prime looked like that."

Gerald scoffed. "Speak for yourself. My Bettey was the apple of my eye. She was a model, too."

"A hand model," Tommy corrected. "And Bettey was pretty, but she wasn't that."

I laughed as the men paid their tabs and kept arguing. When they got up to leave, Olivia strutted over and pressed a kiss to each of their cheeks.

"Leaving so soon?" she asked.

Tommy blushed, taking his hat off his head. "Gotta get this old fart home before he gets too cranky."

"I stay up later than you do," Gerald muttered, jabbing an elbow into Tommy's side.

"You do not!"

Olivia threw her head back and laughed, exposing the column of her throat. "It was so good to see you two," she said, linking arms with each of them. "How often are you here? I need to make sure we can grab drinks again."

"Too damn much," I called out, grabbing a glass from the dishrack and drying it. "It'd be easier to give you a day they're not here."

Tommy turned, pointing a gnarled finger in my direction. "We keep you in business, boy."

"Yeah! If it weren't for us, you'd have no one to talk to," Gerald said.

"And I'd be able to drink my fill," Johnny chimed in.

"Johnny, I know damn good and well that I'm the only sucker that'll still serve you in this town," I deadpanned.

He looked toward Olivia, cheeks heating as Gerald clapped him on the back of the head. "Ow! What was that for?"

"For being a damn fool. Go get in the truck before we decide to leave your ass here," Gerald said, tipping his hat toward Olivia and walking out the door with his brother.

Oliva turned toward me, her smile too goddamn infectious. She sauntered over, taking the stool in front of me. "What's the damage, bartender?"

"It's been taken care of," I said, shaking my head. Gerald and Tommy already paid for it, but I couldn't tell her that. "On the house."

She frowned, jutting out her bottom lip. It was painted a vibrant red similar to the dress she was wearing. "Tell me how much I owe, dammit."

"Already told you." I wiped the beer taps, bracing my hands on the bar to stare at her. "You don't owe anything."

Olivia narrowed her eyes. "Then let me help clean."

"Olivia—"

She hopped off the stool, hips swishing as she walked toward the middle of the room. "If I were a broom, where would I be?"

Ryan finished stacking the last of the chairs on top of the tables and gestured toward the storage area. "Right in there."

She smiled and thanked him, heading around the corner to grab what she was looking for. He stood there, watching her go, until I popped him on the neck with the rag I was holding. "Ow, shit." He turned to look at me, rubbing the red spot with his hand. "Point taken."

"You're done for the evening. Lock the front door on your way out."

Ryan smirked, bringing his hand up to give a mock salute. "Yes, sir."

As he made his way to the door, I added, "If you wanna keep your job, you'll keep your eyes in your fucking head, too."

"Territorial, huh?"

"She's my best friend's sister, dumbass. I'm just looking out for her."

"I'm pretty sure she's a grown woman," he said, failing to hide his laughter. "But whatever you say, boss."

"Get out before I fire your ass," I grumbled. Once I heard the door shut and the lock click into place, I breathed a sigh of relief.

Having Olivia here, so close, and being unable to touch had been killing me all night. It was still fucking killing me, because I had no idea what her plan was. The only thing I knew was that she wasn't going to be driving home.

For better or for worse, she was staying with me tonight.

As Olivia walked back into the room, she looked around, noticing Ryan's absence. "And then there were two," she said, slowly. She brought her hand up, tucking a wild curl behind her ear. "I should probably get out of your hair, too, huh?"

"And go where?" I asked, voice low. "You're not getting behind the wheel."

"I've only had a few drinks—"

"I don't give a shit. You're not leaving."

Though I knew she knew better, she still argued. "And you're not the boss of me."

"I am tonight." I wiped down the bar to give me something to do. "And I have your keys."

Olivia looked down, patting down her dress and freezing when she heard the jingle. Her head snapped up to where I was dangling her keychain in front of her. "How did you get those?"

"You left them behind when you got up to play pool. Didn't want anyone to steal them, so I put them in my pocket for safe-keeping."

"And now you're going to hold me hostage." It wasn't a question, but a statement.

I shook my head. "If you wanna call someone to come get you, you're free to leave."

We both knew she didn't have anyone to call. Lukas was out of town, and Grady was likely already asleep. If he wasn't… Well, I didn't think either of us wanted to interrupt whatever he and Cleo were getting up to.

"Then I guess I'm staying," she said. Her grip on the broom handle was so tight, I could see the white of her knuckles.

"Guess you are," I agreed.

I wasn't sure what the fuck we were doing. Being alone with her felt like tempting fate. We'd been toeing the line in the sand for weeks now. There was no way we'd make it out tonight unscathed.

But even knowing that, knowing I should drive her home and say goodnight, I couldn't find the power to do so. Selfishly, I wanted this time with her, even if I knew it'd ruin me when she left.

Olivia glanced behind her at the jukebox. "Mind if I turn on some music while we clean? It's too quiet in here."

"Go ahead. I'll be in the back finishing up. Let me know when you're done."

She nodded as I walked out of the room and into the cold storage, where I'd half-assed putting up the garnishes. We didn't use much around here. Mostly limes for tequila shots and a few beers.

The jukebox kicked on as I dated the labels and carefully put them away. Olivia's voice quickly followed, though certainly not as off-key as before. I recognized the upbeat tempo as a song from Coyote Ugly and groaned. Images of Olivia dancing on a table, the hem of her dress rising to give me a hint of what was underneath, flitted before my eyes. It was torture knowing she was just on the other side of the wall, likely moving her body to the sensual beat of the music.

I shook my head, trying and failing to clear my mind. What I needed to do was get this bar shut down, but how could I when all I wanted to do was march into that room and kiss her stupid.

Taking a quick count, I realized I'd left a single container of limes out on the bar. It was a weak excuse, but it was all I needed. I marched into the other room before I could talk myself out of it, stopping dead in my tracks when I saw her.

Olivia was still standing near the jukebox, the broom in one hand, while her other was wound up in her hair to keep it off her neck. Her body swayed to the beat, eyes closed, lost to the moment.

I leaned against the bar, unable to stop myself from watching her. Fuck. Olivia really was beautiful. From her soft chocolate eyes to her fuck-me-red lips to the short dress that rode up every time she moved, all of it was captivating. I wasn't sure if I was turned on or relieved that she seemed so free.

As if aware of my presence, she opened her eyes. There was a fire in them. The same one I'd seen the night I watched her step out of her tub and cruelly tease me by dropping her towel. Her lips curved up. "Enjoying the show?"

I nodded. No point in denying it when it was so obvious. "I am."

Olivia set the broom near the jukebox. "You know, I'm starting to think you like to watch. This is the second time in a week I've caught you looking."

"It's been a long time since a woman's caught my attention," I admitted, bringing my hand up to scratch the stubble along my jaw. "Wouldn't wanna miss anything."

Her lips parted in an O shape, and fuck me, I couldn't help but wonder what they'd look like wrapped around my cock. I wanted to ruin her makeup, spreading that bright color along my length as I slid inside. I wanted to see how far she'd take me. If she'd choke or take it all the way.

"Maybe you should take a closer look." Olivia stepped toward me, swaying her hips with the beat of the music. "I wouldn't want you to miss anything either."

I balled my hands into fists as she stopped in front of me, trying like hell to keep myself from touching her.

Once I did, it would be over. I wouldn't be able to stop.

"You know, there's one thing I've always wanted to do," she said, peering up at me.

"What's that?" I grunted.

Olivia glanced down at the noticeable tightness at the front of my jeans before flicking her gaze up. "A body shot."

"What a shame."

"It is." I held my breath as she leaned forward, damn near caging me in as she reached for the bucket of limes behind me. She grabbed one, bringing it between our bodies. "But we could change that tonight."

Goddammit. I couldn't think with her this close. Not when all I could think about now was picking her up, laying her down on the bar top, and running my tongue along her skin. Liquor be damned.

"Do you think that's a good idea?" I asked, voice tight.

I held my breath, waiting for her to step back and tell me I was right. That this wasn't a good idea, but she didn't.

"I've spent the past week doing everything I could to distract myself," she admitted slowly. "But no matter what I do, my mind keeps coming back to you. So yes, I do think it's a good idea. I think if I were going to do something like that, it should be now. Here. With you."

I wasn't sure if we were still talking about the body shots or if she was using it as a way to ask for what she really wanted.

"Are you sure you should be making a decision like that while you're intoxicated?"

Olivia laughed softly. "Duke, I haven't had a sip of alcohol in over two hours. Any lingering buzz is just enough to give me the courage to ask for what I want." She held the lime in front of her face. "So, what's it going to be?"

Slowly, I unclenched my fists and reached forward, letting my fingers dance along the hem of her dress. I waited patiently, waiting for her to tell me to stop, but she didn't. Not even when my touch grew bolder, sliding along her hips to cup her ass and pull her into me.

Olivia gasped as the outline of my erection pressed into the top of her thigh, the sound making me cock ache. It was perfect. She was fucking perfect, and I couldn't stop.

Moving my hands up, I gripped her waist, relishing the feel of her bare skin against mine. I was so close to having what I wanted, and yet I dragged it out, careful not to lose it so soon.

"Duke," she breathed, carefully running her hands up to my shoulders.

It was all the permission I needed.

We moved at the same time, me lifting her into my arms and her wrapping her legs around my waist. I turned us around, perching her ass on top of the bar. I stayed there, enjoying the heat between her legs far too much. Olivia's chest moved rapidly, the skin there a light shade of pink. It matched the flush along her cheeks.

"Pick your poison," I said, stepping back. I took my time walking around the bar, all the while feeling her gaze searing into me. There was something about her attention that made me feel powerful. Like I was worth something. She wasn't the kind of woman to trust easily, yet for some reason, she was here. Sitting on my bar like a goddamn queen.

She cleared her throat. "Tequila."

I nodded, reaching into the small fridge for my personal bottle, which I kept there for special occasions, and a shot glass. If we were going to do this, might as well make it the good shit. "I prefer my liquor chilled. Hope you don't mind." She shook her head. "Good."

I placed the bottle beside her, grabbing a salt shaker and fresh lime, before walking around and seating myself between her thighs. Her pupils were blown as I reached up, tracing the delicate hollow of her throat.

"I'm going to kiss your skin right here," I said, trailing my fingers up toward her pulse point, "so that the salt stays put. Is that okay?"

"God, yes," she breathed, nodding quickly.

"So eager," I murmured, smirking. Her legs tightened around me as I leaned forward, latching my mouth onto the very spot I'd been dreaming of for weeks. I could feel her pulse thrumming through her skin, the pace nearly matching mine perfectly.

Olivia's head fell back, giving me access, as I licked and sucked. It would've been easy to lose myself to the moment, to let my body take over and lips travel across the expanse of her body, but I kept myself contained.

I pulled back, the spot I'd left glistened beneath the neon lights. I brought the salt up and coated the area before it dried.

"A-And what about the tequila?" she stammered.

Olivia was the type of woman who commanded the attention of every room she entered. She didn't balk or trip over her words. It was sexy as hell seeing that confidence slip away, leaving behind a woman desperate for my touch.

My finger ran along her neckline towards the delicate space between her breasts. "The shot will sit right here."

I grabbed the glass and placed it exactly where I indicated. Then I reached for the bottle, unstoppering it with my teeth before slowly pouring the tequila inside. She gasped as the liquor splashed onto her skin, pouring over the lip of the glass and soaking into the fabric of her dress.

"And for the final touch," I said, bringing the lime to her mouth. She opened without instruction, keeping it perfectly poised between her lips. "Good girl. Keep it there for me, okay?"

She nodded, a small whimper escaping her throat as I leaned forward and closed my lips around the patch of salt, cleaning up the mess I'd left on her skin. It tasted better than I ever imagined, and left me feeling drunk before I'd even tasted a drop of tequila.

I met her gaze as I lowered my head to her breasts, running my nose along the fabric and inhaling her scent. Her breathing accelerated as I closed my mouth around the shot glass and pulled it from her cleavage. The liquor burned as it landed on my tongue, but I relished it, knowing I was only seconds away from tasting something far better.

Olivia grabbed the collar of my shirt and pulled me close, sealing our lips together. The tartness of the lime hit me first, quickly followed by the sensual swipe of her tongue.

Fuck me. This was a horrible idea. Probably the worst I'd ever had, but I couldn't stop myself anymore.

I wanted Olivia Hart, and I wanted her now. In this bar. In my bed. In my fucking truck. I wanted to claim her on every surface just because I could. I wanted to hear her moan my name like it was a goddamn prayer.

I pulled back, discarding the lime on the bartop before going in for another kiss. This one was more urgent. Carnal. It was like I couldn't breathe, and she was the air I desperately needed to survive.

My lips moved down, down, down along her jaw to her neck and the hollow of her throat. I nipped at the space, earning a whimper that went straight to my fucking cock. And then I moved lower still, trailing my tongue along her neckline to her breasts.

Letting my fingers move up her arms, I wrapped one around the delicate straps of her dress. "Tell me to stop," I murmured along her skin. "If this isn't what you want, tell me now."

I glanced up, waiting for her to give me a sign this wasn't what she wanted.

But she didn't. Instead, Olivia threaded her fingers through my hair and tipped her head back, a raspy "please" on her lips.

And I was done for.

OLIVIA

SEEING Duke Bennett entirely disheveled and lost to his pleasure would surely be my undoing. He stared up at me, eyes wide, pupils blown, lips wet, and yet clearly wanting more. It was the same desire I felt. The same desire I hoped he saw on my face as clearly as I saw it on his.

"You want this?" he rasped. His fingers toyed with the straps of my dress, slowly pulling it down my shoulder before moving to the next one.

"Yes," I breathed. "I want *you*."

If he took nothing away from this evening, I hoped it was that. While I missed physical intimacy, I craved him more than I craved the act of having sex. Orgasms were easy, but letting myself be vulnerable with someone else was not.

Duke moved quickly, capturing my mouth in a hungry kiss. His fingers gripped my thighs, pulling them up against his waist. I could feel his erection through his jeans, pressing into me. Driving me absolutely crazy.

When was the last time I'd felt like this?

Had I *ever* felt like this?

I spent so much of my life worrying about everyone else, doing the supposed right thing, that I took little stock in the pleasures I chased. Whether that was physical or just laughter for the sake of laughter.

For the first time in my life, I thought it might be possible to have it all.

Duke's fingers tiptoed up to my ass and dug into my skin. I threw my head back as he helped me shamelessly grind my pussy against the rough fabric. The sensation of his mouth nipping at my throat and the rough stubble along his jaw rubbing against my chest was too much. My orgasm was right there, and he hadn't even touched me yet.

As though reading my mind, his right hand trailed to my center, pressing firmly against the soaked fabric covering my clit.

"Fucking hell, honey," Duke breathed against my skin. "You're soaked."

"It's your fault." He slowed my hips, pinning me in place with one hand still on my ass, as his other slipped beneath my panties. I tried breaking out of his hold, to give him no choice but to touch me exactly where I wanted him to, but he refused.

"If you need something—" he nipped at my collarbone "—you should ask for it."

"Maybe you're the one who needs something," I panted. "Like a roadmap to find my clit?"

My playful taunt was enough to spring him into action. Duke struck before I could process what was happening, tearing my panties like they were nothing more than a flimsy piece of paper. The sound made me gasp, looking down to see the crudeness of passion.

My legs were spread, boots resting on the barstools for

comfort, dress hiked up around my waist, and pussy now bared to the room. His throat moved, swallowing thickly as he followed my gaze to the scene. He ran his finger down my center almost reverently. A juxtaposition from how he'd been only moments ago.

Almost as quickly as it came, it was gone. Back was the man, so mindless with need that he couldn't be bothered to slip the fabric down my legs. "I don't need a roadmap," he said, slowly slipping two fingers inside of me.

The fit was tight, so much so that I cried out, clinging to his shoulders as though it would help. He brought his thumb up, circling my clit once, twice, three times, applying just enough pressure to keep me on the edge of an orgasm, but not enough to send me over.

"I know exactly what it takes to make you come." Another circle. Another taunt. "And you're going to do it right here, right now, like a needy little slut."

Nothing had ever felt so good. His fingers moved inside of me, curling up and hitting a spot only my favorite vibrator had ever been able to find.

It was all too much. The pressure, the tightness, his words. As he bent forward and latched his mouth around my neck, I detonated.

My hands clawed at his chest, fingers digging into the fabric until the familiar sound of ripping fabric filled the air along with my screams. My entire body shook as he continued his ministrations, not letting up until I was begging and pleading for him to stop. I was far too sensitive for him to keep up the pace.

Duke didn't stop, but he slowed down, letting me come down from the highest peak while also nurturing the small aftershocks he caused. His lips never left my skin, nipping and sucking and kissing his way across my upper body. There were sure to be marks tomorrow, but I didn't care.

The thought of being marked by him was more intoxicating than any drop of alcohol I could ever consume.

"It's not enough," he murmured against my neck.

"What's not?" I asked, running my hands up through his hair. I cradled him against me, never wanting to let him or this moment go.

Duke pulled back, letting his forehead rest against my own. His breathing is harsh, voice broken and barely restrained as he whispered, "This. Us. I can't let you go yet. I don't want to."

"Then don't." I wasn't ready to walk away. Not when, for the first time in god knew how many years, things felt okay.

I wasn't thinking about work.

I wasn't thinking about being a bad mother or worrying I wasn't doing enough for my daughter.

I wasn't thinking about John's death, or the fact that, at thirty-seven years old, I was standing at a crossroads.

No, all I wanted was Duke.

Forever.

I kissed him, hoping he felt every ounce of desperation I felt. "Take me to bed."

His lips quirked in a small smile. "What about a couch?"

"Even better," I laughed. "Honestly, you could tell me we were sleeping in the bed of your truck, and I'd be okay with that."

"Maybe another time," he said, slipping the straps of my dress back onto my shoulders. "But I don't want to share your screams tonight." Another kiss. "Tonight, they're all mine."

Without breaking apart, Duke scooped me up. I was beginning to see a pattern with him. He loved holding me. Carrying me.

And I loved it right back.

We made our way through the back door, pausing only to lock up, before he made the quick walk to his cabin. With every powerful step, I was reminded of the fact I wasn't wearing anything beneath my dress. I couldn't stop myself from grinding against him, seeking friction to quell the ache he'd created.

"I give you one orgasm and all of a sudden you can't stop?" Duke nipped at my earlobe. "Needy girl."

"I can't help it," I whined. "I need you, Duke."

"Honey, if you don't stop, I'll have to fuck you out here in the open." I whimpered at the thought, and Duke slowed his pace. "You like the sound of that, don't you?"

I nodded, unashamed. I may not have had much sexual experience, but I had an idea of what I liked and what I didn't through romance novels and the occasional pornsite.

I'd read about voyeurism and exhibitionism before. I'd even listened to those erotic audio apps where they immerse you in the story. And nothing got me off quite like knowing I was being watched. It was why, when I discovered Duke had been staring at me through the crack in the bathroom door, I'd dropped the towel.

If it hadn't been for our daughters in the same house, I would've given him a show. Taunting him until he couldn't help but burst through the door and make me pay for being such a little slut.

Duke looked around, walking over and pinning my body against his truck. Oh my god, was he really going to do this here?

He resituated his grip, holding me with one hand while the other slipped back up my dress. His fingers parted my folds, finding my clit and giving it a squeeze. "I'm not going to fuck you here, but," he flicked his gaze down to where his hand played with my pussy, "I am starving. Maybe I should have a snack before I make you scream."

"Yes, please," I nodded. "This snack would very much like to be eaten."

Duke smirked, lowering one of my legs so I could support my weight as he dropped to his knees. He rested the other over his shoulder, rolling up my dress until he was eye-level with my pussy.

"So wet," he murmured. He used his thumb to dip inside me and spread the wetness up over my clit. "Even in the fucking moonlight, I can tell how much you want me."

"Please," I whimpered. "I need—"

But I didn't get to finish my sentence. Not as Duke leaned in, pressing an open-mouthed kiss over my sex. My head fell back against the truck, unable to stop a low moan from escaping my lips at the first flick of his tongue. The realization that we were out in the open hit me hard. That anyone driving by could see us, see him on his knees, devouring my pussy like it was his last meal.

And god, did I love it.

It wasn't just the act of sex in public, but also knowing it was with Duke, that had me clenching my legs together. His coarse stubble rubbed along my upper thigh as he licked and sucked at my clit. He brought his fingers to my entrance, sliding the first into the knuckle before adding another beside it.

I looked down, seeing his bright green eyes already trained on me. Watching as I lost myself to the pleasure he was giving. Seeing him between my legs was too much and not enough.

"Fuck, fuck," I cried. I tried to bring my hand up to cover my mouth, but Duke stopped me, pulling it away.

"You wanted this," he reminded me, pulling away to nip at my thigh. "You wanted to play this game. Don't be shy now."

He was right. I did want this. I wanted to be bad. To be reckless.

I nodded, letting my hand fall to the top of his head. His mouth found my core as I wound my fingers through his hair, tugging and pulling as he brought me so close to orgasm. If it hurt, he didn't let on. If anything, he seemed to take it as encouragement, fucking me with his fingers faster and harder than before.

The sound was obscene. I could hear every move he made, the unmistakable noises of my arousal filling the silent night. My thighs were wet. I couldn't tell if it was from him or me.

"Come for me, Olivia. Come right here, out in the open, on my tongue," he growled. "Let the whole goddamn town hear you."

I moved my hips, grinding against his face shamelessly as my orgasm crested and I dove into a freefall. My fingers wound tighter, holding him to me as he sucked hard on my clit, while his fingers curved up to the same spot as before.

"Yes, yes, yes," I chanted. My body was no longer my own. I couldn't control it, letting it act of its own accord. God, it was perfect. It was everything.

And I still wanted more.

Duke stood quickly, wrapping my legs back around him. He carried me into his cabin quickly. The moment we crossed the threshold, he tossed me onto the couch and climbed on top of me.

We were a mess. A tangle of limbs. Our bodies moved in perfect synchronicity, grinding against one another wantonly.

"You're wearing too many clothes," I complained, pushing at his shoulders. "I want to see you."

Duke pulled back, a brief look of hesitation crossing his face. "I haven't been naked with someone in a long time."

"Neither have I," I huffed. "Nine years, remember?"

"Yeah, but," he paused, shaking his head. "I've seen your ex-husband. We don't look alike."

I leaned up on my elbows, staring at him. No, Duke certainly didn't look a thing like Grady. While my ex-husband was lean and toned, Duke was broad and thick. He must have had a solid fifty pounds on Grady. Possibly more.

A hint of chest hair peeked out through the tear in his shirt, making my mouth water. Whatever he was afraid of, whatever demons he was battling, I wanted to banish.

Duke watched, leaning back on his heels, as I climbed off the couch. "What're you—"

His words cut off as I reached up and slipped the strap of my dress off one shoulder and then the other. Words, I realized, wouldn't be enough to put his fears to rest. I'd have to show him he had nothing to worry about.

"My pregnancy with Charlie was rough," I said, peeling the top of half of my dress down to expose my chest. "And once she was born, I struggled to look myself in the mirror some days."

"You're beautiful," Duke murmured. He couldn't take his eyes off me.

"My breasts aren't as perky as they used to be. My right is larger than my left because that's the one Charlie preferred while breastfeeding." I ran the tips of my fingers across the hardened peaks of my nipples. "My areolas are darker, too."

Then, I rolled my dress down further, past my stomach and hips, until it fell around my feet. "The stretch marks were the most difficult for me to get used to," I admitted, touching the shimmery purple stripes running along the sides of my belly to my hips. "It was further evidence of how my body wasn't the same as it used to be. That *I* had changed and couldn't be put back to how I was before. No amount of money in the world could do that. And my hips are wider, too."

"Why're you telling me this?" he asked, gently.

I stepped forward and cupped his jaw. "Because we all have insecurities, baby. It doesn't matter that my mind is screaming at me to put back on my clothes, or that admitting all of this out loud makes me feel far too vulnerable." I pressed a kiss to his cheek, feeling the moisture there and realizing he must've let a tear slip. "The way you're looking at me right now quiets the noise."

Duke ran his hands from my calves to my thighs and hips, tugging me closer until his face was level with my stomach. He looked up as his lips skimmed over the marks left behind. One after another, he kissed each one. The sentimentality of it was so tender yet powerful.

"You're perfect," he murmured. "Even when you think you're not. You're perfect to me."

His words felt like the admission of something bigger. Of almost, but not quite, crossing the line we'd been dancing around since I got home. The most confusing part was how I didn't feel the need to correct him. To try and prove his opinion wrong, but drawing more attention to the things that'd taken me years to love again.

"I don't know what has you believing otherwise, but I promise there is nothing about you that I don't love," I said.

Slowly, I reached for the tattered remnants of his shirt, tugging it over his head before tossing it to the floor. He waited on bated breath as my eyes skimmed over his body. Along the thick hair across his chest to the line running down his soft stomach and disappearing beneath his jeans.

I threaded my hands into his hair and tilted his head back so that he was staring at me. His green eyes were nearly swallowed by the black of his pupils. "Now that we've gotten that out of the way," I said, earning a slight curl of his lips, "are you going to finish what you started?" Duke moved his hand between my thighs, swiping between my folds. "You've made me so needy. I want more. I want you."

He surged forward, tossing me on my back as he stood above me. I watched, waiting eagerly, as he slowly undid the button of his jeans and slid them down his legs. His briefs did nothing to hide the outline of his hard cock jutting against the fabric.

My core tightened at the thought of how he'd fill me, stretch me. It'd be too much, and yet I yearned for the sting. I wanted it to hurt. I wanted to feel it tomorrow when I sat down, knowing it was from him.

His gaze followed mine, smirking. "This what you want?" he asked, running his hand along his length through the fabric.

I licked my lips. "Very much."

"Take it out," he commanded. "Feel what you do to me."

I scrambled up, reaching out with shaking hands as I slipped inside his briefs and felt his hot flesh in my hand for the first time. It was so soft compared to the rest of him. I stroked him absentmindedly. Not for his pleasure but mine.

His hand gripped my wrist, stopping me. "I said to take it out, not play with it," he said through gritted teeth. "I'm not going to last long if you keep doing that."

"I don't think either of us is going to last long as it is," I said honestly.

"Maybe not, but I don't want to rush this first time."

"So, there will be others?" I teased.

Something flashed across Duke's face akin to sorrow, but it was gone before I could question it. "There'll be as many times as you let me. Now," he placed his hand in the center of my chest and pushed me back onto the couch, "lay there and play with that pretty pussy until I get back."

My hand slid down my stomach, fingers circling my clit, as he walked down the hall and into the bathroom. I was already sore from multiple orgasms, but that didn't stop me from doing exactly what I was told. I didn't want to disappoint him.

Duke strode in a moment later, holding a box of condoms in his hand. He watched as I dipped my fingers inside myself, arching my back as I imagined it was him. My other hand came up, squeezing my breast and nipple.

"Goddamn, this is a good view," he growled. He slipped his briefs down and fished out a condom, making quick work to remove it from the foil. And then it was my turn to watch as he unabashedly rolled it down his length. It was fucking filthy.

I clenched around my fingers, letting out a needy moan. "I can't wait anymore, Duke. I need you."

Slowly, he slipped between my legs, spreading them wider as I continued lazily fucking myself. "It's gonna be a tight fit," he said, gripping his dick. "But I can't fucking wait to see your sweet cunt stretch around me."

"Baby, please," I begged.

I wanted to pull him toward me, but he was just out of reach. His eyes were still trained on my center as he guided his length toward my entrance, knocking my hands away.

"You'll tell me if it's too much, right?"

"It won't be."

"Promise me," he said, meeting my gaze.

I nodded. "I promise."

The moment the words left my lips, Duke began to push.

Already, I could feel the slight burn as my body stretched to accommodate his size. "I'm gonna go slow," he rasped. "Gonna make it feel so good."

His head dropped back as he pushed in halfway. "Fuck, Olivia. Fuck. You feel so good, honey. Oh my god."

I couldn't speak, couldn't think, couldn't do anything other than writhe beneath him as he worked himself inside of me. The stretch was nearly unbearable, but I welcomed the pain.

I wanted more.

"Please, baby. I need you to move," I begged. "I need—"

Duke pulled out slowly, unable to take his eyes off where we were joined. I missed the fullness immediately. My body ground down, searching for more.

His hand pressed gently on my stomach as he pushed back in, setting an even tempo. I could see the desire etched onto his face. The picture of yearning was so perfect and tender that it nearly sent me over the edge before we'd even begun.

"Is this what you need?" he asked, picking up his pace. "To be fucked?"

Yes, oh god, yes. I needed it more than I needed air to breathe. I could die right here, and the only regret I'd have would be not knowing what he looked like when he came.

He leaned forward, covering my body with his own as he slammed into me. Each thrust stole my breath. Each curse falling from his lips was my undoing.

"I'm going to come," I breathed.

"Give it to me, Olivia," he hissed. "Fucking give it to me."

My orgasm hit me like a freight train, body writhing from the heady combination of pain and pleasure as Duke thrust into me once, twice, three times more before letting out his own low growl. His cock twitched inside of me as he came, letting the waves of my own orgasm carry him into his own.

For the first time tonight, I wished we hadn't used a condom. It was a reckless and stupid thought, especially given our fragile situation, but I wanted to feel the warmth of his release, to see it spilling out of me in the most obscene way.

Duke buried his face in my neck, murmuring my name over and over again. His lips moved along my skin, kissing from one side of my chest to the other until his head came to rest on my shoulder.

Wrapping my arms around him, we stayed like that until the

warm sheen of sweat covering our bodies dried. He was still inside of me. A fact I was reminded of every time one of us moved.

It wasn't uncomfortable. It wasn't even awkward. Instead, I felt nothing but peace.

"I hope you know I'm staying the night."

He chuckled, turning to press another kiss onto my neck. "You can stay as long as you like."

DUKE

THE SMELL of citrus and salt was the first thing I noticed as I blinked against the morning sun. I wasn't sure what time it was, but I knew it was late from the light streaming through the windows.

I glanced down, peering at Olivia asleep on my chest. After we had sex last night, it hadn't taken long for either of us to want more. Making her come was like a drug. I was addicted, wanting to see just how many times I could have her crying out. I thought she might have been done after four, but she'd woken me up only an hour later by grinding her sweet pussy against my leg.

Obviously, I had to give her what she so desperately needed.

I ran my fingers down her bare back, waiting for the guilt to kick in over what we'd done, the lines we obliterated, but it never came. I only felt peace.

My mind was quiet for the first time in years. It could have something to do with all the orgasms she'd dragged out of me, but I had a feeling it had more to do with the woman lying in my arms.

The moment she walked into my bar, I knew I was fucked. There was only one question as to how last night was going to end—her place or mine?

We were being reckless. And I was sure that was going to come around and bite us in the ass, but this morning I couldn't care less. Any amount of pain was worth it. Especially as Olivia's eyes slowly opened, and she stared at me with a soft and sleepy expression.

"Good morning," I whispered. Reaching out, I tucked her hair behind her ear. "How did you sleep?"

She smiled, letting out a low hum as her body stretched against my own. I was acutely aware that neither of us was wearing any clothes. "Good," she said, resting her chin on my chest. "And you?"

"Absolutely zero complaints from me."

"Hmm, and here I thought you were going to say something about me taking up all your space."

I slid my hand toward her ass, giving it a tight squeeze. "I like it when you take up my space." My fingers moved lower still, dancing over her sex. She was wet, just like I knew she'd be.

My girl was insatiable. I loved that about her.

I loved a lot of things about her, but none that I could say out loud yet.

We might have known each other our whole lives, but this was different. I should be terrified of the things I felt. Of caring so deeply in such a short amount of time. And on some level, I was.

Whether she wanted to or not, Olivia was still dead set on leaving Pinecrest—and me—behind. I wasn't sure anything could change her mind at this point, but I could try.

"What're you thinking about?" Olivia asked, running the pad of her finger between my brows.

I couldn't very well admit how obsessed I was with her, so I said, "That we should probably check the time. Harper has a soccer game at ten."

Even though Grady offered to take her, I'd never missed one of my daughter's games. I wasn't about to start now.

"Good call," she said, looking around for one of our phones. When she found it, she let out a triumphant sound. "It's only eight."

I lifted my knee until it pressed against her center. "That's good," I murmured. "Means we'll have plenty of time."

Olivia smiled coyly. "Time for what, Mr. Bennett?"

I leaned down, letting my mouth graze the shell of her ear. "For you to ride my cock."

Goose bumps erupted along her skin. It was so easy to rile her up, to have her writhing in my arms.

"You're insatiable," she said, swinging her leg over my waist. "Downright greedy."

"Says the woman who's grinding her hot little cunt against my dick."

She sucked in a breath. I'd never been much for dirty talk in the past. It always felt awkward and forced with Sarah, but I loved watching Olivia's eyes light up at the lewd statement.

We both looked down, watching her easily slide along my length, leaving a sheen of arousal in her wake. It was easily one of the hottest things I'd ever seen, and she smiled as though she was proud.

"You like that, huh?" I brought my hands to her hips, stilling her movement. It was irresponsible to be this close, to know I could slip inside her with little effort.

She nodded, mewling as I canted my hips and notched my head at her entrance. "It feels so good."

It did feel good, and that was the problem. I wasn't worried about getting her pregnant as I'd had a vasectomy a few years after Harper was born. Though we'd never talked about it, I knew both of us were in the clear when it came to any possible STDs.

But knowing what she felt like without anything between us would ruin me.

And yet… I pushed inside an inch, anyway.

"I'm on birth control," she rasped, running her hands through the hair on my chest.

"Vasectomy," I replied through gritted teeth. She was so warm, so wet, so inviting. Goddamn. I wasn't sure how long I'd last, not like this.

"Oh god." Olivia ground her hips against mine, forcing herself down, down, down until our bodies were flush. The fit is even tighter than before, evident on her face as her mouth falls open in a perfect O. "Why didn't we do this last night? It feels so good."

I chuckled, regretting the sound immediately when my cock twitched painfully inside of her. I wanted to move, needed to move, but I didn't want to hurt her.

The moment she circled her hips, I knew she was okay. "We're doing it now," I said, gently bucking my hips up. "And we'll do it again—" *thrust* "—and again—" *thrust* "—and again." Her hands clawed at my chest as she met my movements. "Just say the word."

All she had to do was snap her fingers, and I'd travel wherever she was. I'd fly halfway across the world if she asked me to.

Which was insane.

Olivia dropped her head as I bucked faster, pounding into her from below. The sounds she made, the keening wails for *more, more, more* made me lose my mind. It was hot as fuck watching her unapologetically chase her own pleasure. I could watch her all day. Hell, I *wanted* to watch her all day. Every day.

A single bead of sweat ran down her neck. I couldn't help myself, leaning up to catch it with my tongue. My hands gripped her ass, helping her move in the new position. It wasn't long until her legs began to tremble. She was close. So goddamned close. And I wasn't far off either.

"Tell me where to come," I panted, voice broken with restraint. It was hell trying to hold myself back, but I had to. "I need to—I want to come inside of you."

"Yes. I want to feel it, want to—oh *shit*." I reached forward, needing no further instruction. I pinched her clit, watching a brutal climax wrack her body. Her pussy squeezed my cock like a goddamn vise, and I could no longer ignore the sensation building at the base of my spine. It only took three more stuttering thrusts before my own release found me, and I was emptying myself inside her.

It was so fucking powerful, knowing my cum was filling her up. That it'd be leaking out of her all day. I could feel it even now, running down my length and pooling beneath us.

Jesus Christ. What the hell was this woman doing to me?

Olivia pressed a kiss to my lips as we rode out our highs together. I knew we should move. Knew we should take a shower and clean ourselves up, but I wanted to steal another moment with her just like this.

"I don't think I've ever seen anything so beautiful," I said, running my thumb along her bottom lip.

She nipped the pad, taking it into her mouth, and I groaned. "You can't fucking do that. We don't have time."

"I know," she sighed. "Fine, fine. I'll behave."

She tried to move off me, but I stopped her. "Will you come to the game with me? I know it's your free day, but—"

She cut me off with a kiss. "I'd love to, but we'd have to hurry. And you'll have to run out to my car and grab the bag in my front seat."

"Packing an overnight bag?" I quirked a brow. "Someone was confident."

"It was just in case I needed to crash here," she said slowly. "But I'll admit I had a few hopes for the evening."

I wrapped my arms around her waist, holding her to me as I stood from the couch. She laughed as I made our way into the bathroom. "You have a thing for carrying me around."

I set her down outside the stall, reaching inside to turn the water on. "Is that a problem?"

Honestly, I wasn't sure why I liked it as much as I did. It just felt natural at this point.

Plus, she felt good in my arms.

"No, no," Olivia said quickly. "I love it. I think it's very endearing, actually."

"Good," I said, giving her a chaste kiss. "Now get your cute ass in this shower so I can dirty you up once last time."

OLIVIA STOOD UP, placing her fingers in her mouth to let out an ear-splitting whistle. "Let's go, Harper!" she screamed.

My daughter ran down the field, effortlessly dodging the other team as they attempted to steal the ball. She'd been on fire all morning, having already scored three out of the four points on the makeshift scoreboard.

We watched, literally on the edge of our seats, as Harper took aim and launched the ball into the net. The goalie leapt, but it was too late. The ball was in, and the crowd went wild.

I jumped up, clapping and whooping loudly as Harper jogged to the sidelines with her team. She glanced over, smiling and waving at our group, before taking a seat next to one of the other players. My face echoed the joy in her own, though I wondered whether it had more to do with Olivia squeezing my hand the moment my daughter turned her back on us.

It was difficult to be so near her and yet not be able to touch. Even if we blew past the line in our relationship, we still had to dance around it in public. Friendly, but not too friendly. Cozy, and yet distant. My scowls were out of practice. If anyone looked too closely, they'd likely find it was impossible to do so when Olivia was around.

Grady stood up. "I'm going to grab a water. Y'all want anything?"

"I'm good. Thank you!" Olivia said, turning her attention back to the game. Grady turned to me, and I shook my head. The one thing I needed, I couldn't have right now.

"Can I have sour Skittles?" Charlie asked, glancing between her parents. They shared a look before Olivia nodded.

"Sure you can, sunshine."

Charlie cheered, grabbing Grady's hand to pull him toward the stand.

"It's so strange," I heard someone say from behind me. "She's here with her ex-husband."

"I wonder what his wife thinks of that," another answered. "I, for one, wouldn't let my husband hang out with an ex." Her nasally voice grated on my nerves, but the topic of conversation had me seeing fucking red.

How dare they judge her without knowing her situation? How dare they make comments on shit they didn't understand?

I went through a similar situation when Sarah left. But instead of being met with viper-like jealousy, I was forced to bat away single moms who refused to take a hint. No matter how many times I declined their invites to coffee or dinner, they kept coming back like flies to shit.

"You know, she's been hanging around Duke Bennett so much lately." I felt their gazes land on my back. "I have to wonder what she's playing at."

"It won't last," the nasal lady said. "Duke hasn't looked at another woman since his ex-wife left him. Little Miss Celebrity isn't going to change that."

"She's not even that pretty."

And then they laughed. Fucking laughed like the comments on my romantic life were any of their business. Like they had any right to talk about Olivia as anything other than spectacular.

I couldn't take it anymore. I had to say something. Anything.

I moved to turn around, ready to give them a piece of my mind when Olivia's hand landed on mine. She was still looking forward, smiling as she watched the girls run the ball down the field. "It's not worth it."

"Someone should put them in their fucking place," I growled.

Olivia laughed. "What would that do other than give them yet another thing to talk about? It's all gossip, Duke. It doesn't matter."

"They shouldn't even be talking about you."

"And yet they are." She laughed, turning toward me. "Whether you say something or not, our names will be on their lips."

At the mere mention of her lips, my gaze dipped to her mouth.

"Insatiable," she muttered, shaking her head.

"Let me set the record straight," I said, leaning forward. "Let me give them something better to gossip about."

Olivia was quiet for a moment, glancing to the concession stand where Grady and Charlie were still in line. "If they start talking, you know it'll be around town before we ever leave the game."

"So?" Honestly, I didn't care. Let them know. Let them talk. I wanted the whole goddamn town to know she was mine.

Even if she hadn't admitted it to herself yet.

"You will when kids ask Harper about it at school. Or when my brother questions you about what's going on."

I snorted. "Harper loves you. She'd understand that this is the happiest I've been in years. And as for your brother, remember that he's already asked me about my intentions toward you. Your ex-husband, too."

"Oh my god," she muttered, covering her face with her hands. "They're so embarrassing."

"They care," I said, prying her hands away. "I'd do the same if I were in their shoes."

I could see the gears turning, the mental battle she was waging against herself. "Duke, I—"

"Come on… Let me show you off, honey."

We'd gravitated so close without realizing it. My gaze dipped to her lips yet again.

"Mom, look! Dad let me get two bags of sour Skittles!" Charlie came bounding up, holding two lime green bags of sweets.

Olivia forced a smile. "He did, did he?" She looked up at Grady, clearly judging him for being so wrapped around their daughter's finger. "He just can't say no."

"Nope!" Charlie beamed. "I'm going to go give the other bag to Harper." She ran off toward the sidelines, sitting on the ground next to her best friend.

"*He*," Grady emphasized, returning to his seat, "was trying to buy you two idiots some time so you'll quit eye-fucking one another and make a move so those bitter bitches behind you will finally shut up." He took a sip of his drink. "They're getting on my nerves."

Olivia's jaw dropped, and I couldn't stop myself from laughing. "Oh my god, you're the worst."

Grady turned toward her, lowering his sunglasses to peer

over the top of them. "Consider it payback. You were insuffer-able when I was trying to navigate my relationship with Cleo."

"I—That was different!"

"Was it?" He readjusted his glasses and looked back toward the field. "Doesn't look like it to me."

Olivia turned back toward the field, arms crossed tightly over her chest, clearly irked. Honestly, it was cute as hell knowing how easily Grady had ruffled her feathers.

As the game came to a close, I began gathering up the chairs. Harper and Charlie were talking to some of their classmates on the field. Parents said their goodbyes before heading off to their vehicles.

I thought I was going to get away unscathed when I felt a hand run along my lower back. "Duke, it's so good to see you."

Turning, I realized it was one of the women who'd been cruelly gossiping behind us. She was pretty enough, but rather plain. Nothing like Olivia.

"Just like every Saturday," I deadpanned.

The nasal lady threw her head back in laughter. "I know I've asked before, but we really should get the girls together for a playdate. My Taylor has been begging me for weeks."

Her daughter was clear across the field, rolling around in the grass with one of her teammates, but I sure as hell wasn't going to bring an eight-year-old into the discussion.

"I don't think—"

"There you are." Olivia breezed over, placing her hand on my arm. "Grady's going to take the girls for the night, which means we," she gestured between the two of us, "are free for the evening."

"Olivia." The lady in front of us cleared her throat. Her eyes landed on the spot where Olivia's hand was touching my arm. "Duke and I were actually just discussing something."

Olivia turned her attention to the woman. The smile she

wore was sickly sweet. "I'm so sorry. I'm afraid I must cut it short. You see, I've got an ache Duke has just been *dying* to clear up for me, isn't that right, baby?"

I nearly choked on my own spit from trying to stop the laugh bubbling up. The lady's face turned bright red. "I didn't realize the two of you were—"

"A *thing?*" Olivia finished for her, earning a rueful glare. "Yes, well, I don't really see how that is any of your business, is it?" Then she leaned in, dropping her voice. "Let this be a lesson for you. No means fucking no. Duke has expressed his disinterest multiple times. It's not cute to keep asking."

And then she grabbed the collar of my shirt, pulling me in for a quick, yet searing kiss I felt all the way to my goddamn toes. People murmured around us, whispering harshly about my being off the market.

While it may not have been entirely true, it was one rumor I had no intention of debunking.

OLIVIA

ON THE WAY home from Harper's game, Duke insisted we stop by the grocery store for supplies before heading to the guest cottage. Since we were both child-free—and his amazing staff agreed to cover the busy Saturday evening shift—we decided to close ourselves off from the rest of the world and spend our day in ignorant bliss.

Kissing him at the game was a mistake. I should feel guilty about setting the rumor mill turning, but I didn't. Much like everything else we'd done last night, it felt right claiming him so publicly.

I'd heard every word the women at the game had said. It wasn't the first time they'd talked about me, but I'd just ensured it wouldn't be the last. While I'd been content to let things go, seeing Duke grow so protective was far too hot to ignore.

And yes, I could admit that Grady's taunts had only fueled the flame.

I had, of course, played wingwoman to him when he'd gone down to Texas to win back his high school sweetheart. I'd also been the one to draw up our divorce papers before he ever asked, forcing his hand because I knew he'd struggle with the decision himself.

We all needed a little push sometimes, and I'd been happy to give it to him. But my situation with Duke was different. We didn't have a history to build on. We didn't—we couldn't—even have a future.

If I were a smarter, better woman, I would've let Duke handle the nosy woman himself and told him I had things to do around the house. I would've told him that as wonderful as last night had been, it couldn't happen again.

Instead, I'd gripped his hand, pulled him toward our vehicles, and kissed him before begging him to stay with me tonight.

I rationalized my decision by telling myself Duke knew I couldn't stay, and yet he chose to dive headfirst into the precarious waters anyway. If we were going to drown, it seemed as though we were going to drown together.

Now, as I looked over and saw him standing at the grill, so carefree with that easy smile on his face, I couldn't bring myself to regret jumping in without a life preserver.

I stood from the lounger, walking over and wrapping my arms around his waist. "What gourmet dish can I expect from you today?" I asked.

He turned, giving me a quick kiss. "Burgers."

"Burgers?" It did smell amazing, but I was expecting something different when he'd walked out of the store with a ridiculous amount of grocery bags. "What's on them?"

"Whatever you like. I know your taste may have changed from when we were younger, but I remember you dousing your food with hot sauce and jalapenos."

I smiled against his back. The fact he remembered was so damn endearing. Honestly, I needed him to stop because it was getting harder and harder not to fall in love with him.

As if I hadn't already.

"So, I made a quick habanero aioli for you. Figured I'd toss some jalapenos on the grill." He turned over his shoulder. "Unless you prefer fresh? I also got pickled and—"

"Oh my god, stop," I laughed.

He looked down, a deep crease between his brows. "Is it too much?"

"No." I shook my head. God, the last thing I wanted him to think was that he was too much. Especially when it was the most thoughtful thing anyone had done for me in a long time. "It's perfect. You're perfect."

"I just wanted to impress you." Duke turned, paying an awful lot of attention to his burgers. "You deserve the best."

"So do you," I whispered, tightening my arms around his middle.

So much better than me was what I wanted to say, but didn't.

One day, I would be forced to smile and put on a happy face when he found someone who could give him all the things I couldn't. Because the worst part of our situation was that neither of us would be given a clean break. Whether I was Lukas's sister or Charlie's mom, we'd always be in our lives in one form or the other.

Duke squeezed my hand before letting it go. "Wanna grab us some plates?"

"Sure. Do you want to eat inside or out?"

"Out, if that's okay with you. I like the view." I knew he was talking about the green acreage and grazing horses just beyond the fence, but he was staring at me the entire time.

I walked into the house, calling over my shoulder, "You're a terrible flirt!"

"Actually, I think I'm pretty damn good at it!" His laughter followed me as I went to the kitchen, grabbed plates from the cabinet, and set out the toppings along the counter. He really had thought of everything. Tomatoes, lettuce, pickles, and onions were the staples, but he also had an array of vegetables, such as sautéed mushrooms, sliced avocado, and grilled jalapenos.

Duke walked in carrying the tray of burgers and bacon, set it on the stove, and then turned toward me. "You got enough food to feed twelve people," I laughed. "Did we really need all this?"

He shrugged, a tinge of pink coloring his cheeks. "Like I said, I wasn't sure what all you liked and wanted to make sure we had it."

I pressed him up against the counter, running my finger down his chest. "You could've just asked me, you know?"

"And ruin the surprise?" He leaned down, mouth brushing my cheek. "Where's the fun in that?"

I tipped my head back as his lips ran lower, sucking gently on my neck. "If you don't stop, we're going to get distracted, and this wonderful meal you've prepared is going to get cold." Placing my hand on his chest, I pushed him back. "And you've kept me waiting long enough. I'm already on the verge of being hangry."

"Well, we don't want that." He stepped to the side to begin fixing a plate. "What do you want on your burger?"

"I can make it," I said, grabbing for the plate, but he held it out of reach.

"Nuh-uh. You're going to tell me what you want on it. Then you're going to sit your sweet little ass down and wait for me to bring you a plate."

It was pointless to argue, but I was going to do it anyway. "Duke, seriously—"

"Honey, you're not gonna win this argument, so you might as well just do what I say for once and take a seat."

He was trying to put on his best grumpy scowl, but his eyes were alight with amusement. This playful side of him was new, but it was quickly becoming my favorite.

"Fine. Tomatoes, grilled jalapenos, onions, aioli, and pickles, please," I said, stepping back. "Am I allowed to grab two beers from the fridge for us, or is that crossing some imaginary line you've set?"

Duke's lips twitched. "I'll allow it."

"Oh, good. I'm glad to know where you've drawn the line."

Walking back outside, I stopped at the plain white appliance Lukas had affectionately dubbed the beer fridge and grabbed two from inside. Duke was already headed outside by the time I made it to the picnic table.

He placed my plate in front of me, giving a dramatic bow when I took my seat. "Your dinner is served." Then he took the seat opposite of me as I slid his beer toward him.

Duke watched me nervously. I couldn't help it. I moaned the moment I took a bite. The flavors were unreal, and the aioli was the perfect touch of searing heat.

"Oh my god," I mumbled. So what if I spoke with my mouth full? He deserved every ounce of praise. "This is the best burger I've ever had in my life."

Duke picked up his burger, hiding his smile behind his food. "You don't have to kiss my ass. I already cooked for you."

"It's not kissing your ass if it's true." I took another bite. "Like seriously, Duke. I didn't know you could cook like this. Where'd you learn?"

"Would you believe me if I told you I was self-taught?"

I shook my head. "There's no way. It's too perfect."

"Better believe it, honey," he said, putting down his burger. "I knew the basics coming out of college. Mostly because Lukas couldn't be trusted not to burn toast."

"No, I remember he literally set the carpet on fire when we were kids. He was trying to make eggs for our dad and set a paper plate too close to the burner."

"Exactly," he laughed. "So, you can see why I needed to be

able to take care of the basics. We would've starved if I hadn't taken over. And then it just kind of evolved from there. Sarah didn't cook much. Harper was a picky eater, so I had to get creative at dinner time. Turns out I like it. It's a rare moment during the day when I can be by myself."

I leaned forward, resting my chin on my palm as he spoke. Duke didn't talk much about himself. The fact that he was giving me this much didn't go unnoticed. I didn't want to miss a single detail, determined to soak up as much from him as I could.

"Charlie was the same. Always picky, I mean. Grady was more of the cook in our household. I'm ashamed to admit I'm not much better off than my brother."

Duke grinned. "Maybe I could give you a lesson or two."

"I think I'd like that. At the very least, I need to be able to make this burger again." I grinned. "Now that I've tasted it, I'm not sure I could go back to anything else."

And I wasn't just talking about the food.

How the hell was I supposed to walk away from this? From him? It was nearly too much to bear.

I reached for my beer, taking a swig before the moisture lining my eyes could fall. Out of all the conversations we needed to have, I wasn't ready for that one yet. I wanted to live in bliss for a little while longer.

DUKE

AFTER DINNER, I cleaned up the kitchen, washing all the dishes and putting away the leftovers. Olivia had been down-right pissed about it, insisting that she should be the one to clean since I'd done the cooking, but I refused.

I was enjoying the brief glimpse of what domestic life would've looked like with her. It wasn't flashy or over-the-top, but rather simple. She enjoyed reading books and going for walks in the pasture. And at night, as I was informed only moments ago, she enjoyed soaking in a bathtub when her schedule allowed.

Walking down the hall, I pushed open the door to Olivia's bedroom. I followed the scent of rich amber and vanilla into the bathroom, finding her already neck deep in bubbles with a glass of wine sitting on the standing tray near her head. Her hair was up, piled into a messy bun.

I was immediately taken back to the night I'd watched her through the cracked door. When she'd dropped the towel and given me my first glimpse of her.

My cock hardened at the memory. Especially knowing she was naked beneath all those bubbles right this very moment.

"Kitchen's clean," I said, resting my shoulder against the doorframe. "Even wiped down the counters for you."

Olivia grabbed her wine, taking a hearty sip. "You didn't have to do that, you know."

"I wanted to."

"Well… Thank you," she said. She gestured toward the water. "Care to join me?"

"Honey, I don't think—"

She rolled her eyes. "This tub is massive, Duke. Get your ass in here before I drag you in."

"I'd quite like to see you try," I said.

I pushed off the frame and started toward her, reaching behind my neck and pulling my t-shirt off. It hit the floor with a soft thud, followed quickly by my sweats and briefs.

She sucked in a breath as her gaze dipped down my body. It was a strange sort of confidence. One I wasn't used to.

I'd always been a bigger guy, which hadn't bothered me until much later in life. Sports and the gym kept me lean enough, but I was never going to be the man to have washboard abs and blatant muscle definition.

Last night, Olivia had taken those fears and squashed them beneath her red-bottomed stilettos.

"Scoot up," I said, stepping into the tub.

Water sloshed over the side as I settled in behind her. She leaned back, resting her head on my shoulder as my arms found her waist. Classical renditions of pop songs played softly in the background.

It was peaceful.

She was peaceful.

"I like these moments alone with you," I quietly confessed. "They feel special."

Olivia was silent for a moment before nodding. "They're my favorite. It's like we're the only two people in the world."

I pressed a kiss to her temple, savoring the heat along her skin. There was so much I could say, but what good would it do? I was terrified of breaking us out of this bubble we'd found ourselves in. It felt safe here.

Even if all we were doing was slowly breaking our own hearts.

"If you could go anywhere in the world, where would it be?" I asked.

She hummed, taking a sip of her wine. "Who's going?"

"As much as I love the girls, they're staying home this time," I said.

"I've been to so many places. London, Paris, Milan." She listed each one, ticking them off her fingers. "And they're extraordinary, don't get me wrong—"

"But?" I couldn't help but run my fingers across the expanse of her stomach and up to her breasts. Soon, I wouldn't be able to do this whenever I wanted, so I needed to take full advantage of it while I could.

"But, other than this tub in this cottage right now," she said, smiling. "I'd most like to go back to that cabin John rented for us."

"The one from graduation?"

She nodded. "It felt simpler back then. I still had my whole life ahead of me. No kids or ex-partners or careers. It was just you, me, Lukas, and John for one full weekend." Her words trailed off. "I don't even know if it still exists, but in a perfect world, I imagine it does and that's where I'd like to go."

"There's an easy way to find out. You could go there any time you wanted," I said, bringing my hands up to her shoulders. The muscles beneath my fingers were tight. I rubbed them gently, enjoying the way she melted into my touch.

"It wouldn't be the same without you." I waited for her to say more, to add in Lukas at the very least.

It wouldn't be the same without *me*.

"Maybe we can make that dream come true sometime," I murmured, kissing the spot beneath her ear.

"Really?"

"I think—I hope—you know by now that there isn't much I wouldn't do for you, honey."

We let the weight of my words settle between us like an anchor sinking to the bottom of the sea, understanding there were so many meanings to them.

Olivia's chest shuddered as she let out a quiet sob. She quickly covered her face with her hands as I held her tighter to my chest. "Hey," I crooned, nuzzling her neck. "Don't cry, baby. Please don't cry." When she didn't stop, my own voice broke. "I didn't mean to make you cry."

"It's not you," she whispered. "I just hate that I've gotten us into this mess and have no way of getting us out. No matter what decision I make, I'm going to hurt someone."

I didn't speak for a moment, giving her the space to feel the grief and rage of our situation. "You could stay," I offered quietly.

"I can't—"

"Give me a good reason why you can't."

Olivia turned toward me. The grief-stricken expression on her face was nearly my undoing. "Because of my job. I have an obligation to my family to carry on the legacy at Hartstrings. It's got our family name, for Christ's sake." She laughed, but it was laced with resentment. "And Lukas has said time and time again he has no interest in taking over, so that leaves me to be the one to carry the brunt of the work. I have no one to tag me out of this mess, and so I have to see it through."

"Even though you're miserable?"

"I'm not—"

Olivia tried to pull away, but I cupped her face and forced her to stare at me. "Honey, look at you. Don't even try to deny it. The thought of going back to a career where you're overworked and underappreciated is killing you. And the fucked up truth is that John died before he could understand the toll it's taken on you."

I watched the fight leave her eyes as she crumbled into my arms.

"I'm not trying to tell you what to do, Olivia. But I want you to know that you have your family's support. You have my support."

I pulled her into my chest, surprised she was even willing to go. We laid like that until the water was cold and the wine was gone. Neither of us spoke. At this point, words would only cause more harm than good.

Standing up, I helped her out of the tub. She reached for the towel, but I shook my head. "Let me do this."

She didn't argue, letting me run the soft fabric over her skin until she was dry. And then I picked her up, carrying her bridal style to the bed. She slipped wordlessly under the sheets, watching me as I followed in after.

Olivia reached out, carefully tracing the lines of my face. Whether it was to commit to memory or just in reverence, I didn't care. As she reached my lips, I kissed the pad of each finger before reaching for her other hand to do the same.

"Will you hold me?" she asked, looking up at me through thick black lashes.

"Always."

I opened my arms in response, welcoming her. It was amazing how perfectly her body fit against mine. Like we were two halves of a whole. Meant to be. Written in the stars. All the lovey-dovey bullshit I hadn't believed in in years.

We fell asleep like that: safe, warm, and content.

And when she woke me up in the middle of the night, kissing my neck and stroking me to life, I welcomed that, too. Returning her soft touches with ones of my own. We murmured things we shouldn't have. The gently whispered, "I'm yours," echoed on each other's lips, signaling something bigger than either of us had anticipated when we ran into one another at the grocery store. I claimed her body as much as I claimed her heart, and she'd done the same to me.

It wasn't just sex this time. No, this was different.

It was a promise. A commitment to love and cherish not only the other's mind, but body as well. It was two souls coming together, binding themselves to one another in a way that time, distance, and obligation could never break apart.

It was also, unfortunately, a lie.

OLIVIA

THE NEXT WEEK passed by in a blur of sex and denial.

When Duke and I weren't sneaking around, desperate to spend every possible free moment with one another, I was fielding calls and emails from the Hartstrings board.

They all asked the same question: to know whether someone was going to inherit control or whether John's stocks were up for sale. And each time I answered, I told them the same thing.

I didn't know.

After day two, I was tired of repeating myself, so I asked Darcy to make up some bullshit excuse about not taking calls until the reading of the will next week.

As grateful as I was for the extra time in Pinecrest, I had no idea what Uncle John's reasoning for the delay was. Even Carl had said it was most unusual for it to have been written in. We couldn't have forced an earlier reading even if we wanted to, which left us to hold our breath and bide our time as we watched the meeting tick closer.

But now the waiting game was coming to a close, and I'd never felt so scared in my life. Sometimes, I just lay awake at night in a state of panic. Unable to do anything other than stare at the ceiling while my heart felt like it was about to beat out of my chest.

Would it have been easier if I'd just gone back to Nashville after John's death? If I had, it would've been a clean break. If I had, I wouldn't have known what it felt like to be loved—yes, *loved*—by Duke Bennett.

But even knowing now what I didn't know then, I couldn't bring myself to regret it. The thought of living a life without ever experiencing the kind of tenderness he showed me was not one I wanted to live.

Despite every red flag and warning bell telling us not to go there, I was sure neither of us would go back and change what was happening between us.

Duke and I hadn't talked about what happened last Saturday night. We hadn't spoken about the fact that he'd asked me to stay. Anytime we veered too close to ardent promises and hopeful wishes, one of us was forced to navigate toward safer water rather than the terrifying cliff's edge we were charted for.

My duty to my career and my family was at war with the duty to my heart. Even though I knew which option would win out, I was praying for some kind of miracle that could have me being a part of my family's legacy *and* with those I loved.

I wanted to stay in Pinecrest more than anything. I wanted to spend my days with my daughter and not find out about her life secondhand. I wanted to see my brother more than once every six months if we were lucky. And I wanted to spend every night with Duke, curled in his arms.

I wanted to make plans. To live my life as I saw fit, without worrying about profit margins or acquisitions.

"Mrs. Thompson said I was the best singer in class today," Charlie boasted from the back seat. "She said I have a real talent."

I glanced in the rearview mirror and smiled. "That doesn't surprise me at all, sunshine. You're pretty amazing."

"I can't wait for you to see my play, Mom."

Guilt struck hard and fast, not knowing whether or not I'd even be here by then. With John's original prognosis of three to six months, I'd hoped it wouldn't have been an issue. Now, I had no idea what my future looked like.

I wasn't sure what to say, so I just mumbled, "It's gonna be great."

My daughter was quiet for a moment, her little voice barely above a whisper as she asked, "You're going to be there, right?"

Thrusting a knife into my heart would've hurt less than the subtle heartbreak behind her words. Knowing my daughter was already expecting me to cancel was the shittiest feeling in the world. And I couldn't promise a damn thing because I truly didn't know where I'd be or what I'd be doing.

"I'm going to try," I said, attempting to sound convincing. "I don't know what work is going to look like, and—"

There was a long, insufferable sigh from the back seat. "Yeah, okay."

"Charlie, it isn't like I don't want to be. You know that, right?"

My daughter looked out the window. "I get it, Mom. You're busy."

I drove in silence, trying to blink away the moisture pooling along my lash line. None of this was fair. Losing John, finding Duke, spending time with my daughter. It was all too fresh, too new. I didn't want to lose any more than I already had.

It wasn't as simple as walking away. Even if I found a way to leave Hartstrings, it would take months at best. Years at worst. And, depending on what happened in the upcoming meeting, it would mean leaving behind a company that has meant a great deal to the people who matter most to me.

My voice broke as I said, "I don't want you to think I'm too busy for you, sunshine. I'm going to do everything I can to be there."

She nodded, clearly uninterested in speaking about it further. If I didn't already hate myself for my situationship with Duke, Charlie's cutting disappointment was the final nail in my coffin.

The rest of our ride home was quiet, save for the radio playing softly in the background. As much as I wanted to ask questions, to know more about her day, I knew my daughter well enough that she would only shut down further if I tried.

She was a lot like me in that way.

As we pulled up to the cottage, Lukas and Duke's trucks were both parked outside. There was a flash of red hair at the window before Harper ran outside to our car the moment we came to a stop.

"Charlie! Oh my gosh, come on! You've got to pack."

I stepped out of my car, holding a hand up as they tried to run back into the house. "Whoa, whoa, hold up. What's going on? What do you mean by "pack"?

Lukas strolled out of the house, holding a phone up to his ear. He quickly said goodbye before stopping next to me. "Didn't you get my text?"

"I was driving, so no. Mind filling me in?"

My brother smiled. "You remember that trip we took after graduation?"

"Uh, the cabin?" I asked slowly.

"That's the one."

I stared at Lukas, waiting for an explanation, but he just smiled broadly. "Mind filling me in?"

"Turns out it's an Airbnb now."

"And?"

"We're going away for the weekend," Duke said, strolling out of the house. My mouth watered at the sight of him in a maroon henley and jeans. It was different from his usual plain black t-shirt. Both delicious, but in different ways.

"To the cabin?"

Lukas shot me a wink, ushering the girls inside the house to pack as Duke walked up and placed his hand on my lower back. He pressed a kiss to my temple, holding me steady. "Are you surprised?"

"Yeah," I laughed. "And maybe a little confused, too."

"Hardest surprise of my life to keep. I've wanted to tell you for days."

"Days?" I turned to look at him. "Just how long have you been planning this?"

"In my defense, your brother helped. I was simply the source of information."

Suddenly, our conversation from last weekend came hurtling back. How he'd asked me where I'd like to go if I could. I'd said the cabin because it was the last time I remembered before I was bombarded with obligations and expectations.

I missed the days when the only thing causing me anxiety was a calculus test.

"What would you have done if I said Paris?"

Duke smiled. "Well, we might have had to wait on that one a bit. Can't be gone from the bar for that long. But a weekend is manageable."

My god. Could everyone in my life stop making me so damn emotional? It was too much for a girl to handle. I stared up at him, searching his green depths for comfort. "How?"

Duke pursed his lips. "It's likely your last weekend at home. I wanted it to be a good one."

The reality of our situation was like a lead weight sinking to the pit of my stomach. I could feel it there, the pressure and dread of the next few days nearly making me want to vomit. I didn't want to admit it, but there was a chance this was my last weekend for a long time with the people I loved. Depending on how the reading of John's will went, I could be boarding our jet as early as Tuesday and heading off to handle some godforsaken crisis.

"You didn't have to do all this."

Duke cupped my face, pulling me back into this rare, private moment with him. "Hey, I can't take all the credit. Your brother wanted to throw a party, but that seemed like the last thing you'd want." I snorted, loving the way he knew me so well already. "So I proposed this. Grady and Cleo are coming, too. It's a whole family affair."

"Thank you," I said, leaning into his touch and pressing a kiss to his palm. "I can't tell you what this means to me."

He slid his hands down my body, tugging me into him. "You're worth it, honey."

OLIVIA

"PIZZA OR BURGERS?" Lukas asked, scrolling his phone for the nearest restaurants.

The cabin was about three hours from Pinecrest, tucked in a thicket of trees on the lake. By the time we made it there, it was dark and well past everyone's dinner time.

Charlie and Harper had already reached the hangry stage, and were on their way to full-blown meltdown as we parked our vehicles. We'd had to stop at a gas station after only an hour on the road, just so they wouldn't completely lose their minds before we got to our final destination.

"We should've stopped somewhere on the way," I said, yawning. Grady, Duke, and I sat on the porch while Lukas and Cleo graciously agreed to keep the girls distracted inside. Judging by the overall silence and sporadic giggle we heard, I'd say they were doing a damn good job.

"Well, we didn't," Grady muttered.

"I forgot how bitchy you get if you're not fed every ten minutes," I sighed, running a hand through my hair. "Our daughter sure didn't get that from me."

Grady opened his mouth to argue, but Duke stepped between us. "We'll do pizza. It's easy and fast. I think I saw a place on the way. It's about twenty minutes back into town. I can go." He turned to me. "Unless you wanna come?"

"You're asking if I'd rather sit in a house where everyone is grumpy or enjoy some fresh air with you?" I looked toward Grady, who was now wearing a scowl. "Yeah, I'll be coming with you."

"Just get a variety, please," Grady called as I followed Duke down the steps. "I know you like weird shit."

"That's rich coming from the man who likes pineapple on his pizza!"

"It's good!"

"It's a travesty, Grady, and immediate grounds for divorce."

He chuckled at that. "I wondered why you were so quick to draw up those papers."

Duke climbed into his truck and started the ignition. I slid in beside him, pulling out my phone and searching for a place even remotely close to what he described. Sure enough, on the edge of town, was the only pizzeria within thirty miles.

"This place looks good for a small-town hole-in-the-wall kinda place," I said, skimming the menu. "Oh my god. They have something called Reaper Roulette."

"That sounds terrifying," Duke muttered, typing the address into his GPS.

It was, but that made it so much fun. "Basically, they put this really hot sauce on one single slice of pizza, but you don't know which one. It isn't marked or anything." I turned to Duke. "It could be fun."

"Honey, that sounds like a recipe for disaster."

"Hear me out!" I said, turning to face him. "Grady and Lukas are the only ones who like Hawaiian style. They get to have their pizza, and we get to have a little fun. It's a win-win."

Duke chuckled, reaching over the console to grip my thigh. "You're gonna get us in trouble."

I shifted my hips, drawing his touch closer to where I wanted it. It'd been a long trip without being able to touch him. With Harper and Charlie in the truck with us, we couldn't exactly kiss and hold hands.

But now we were alone…

"Don't you like trouble?" I asked coyly, squeezing my legs together.

"You know I do," he muttered, sparing me a glance.

"Perfect. Then it's settled," I said, turning back to my phone. "Do you have any special requests? Or Harper? I figured I'd get a large cheese and a large pepperoni because everyone will eat that. Cleo keeps it pretty simple."

"Harper and I both like the supreme, but no olives." He said it so casually, yet his hand was still lingering between my thighs, stroking the skin there. Goose bumps traveled along my skin.

"P-Perfect," I stammered.

"What about you?" The tip of his finger was dangerously close to the edge of my cut-off shorts.

"What about me?"

"What do you like?"

I chuckled nervously. "That feels like a loaded question when you're playing with the fringe of my shorts."

Duke lifted one shoulder in a shrug, so casual and cocky. "Just making conversation. You gonna put that order in?" He glanced at my phone. "Might take'em a minute to get everything ready, and I'm trying to avoid pulling up at the house to pitchforks and screaming."

"Right," I breathed, pressing the phone number on the website.

The moment I brought it up to my ear, the unmistakable

sound of a ringing line over his Bluetooth speaker, his fingers slid up higher.

"What're you—"

"Nocturnal Pizza," a bored voice said. "What can I get ya?"

I stopped breathing entirely, too aware of his touch to think. Duke raised his brows, eyes flicking to the phone in my hand as he pushed the fabric aside and caressed my center. "Order," he mouthed.

"Hello?" the young woman asked. "Billy, if this is you, I'm calling your mom. The whole heavy breathing thing is weird."

"S-sorry," I stammered, looking straight ahead. I couldn't stare at him, or else I'd lose track of every semi-coherent thought in my brain. "Must've lost signal. I need to place an order for pick-up."

"Okay... What do you want?"

"C-Can I get a large pepperoni, a large cheese, a medium Hawaiian, and a medium supreme?" I rushed out just as Duke pressed a single finger inside of me. "Shit," I cursed.

"No olives," he whispered. There was no hiding the smirk on his face as I turned to face him. He was thoroughly enjoying himself.

"Oh, and no o-olives," I hurried.

Duke's pace was leisurely. Like fingering me in the truck while I was on the phone with some unassuming cashier was a totally casual thing for someone to do. I tried my best to stifle my low moans as the woman prattled on about extras and dipping sauces, but I lost that battle as Duke added another finger.

"Shit." It came out as more of a low whine, and I threw my hand over my mouth to stop whatever might come out next.

"And do you want to try our Reaper challenge?" she asked. "It's free. You just tell us which pizza you want it on and we'll handle the rest."

I circled my hips as Duke kept his unrelenting pace. Each thrust of his fingers sent me higher, but it wasn't enough to get me there entirely. Now that we'd spent the last week worshipping each other's bodies, I realized that while I loved the feeling of being stretched, I needed the clitoral stimulation to truly push me over the edge.

Which was why Duke seemed keen on touching every part of me, save the one I wanted most.

I whined as he rested the heel of his palm on the outside of my shorts, pressing hard enough for me to know it was there. Every time I got close, he'd take it away.

"Please," I panted, talking to both at the same time.

"You have to tell me which one," the woman deadpanned. "Or I guess I could add it to all of them if you really wanted me—"

"No! Sorry. The Hawaiian, please." The sound of my arousal was steadily filling the cab, no longer muffled by the fabric covering my lower half. Duke pulled my shorts and underwear to the side, exposing me to the cool air as he fucked me relentlessly.

I wasn't sure I'd ever been so turned on in my life. Here we were, messing around like two young kids with their lives ahead of us, not the two-grown ass adults we were. Even when I was younger, I never got to experience that *"can't get enough of you"* kind of excitement.

"'Kay. Be ready in twenty. You'll have to come in and get it. The drive-thru window is broken."

The moment the call clicked off, Duke pulled over on the side of the road. He withdrew his hand as I scrambled to undo my seatbelt. I paused as he brought his fingers to his lips, catching the sight of my arousal in the moonlight. And then he slowly licked them clean of any evidence.

"I swear to god, if you don't fuck me—"

He flipped the console up, and I made quick work of my shorts and underwear. I straddled his legs, feeling the hardness beneath his jeans. My fingers worked quickly to undo his belt and tug down his zipper.

"I can't wait," he growled. "Need to be inside you. Need to make you come. Need to fill you up."

I wanted that, too. Needed it more than anything in my life. His very touch had set my body on fire.

Duke lifted his hips as I tugged down the fabric separating us. Without preamble or pause, I slid onto his cock. He captured my mouth in a fierce kiss as we let out whimpers of mindless need.

"Fuck, honey," he gasped as I rolled my hips. "*Fuck*. Just like that."

There was nothing tender about this moment. No sweet whispers or tender caresses. I'd have bruises tomorrow along my hips where he grabbed me. Yet, somehow, we still felt closer than any two people had a right to be.

Each shared breath, each pathetic whimper, each garbled curse was like a language of our own. Neither of us had to direct the other on what we liked. It was instinct. It was perfect.

"Duke, I'm so close," I panted, digging my fingers into his neck. The cab of the truck was completely fogged up now. While it offered us a semblance of privacy, it was fake. Anyone who drove by would know what we were doing, made only more obvious as I dragged my hand through the condensation and left a desperate mark behind.

His head fell back against the seat, but he kept his eyes on my hips. "Touch yourself, honey. Let me watch you come all over my cock."

Leaning back on the steering wheel, I slid my hand between our sweat-slicked skin. The moment I grazed my clit, I was done for. Everything was too hot, too tight, too much. My fingers moved in short, fast circles as Duke bucked up into me furiously.

My eyes closed as the orgasm took over, crashing over me in waves. He fucked me through every second, not letting up even as I screamed. I allowed my release to pull every ounce of pleasure out of my body until I felt Duke's grip tighten around my waist, bringing me back to the present.

He let out a strangled cry as he came, holding onto me like I was the only thing keeping him on the ground. His cock twitched and pulsed inside me as he drew out our climaxes with slow, punctuated thrusts.

Other than the sound of his truck, the only thing I heard were our gasps for air. I fell back against the steering wheel, my body limp, as the scent of sex hung in the cab. Duke popped open an eye, giving me a lazy smile. "I can't get enough of you."

I let him pull me closer even though we were a sweaty mess of limbs. We didn't even really have time to linger, and yet we did anyway. His lips grazed the top of my head, then my temple and cheeks, before finally landing on my mouth. I melted into it for one second before pulling back.

"We've got to go. We're still at least ten minutes from the store," I complained.

Duke sighed, tapping me on the thigh. "Can you reach into the glovebox? I've got some spare napkins we can use to clean up."

"Or," I said slowly, a sudden idea taking shape. "I could take care of it."

Admittedly, I wasn't really sure what I was doing. It sounded hot, but my experience giving head was limited. Surely there wasn't a wrong way to do it, right? Just avoid the teeth, and it'd be fine.

Before I could talk myself out of it, I slowly lifted myself from Duke's lap. Wetness seeped between us, slipping down my thighs and coating his cock. He held my hair back as I gripped his erection and slowly slid him inside my mouth.

"Fuck, fuck," he hissed. The grip in my hair tightened, making my eyes water, but it was the best kind of pain.

The taste of him was salty. Not entirely unpleasant, but not my favorite flavor. Duke guided me gently, offering sweet whispers of encouragement as I swiped my tongue down his length and cleaned away our releases.

"Stop—*I can't—*"

I lifted my head, staring up at him with a smile. "Something wrong?"

"Too fuckin' sensitive," he gasped, tucking himself away. I stayed put as he collected himself, chuckling at how pained he looked to be doing so. "As much as I enjoyed that, the napkins were for you, honey."

Right. That probably would've been the smartest move. I was sure I was a goddamned mess. "Oops."

I was about to reach for the glove box before Duke opened his door and stormed around the truck. I scrambled to cover myself up as he ripped open my door and stood above me. "Have you lost your mind? What're you doing?"

Duke smiled, tugging me out of the truck and bending me over. I felt him fall to his knees behind me, his breath skittering along my most sensitive parts. "Cleaning up *my* mess."

DUKE

I WATCHED from my spot on the man-made beach as Charlie and Harper held hands and plunged into the cold water below. They'd been at it all afternoon, wearing Grady, Lukas, and me out by seeing how far we could launch them into the lake.

I was, of course, the winner.

The girls had it easy, though. Olivia and Cleo were floating on the water in giant pink and red inner tubes, margaritas in one hand and books in the other. They'd occasionally come ashore to grab a snack or refresh their drink, but somehow we more often ended up swimming out to them with refills.

Grady walked back to Lukas and me with a towel slung over his shoulder and water droplets clinging to his hair. I fished out a fresh beer from the cooler beside me, holding it out as he plopped down in his chair.

"I didn't realize I planned this trip for us to end up at their beck and call," Lukas grumbled. "So far, I've done more running around for other people's drinks than I have for myself."

"You'll understand it one day," Grady said, nodding in thanks for the beverage. He stared at his wife on the water, smiling like a goddamn fool.

Lukas huffed. "I will not."

"It's called Marriage 101. Happy wife, happy life. And I, for one, want the best of both worlds."

"You're so pathetically obsessed," Lukas said, blowing out a breath. "It's disgusting. See, this is why I'm never getting married." He paused, reaching over to try to tap his bottle with mine. "At least Duke agrees with me."

I shook my head, jerking away my drink before he could make contact. "Sure don't. I'd spend the rest of my life bringing your sister those fruity little cocktails she loves so much if she'd let me."

If she'd stay.

While this weekend had been great in so many ways, it was like a false sense of security. We all saw the massive elephant standing in each room we entered, but no one spoke about the meeting with the lawyer on Monday. No one uttered a word about the possibility of Olivia leaving. It was like it didn't exist.

Only it did, and it was damn near all I could think about.

"Scratch that, Grady," Lukas mumbled. "This one's pathetic too."

"I'm not pathetic."

He tilted his head to the side. "Your actions say otherwise."

"Weren't you the one wondering what my intentions were with your sister?" I snapped. "Well, now you fucking know."

My mood had grown worse as the day dragged on. I wasn't going to let the girls see the shift, but I was done pretending around Lukas and Grady. They were just going to have to deal with my sorry ass sulking around as the weekend came to a close.

"What crawled up your ass and died?" Lukas asked.

I knew what my best friend was doing. He wasn't stupid. He was, however, an asshole who would force me to confront my feelings rather than let me dig myself into a hole I'd struggle to climb out of.

I stared straight ahead, watching the sun dip lower in the sky. It nearly kissed the tops of the pines. "I love her."

The words were little more than a whisper, but they felt like a scream. It was exhilarating and terrifying at the same time. When Sarah and I divorced, I swore I'd never let myself end up in this position again. Not just because of Harper's feelings, but my own. The depression I fell into after realizing my marriage had fallen apart had nearly destroyed me. It'd taken a long time, but with help, I managed.

Being with Olivia had changed me. It made me want and wish and dream for a life better than the one I was going through the motions in. I laughed more now than I ever had with my ex-wife. Loved harder, too.

Harper's happiness seemed to improve tenfold. She spoke confidently about things she wanted, and didn't spend her days hiding away in her room when it was just the two of us. We ate most meals together, and she even came over to the bar sometimes to help us get ready for opening.

For the first time in years, the family I always wanted was right within reach.

"Well, no shit, Sherlock," Lukas grumbled.

"Glad you finally pulled your head out of your ass," Grady added. "Do I need to give you the stern ex-husband talk?"

"Why are we talking about my ass so goddamn much?" I asked.

"I already pulled my big brother card," Lukas added. "You're safe."

I glanced between the two, who had shit-eating grins on

their faces. "Alright, then why're you asking me stupid questions then?"

"I didn't ask you if you loved her, I asked what has you in such a pissy mood. I'm not an expert, but I don't think love is supposed to look like that." Lukas gestured toward me. "You look like the old Duke. The one who never smiled and only spoke in grunts."

I ran my hand through my hair, ignoring his jab. "I can't just tell her—"

"Why not?" Grady interrupted. "Worked for me."

"Yeah, well, it's not the same, is it? You and Cleo were a thing before you decided to beg your way to a second chance."

"Third," Grady corrected.

"Whatever." I waved him off. "The point is, I don't have that with Olivia. I may have known her my whole life, but not romantically. It's fucking crazy to ask someone to stay for something that's not even two months old."

"No, it's crazy *not* to if that's how you feel." Lukas leaned forward, bracing his elbows on his knees. "I may not be an expert on love or the fine rules of marriage, but I know if you find something worth holding on to, then you should fucking try."

"Are you just saying all that because it's your sister?"

"I love my sister. I want the best for her, but I want the best for you, too. You're the closest thing I have to a brother—"

"I take offense at that," Grady mumbled.

Lukas paid him no mind. "You deserve everything you've convinced yourself you don't deserve."

Some part of me wanted to agree with him. I'd done so much work in therapy to get to where I was today. I was a proud father. I was a good man with good intentions. I was a business owner who, albeit in a weird way, brought something meaningful to the community.

And I loved a woman with every desperate part of my soul.

But is it enough? Am I enough?

"She deserves more than the life I can give her," I said.

My eyes slid to where she sat in the water, head thrown back in laughter as Charlie and Harper snuck up behind Cleo to push her overboard. They screamed and howled with laughter right before Cleo tugged Olivia in after her. Her arms flailed as she tried to catch herself, but she was slipping beneath the surface, drink and all, in a matter of seconds. When she came back up, all four of the girls began pushing water toward one another. They all sounded so happy.

"More than what? No, I'm serious. What more do you think she needs?" Grady asked. "You *know* her, Duke. You know that she pretends to be all diamonds and class when in reality she hates the front she is forced to put on.

Liv's my best friend. When we got divorced, I was worried about her. That woman works too damn much and looks for any excuse not to sit still in one place for long, and hardly takes care of herself. But now?" He shook his head. "I've never seen that woman as happy as I have with you—despite the shit circumstances that led her here."

"I can't give her the life she's used to. I own a small town bar, not a multi-billion-dollar company. What can I offer her that she can't get on her own?"

"Jesus, man. You think that's what she wants?" Lukas questioned. "She doesn't give a shit about any of that. She plays the part because there are sharks in the water watching and waiting for her to make any mistake so they can swoop in and destroy her."

Grady pointed his bottle toward Lukas. "Exactly. And you said it yourself. Olivia Hart can get anything she wants, but what she wants is *you*. If she was looking for a man to hang off her arm, don't you think she would've found that already?"

"I guess I hadn't thought of that."

"Y'all are both such idiots," Lukas muttered. "You said it best yourself. There's nothing you can specifically offer, financially, that she couldn't handle on her own. If she wants a trip to Paris, then guess what? She'll fire up the jet and be on her way. But you showed her something she can't give herself."

"What's that?" I huffed.

Grady's face softened. "A partner she can rely on. Someone who sees her for who she is, not the face behind the company. You may not see it, but we do. She doesn't shy away from you."

A commotion drew our attention to the girls. Charlie and Harper were racing toward the shore as Cleo and Olivia took their time bringing back their tubes. It was getting dark, and I was sure we were about to be asked by two very inquisitive children if the bonfire was ready.

Harper came up first, colliding into me so hard that my chair nearly toppled over. Charlie followed suit with Grady.

"Daddy, is it time for s'mores yet?" Charlie asked, looking up at Grady through thick lashes.

I may have been wrapped around Harper's finger, but Charlie had her father completely under her spell. I was sure that if she asked him to do a dance on live television in a hot pink ballgown, he would've called his fancy agent to make it happen.

"Your dads were too busy yapping to light the fire, but your uncle Luke will take care of everything," Lukas said, pushing to his feet. They cheered and danced as we grabbed their towels and quickly wrapped them up.

"I take it you agreed to s'mores?" Cleo said, walking up and planting a kiss on Grady's cheek.

"Sure did. Thankfully, Uncle Luke is going to get everything started," he said, returning the gesture as Charlie fake vomited.

"Y'all are gross."

Olivia stopped beside me, collapsing into Lukas's vacated seat. She had this adorably dazed smile on her face. The kind you get from being tipsy on the water all day. Her olive skin was glowing, sun-kissed and radiant.

"Did you have fun?" I asked, pulling Harper into my lap.

Olivia bit her lip and nodded. "I think I needed this more than I realized."

"Good. I'm glad we could give it to you."

Without thinking, I reached out and squeezed her thigh. It wasn't like everyone around us hadn't seen the longing glances we'd given one another, but this was the first time we did so in a way that felt free. It couldn't be excused as my offering comfort in a moment of grief, nor was it the casual touch of a part-time lover.

It took me only a moment to realize Lukas was lingering out of direct sight, watching the four of us with our kids. He was too far away for me to get a read on him, but I swore I saw something like longing there, which was strange.

Lukas had always been adamant about never getting married. He wanted to live his life freely and was content being the fun uncle, but I wondered if that was really true. I wondered if losing John and seeing Olivia's struggle to balance her career and her heart weren't weighing on him in more ways than one.

"Did Luke go to the house?" Olivia asked, turning to find her brother. She spotted him as he slipped inside the cabin and frowned. "Is something wrong?"

"I think he's having trust issues with anyone else handling the food. He hasn't forgiven us for the reaper slice last night." She grimaced. "But he'll be back. Oh, and we still need to remake our picture from when we were kids."

Olivia laughed. "We were eighteen and twenty-three."

"Like I said," I deadpanned. "Kids."

She looked toward the lake and pushed to her feet. "Oh, well. Guess we'd better head inside then—"

"Oh, no, you don't," I said, snatching her around the waist. I tossed her over my shoulder, playfully smacking her ass as I turned away from the kids. Cleo and Grady cheered as I jogged with her to the dock.

Lukas appeared on the porch a second later, a bag of marshmallows in one hand and a box of graham crackers in the other. "Wait for me!"

"There's no way I'm going to let you toss me in the water, Duke Bennett!" she cried, kicking her legs wildly. "I refuse!"

"Come on, honey. I know you're already wet for me." She guffawed at my joke, pounding my back with her fists.

Lukas was out of breath as he skidded to a stop in front of us. He called for Grady to grab his camera. "It's tradition!"

"I don't think doing something one time is considered a tradition," Olivia interjected. I kept her in place over my shoulder, knowing with certainty that she'd run off if I let her.

Lukas peeked at his sister. "Well, this makes it two times, so…"

"Kind of feels like we're making a tradition," I agreed.

"You guys are the worst."

As Grady came running up with the girls in tow, I helped set Olivia down on the dock. The moment her bare feet hit the sun-warmed wood, Lukas and I grabbed an arm and a leg, swinging her back and forth over the water.

"I'm so going to kill you for this," Olivia squealed as we tossed her into the water.

As she surfaced, I pushed Lukas in next, and then followed suit. Before long, all six of us were wading around, sending waves of water speeding toward each other.

Olivia tried to sneak toward the shore, but I grabbed around her middle and yanked her back to my body. "Where do you think you're going?" I whispered in her ear.

"Away from you," she said, kicking her legs in the water. "You don't fight fair."

"When it comes to you?" I pressed a kiss softly along her neck. "Never."

OLIVIA

THE ORANGE GLOW of the fire danced along my skin as I watched Harper struggle to put the sticky marshmallow on the skewer. "It's so sticky," she complained, staring at her fingers. "Why is it so sticky?"

"It's basically all sugar," I laughed. "Here. Let me help."

She quickly shoved them into my waiting hand before plopping on the ground in front of me. The flames really brought out the red in her hair. It seemed much more vibrant after being in the sun all day. After we went swimming, I carefully combed and detangled it, then braided it to keep it out of her face. Duke had offered, but Harper insisted I do it, which made me feel warm all over.

Grabbing a new marshmallow, I placed it on the skewer and handed it back to Harper. "Good as new. Now, gently place it in the fire."

She thrust the entire thing into the flames, engulfing the pillowy confection. I laughed and pulled it back until it hovered over the heat. "Not quite. Like this. See how it's slowly turning golden?"

"Why does my dad keep burning them?" Harper asked. I followed her gaze to where Duke was currently sandwiching something charred between his graham crackers. When he realized we were staring, he paused, sticking his thumb in his mouth to clean it off.

The move shouldn't have had heat licking at my skin, but it did. At least I could blame my flush on the fire.

"Well, there's no accounting for taste," I murmured, pulling back the stick. It didn't take long at all until I had the white, sticky goo all over my fingers as well. "I don't think you'd like it like that. Try this one first and let me know."

Harper took it with a smile, heading over to where Charlie sat with her uncle. Both their cheeks were puffy and swollen as they yelled, "chubby bunny," at one another in between stuffing their mouths with more marshmallows.

I looked at Grady. "That's going to be your sugar crash to mitigate later."

"Why?"

"Because you started that battle in the first place."

His lips twitched. "Just because I bet Lukas he couldn't fit ten full-size marshmallows in his mouth doesn't mean I'm to blame for our daughter's involvement."

"You know damn well he influences her," I hissed. "Besides… I may have plans tonight."

"Ding, ding, ding. There it is," Grady said. "Off on a midnight rendezvous with a certain mustached bar owner?"

Across the fire, Duke pushed off his log. "Something like that."

Cleo sat beside her husband, wrapping her arm around his. "We'd be happy to. The girls mentioned wanting to stargaze tonight, anyway. I'm sure we could keep them occupied chasing constellations for a while."

I wasn't sure how I got so lucky with her. Honestly, Grady's just lucky he proposed first; otherwise, I might have claimed her. She gave me a wink just as Duke stepped up beside me.

I glanced up, noticing the nervous shift of his weight from one foot to the other. "Have you come to pour me a drink, bartender?" I asked, shaking the fancy red solo cup in his direction.

"Was actually wondering if you might take a walk with me?" He slipped his hands into his pockets. "It's a really beautiful night." His gaze heated, warming me from the inside. "I think I should spend it with beautiful company."

"Get a room," Grady murmured before Cleo slapped her hand over his mouth.

I stood from the log, dusting myself off. "A walk sounds great. The company here, save for Cleo, is certainly lacking."

Duke helped me stand and led the way from the fire toward the lake. The dock was just out of sight from the fire pit behind the house, so we wouldn't have to worry about prying eyes. Neither of us spoke as we walked. With my hand in his, I felt comfort in the quiet.

The waves quietly lapped against the wood as we took our seats. Duke made quick work of my sandals before slipping his off. We dangled our feet above the water, letting the crickets' songs lull us into a false sense of security.

"I don't know if I ever properly thanked you for all this," I whispered, tilting my head back to stare at the moon. "It's been perfect."

Duke opened his arms, and I slid over, letting his warmth envelop me. "There's not much I wouldn't do for you. I hope you know that."

"I do."

I knew that more than anything, yet all it did was fill me with dread.

The thought of walking away from Duke and Harper after

everything was inconceivable. I found myself more attached, more drawn to them than ever before. It felt good to have them around Charlie and me. We felt whole.

"Sarah and I met in college and dated throughout. We got married shortly after graduation. I went to work at the mechanic's shop. She was a teacher. And then she got pregnant, and we had Harper." I glanced up, noting the faraway look in Duke's eye. "It was simple between us until it wasn't."

I snuggled closer, held him tighter as I asked, "When did you know that it wasn't going to last?"

"You know, I've been trying to figure that out. I felt blindsided at first. There was no suggestion to attend couples counseling, no knock-down, drag-out fight, or begging not to leave. I came home after work one day and saw her suitcases piled by the door. I asked her why, and she told me that she wasn't happy. That she was sick of putting on a smile and pretending everything was okay when it wasn't." He shrugged. "That was it. The craziest part was how she didn't even tell Harper. She left that to me, and when Harper asked me why her mom would leave us, leave her, I didn't know what to say. Nothing Sarah told me would bring Harper comfort. And when our daughter tried calling, it went to voicemail every time."

"Oh, Duke."

He squeezed my hand, but didn't look at me. It was breaking my heart. "I'm sure it was glaringly obvious how bad a spot I was in when you first saw me. I'd been in survival mode for two years, going through the motions just to get me to the next day. My depression was eating me alive. I drove to John's house after Harper and I moved into that shitty little cabin. I remember falling to my knees and confessing my darkest secret. That I wasn't sure I could live this life anymore. I was in more debt than I could possibly pay off. Harper would barely speak to me. My mom had just had her stroke, and there wasn't a damn thing I could do to get her the help she needed." His voice broke as he uttered, "I was drowning."

From the little Duke had spoken about his divorce and his mental health, I'd guessed as much. But hearing it out loud from his lips was another thing entirely. Now that I knew Duke, the *real* Duke, I couldn't imagine a world without him in it.

"John made sure I got the help I needed. He made sure I was back on my feet and seeing a therapist regularly. He forced Harper and me to come over for dinner at least twice a week. Lukas, too."

I couldn't stop a tear from falling. "I'm glad you had that support."

"So am I." Duke pressed a kiss to my head. "And then you swept in, dumped a gallon of milk on me, and woke me up. Despite John's passing, despite the storm cloud hanging over our heads, these moments with you have given me purpose again. I want to *live*, not just exist. I want to love and be loved back."

I wanted that, too. God. And I wanted it with him most of all.

"I'm not good with my words, honey. You should know that by now. I'm better at proving how I feel with my actions, but," he glanced down at me, running a finger along my jaw, "I want you to know that I love you, Olivia Hart, with everything that I have. Every last, broken piece of me. You've brought color to my life again. To Harper's life, too. And I don't want to lose you."

I closed my eyes as I let his words, his declaration, wash over me. It was everything I wanted and everything I didn't deserve. Duke deserved better than me. He deserved someone who could give him everything. A person who wouldn't need to make concessions to spend time together or be gone for weeks on end.

"Say something," he whispered, and it made me want to die. "Please? I just—*fuck*—I shouldn't have said anything."

"Duke, I—" I stopped, pulling back. I could say the thing I longed to say most, but wouldn't that be worse? Like pouring salt in a fresh wound. I loved him, but I couldn't be with him. I couldn't stay. "You know I can't—that I don't know—"

Gently, he untangled his arm and stood, quietly slipping on his shoes as I sat there, still dangling my feet in the water. I looked up in time to see him swipe a tear from his cheek as he stared out over the lake.

"Thank you for the walk," he said, clearing his throat. "It's been a long day. Too much sun. I think I'm going to get some sleep."

Duke didn't say anything else as he turned and headed for the house, and I said nothing to stop him. I was left sitting in silence, too dumbfounded and stunned to speak.

While I was heartbroken and devastated for the truth of our reality, I also found myself growing angrier at the way we'd both handled things. How many times had we spoken about what we could or couldn't do? How many times had I mentioned I couldn't stay? That I had a duty to my family's legacy before I had a duty to my heart?

We might not have explicitly said we shouldn't go falling in love with one another, but I thought it was implied. From the very beginning, we acknowledged the fact that starting anything between us would only end in heartbreak.

Before I could stop myself, I was angrily pushing to my feet, shoes be damned, and storming into the house after him. I could hear our family outside, laughing and joking and having a wonderful time, while Duke and I were fighting for our lives.

By the time I made it up to my room, I saw Duke standing near the window, staring down at the scene below. His back was straight, muscles coiled with tension. He ran a hand through his hair and sighed. "Olivia, I can't—"

"You could've stopped it too, you know," I said, stepping into the room. I closed the door behind us, hoping it would muffle the noise of our argument. "I didn't ask you to fall in love with me. And I didn't—Duke, I *tried* to tell you I couldn't stay. I tried to tell you time and again, but you wouldn't listen. And now look at us! We're both in fucking agony."

He didn't turn around, didn't even spare me a glance. "You're right. I knew better than to hope you could love me, too. I thought..." he trailed off, shaking his head. "I don't know what I thought, Olivia. That I could change your mind, maybe? That I was worth staying for—"

"You are!" I said, storming over to the bed. It was taking all I had not to come any closer. "You're worth that and more. You deserve someone who will put you and Harper first. I can't be that woman right now. If John were still alive, then maybe we would've had a chance. I could've spoken to him, figured out another solution, but he's gone and I can't."

"Why do you want to run this company, Olivia? I mean, truly. What do you get out of it? Because it sure as fuck doesn't seem like enjoyment."

"It's my family's company. It was passed to me in a trust set specifically by my father. He wanted me to run it someday, and that's exactly what I'm doing."

"It won't bring him back, you know," he said solemnly.

His words were like a slap. "What did you just say to me?"

"Working this job, it won't bring your father back." This time, he turned to face me. His expression was nearly unreadable. "It won't bring John back either. It doesn't matter what they want because at the end of the day, they lived their lives the best they could, but you're ruining yours by trying to make everyone else happy. Why can't you see that?"

"How dare you—"

"How many times have you told me how unhappy you are?" He turned on me, encroaching on my space until I stumbled into the bed. "How you wish things could be different? That you didn't have to go?" When I didn't answer, he raised his voice, "How many times, Olivia?"

I tried to think back, but couldn't. Everything was blurring together until I couldn't pick apart what was real and what was in my head. Or maybe it was the tears that'd finally started to fall? "I don't know—"

"Three times I asked you to stay. Three times I tried to convince you this was worth fighting for. And not just for me, either, but for your family out there who love you just as much as I do. And each time you said no. You told me you had to do what was right, even if it made you fucking miserable."

I was rapidly losing control of my body. I couldn't breathe through the pain anymore, so I let it consume me until I was numb. Until I could barely register the simmering rage behind his gaze. It wasn't even aimed at me. Rationally, I knew that. And I knew we'd both look back on this argument with regret, but we were too far gone to pull ourselves back now.

"It was—We were—"

"Don't you *dare* call what happened between us a mistake." His voice broke, bright, beautiful green eyes lined with silver as he stared down at me. "I can handle a lot, but I cannot fucking handle that."

"I wasn't—I couldn't ever say that, Duke," I murmured, stepping forward. I reached for his hand and brought it to my lips, pressing a gentle kiss along the rough surface. "Our time together means more to me than anything."

"Then I'll ask again." Duke's eyes were locked on mine, trapping me. I couldn't move. Couldn't think. Couldn't breathe. "*Stay.*"

"Duke, I—"

"I haven't asked for much, Olivia. In fact, I make a habit of not asking anyone for anything. I'd rather punish myself than inconvenience someone else, but I'm fucking asking for this now." Before I could speak, he plowed forward. "Scratch that. I won't even ask you to stay. Just don't say goodbye. Don't say this is the end. We can figure something out."

"Are you telling me you'd be okay with long distance? Because somehow, I don't think that'd suit you very well."

He knew it just as much as I did. Duke was an all-or-nothing man. He didn't do anything half-assed, and when he loved, he loved with everything he had.

"Do I want to do it forever? Fuck no. But would I do it for a while if it meant you were still mine? In a heartbeat."

All of that sounded great. Fantastic, even. But neither of us knew how long I'd have to be gone, especially if whatever was included in his succession plan forced me to board a plane without looking back.

Duke braced himself upright against the dresser. When I said nothing, he sobered. "It doesn't matter, does it? It doesn't matter what I say or if I get down on my knees and beg." He ran a hand through his hair. "You've made up your mind, and that's it."

I'd never hated myself more than I did in that moment. Seeing him break was more than I could stand, and yet I forced myself to watch as the first tear fell down his cheek.

I did this.

I broke a good man's heart because I was too goddamn scared to break a promise to a dead one.

This was why I didn't let anyone see the real me, because it was all a lie. The real Olivia was a scared little girl who'd never found her voice. And she was about to let one of the best things that'd ever happened to her walk out the door because she couldn't speak up.

Just tell him you love him, Olivia. Tell him to wait. Tell him that time and distance and whatever other bullshit doesn't matter. Tell him he's yours and you're his.

But I didn't. And I couldn't.

"I'm gonna sleep down the hall tonight," Duke said, crossing the room to grab his packed duffel bag.

"No, *please...*" I said, dropping off the bed to my knees. I reached for his feet, but he stepped away. My panic rose until it was nearly suffocating. "We could have one more night. We could—"

"Olivia," he said, shaking his head. "I can't lie next to you in that bed and pretend anymore. It's fucking killing me. This," he waved his hand in the air, "is fucking killing me. I've been the second option before. While I want to believe we'd find a way to work it out, I just don't know that I believe you'd ever step away. I can't—I won't—let myself hope for a scrap of your time and attention if it isn't headed for forever."

I watched him trudge to the door. He opened it, letting his hand rest there for a moment. "I hope you find something or someone that brings you enough joy to want to stay one day." He patted the frame. "I just wish it'd been me."

Everything stopped as I slid to the floor. The world stood still as I stared at the place Duke Bennett had just been.

I didn't hear the sound of his footsteps down the hall, nor the sound of my family creeping up the stairs.

I didn't see Cleo open the door.

I didn't feel her arms around me as she helped me into bed and held me as I cried.

DUKE

ROLLING OVER, I blinked at the harsh light streaming in from the window overlooking the lake. I hadn't slept for shit, spending most of my night pacing a hole in the floor outside Olivia's room to keep myself from going in. It'd been hard enough to walk away. To force myself to leave her sobbing on the bedroom floor and close the door behind me.

I didn't remember how I got outside, but when Cleo saw me sitting by myself on the porch steps with my head in my hands, she immediately went to check on Olivia.

At least she wouldn't be alone.

It'd taken every ounce of self-control I had not to immediately barge back in, pick her up, and tell her how sorry I was for the mess I made. After all, she'd told me time and again that she never intended to stay in Pinecrest, but I hadn't listened. Or maybe I was just delusional enough to think I could change her mind.

I should've known better than that.

What we had together had been too good not to pursue. Even if I could go back in time and tell myself then what I knew

307

now, it wouldn't change anything. I'd still take that shot with her, knowing how badly it'd burn in the end.

I did, however, regret using John's words as ammunition in my anger. Saying that her choice to remain in a career she hated wouldn't bring back two of the most important people in her life was a low fucking blow. The words had tumbled out before I could stop them. I hated myself for it.

I sat up, scrubbing my hands over my face. I had no idea what was waiting for me outside these walls. How was I supposed to act like Olivia and I weren't in the worst sort of pain imaginable? The wound was too fresh.

When Sarah left, she hadn't lingered. She just packed up her shit and drove off into the sunset, but I still had to linger in Olivia's presence until I was safely home in my cabin. Even that wasn't free of her presence. I'd still get whiffs of her sweet perfume as I slept. Or picture her spread out on my bar when I went to work.

Now, I'd have to live with those memories haunting me forever, and mourn them when they finally faded.

There was a soft knock on my door and Harper stuck her head in. The Dutch braids Olivia had done the night before were somewhat intact, albeit much frizzier after she'd slept in them.

"Dad? Are you up yet?" she called softly, creeping into the room. "It's, like, nearly time for breakfast."

With a sigh, I sat up in bed and patted the spot beside me. "Come here. Let me fix your braids. That one's about to fall out."

"But Miss Olivia did these. I want to keep them." She touched her hair.

Knife, meet heart.

"I won't mess them up. I promise. Let me just tighten them a bit, okay?"

Harper nodded and sat down in front of me. I didn't have a brush, but thankfully, my daughter wasn't tender-headed. I made quick work of clearing any small tangles before following the same Dutch pattern Olivia had used before.

"Did you have a good weekend?" I asked.

"This was a lot of fun, Dad. I didn't realize s'mores were so good."

I chuckled. "Yeah, it's been a while since we did any camping, huh?"

The thought was sobering. When was the last time I did anything fun like this with my daughter? Something outside of our normal day-to-day routine? Since Sarah left, I'd been so preoccupied with running the bar and making sure we could pay our bills that a getaway of any kind was out of the picture.

Until Olivia swept in and disrupted our complacency with her coordinated chaos.

"I'm sorry about that, Harper. No matter what was going on in my life, I should've made sure you were my priority."

"S'okay," she mumbled, chewing on her nails. "I'm, um, really glad you have Miss Olivia to help you. I like hanging out with her."

"Yeah," I said, securing the hair tie. *I do, too.* "It's been nice, huh?"

She nodded. "You haven't been as grumpy."

"Grumpy, huh?" I asked, gently pinching her arm.

"Yeah, you never smiled or anything. But you do now."

With a sigh, I pulled Harper into my chest and let my chin rest on top of her head. "It's been a tough few years, Harp, but you shouldn't have had to know I was struggling to keep it all together. I'm sorry for not being more present." I pressed a kiss to her temple. "Things are going to change around here. I don't want to go back to how things were before, do you?"

"Not really."

"Then let's make a promise. At least once a month, you and I are going to do something together. We'll take the whole day and—*I don't know*—take a hike or something."

Harper scrunched up her nose. "I don't know that I want to hike, Dad."

"Honestly, neither do I. I don't know why I said that," I confessed quickly. "But we'll do something actually fun, okay?"

"And maybe we could invite Charlie and Miss Olivia. I bet they'd love to come, too."

I sat there, not knowing entirely what to say. While I didn't want to set Harper up for disappointment, I sure as hell wasn't about to tell her that wouldn't be an option.

"I'm sure if they're available, they'd love to come." Wasn't that the worst part? Knowing without a doubt that if Olivia were in town and Harper asked her to come over, she would without question. No matter how uncomfortable it might be between us, she'd put the girls first.

Harper hopped down and ran her hand over her braid, making sure I hadn't messed anything up. When she was satis-fied, she gave me an approving nod before heading toward the door. "Come on, Dad. I'm starving, and Uncle Luke promised everyone donuts this morning."

I snorted. There was no way in hell Lukas had gotten up and driven into town for donuts. "Well, you'd better make sure he's awake. If not, he'll sleep in, and then you'll have to wait until tomorrow morning for some."

My daughter turned on her heel and ran from the door. I heard her feet thud against the hallway only a moment before the knocking began. "Uncle Luke? Are you up?"

A second later, another voice joined the fray. One that wasn't nearly as understanding as Harper's. "Uncle Luke! You promised us donuts!" Charlie shouted. Her fist banged rapidly on the door until I heard Lukas's muffled, "Oh my god, I'm up!"

I shook my head and walked into the bathroom to brush my teeth and change clothes. There wasn't much I could do about my appearance. My face showed every bit of the exhaustion I felt.

After doing a quick sweep of the room, I grabbed my duffel and headed down the stairs. Voices carried in from the kitchen, but I slipped out the back unnoticed. I wasn't quite ready to face the music yet.

I opened the back door of my truck to toss my duffel inside, but was immediately halted by the sweet, honeyed scent of Olivia's perfume. It lingered better than any freshener I'd ever bought, which was a real fucking problem, seeing as that was the last thing I wanted.

Get it the fuck together, Duke.

And then I saw the small travel purse she'd tucked beneath my seat. I'd told her it wasn't a good idea to leave her things behind, but she did it anyway. Completely and totally determined not to listen to me.

Grabbing the back, I closed the door and headed back into the house. I'd just rounded the truck when a hard body collided with mine.

Olivia's hand gripped my forearm to steady herself, digging her nails into my skin as she looked up at me.

"Shit, sorry," she murmured, taking two quick steps back. "Didn't see you there."

"You didn't see me?" I asked slowly.

I was fucking six foot four. How did she not see me?

"Must not have been paying attention." Her gaze dipped to her purse. "Ah, but I was coming out for this. Sorry. I know you said not to leave it in there. Guess if I'd listened, it would've saved us this weird conversation, huh?"

"Probably." I held it out, and she quickly took it from my grasp. Neither of us attempted to move or speak. We just awkwardly existed in each other's company. There was so much I wanted to say, but where the hell was I even supposed to begin?

"Cleo and I'd like to take the girls in her car, if that's okay. Figured you boys could ride together in your truck," Olivia said, breaking the silence. "Might make it less awkward and all."

"If that's what you want," Olivia muttered something beneath her breath, but I didn't catch it. "Sorry. What was that?"

"Nothing." She blew out a breath, forcing a smile. "That is what I want. We can trade off when we get to Lukas's house."

"You make it sound like we're getting a divorce. Trading off the kids like that."

"Yes, well, that would be silly, wouldn't it? Seeing as we were never even really together."

Olivia wouldn't meet my eyes. Hell, I couldn't even blame her. I scratched the back of my head. "That's not what I meant. The divorce thing—it was just a bad joke."

"It's fine, Duke. It's for the best. I mean, it's not like we'll ever be rid of one another, so we might as well get used to it."

I didn't want to get used to it, though. "It sounds terrible," I admitted. "Feels pretty shitty, too."

Her smile faltered. "Yeah, it does."

There was so much I wanted to say. Yet I couldn't. The words wouldn't come. They were struck, lodged in my throat like bitter bile. It would only make things worse between us, and that was the last thing I wanted.

Olivia held up her purse. "Thanks for this."

I dipped my chin. "You're welcome."

When she left, she took what was left of my barely beating heart with her.

OLIVIA

THERE WAS a paint chip on the wall directly behind what used to be my uncle's desk. I'd never noticed it before. Why would I, when I'd spent more time sorting files in this room than appreciating the years of wear and tear?

What else had I not noticed?

The walls were lined with photos from his years of travel. There was one of us on my first trip to Paris. John had taken me there not long after my father died because he thought it'd take my mind off the horrors back home, but it hadn't worked. All I could think about as I meandered down miles of museum hallways was how Dad would've loved it, which only made me miss him more.

And then there was the same picture that sat on my nightstand. One of Duke, Lukas, and me on the same dock I'd stood on only yesterday.

I quickly looked away, unable to stomach their smiling faces.

My conversation with Duke had played on a loop through my mind over the past thirty-six hours. The false sense of safety on the dock, the itch of desperation as I watched him walk into the house without me, and then the crash that set everything on fire.

It's for the best, I tried to convince myself, but the lie was hollow. Not even the most pessimistic part of me believed it.

I heard voices coming from down the hall, and straightened in my seat. Lukas and a woman I didn't recognize came striding in moments later. My brother took the seat beside me, the leather creaking as he shifted his weight.

Despite having ridden over to John's house together, we hadn't spoken much all morning. He tried, but after a handful of attempts crashed and burned, he realized I was a lost cause. I hadn't talked to anyone outside of Charlie, who, unfortunately for me, kept talking about the two of us going on monthly dates with Duke and Harper.

The woman took a seat behind the desk. She pulled out a small tablet and positioned it toward us. The next moment, a familiar face appeared on the screen.

"Mr. Hart, Ms. Hart. Though I wish it were under better circumstances, I am delighted to meet you. John was an extraordinary man who lived an extraordinary life," she said.

I dipped my chin. "Thank you. I'm sorry, but I didn't catch your name."

"Forgive me." The woman held her hand out. "I'm Allison Reid. I had the pleasure of working with your uncle regarding his estate. And Mr. Carl Johnson," she gestured toward the tablet, "is here at his request."

Carl handled commercial and entertainment law for Hart-strings. Having him here didn't make any sense. As though reading my mind, the lawyer chuckled over the line. "I'm not sure why I'm here, either. Mr. Hart didn't leave me any instructions."

"Hopefully there's some in there," Lukas said, gesturing toward Allison's suitcase lying on the desk.

"Of course." Allison smiled and pulled out a large manila folder from inside.

Final Wishes and Directives of John Hart was written in neat cursive at the top. She flipped it over, swiping a sharp nail beneath the seal. Inside was a leatherbound binder and two envelopes.

"Those are for us?" I asked, clearing my throat of the emotions threatening to surface.

The jagged scrawl across the top of the envelopes was one I instantly recognized. I'd stared at thousands of handwritten notes from my uncle over the years. He'd leave them throughout my office for me to stumble upon randomly.

Allison nodded. "They are. I have no idea of the contents. They were added to our files after Mr. Hart's passing. We received them in the mail, with instructions to ensure they were given to you directly. Additionally, I can confirm that a third letter was mailed to a family member whom Mr. Hart asked not to be present."

Lukas and I shared a knowing look. We'd both wondered whether our mother would be in attendance. Neither of us had been surprised when we pulled up to find the house empty.

I suppose it made me feel slightly less bitter knowing she was asked to stay away, and not that she couldn't be bothered to show up.

Allison slid the letters across the table for us to take. My thumb traced the slight indentations in the paper as a wave of grief washed over me. I'd done such a good job since his death, pushing everything down, down, down until I nearly had myself convinced it wasn't real.

But I couldn't do that anymore. Sitting in a room with two

lawyers and an envelope marked with his shaky scrawl made it irrefutable. John was gone, and we were still here. Forced to go about our day-to-day lives as though we hadn't lost the one constant we had in a world of variables.

I'd been so angry at myself for not being there when he died. I knew he hadn't been feeling well, and yet I left him as though the man had all the time left in the world. There wasn't a chance to have a deathbed confessional for all the things that went unsaid. There wasn't even a goodbye.

But these letters gave me hope for guidance. Or at the very least, closure.

"I should mention that a will reading like this isn't a normal procedure. The movies make my job seem much more suspenseful than it really is," Allison said. "But as this was a specific request made by Mr. Hart, my firm decided to honor it. We will discuss the will first before moving on to your letters."

She opened the binder, flipping to the first page, and began reading. "I, John Hart, being of sound mind and body, declare this to be my last will and testament, hereby revoking all wills made by me. I appoint Olivia Hart as the Executor of this will. Should she be unable in any capacity, I appoint Lukas Hart as the Successor Executor."

We both nodded. That wasn't a surprise to either of us. John had made it clear early on that I would be the one handling his estate. It was why I spent the majority of my time in this office, sorting through more paperwork than I'd ever seen in my life. John had saved damn near every scrap of paper that ever crossed his desk.

"In regard to my monetary assets, stocks, and bonds, forty percent each will be gifted to Olivia Hart and Lukas Hart, while twenty percent will be gifted to Susan Hart, with the condition that she successfully completes a regimented recovery program."

"I hadn't expected that," Lukas said.

I shrugged. "I assumed she was going to get some kind of stipend. I'm sure Dad's was set to dry up at some point."

"In regard to my home and the possessions within, Olivia Hart will be the sole beneficiary. She is welcome to make any changes she desires. However, should she wish to sell the property, the Hart Family Trust must be given first right of refusal."

Now that was a surprise. I never thought about who might inherit the property, but for whatever reason, I hadn't believed it would be me. Lukas seemed the likely benefactor. He lived in Pinecrest after all.

I did not.

But maybe it wouldn't be terrible having my own place to stay when I came home. At least I wouldn't have to crash in Lukas's guest house anymore. And Charlie could have a sense of stability. She could pick any room she wanted and decorate it however she saw fit.

There was a little flutter of excitement before I remembered any stay here would be short-lived. It wasn't permanent.

But it could be.

"And finally, in regard to the majority shares I hold of Hart-strings Records," Allison paused, glancing up at us before continuing. "I hereby gift them in their entirety to Olivia Hart. She is free to do with them as she sees fit. If shares are sold, she is entitled to ten percent of the proceeds, while the remainder is to be deposited back into the trust."

Even though I'd been expecting the news, all the air left my lungs as Allison finished speaking. I waited in tense silence, hoping to hear the caveats I craved, that there were stipulations and red tape and a million other stipulations that'd free me, but she simply sat back in her chair.

"What about my job?" I asked. Carl's presence here suddenly

made sense. "Can I be CEO and majority shareholder at the same time, the way our company agreement is designed?"

He tapped his fingers against his desk. "It's not entirely uncommon, especially for some smaller companies. I don't believe it's against any of our clauses, though I'd need to verify."

"And what are my options if it is?"

"Well, to be frank, you would have a decision to make—to keep your role as CEO of Hartstrings Records, or become the majority shareholder. From there, depending on your answer, we'd begin the transition."

He said it so casually, as though it were really that easy. But how the hell were we going to do that when I didn't even know what they were? All of this was too much. I didn't have the capacity to make any more decisions right now. Especially not when the last one I made was still haunting me.

"How long will it take you to look up the specifics?"

Carl chuckled. "I'm pulling up the documents as we speak. Would you be available tomorrow morning? As you may know, the other shareholders are dying to dig their claws further into the business. The sooner we figure out the company's path, the sooner we can get them off our backs."

Tomorrow. It was too soon. I didn't want to leave. There were still so many things I wanted to do while I was home, but there was no time left.

Charlie. Lukas. Grady. Cleo. Harper.

Duke.

I'd have to leave everyone behind, going back to living out of hotels and eating takeout, alone, in front of the television. Compared to the past two months, that might as well have been my fucking nightmare.

The chair squeaked as my fingers dug into the armrest. Panic clawed at my throat, threatening to tear me up from the inside. I was vaguely aware of someone saying my name.

"Livvy?" Lukas asked, drawing my gaze toward him. Concern hardened his eyes. "Are you okay?"

"Y-Yeah, sorry." I smiled weakly. "I just started thinking about everything I need to get done before this meeting tomorrow. Are you in the Nashville office, or am I flying out to L.A.?"

Please say Nashville. Please say Nashville.

"L.A., unfortunately." My heart sank. "I'm already rescheduling my day to ensure we have enough time to take care of everything. If you're okay with it, I'd like to start first thing at eight?"

I nodded. If I were going into the office that early, I'd barely have enough time to say goodbye to Charlie before I left. The pit in my stomach grew tenfold.

Carl was quick to depart, eager to get started on his research, leaving the rest of us to sit in silence. Allison slid the binder across the desk toward me. "Here is the will in its entirety. I know it's soon, but we should also schedule a meeting sometime this week to go over your duties as executor."

"I'll have my assistant reach out to schedule a time," I said, shaking her hand as she stood.

Her gaze traveled to the unopened letter I'd set down. "Please don't forget to read that. It's imperative that you do so as soon as possible."

"Why?" I asked. "What's a few more days when we've already been waiting weeks?"

"Mr. Hart was clear in his instructions that you were both meant to read the letters the day you received them." Allison stepped around the desk. "He seemed like a deliberate man. I would assume there's a reason for his urgency."

Lukas escorted Allison down the hall, leaving me alone in the office. I collapsed back into the chair and stared at the letter. If the law office had received it in the mail only a day or two after his death, it meant this was one of the last things he wrote.

Seeing his final thoughts was a privilege, but having them immortalized in writing was even more so.

"Surprised you haven't opened it yet," Lukas asked, leaning against the door. "Curiosity would've gotten the best of me by now."

"Thankfully, you have your own letter to satisfy you," I muttered.

"You're not even a little bit curious?"

"Obviously, I am."

He scratched his neck. "See, Sis, I'm failing to see the hang-up here."

Of course, he didn't understand. I loved my brother, but our priorities had always been different. "Opening that letter feels too real. I know John's dead. I know he is, but seeing his final thoughts on paper makes it tangible. Its closure. It's goodbye." I placed my hand over my heart, voice breaking. "I'm not ready for this to be over."

Lukas came to a crouch in front of me, placing his hands on my knees. "Liv, it doesn't have to be. You don't have to take the meeting tomorrow. Put it off for at least a few days. That'll buy you some time to figure out what the hell you want to do."

"If I don't do it now, my anxiety is only going to get worse. I'm already nauseous. I don't know how much more I can take." I tried to joke, but Lukas didn't look convinced. "I'm fine, Luke."

His gaze softened. "Open the letter."

I put up my finger. "I'd rather do it alone, actually. You don't get to see my tears."

"Open it, Livvy."

I stared at the letter for only a moment before I swiped it off the table and tore it open. There was the faintest whiff of John's aftershave on the paper. I closed my eyes, thinking back to all the times that scent brought me comfort.

It was like he was in this room with us. I could picture him sitting right behind the desk, like he so often was growing up. Or us sitting together in this garden as we watched the sky turn pink at dusk.

I'd give anything for that to be true.

Glancing up at my brother, he gave me a nod. I could do this. I *needed* to do this.

Olivia,

I don't have long to write this letter. You'll be back from town any minute now. I'm glad you have a soft spot for old men who are dying and love chocolate. It works out very well for me, especially when I have a couple of things I need to say.

First, you need to know how proud I am of you. I've never seen anyone work quite as hard as you—including your brother, and he builds houses. (Please don't tell him I said that. I don't need him haunting me in the afterlife.) No matter the challenge, you've risen to every occasion. I'm convinced there isn't a single thing you couldn't do if you put your mind to it.

Which brings us, not so gently, to the next matter.

From the time you were old enough to walk, music was your passion. You begged your parents to train you on all manner of instruments—some of which you excelled at, while others you did not. Do you remember your harmonica phase? Because I still have a headache from those excruciating months. Your father had to bury the damn thing just to get you to move on to something else.

But you never gave up. Music is in your blood. It's a part of who you are. Which is why your father planned to entrust you with the company when you got older. We both know now that the handover came too soon. You were just a child grieving, and yet you were already being groomed to over take the company.

At first, I thought your fierce allegiance to Hartstrings was what we needed. In a way, I was right. Only someone with your level of determination could have taken a successful venture and grown it tenfold. When your grandfather founded this business, I can tell you with certainty that he never dreamed it would be what it is today.

But that has all come at a cost I perpetuated, I fear.

You see, I pride myself on having lived a life without regrets. I never felt the absence of a spouse or children because you and Lukas brought more than enough light to my life. I never dreamed of more money because I inherited more than I could ever spend in a lifetime. I never wanted to slow down in my career because it was a part of who I was. It was my purpose in life.

<u>*Do not let it be yours.*</u>

I've sat back and watched you struggle to balance who you believe you have to be with who you are. Let me tell you now that it doesn't have to be this way. You don't have to choose between being a mother or wife and having a career of value. Nor do you have to continue down a path you no longer recognize for the sake of doing what you believe is right or the only choice.

Olivia, you can have it all.

My one regret in this life is not telling you these words sooner. I helped you pursue a career at the top because I believed it was what you truly wanted, but I worry that was a mistake. We never really talked about it, did we? Before I shoved you in front of that boardroom and paraded you around as the future of the company.

For that, I am terribly sorry. I will never forgive myself for any harm I've caused. Please know it was never done with ill intent. I wish I had more time with you to make it right.

By now, my lawyer has informed you of your inheritance. This was not a decision I made lightly, but I trust that, after reading this letter, you will do what you feel is right. Whatever that may be.

My dear, I wish I could've said these words and so many more in person. I wish we had more time, but time is the one thing we

*cannot manufacture, so I hope these scribbled apologies on a piece
of paper are enough.*

*Live your life, Olivia. Live it boldly and without fear. Live it
for you and no one else, and know that no matter what your decision may be, I will always be endlessly proud of you.*

Your biggest fan,

Uncle John

Droplets splattered against the paper as I looked up, blinking away the torrent of tears running down my face. Lukas stared at me, his eyes so full of concern. "That's not really giving me a lot of hope for my own letter, you know." I chuckled, but immediately delved into a hysterical sob. "Okay. No to the bad jokes," he said, scooting closer. "Got it."

"No, it's fine," I said, wiping my nose on the back of my sleeve. "I don't know why I'm crying."

"Because it's a lot to take in at once. The letter, the company, all of it."

My lip trembled as I murmured, "I don't know what to do, Luke. Everything feels so out of my control right now."

"Livvy, you've never had more control than you do right now. The company is yours to do whatever you want with. You can run it however you like."

But that was the problem. What if I didn't want to run it at all anymore? Sure, I could sell, but then what? The independent label created solely to give smaller artists a voice would be gone. The legacy my father left behind, the one my uncle protected, would be destroyed. The sacrifices I made wouldn't amount to shit.

All the school productions, soccer practices, and ballet recitals I tearfully watched on a small screen while away at work would be for nothing. Unlike John, I looked back on my life and saw a graveyard of poor decisions. It would be easier to name the things I didn't regret at this point.

"I know it terrifies you, but you're the one in control here. Only you can decide how to live your life." Lukas squeezed my hands. "So, what do you want to do?"

Taking a deep breath, I met my brother's gaze. "I need you to do me a favor."

DUKE

I BLEW out a breath and tossed my phone on the dashboard. There was no use in staring at the damn thing. It sure as hell didn't make messages appear out of thin air.

I would know. I'd been doing it all day.

The sky, a perfect reflection of my mood, was cloudy and grey. By this evening, there'd be a massive storm rolling in, which would scare away even my regulars. No one wanted to be caught on those roads in the dead of night while it was pouring rain.

Harper and I would be lucky to make it home before it hits at this point.

When the school bell rang, students poured out of the doors, hurrying to their parents' cars. Harper's auburn hair stood out amongst her classmates. She walked up to my truck, tossing her backpack on the floor before climbing into the backseat and buckling up.

She murmured a hello before turning her head and staring out the window.

"How was school?" I asked, starting the truck. "Did you have a good day?"

Harper shrugged. "It was fine, I guess."

I didn't consider myself an expert on much, especially when it came to my daughter, but I did know a thing or two about women in general. Like when they said something was fine, it was inherently not.

Drumming my fingers on the wheel, I tried again. "It doesn't sound fine. Wanna talk about it?"

She was silent for so long that I assumed the answer was no, but then she surprised me. "Charlie got signed out of school early today. Her Uncle Lukas stopped by to get her."

"She did, huh?" My drumming immediately stopped. "What for?"

Harper's eyes met mine in the rearview mirror. "She said it was probably because her mom was leaving town and she had to go see her before she left." *Fuck, fuck, fuck.* I tightened my grip on the wheel. "Is that true, Dad? Is Miss Olivia leaving?"

"Well, sugar, Miss Olivia has to go back to work for a little bit but she'll be back." *I fucking hope.* "It's only for a little while."

"But I didn't get to say goodbye." My daughter was trying so hard to hold in her emotions, but in the end, they won out. A quiet sniffle escaped, and I realized she was quietly crying. "I'll miss her."

Goddammit. I fucking hated this. Everything was out of my control, and there was nothing I could do about it. How the fuck was I supposed to tell my daughter everything was going to be okay when every alarm bell was ringing in my mind, telling me otherwise?

This scene was so similar to Sarah leaving, except that, instead of being too young to understand, my daughter was, unfortunately, aware of being left in the dark this time.

"Harper, baby, don't cry. I'm gonna miss her, too." I reached back with one hand and squeezed her knee for comfort, but it didn't help. If anything, she seemed to cry harder. I glanced at my phone on the dashboard and grabbed for it. "What if we give her a call? She may already be in the air, but we can leave a voicemail. Would that be okay?"

I was setting us both up for further disappointment. There was no way in hell Olivia was going to answer, especially when she saw my name on her screen, but if it stopped Harper's tears even for a second, I'd try.

My daughter nodded and reached for the phone. She found Olivia's contact and pushed the call button. Loud ringing filled the cab as we both sat in tense silence, waiting to see if she would pick up.

I was about to give up hope when a soft-spoken, "Hello?" reached my ears.

It'd only been a day, and I was already weak in the fucking knees for the sound of her voice. How the hell was I supposed to go days and weeks and months without it?

"Miss Olivia, I just wanted to tell you bye before you left since I didn't get to before."

It was impossible to miss the little catch of her breath at Harper's woeful voice. "Oh, Harper. I'm so sorry I didn't tell you yesterday. It's just that I was hoping I could stay a little while longer."

"But you can't?"

"Not this time," Olivia whispered. "But when I come back, I'll make sure you're the first one I come to visit, okay? I promise."

"And my dad?" Harper chewed on her bottom lip. "He said he's going to miss you, too."

"Y-Yeah," she stammered. "Of course. I'll visit your dad, too. You're a package deal."

She was trying so hard not to let Harper down by carefully picking and choosing her words, but I heard the hesitation. Olivia would keep her word because she had to, but we both knew it wasn't for either of our benefits.

Did it make me pathetic that I didn't care what the reasoning was, so long as I laid eyes on her at all?

"When do you leave? Are you already in the air?"

Olivia chuckled. "Well, I couldn't be talking to you if I were, so no. My brother is taking me to the airport now. We're about ten minutes away."

"Oh." Harper glanced down at her feet. "I was hoping we could see you again before you left."

There was a beat of silence before Olivia cleared her throat. "Not this time, sweet girl. But I promise I'll let you know when I come back, okay? We can plan a sleepover and everything."

Harper nodded. "Okay, I'd like that. Maybe we can dress up like we're going to the Met Gala."

"I'll bring the dresses," she said. There were voices on the other line before she came back. "Harper, I'm going to let you go, okay? We're almost to the plane, and I need to get my things together."

"Will you let me know when you get wherever you're going?"

Olivia hesitated. "I'll text your dad."

Harper looked at me, and I nodded. "I'll let you know the moment it comes in."

"Even if I'm in bed?"

"Even if you're in bed."

"Okay. Be safe, Miss Olivia."

"Bye, Harper." Then Olivia softly whispered, "Bye, Duke."

My daughter ended the call and handed my phone back to me. Even if she looked better than she had when I picked her up, I could still see the dried tear tracks on her cheeks.

"Hey, you want to watch a movie tonight?" I asked.

Harper's brows scrunched together. "Don't you have to work?"

I shrugged. "It's gonna rain. There's no point in being open if no one's going to come in. Especially if it's gonna take me away from my favorite girl. Besides, I think we could both use something to cheer us up."

For too long, I'd been prioritizing Frank's over my relationship with Harper. I was too worried about paying bills and saving money after Sarah left. Every dollar was counted, every penny was pinched. While being able to buy groceries without worrying about overdrawing my account was great, it wasn't everything.

Having Olivia around showed me how much I was missing by hiding myself away at the bar. These were some of the best years of my life, and yet I was just letting them slip by.

Harper's lips twitched. "Can I pick the movie?"

For the first time all day, the knot in my stomach loosened a fraction. "Sure, sugar. You can pick the movie."

DUKE

TWO MONTHS LATER

LUKAS STARED at the help-wanted sign hanging above the cash register. "I'm so proud of you, man. I never thought I'd see the day."

I snorted, grabbed the cleaner, and sprayed down the bartop. "What? That I'd ask for help?"

"Yeah. I thought you were allergic to it or something." He leaned forward. "What if I applied? Would you hire me? I know the owner."

"Fuck no." I shook my head. "You'd drink my entire stock before we opened, and I'd catch you passed out behind the bar or some shit."

"Ye of little faith. I haven't done it yet—"

I raised my brow. "You literally did it the night I got the keys to this place. I found you curled up on one of the tables out there."

Lukas pointed at me. "Don't pretend like you weren't outside of the freezer, shirtless."

Okay, maybe I had been, but that's beside the point.

"But I am proud of you. I know the past few months haven't been easy, so I'm glad to see you prioritizing yourself."

If there was one thing Lukas and I did well, it was avoiding talking outright about his sister. He tried on two different occasions—both of which I quickly shut down—which left him toeing a line he knew he shouldn't cross.

Even though I desperately wanted to talk to someone about her, I couldn't let myself go there. There wasn't much of a point to asking Lukas how she was, because I knew my girl well enough that she wouldn't tell her brother the truth anyway.

So, I was left to wonder.

I hadn't heard from her in nearly two months. The last text I had from her was when she landed and messaged Harper as she promised. Sometimes I found myself staring at our conversation thread. Late at night, when I was too exhausted to pretend I wasn't in any pain, I'd just watch the screen, hoping for three bubbles to pop up that never seemed to appear.

"It's time. Harper's out of school for the summer, and I made promises I intend to keep," I said.

Sawyer and Ryan agreed to work the bar this weekend so Harper and I could go camping. It wasn't a giant cabin on the lake, but my daughter wanted the real-deal experience, complete with a tent, sleeping bags, and a fire pit.

So, that was exactly what we were doing.

Thankfully, there were public restrooms and showers at the campground because I wasn't entirely sure either of us could handle shitting in the woods.

"No, I get it. Like I said, I'm proud of you. Has anyone filled the position yet?"

I shook my head. "Nope, but I'm hoping that someone will come in while I'm gone and apply. People seem to like Sawyer better, anyway."

"Well, duh. She's more personable."

"I've never heard you use that word in your life."

Lukas put his hand over his heart. "I do run a very successful business. I know a thing or two about customer service."

Lukas checked the time on his phone. It was nearly midnight. He'd stayed well past all my regulars, and it was about time to close shop.

"You sure you don't wanna crash on my couch? I've been told I'm a great cuddler."

Lukas scrunched up his face. "By my sister, man. And I don't really wanna think about that."

Fair point. I didn't either.

"Nah, I'm gonna head home. I've got an early job tomorrow. Today was slow."

"Alright, man. I'll see you when Harper and I get back."

"Don't forget to take pictures!" he called over his shoulder as he strolled out of the bar.

Looking around, I took a tally of everything I still needed to get done. Since Lukas had been there to help, or yap long enough to distract me while I mindlessly took care of it, I didn't have much to do. I'd already balanced the register and washed the dishes. All I needed to do now was put away the garnishes and lock up the back.

I grabbed the metal containers and walked into the freezer, marking them with today's date. I'd just finished when I heard the front door open.

"What'd you forget?" I asked as I stepped out of the cold storage. "My tip?"

I rounded the corner, prepared to hit him with an old man joke, when I slid to an abrupt halt. Olivia Hart was standing behind my bar, only twenty feet ahead of me. She had two shot glasses and a bottle of tequila out. "Hi, Duke."

"Olivia? What're you doing here?"

A shy smile curved her lips as she pointed to the door behind her. "I couldn't help but notice the help wanted sign on your door. Is it still available?"

It might've been the old age, but I was struggling to wrap my head around what was going on. "I'm sorry, I don't understand…"

She took a step forward, dusting her hands on her jeans. "Well, it's pretty simple. You have—*presumably*—an available job, and I happen to be in need of employment." She gestured toward the tequila. "Thought maybe I could show you my skills. It seems like we might be able to help each other out."

I laughed nervously. There was no way in fucking hell I was about to get my hopes up about a scenario I wasn't even sure had happened.

Because it sounded a whole hell of a lot like she was saying that she was no longer CEO of Hartstrings Records. And if she was looking for a job here, in Pinecrest, that meant she had plans to stay.

Surely she wouldn't pull a joke so cruel.

"Don't you have some fancy pants job already?" I asked, crossing my arms and widening my stance.

Olivia gestured toward the bar. "Wanna take a seat?"

I strolled over and pulled myself cautiously onto a stool. She looked good. Far better than the last time I saw her. There were no red-rimmed eyes or dried tear stains. No mascara smudges lingering beneath her lashes or pity in her gaze.

She leaned forward, bracing her elbows on the old, worn wood. I couldn't help but think about the last time she was here. When I had her spread out before me.

Get it the fuck together, man.

"I'm sorry I haven't called or texted these past few months. As you can imagine, I've been a bit busy dismantling the stability of my family's record label." She winced. "Correction. My family's *former* record label. That's going to take some getting used to. It's just such a habit." Her fingers tapped anxiously against her biceps as she eyed the bottle in front of us. "Would it be terribly inappropriate to take a shot during a job interview? I'm going to do it anyway."

Olivia quickly poured two shots, sliding one my way before bringing the other to her lips and knocking it back. I just sat there, gaping like an idiot, at the news she just dropped. "You sold?"

"Is that a no to the tequila, then? Because if you're not gonna drink it, I will."

"Until you tell me what the hell is going on—"

She ran her hands through her hair, gripping the roots tightly for a moment before releasing. "I didn't want to live another day in a life that didn't feel like mine. I didn't want to go through the motions just to make everyone else happy." She closed her eyes, exhaling slowly. "I didn't want to be on my deathbed and see a graveyard of missed opportunities. So yes, I sold the company. I tendered my resignation the day I signed on the bottom line to hand over control."

This woman. I had so many questions, and yet all I wanted to do was walk around this bar and pull her into my arms. But I couldn't. Not yet. Not until I knew exactly what she was saying and what she was asking for.

"How does it feel?"

"I see you have your therapy hat on," she laughed, looking away. "Um, I'm going a little crazy. Idle hands, and all that. There have been so many meetings with so many goddamn lawyers and men in suits that I thought having nothing to do would be a nice change, but I was wrong. Hence why I'm already back on the hunt for work."

I leaned forward, mimicking her stance with my elbows on the bar. "Olivia, you can't work for me."

She reached across and laid her hand on my arm, pleading. I

relished the heat radiating off her skin. The softness of her touch. "Come on, Duke. I'm desperate. I can't shadow Lukas again. I've been doing it all day, and he drove me out of my mind."

"You've been in town all day?"

"I got in this morning. Lukas had to run some errands, which meant I was forced to tag along. Believe me, it was not my idea of fun."

I shook my head, focusing on playing the interviewer. "I need someone who lives locally, Ms. Hart. I'm afraid that disqualifies you from the job."

"Actually, I am local." Olivia reached across the bar for her purse. Inside, she grabbed a small pink-and-red polka-dotted keychain that held a single key. "This is the key to my new house. I can even provide proof of residency if you need it."

Stay calm, Duke. Stay. Fucking. Calm.

"You're staying in town?"

"There's no place I'd rather be," she said, hesitating with a smile on her lips. "Everyone I love is here."

Everyone I love is here.

Everyone I love.

"Yes, idiot. I'm talking about *you*." The sweetest pink hue swept across her cheeks. "I'm sorry it took me so long to say it back, but I do. God, I love you so much. And I know it's crazy. It's so fast, but I couldn't wait another day to tell you. It's why I had to stay away until now. There was no way I was coming back unless I could commit to being all in with you."

"Olivia—"

"And you might not even want to be with me anymore, which is completely fine. I mean, that would really suck, honestly. It's not going to change the fact that I'm here to stay, though. I'll help at the bar or with Harper or whatever needs to be done." She burst out laughing, and the sound startled me.

"You know, I have no idea what I want to do with my life, which is a terrifying concept at thirty-seven. But it's also thrilling in a way? I get to start over. I get to build a life I want—no matter what that looks like or what other people expect. I just get to be me."

Her chest was heaving by the time she was done. It was kind of cute how she was staring at me, exasperated by my silence.

"Well, are you going to say anything?"

My lips twitched. "You didn't need to confess your love in such a dramatic way, you know. My attention was already yours."

"You ass," she murmured. The smile didn't leave her face. "Don't make me laugh." She glanced down coyly at the empty shot glasses. Pulling up the bottle, she shook it lightly. "What do you say, Mr. Bennett? Up for one more round?"

Without breaking eye contact, I stood up and slowly walked around the bar. Her back hit the counter as I caged her in. I leaned forward, skimming my lips along her neck as my hands found her ass.

Hoisting her in the air, I set her on top of the counter. There was something so carefree about her. The way her laugh sounded like the tinkling of wind chimes, or how she kicked her feet like a woman who felt free for the first time in her life. It was magical. She was magic.

And she was mine.

"Only one?" I asked.

"Maybe two or three..."

I brought my hand up and tucked a loose strand of hair behind her ear. Olivia leaned into my touch, kissing the palm of my hand. "How about every single one for the rest of my life?"

"That sounds like a plan to me."

EPILOGUE
OLIVIA

"WE DON'T HAVE TIME," I moaned, letting my eyes slip closed as Duke crowded me against the bathroom counter. The trail of his lips down my neck left goosebumps in their wake. "We have to go."

"The fuck we do," he growled. "It's our party. All those other fuckers can wait."

"They're our friends."

"And you're my priority. I don't give a fuck about anyone but you and the girls—who I know are more than taken care of right now." I smiled as he pressed a kiss beneath my ear. "So, let me take care of *you*. You've been working so hard, honey. Don't you ache? Don't you want to feel good?"

My head fell back against Duke's shoulder as he reached around and slowly undid the tie holding my robe together. Cold air nipped at my skin, causing my nipples to go painfully taut as his fingers delicately caressed my breasts.

"Come on, Olivia. Don't make me beg."

Sliding my hand up, I cupped his cheek. "But I do so like it when you beg."

Immediately, his body and warmth were gone. I stumbled forward, catching myself on the countertop as I looked dead ahead at the man smirking at me in the mirror.

He stepped back, choosing to lean casually against the wall. His long-sleeve shirt was unbuttoned, revealing the smattering of hair along his chest and the trail that disappeared beneath his jeans. This morning, he'd cleared away the stubble he loved so much, leaving only that slutty little mustache behind.

Duke Bennett was too goddamn handsome for words, and he was all mine. Since the moment I came back home and announced my retirement from Hartstrings six months ago, neither of us had been able to last long without the other. It'd only taken us a month to move in with one other.

We told everyone it was the most practical thing to do, seeing as Duke was sleeping on a couch in a cabin that wasn't even big enough to fit my wardrobe. But it was really just because we couldn't stand waking up every morning without the other person beside us.

John's house had taken a while to clear out, but we were finally beginning to make it our own. Charlie and Harper's rooms were the first we renovated, followed quickly by the primary bedroom. Duke and Lukas spent their weekends painting, while the girls and I did more shopping than we ever had before—much to the boys' chagrin.

While I hadn't been hired for the bartending gig I interviewed for when I came home, I'd been busier than ever helping Duke run the business side of things as he trained not one, but two, new employees.

Coming on board as his business partner was slightly terrifying at first. I didn't want him to think I was going to change everything at once, or take over completely, but all my time at Hartstrings taught me a thing or two about running a business. I had the experience and the degree to back me up.

As of tonight, it was official. We signed a new partnership agreement this morning, splitting ownership and creating our own legacy from the solid one Frank's Bar already had.

Now, all of our friends and family were waiting for us to show up, cut the cake, and drink our fill of good liquor and beer.

"You don't play fair," I said, turning around with a pout.

"Never said I did."

Duke's eyes burned a path across my body as his gaze slid down to my aching center. I was completely bare beneath the robe, and there was nothing for me to rub against for friction.

Without warning, I slipped to my knees and slowly crawled across the floor to him. There was no set dynamic between us. We loved switching things up to keep it interesting. But if there was one thing I knew the man loved... It was me on my knees for him.

The bulge in his jeans was hard to miss as I sank back onto my heels. My robe was open, revealing my heavy breasts. I waited to see what he would do or say, but Duke kept silent as I walked my fingers up his denim-clad thighs to the bronze button keeping him in place.

"Is this what you wanted?" I asked, popping it free. His nostrils flared as I slid the zipper down and tugged at the fabric until it fell into a puddle at his feet. "Maybe I should take care of you instead."

I leaned forward, letting my nose run along the bulge in his briefs. There was a wet spot on the fabric where he was already leaking. My mouth watered at what was hidden away.

Reaching inside his boxers, I pulled him free. His cock was hard and heavy in my hand. I swiped my thumb across the pre-cum leaking from the tip and placed it in my mouth, humming as I glanced up at him beneath thick lashes.

"Maybe you should," Duke murmured, reaching down to run

his hand along my hair. His fingers laced through the strands, tugging hard enough that I gasped. His cock was right there, pushing gently against my lips.

Like the good girl I was, I opened for him.

Duke groaned as he slid against my tongue, moving in slow, shallow thrusts as I let him use me. We'd played this game a thousand times, and it still hadn't gotten old. "Fuck, Liv." He looked down, mouth parting slightly as he watched. "Just like that."

The scent of mint washed over me as he spoke in a harsh whisper that made my toes curl. "Show me what that perfect little mouth can do when it's wrapped around my thick cock, honey. Drive me so crazy that I have no choice but to pick you up and fuck your sweet, tight cunt until I fill you up." I whimpered at his words, shifting my weight to ease the ache at my core. "Yeah, you'd like that, wouldn't you? Gonna be leaking me all fucking night. Might have to fill you up again. Sneak away to the bathroom when no one's looking and bend you over the sink. I'd just have to lift that pretty dress up, pull your panties to the side, and slide home."

His cock hit the back of my throat, making me gag for only a second before he pulled back. I'd already done my makeup. As much as we'd both like to get messy, we truly didn't have time for me to start from scratch again.

"Duke, I—"

Before I could say anything, before I could tell him that was exactly what I wanted, Duke bent down and scooped me up beneath my arms. He tore off the robe, leaving me naked, as he bent me over. My face lay against the cool marble. I could lift it just enough to see Duke standing behind me.

He reached down, pulled my right leg up, and placed it on the countertop. I felt so exposed, so vulnerable, in this position.

Duke could do anything he wanted to me, and there wasn't a single thing I could do but beg or cry for more.

"So fucking wet," he murmured. The thick head of his cock notched at my entrance, but he didn't push forward. Not yet. "Is this what you want? To be fucked and filled, honey?"

I nodded my head, unable to think as he dragged himself down to circle my clit. The scent of my arousal hung in the air, making me dizzy with need.

"Words, Olivia. Tell me how badly you want this."

Duke tipped his hips forward, pushing into me an inch. My body welcomed the intrusion, though it did nothing to clear the lust-filled fog rolling in. "Please, Duke…" I whimpered. "Please fuck me. Please make me come. I want to feel—" my words cut off as he pushed in further, but he waited for me to continue. "I-I want you to use me to make yourself feel good."

"Shit," he cursed under his breath. His fingers found the divots in my hips, pushing them down for better leverage. I felt impossibly full and cried out as our bodies slowly grew flush.

I glanced up, watching him. Duke's breathing was labored as he fought for control. Every muscle in his body twitched as he denied himself—and me—what we both wanted. "Goddamn, you feel so good."

Our gazes locked as he began to move. His green eyes were like flames, burning me from the inside out and making me sweat. Leaning forward, his hot breath caressed my neck. "Little cock tease. You drive me fucking crazy, you know that? I've been watching you walk around all afternoon in this tiny little robe, trying to behave, but you make that impossible."

"I wanted to see how long you'd last," I confessed. His hips slammed into me, stealing my breath. "You almost took too long."

"Did you think a party was gonna stop me?" he cruelly chuckled. "Nah, honey. Like I told you earlier, I don't give a shit who's around. If I want to fuck this sweet little pussy, that's exactly what I'm going to do."

Duke straightened, tightening his hold on my waist. I couldn't move as his shallow thrusts turned frenetic—the countertop bit into me with each slam of his hips. I'd definitely bruise, but I didn't care. I loved the pain. Loved the way he owned me.

His skin was hot against my own. Each rough movement, each panting breath, brought me closer to the precipice. Desire coiled tight in my belly, an incessant reminder of how close I was to careening over the edge. Every time I drew close, Duke slowed down.

I could feel myself leaking down my thighs, hear the slick sound of my arousal as Duke pounded into me without mercy. I tried to snake my hand between our bodies to my waiting clit, but he slapped it away. "No. I control when you come, Olivia. *Me*. Not you. And it's not time. This cunt feels too good."

"Please," I begged again. It seemed to be the only thing I could do to get his attention. He was too far gone to his pleasure. "I need to come. I'm so close."

Threading his fingers in my hair, he pulled my head up. "Look in the mirror," he rasped, tightening his hold. The angle was awkward, but it forced me to stare dead ahead at the two of us.

Duke owned every part of my body, forcing me into impossible positions just for the fun of it. A bead of sweat trickled down his face from his temple as he continued his lazy fucking. No matter how much I whimpered or begged, he was intent on taking his time.

"See how goddamn beautiful you are taking my cock, honey. Fucking made for me, aren't you?" I nodded, unable to speak as he picked up the pace. "Touch yourself. Make yourself come right now."

My mouth fell open on a silent scream as I did what I was told. My fingers grazed the point where we were connected as I dragged my wetness up and circled my clit. It wouldn't take me long to fall over the edge, especially not as I watched the ferocious way he claimed me.

"Fuck, fuck, fuck," I squealed as Duke slammed home one last time.

His growl reverberated through the space as his cock twitched, filling me with his cum. He doubled over, hips stuttering as he fucked me through our orgasms. Soft lips came to rest over my skin, peppering hot kisses along my shoulders and neck.

I rolled my forehead against the cool marble, trying to catch my breath as Duke sat up. Hands fell on either side of my ass, exposing me as he slowly slipped free. His fingers gently probed at my entrance as he watched his release leak out.

Then he pushed it back in.

His fingers slowly scissored inside of me as I groaned. "Duke, I need to clean up, or else I'll get a UTI."

With a sigh, he grabbed a washcloth and ran it under warm water. He was gentle as he reverently washed me, though I suspected he was getting more enjoyment out of it than he let on. When he was satisfied, he helped me stand and handed me my robe.

"I'm going to finish getting dressed," he said, leaning in to kiss me. I grasped his shirt, pulling him closer until I was satisfied. "You're gonna be the death of me, woman."

"You started it," I said, playfully swatting his ass as he walked out.

"Well, with a woman like you," he said, pausing at the threshold. "How could I not?"

EPILOGUE

DUKE

"WHOSE IDEA WAS it to get them together?" I asked, gesturing toward the jukebox where Olivia was talking excitedly with Cleo and her sisters. Sawyer was behind the bar pouring a round of drinks. We'd closed the bar down tonight. Their whole family had flown in yesterday to help celebrate my girl and me as we grew our business.

Or so she thought. I may have had something else up my sleeve, too.

I'd met the Hayes family when I bought the business from Lincoln Carter. He worked this place directly under the bar's namesake for years before Frank passed it on to him. Fortunately for me, as much as Lincoln loved this bar, he loved his wife, Josie, more. The two of them lived in Texas on Black Springs Ranch with their two kids, Stella and Poppy.

Cleo and Josie's younger sister, Lennox, was also in tow, though she was sitting off to the side as she rubbed her very pregnant belly and laughed. Her husband, Bishop, had been standing behind her the whole night like a goddamn sentry until Lincoln and Grady dragged him over to the bar. It didn't stop him from looking over his shoulder every time he heard her laugh.

"Yours," Lukas said, pointing his beer my direction. "In fact, all of this is your idea." He leaned forward, lowering his voice. "*Brother.*"

"It's just a label," I said, trying to hide my smile. I was failing miserably, but it was the thought that counted.

The ring, now hidden in my pocket, had been tucked away at the back of the closet for the past month. It wasn't overly grand or flashy—just a single solitaire diamond on a gold band I'd been saving up to buy. Harper and Charlie had both helped me pick it out. They assured me Olivia would love it.

I hoped they were right.

Ever since I first held it in my hand, it was a struggle not to drop to one knee and ask her right then and there to be mine forever. Each morning when she was in the kitchen making breakfast, or when she'd slide beneath the covers after soaking in the bathtub every night.

But I wanted to do this right. I wanted to make sure she knew just how loved and cherished she was.

"You know, I thought it was going to be us bros forever," Lukas grumbled. "But now, here you are, all moon-eyed over my sister. I can't believe this."

"One. Don't ever say the word 'bros' again. You're a forty-two-year-old man. Two. Your sister's hotter than you are," I countered. "It was an easy choice."

Lukas placed his hand over his heart. "Okay, ouch. You didn't need to cut me so deep."

I just shrugged. "The truth hurts sometimes."

"I'm telling you… This bar is magic. I proposed to Josie right there only two years ago, and look at us," Lincoln said, gesturing toward the charcoal band on his left hand. "Happier than ever."

"Yeah, suffocatingly so," Bishop muttered. "I keep waiting for your honeymoon phase to go away, but it hasn't yet."

"Says the man who won't let anyone even remotely close to Lennox. Tell me, has she threatened to castrate you yet?" Lincoln shot back.

Bishop shifted on the stool, adjusting himself. "She says I'm overbearing, but I just want to protect her. Not my fault she has a knack for getting herself into trouble. Gotta protect my woman and our babies."

"I'll give you this, old man. I wasn't sure you still had it in you. Twins? At your age?" Grady shivered. "Keeping up with one kid that young was hard enough."

"Yeah, well, I'm not a pussy," Bishop snapped, taking a swig of his beer. "And my swimmers are very strong. Thank you very much."

Lukas chuckled. "I'm glad I don't have to worry about that shit."

"Nah, I said that, too. Now look at me. Married to a woman I can barely keep up with two babies on the way. Life's weird, man," Bishop said.

"I'm not holding my breath," Lukas chuckled, but it was hollow. He glanced down at his beer, fiddling with the label. "Don't think any of that is in the cards for me."

Lukas and I had this conversation more times than I could count. He truly believed there wasn't a single woman out there capable of changing his mind, but I knew it was bullshit. I'd thought the same thing after Sarah left, and yet here I was preparing to propose.

"Hey," I said, clapping him on the shoulder. "Somewhere out there is a woman who's gonna knock you straight on your ass when you least expect it."

"I think I'll keep standing on my own two feet, thank you very much," he said, settling back in his chair.

The lights overhead dimmed, causing all of us to turn around and glance toward where Lennox and Sawyer were standing off to the side. The latter held a makeshift spotlight toward the bar.

"What the hell?" Bishop muttered, pushing to his feet. The moment he stood, a familiar song sounded out from the jukebox, and I groaned as Cleo and Josie lifted Charlie and Harper onto the bar before following suit.

"Uh, what's going on?" Lukas asked.

Lincoln leaned back in his seat, a maniacal smile on his face as Josie winked at him. "I don't know, but I'm damn sure going to have fun finding out."

"Our daughters are up there, you asshat," Grady said, smacking the man on the back of the head. It didn't deter Lincoln one bit.

As the lyrics started, Olivia appeared between the other girls, casually climbing up onto the bar. Each of them swayed their hips to the beat, dancing in a perfect rhythm. It was clear they'd modified the routine, so it wasn't too provocative for Harper and Charlie.

"Isn't this from that movie?" Lincoln asked, turning toward me. "You know the one—"

"Liv always did like the dramatics. Wonder how long they've been planning this," Lukas said.

Bishop looked over at Lennox, who was miming the words. "So, that's why she's been pouting all night," he said.

The guys and I watched the girls dance on the bar, hooting and hollering as they took turns in the spotlight. By the time the music cut off, we were all on our feet giving them the round of applause they deserved.

I walked over, holding my hands out for Olivia to take. She did, jumping down in front of me. "You better not have scratched my bar," I said, giving her a kiss.

She smiled up at me, her blonde curls a sweaty mess. "*Our* bar, baby. Remember that."

"How could I forget?" I pulled her closer, letting her body melt against my own.

Her hand came up, playing with the hair along my neck as she whispered. "Is that a ring box in your pocket or are you just happy to see me?"

What. The. Fuck.

She pulled back, a knowing smile on her lips at my stunned expression. "I—Well, I—"

"Oh, please. I found that thing the first time I did laundry, Duke. We really need to work on your hiding spots?"

Goddammit. My heart sank. Suddenly, it felt like the night was ruined. I wanted to surprise her. "You knew?"

"It has literally been killing me. Honestly, I'm glad you're not making me wait anymore." She slipped her hand inside the front pocket of my jeans and pulled out the small box. It lay flat in the palm of her hand.

I took it from her, pulling out the golden band before dropping to one knee. It wasn't at all how I pictured it, but it was perfect all the same. Here, in our bar, surrounded by friends and family, I stared up at the most beautiful woman I'd ever known.

"I'm not good with my words, so you'll have to bear with me as I stumble through this," I said, eliciting a laugh from those around us. "A wise man once told me that regrets are for fools. Since then, I've taken those words to heart and tried my best to live by them. If you would've told me that I'd be getting down on one knee for the annoying girl I used to throw into the lake when we were kids, I'd have probably said you were crazy."

"Hear, hear," Lukas chimed. "Back when I was the most important Hart in your life."

Olivia rolled her eyes, reaching over to pinch her brother.

"You're just mad because your best friend would rather play with me instead."

Lukas scrunched up his nose. "Nope. I don't want to think about that."

I looked between the two of them, waiting. "Can I get back to what I was doing?" Lukas held up his hands as Olivia turned back to me, bright eyes shining as she glanced down. "But now, there's no one else I could imagine spending the rest of my life with. You're an amazing woman. An amazing mother. I'm so glad Harper and I get to share a life with you and Charlie." I glanced around at all the tear-filled eyes trained on us. "And everyone else, too."

"Oh, Duke…" she whispered.

"Olivia Hart, will you marry me?"

Olivia smiled, one side of her lips kicking up a smidge higher than the other. "That must have been one wise man."

"He was pretty great."

She glanced down at the ring and bit her lip, nodding. "I would love to marry you, Duke Bennett."

The bar broke out in a thunderous applause as I stood and picked Olivia up, kissing her senseless. She wrapped her legs around my waist, locking us together.

"Get a room," Lukas boomed as I set his sister down. He pulled me into a hug, clapping me on the back. "Proud of you, brother."

Charlie and Harper ran up and grabbed Olivia's hand. "Look at our shirts!"

She glanced down at the matching pink and purple shirts with the word "sister" in bright glitter on the front. Cleo had helped them both make them last weekend when Olivia and I were working.

"Oh, girls. This is fantastic!" Olivia said, giving me a wink and smiling before pulling Harper and Charlie into a hug. "I love it. Do you think we could make one for your dad and me? That way we could all match."

"I'm not wearing glitter," I murmured, pulling her to my side.

"What about pink? Does that offend your delicate sensibilities?"

"I'm a girl dad. Of course, I'll wear pink."

Olivia nodded. "Good. Because I have all kinds of plans for this bar."

I pulled back with furrowed brows. "Hold up. Wait. You're not painting my bar pink."

"I've been talking to Lennox and Sawyer all night about ideas. We could get a disco ball, at least," she said, kissing my cheek.

We didn't really need a fucking disco ball, but if she wanted one… I might be able to make it happen. "You'll have to get your brother on board with that."

"Oh, he's easy to manipulate. I can handle him."

Olivia settled her head on my shoulder as we looked out at the bar. At all of our friends and family who'd gathered here not only to celebrate the start of something new but to show their unwavering support for Olivia and me, I couldn't help but be grateful for how things fall apart before falling together.

"I thought my life was over after the divorce," I said, capturing Olivia's attention. "But it was just getting started."

She curled into my side, nuzzling my neck. "We both deserve a fresh start."

I kissed her forehead. "I'll drink to that."

WHAT'S NEXT?

MEET SAWYER AND BECKETT!

When small-town bartender Sawyer Sutton catches the eye of Beckett Montgomery, their connection burns as bright as the fireworks at the country fair. She isn't afraid to tell the wealthy property developer what she thinks of his profession, and he finds her passion for the community endearing, even if old-fashioned. After a fervent one-night stand, they go their separate ways with only memories to remind them of what they shared.

Or so they thought.

Six weeks and two pink lines later, Sawyer and Beckett find themselves tied together in ways they never imagined. Becoming parents wasn't something either of them had planned, but as the countdown to the due date begins, the two must learn to work together despite clashing personalities. The more time they spend together, the harder it is for them to ignore the sizzling chemistry that got them into this position in the first place. The only thing standing in their way now is themselves.

Can Sawyer show Beckett there's more to life than dollar signs? Or will her insistence on independence be their undoing?

COMING SEPTEMBER 15, 2026

ALSO BY AMBER PALMER

<u>**Black Springs Ranch**</u>

Between the Pines

Through the Dust

After the Rain

<u>**Pinecrest Ridge**</u>

One More Round

Make it a Double

ACKNOWLEDGMENTS

When I wrote Between the Pines, I had no intention to ever visit the fictional town and bar featured at the beginning of the book again. It was meant to be a one-off, but I couldn't stop thinking about it. Returning to Pinecrest felt like coming home.

And who better to take us there than Olivia and Duke? From the beginning, I knew their story would be one about second chances—though not in the way we often think about in romance books. It's a reminder to follow your dreams, no matter what they are or how long they take to achieve. Life's too short not to do what you love.

Growing up, I thought if I didn't have my life together by the time I was 25, then I was doomed. (I wish I were kidding, by the way. I really was that dramatic.) But I am so glad I was wrong. I'm glad that I surrounded myself by people who lift me up, who support me no matter what.

One More Round is my first book as a full-time author, which is frankly a little insane to me. But I never could have done it without a few (many) people who helped make this book a reality…

Mr. Palmer, you have remained my rock throughout this transition. I couldn't have made it without your unwavering support. Hearing your wife say she wants to quit her job and write full-time was probably a little scary at first, but you've taken it in stride.

To Heather, my writing wouldn't be half of what it is today

without. Thank you for taking my (sometimes) jumbled words and making a coherent thought out of them. You're the best sounding board in the business.

Holly and Lauren, just look at your girl! She did the damn thing! This whole crazy journey is really your fault—or brilliant idea. Depending on how you look at it. I'm so grateful for your constant encouragement.

To Anna and Ceilidh, thank you for letting me cry in long voice notes when the story felt like it was getting away from me. You two truly helped shape this book into what it is today, and I'm so grateful for your brilliant minds.

To Colby and Jenna who helped keep my socials running when I was on a deadline. You guys saved me countless hours of doomscrolling when I should've been writing.

A special shoutout to my ARC and content teams for keeping the buzz around Olivia and Duke going strong. I'm constantly amazed at how creative y'all are because a girl (me) could neverrrrrr.

Of course, these books would be nothing without the jaw-dropping cover. A huge thank you to Viki with Forensics and Flowers for successfully putting me in my pink era. I didn't think it was my color, but you've helped prove me wrong.

And finally, to you, dear reader. Thank you for giving me a platform to use my voice. For allowing me the space to share these characters stories and give them life. I hope you love Duke and Liv just as much as I do.

MEET AMBER

Amber Palmer is a contemporary American romance author. Born in Arizona and raised in Texas, she's the proud parent of two mischievous cats and one playful pup. When she's not devouring spicy romance novels, you can find her curating bookish Spotify playlists or jotting down ideas for her next project. A fierce advocate for mental health, Amber crafts characters who face and heal from deep traumas. She's unapologetically passionate about all things spicy—both in books and life—and loves gaming with her husband in her downtime.